Better Days

Better Days

by
Kate Kasten

ISLET PRESS · IOWA CITY

By the same author

The Deconversion of Kit Lamb
Ten Small Beds
Wildwood: Fairy Tales and Fables Re-Imagined

Islet Press, Iowa City
www.katekasten.com
Copyright © 2013 Kate Kasten.
All rights reserved.
ISBN: 978-0-9831959-3-1
Cover design by John Evans and Chait Galleries Downtown
Typeset by Sara T. Sauers

To my brothers
Fritz Kasten and Sam Kasten
for their unfailing encouragement
and
To my dear friends
Sandra de Helen, Lorie Hill, Marcia Smies, and Jean Walker
so far and yet so near

MEMORIAL DAY
2010

i.

NEITHER OF THEM BETRAYED the smallest interest in the black cloud coming steadily like a huge, soundless dirigible in the blue sky.

The air shimmered over the lake, where Cal and Wayne sat in the boat, waiting for something to bite. The bill of Cal's old seed cap and the brim of his son's new straw panama were pulled down to protect their broad, nearly identical noses. Wayne took out a handkerchief to mop the sweat from the bald spot on the back of his head. Before replacing his hat, he ran his fingers through the dark hair spilling over his ears, and Cal noticed there were streaks of gray glinting through the black.

Wayne opened his mouth to speak, and Cal, leaning forward, thought, he's going to say something about that cloud now. But Wayne said, "You want to try one of these lures I brought?" Cal shifted his weight on the faded orange life jacket he'd slipped under himself for padding. He was finding it hard to ignore the discomfort of a backless metal seat these days, and he was only seventy-two.

"Where'd you get those lures?" he said. "At that Reels and Rifles place? What'd they hit you up for 'em?"

Turning from Cal to face the bow of the boat, Wayne didn't answer. Cal took the opportunity to stare outright at the huge cloud gliding in from the west on an invisible path set to pass directly over their heads. An enormous black anvil now, the cloud rose many thousands of feet into the air, its flat underside so low it seemed to touch the top branches of the alders fringing the water. Slowly, steadily, it came on.

Cal reeled in his line. He thought, we ought to turn around right now and get the hell off this lake. But he cast his line out again, whipping it past his son's shoulder. The line sank in the murky, unmoving water just ahead, where bass liked to wait in a cover of drowned trees for food to swim by.

Wayne said, "Sorry we couldn't make it up to the cemetery this morning."

"You weren't there?" Cal replied. "Darned if I didn't notice."

Wayne shrugged. "Got delayed," he said.

Delayed. Right. Cal pictured his wife Helen and daughter Barb shedding tears silently with their arms around each other. Cal had stood off to the side with Barb's husband and the grandkids. Wayne had called Barb on her cell phone earlier to say they were "running late," that the family should go on up to the cemetery without them. What the hell was the point of Barb and Helen working on Wayne's wife to get him down for Memorial Day when he fixes it so he doesn't make it to the cemetery? Cal didn't like being there either, but he did his duty and came.

Every Memorial Day, Cal had to climb the cemetery hill with Helen and whatever family members were in town to lay a wreath on Tom's grave. This morning Helen and Barb had inserted the wreath into the ground. Helen knelt, as usual, to get the angle right, leaning the wreath this way and that, as if such a thing mattered.

Barb just stood there, staring at the face of the stone through the circle of flowers. Twenty-six years ago she had argued for some kind of epitaph to be carved on her brother's marker. She was only fifteen at the time. Every year since, she always commented on the meagerness of the bare name and dates chiseled into the stone. Cal thought maybe they should have honored that simple request, honored the open and abiding sorrow she carried for the easy-going, sweet-natured brother she had adored. Even now it wasn't too late, but Cal couldn't bring himself to suggest it.

The depth of Cal's own grief during that unreal time had embarrassed him. He and Helen had barely talked about Tom's death, and cried separately. What Wayne felt about his brother's death Cal never did know.

Wayne hadn't been there the day it happened. Twenty-two years old and keeping as much distance as he could from the family, he'd been off on one of his painting trips. When they finally got hold of him by telephone in some small New Mexico town, he'd sounded irritated just before they gave him the news. He was silent for a while afterward. Then he said, "Okay. I'll come right home."

The business of arranging for the funeral, ordering a casket and tombstone, Cal couldn't even remember. He guessed he'd done nothing until Helen took over the job. Maybe she'd felt about the inscription the way he did, unwilling to squeeze her grief for their boy into a few words on stone.

Cal and Wayne fished in silence. A breeze started up, just a hint of cool air, and Cal glanced toward the oncoming cloud, then quickly away as Wayne twisted on the bench seat to talk to him again.

"Barb brought her kids to the cemetery, though, didn't she?" Wayne said.

"Gordon Jr. and Mason came," Cal said. "Cindy was on a Girl Scout trip."

"So there was plenty of family there, anyway."

"A quorum," said Cal, dryly.

On the morning of the day Tom died, there had been a short line of squalls with distant bursts of lightning, but it was way off at the horizon and seemed to be holding there in no special hurry to move in. New rain wasn't due sooner than midday. There was bright blue sky overhead.

All that spring it had stayed wet. Then it got dry enough to go out in the fields for half a day before the rain was supposed to start up again. That morning, Cal had gotten a head start on the disking and finished half the field near the house. Tom, at the end of his college semester, had promised to hurry over as soon as he finished an early morning exam. When he arrived to help, Cal was driving the tractor back toward the shed and swearing at the disk. There was a stress crack in the tongue.

Cal told Tom, "If we don't get this corn in pretty quick, we might as well just pack it in." He remembered them both looking back toward the line of squalls, and Tom's saying, "Not to worry, Dad. Go fix the disk, and I'll plant this section you have ready."

Which job either of them chose would have been a toss-up, just a matter of chance, since Tom—even at twenty—was as handy at one as the other. Tom offered to put in the corn.

Cal helped Tom hitch the planter to the tractor and watched him drive up the lane past the yard. He saw the boy wave at his mother as he passed. She looked up from where she was planting peas along the garden fence, and smiled. Cal walked down to the barn.

He was just finishing the weld on the disk tongue when the door-way and all the gaps in the walls filled with a brilliant, white light. Cal dropped the welding rod. An instant later, the single, enormous bang startled him backwards into the work table, reverberating through his ribs and setting his ears ringing. He stood there stunned for a moment before he knew what had happened. Then he wrenched off his helmet and thick welding gloves and ran out of the shed.

Wheeling around the barn, he heard Helen scream his name and saw her, far ahead of him at the top of the driveway, dashing through the open gate. By the time he got up the hill to the gate, she was only a small figure in the middle of the field, disappearing behind the rider-less tractor. At that moment the smell hit Cal. The acrid combination of ozone and seared flesh. Even so, leaping across the deep furrows, he thought, there is no way a thunderbolt could take away Tom's life.

When he came near, Helen was twenty yards the other side of the tractor, bending over the white figure on the ground.

The lightning had reached out a five-mile arm, torn Tom off the tractor, and flung him across the dark, rich soil he had just planted. It left him sprawled on the ground, his clothes ripped off, cap and boots scattered hundreds of feet away. Just the shred of undershorts hanging off his hips. Like the crucified Christ in his loin cloth, Cal thought every time the scene thrust itself into his mind for years afterward. A black brand scorched the boy's flesh from his right temple to his right foot. At first, in his irrational hope, Cal mistook it for dirt.

Helen had fallen to her knees and grabbed up Tom's limp torso. She was screaming and screaming the word No. When Cal finally knelt beside them, he saw that the boyish, thatchy red hair on Tom's head was sticking straight out, and all the gold hair on his freckled arms and chest stood on end. Helen turned to Cal, the screams still bursting from her, but Cal, staring into Tom's dead, startled eyes, had no idea what to do.

Some months later, Cal read that lightning victims could sometimes be saved if artificial respiration was started immediately after the strike. He wondered then if he should add his ignorance of CPR to the thing he asked himself every time he saw a young man on a tractor: was it such a terrible sin of selfishness to let your twenty-year-old son, home from college, plant your field for you? Was it so bad it warranted the sacrifice of the boy's life?

Now, with Wayne's back to him, the right shoulder, like his own, held higher than the other, he remembered that when he was running toward that scene in the middle of the field, so sure that lightning couldn't kill Tom, he had thought, with a strange matter-of-factness, "Now, if this was *Wayne*, it might be a different story, but Tommy?"

Today he had to carry out this duty his wife and daughter had charged him with. They informed him that he would invite Wayne to go fishing and that they would talk together and enjoy each other's company. If he didn't attempt at least some sort of conversation, he would be called to account later.

"You should have brought your painting gear," Cal offered.

Wayne continued to face the front of the boat. "Why?" he said.

"Artists like drawing pictures of this stuff, don't they?"

"Fishing's fishing. Painting's painting," said Wayne. The breeze was cooling things off now. Cal saw his son's head tilt slightly upward, and felt sure Wayne had taken a sidelong glance at the black cloud. Wayne turned back to gaze at his father and—as it seemed to Cal—with calculated afterthought, added, "What 'stuff'?"

Cal kept his eyes off the oncoming cloud. "Scenery," he said. "Don't you paint that kind of thing?"

In fact, he thought, most of Wayne's paintings didn't look at all like scenery or anything else you could recognize.

In April, Wayne had put up another exhibit of his paintings at a gallery in Minneapolis. Cal and Helen wouldn't even have known about it if Barb hadn't mentioned it. Helen thought she and Cal should go to the opening. The pictures were great big things that took up half a wall, paintings of colored triangles—green, red, yellow, and white—on a brown background. When everyone was standing around the gallery, holding plastic cups of wine, Cal asked Wayne, "What are these pictures supposed to be about?" Wayne laughed his dry, hard laugh that made you wonder who he was mocking, himself or you, and replied, "Us."

"You and me?" Cal glanced covertly at one of the larger canvases. He wasn't sure if Wayne was pulling his leg, so he made a joke. "You saying we have pointy heads?" Wayne gave another of his mocking laughs and turned away to talk to someone who had just come in, and Cal never did know if he'd been serious or not.

Neither Wayne nor Cal had his eye on the cloud now, but Wayne said, "If *you* were painting this scene, what would *you* put in it?"

Cal wasn't going to be trapped.

"I'd draw one old coot and one middle-aged coot in a rowboat, not catching any fish."

"That's all you see, huh?" said Wayne.

The cloud was moving past the line of trees, its reflection darkening the water near shore so there seemed to be two clouds, the one in the sky a colossal, hovering spacecraft out of science fiction, the one in the water like a menacing submarine. Both moved in eerie silence toward the boat, while the surrounding sky remained as blue and clear as ever. Cal listened for thunder and thought he might have caught a faint rumble but couldn't be sure. There was the rustle of a small, breeze-blown paper bag in Wayne's tackle box, it could have been that.

The cotton life jacket between him and the metal seat had no insulating value whatever, of course, and it had metal fasteners. Instinctively, Cal slouched, making himself a lower target by several inches, and inadvertently triggering the familiar lumbar ache and the newer twinge in his right hip. For twenty-six years, every single time Cal had gone out to plow or plant or harvest when a storm threatened, he had been afraid. On the day he rented out the last of his land, his first thought was: I'll never have to take a tractor into an open field again.

The cloud's image on the water had left the shore now and was coming across the lake. With Wayne's back toward him once more, Cal could openly watch the cloud's progress as it moved slowly in their direction. It made him think about the explosion of the Hindenburg, its passengers jumping to their death, with fire raining down on the crowd below. It happened two years before he was born, but he always remembered his mother describing it, the announcer on the radio sobbing as he tried to report the disaster, his choked voice crying: "This is one of the worst catastrophes in the world!" and "Oh, the humanity!" When she recalled it, Cal's usually reserved mother dabbed a tear from her eye.

As the cloud mass drew nearer, Cal looked up at its vast underside and was hypnotized by the sleepy, graceful boiling motion that he knew signified millions of volts of charged air. The closer it came, the lower it descended, as if it might actually set itself down on the water and envelop them. It was about to move in over the boat now.

9

The accompanying downdraft cooled the sweat on Cal's shirt, stirred the lake, and tugged at their lines.

Wayne threw a leg across the seat to straddle it and looked steadily at his father. "So what do you think?" he said. "You going to quit being stubborn?" He reached down into the tackle box. "You going to try one of these new lures?"

Cal let his breath out. "No. I guess I'll stick to mine."

Wayne continued to watch him. "What have you got to lose?"

Cal kept his eyes focused on the lake. He reeled in his line, pulled a clump of muck off the hook and cast it out again. "Well," he said, "I'd have to mortgage my house if I lost one of those lures and had to pay you back for it."

"Oh, so you're saying you've got bass in this puddle big enough to snap a line?"

The sky suddenly darkened. Sunrays flung themselves out from under the edge of the great cloud, like imploring arms, before disappearing into it as it rolled over them.

For the first time, Cal saw Wayne look directly at the massive cloud. Wayne pushed his hat back and gazed up with his rod resting on his knee. Cal clamped the butt end of his rod between his forearm and his side as if he expected momentarily to reel in a battling fish. They stared silently at the great moving island overhead, solitary in the sea of blue sky, where a half dozen white clouds were just now beginning to appear along the horizon.

Cal's pick-up was parked by the boat landing. He knew better than to believe you were one hundred percent safe inside a truck, but at least it gave you a fighting chance, unless it was a tornado that got you, and then you were probably finished.

Out of the corner of his eye, Cal examined Wayne's expression, the set of his jaw, his posture. Wayne didn't have the look of a person threatened with sudden annihilation and trying to hide his fear, and that surprised Cal, because he'd thought that Wayne was just trying to bluff it out, to outman him.

What he saw now in Wayne's stooped shoulders and slack jaw—hanging a little jowly these days like his own—and in the caved-in look of Wayne's chest and the fingers of one hand limp across the fishing pole, was that maybe Wayne didn't care much, one way or another, whether he left this world or not.

He glanced at Wayne's face, which failed to give away whatever he might be thinking. Cal thought about Wayne's drifting style of life, his not getting married until he was thirty-seven. Was it deliberate, he wondered—Wayne waiting so long, then hooking up with a woman who was done with having kids? Wayne's stepson was a good enough boy, Cal liked Jake, but he couldn't pass on the name, could he? With Tom gone, that was it. End of the line. Anger rose up out of the resentment he habitually felt around his son.

He thought, what's the point of being out here on this lake? The weather's wrong. Any fish with sense are hunkered down at the bottom, keeping cool. We ought to head back to shore right now.

Helen had told him: Don't let the chance pass you by. Have a decent conversation, just the two of you. But Cal thought, you don't talk while you're waiting for fish to bite. It scares them off. Fishing's fishing, talking's talking. And what was he supposed to talk *about*, anyway?

Cal stole another look at the black cloud, almost dead center over their heads and moving so slowly it seemed to be coming to a stop to consider just how to deal with them. Cal reeled in his line. Gooseflesh rose across his back where his shirt was clammy with sweat. He turned to his son and saw that Wayne was eyeing him. Cal cast his line out again.

In a conversational tone, he said, "How's Jake these days? He still working on you to let him have that bike?"

"He's not getting a motorbike. It's dangerous," Wayne answered tersely.

"I have no objection to him riding it around our place if you bring him down for a visit."

"He's too young."

"How old is he?"

"Thirteen."

"What's his dad say about it?"

"His dad doesn't have a say about it. He'd let him have it, no questions asked. But he doesn't give a damn about Jake. Never did. Puts him on the front of a dirt bike when the kid's three years old and takes him down those quarry cliffs." Wayne was silent for some seconds before speaking again. "At least Jake knows I'm looking out for him. He's pissed off about it, but at least he knows I'm looking out for him." Wayne fell silent again. Then he said, hotly, as if someone had been arguing the point with him, "I could get myself a cycle and go out hot dogging with the kid. Make him think I'm some tough guy. But that's not what he needs." He looked straight into Cal's eyes now. "I don't care how old your kid is, unless you're drooling into your oatmeal, you always have the responsibility to look out for him. Jake's the only son I've got. "

Cal gripped the fishing rod with both hands. Anger spread down into his arms. He thought, why doesn't he damn well just say what he means: you made Tom go out there on that tractor, with a storm coming up. Cal looked down at the butt of the fishing pole and felt like hitting Wayne with it.

Like I could have *stopped* Tom, he thought, furiously. Like he didn't *ask* to help me. Even if there'd been a reason to tell a twenty-year-old grown boy he couldn't help, the boy wasn't going to take no for an answer after following me around the farm like a puppy since he was a child. You couldn't get him *off* the tractor, *or* the combine, or any *other* damn machine around the place. And Wayne, you couldn't get him *on* one, disliked farm work from day one. It wasn't *Tom* who hated farming. With *Tom*, it was always, Dad, let *me* do it.

Grief welled up in his throat at the sudden recollection of Tom's voice, something Cal thought he'd forgotten forever. That adolescent crack in it that hadn't quite left him at the age of twenty. And a much earlier memory: Tommy at five years old standing by the tractor holding his arms straight up in the air for Cal to reach down and hoist him onto the seat. The feel of Tommy hanging by his outstretched arms, so lightweight and so trusting in that moment before Cal swung him onto his lap. He could almost feel the small wrists now, in his calloused old paws wrapped around a fishing pole.

The seething dark mass hung directly over the rowboat now. Wispy blue-black index fingers poked from under the cloud and crooked skeletally at the men as if to say, "Next?" then curled into themselves and drew back. It seemed to Cal he could have touched the cloud's underbelly if he'd stood in the boat and reached up.

Father and son fell silent. Cal studied his hands for some seconds and rubbed the back of the one holding the rod. He stared unseeing at the familiar white stump of a thumb where he'd lost the tip and nail years ago, trying to pull the engine out of the Farmall without help. He looked toward the sky again. "Well," he said, "at least it'll be cooler now."

"At least?" said Wayne, his eyes on his father's face.

"Even if it's fixing to rain."

"Rain, you'd call it?"

"Probably just pass us by," said Cal. Forcing himself to look away from the sky, he played his line casually up and down and leaned out the side of the boat, as if to study the water for some action.

His skin prickled and the hair on his arms rose. The temperature had dropped fifteen degrees in the last few minutes. It sent a shiver down his back, which was tight and aching now. He had to grit his teeth to keep from throwing down his rod, taking up the oars and rowing, flat out, to shore. For this, he felt enraged just to look at his son. Then he noticed Wayne's hands. The fingers of his right hand lay slack on top of the reel, but the thumb and forefinger of the left one were pinching a fold in the front of his shirt so tightly that the nails had gone white.

Looking away, Cal thought of how Wayne used to hold on like that, for dear life, to a piece of his blanket when he woke from a nightmare as a child. He'd been prone to nightmares. After Tommy was born and Helen was tired from getting up for feedings, Cal was the one to go to Wayne when he cried out in the night. Wayne would be in bed clutching his blanket to his chin. But you couldn't pick him up and walk around the room with him, couldn't jolly him out of it like you could with Tommy when he got to be that age—Tommy would curl his arms around your neck and lay his cheek against yours. Wayne was bristly, stubborn, even at two years old. He'd stiffen and fight you if you tried to hold him. Especially after a nightmare, you had to approach him like you would a leery cat.

Cal would sit down by the bedside, lay a hand on top of the boy's head and pat his hair lightly. Wayne's hair was dark and curly and soft, Cal remembered. It got springy like his own when he grew older, but when he was two, it was silky as a spaniel pup's. After a while Wayne's crying would subside and his fingers gripping the blanket would relax, falling away, palms upward, and he'd drift off to sleep. There would be salty paths down his cheeks where the tears had dried up.

Under the cloud's vast shadow, the lake looked black, cold and bottomless. Cal saw Wayne look up at the sky again. Then Wayne shifted on his seat and cleared his throat.

"You know—" Cal heard him say, and Cal's heart raced a little. Unconsciously, he jutted out his jaw.

Suddenly there came a sharp, metallic report. It reverberated where his hand rested on the side of the aluminum boat. At the same instant, Wayne gave a loud grunt, and as Cal whirled himself around to look, he saw Wayne rise up and lurch toward the bow of the boat. Cal scrambled off his seat and lunged for his son, throwing his arms out in time to catch Wayne around his waist and pull him back, tumbling with him down between the seats with a painful bumping and confusion of arms and legs, as the boat pitched wildly.

Cal lay still with his arms around his son, his face pressed into his back. Wayne said, "What the hell, Dad?" and his deep-pitched voice resonated through Cal's ribcage and against his cheek. The rich smell of Wayne's sweat filled Cal's nostrils. The surprising childlike softness of Wayne's midsection and the strangely familiar rhythm of Wayne's heartbeats dazed Cal for a moment. He felt as if they were floating interlocked, the way a tree bough and a scrap of lumber will get caught in each other and bob along a river in the aftermath of a flood.

As the boat's rocking motion started to subside, Cal released his son and began to untangle himself.

Wayne disengaged himself, too, easing back onto the seat. He rubbed an elbow, then reached out a hand to help Cal up. When they were both sitting, Wayne turned and looked down into the lake at the spreading ring where the reel had hit the water first, after bouncing off the side of the boat. His gaze followed the shallow wake marking the path his rod had taken toward the stand of drowned tree stumps and sunken brush where it was dragged under. Cal followed his gaze. The report he'd heard was Wayne's reel whacking against the metal boat as a hooked fish jerked the line. Wayne had lurched up to try to catch his reel before it fell in the lake.

"Shit, Dad!" Wayne said.

Cal couldn't answer. His heart was pounding like a herd of stampeding cattle and his breaths were coming short. The boat was still rolling from side to side as if someone had set a cradle in motion. Cal had the strange sensation that if he opened his mouth to speak, he might cry.

Wayne looked down at himself, at the front part of his shirt flapping in the breeze. The side seam had ripped open where Cal had grabbed it. Wayne took the fabric between his fingers and held it for a moment as if testing it for something. He looked back at his father.

Cal thought that when he got himself calmed down he would apologize about the shirt. It was an old, paint-stained one he'd seen on Wayne a lot.

To disguise his gasping breaths, Cal turned to search for his own fishing rod, which was trailing in the water off the right side. The reel, having caught on the edge, had saved it from falling in when he dropped it.

Wayne got up and retrieved the rod. He gave it to Cal, who laid it down immediately when he noticed it trembling in his hands. The rod fell with a clatter onto the bottom of the boat. For a few seconds, the men sat in silence.

Cal felt the sun hit his back. On the pretext of replacing his cap, which had been knocked askew, he stole a glance upward. Bright white sunrays were fanning out from the edge of the retreating anvil cloud.

Wayne nudged Cal's boot with the toe of his shoe. "What'd you grab *me* for?" he said.

Keeping his voice under control, Cal, said, "Just grabbed whatever was handy, I guess."

Wayne's chin worked and his lips pursed up the way they did when he was trying to get the better of a smile. He looked across the water again to where his rod had gotten dragged under.

"Well," Wayne said, "I guess I was wrong. This little old pond has bass big enough to make off with a whole *rod*."

Cal's breath was coming a little easier now. He looked at Wayne full in the face and cocked his eyebrow.

"Either that," he said, "or that bass was so impressed by your Reels and Rifles lure, he was hell bent to take it home and show it to his wife."

Cal said it jokingly, but he felt a stab of pity. He imagined the bass dragging the rod back and forth underwater, trying to be rid of the torturing thing. He wondered how long it would take, if the line didn't snap, before the pain and effort would finally just wear the fish out.

ii.

"I wish I'd stop counting red cars," Helen's sister Margaret said, as a red convertible sped past.

"That one would be hard not to count," replied Helen. "It's pretty sporty."

There was a lot of traffic on the interstate. It wasn't long before another red car went by. Margaret said, "I have to count red cars. I wish I could stop."

"Is it getting on your nerves?"

"It sure is!"

Helen wondered how Margaret was holding on to the count. Did she keep starting over at one? Or did she use whatever number came to mind? Maybe she *could* keep track, though. It was hard to tell about Margaret. Just when Helen thought, well, here's another thing the Alzheimer's has taken away, Margaret surprised her.

Watching the cars coming toward them in the opposite lanes, Margaret suddenly laughed. "I found a way to stop counting red cars!" she said.

"How did you do that?"

"I just tell myself to *notice* them, but I don't have to *count* them."

Helen turned the air conditioner down a notch, now that the car was cooler.

She was sad that it had turned out so unusually hot and humid for Memorial Day. She had wanted to get Margaret out earlier in the morning before the sun was high. But they had waited for Wayne and JoAnna and Jake to show up at the cemetery to participate in laying the wreath on Tommy's grave, and then they had to go ahead without them. When they finally arrived, there was all the fuss about who should ride back to the house with who, and Cal was starting to quietly balk about the fishing trip with Wayne, and by the time all that was sorted out, the sun was high, and it was hot as blazes.

Heat or no heat, it was getting harder and harder to convince Mar-

17

garet to leave her assisted living apartment. All their time together lately took place in those two tiny rooms. Only after a great deal of coaxing had Margaret agreed to a day out. Then when they'd stepped from the lobby into the sun, Margaret halted in her tracks and stood in bewildered horror at the blast of heat that struck her.

Before she could find the words to express her need to go back inside, Helen had hustled her into the waiting car and turned the air conditioning on high, declaring in an artificially upbeat voice, "The cold air will kick in in just a minute, Margaret, and then we'll be as cool as cucumbers." Helen would have left the car running while she went in to fetch her sister, but she knew that if Margaret wasn't already dressed, the procedure could easily go to a half hour or more and there could be no rushing it.

"What are we doing?" said Margaret, touching the unfamiliar opening and locking devices recessed in the car door.

Helen pressed down on the automatic lock. The clunking noise made Margaret glance around the car's interior. "What was that sound?" she said.

"Just the doors locking," said Helen. "You want to put your seat belt on? We're going to take a drive out to your house. We'll stay overnight, and you can spend some time in the country, for a change."

After only one missed try, Margaret succeeded in buckling her own seatbelt. Helen's anxiety lightened a bit.

A red pick-up went by, and Margaret said, *"There's* one!" She stared out the window for a while and said to herself. "It's a good thing I don't have to count red cars, now."

"Yes, I guess that's a relief, to notice them instead."

"I just say: there's *another* one."

At that moment the gleaming red cab of a massive semi-truck pulled alongside with a noisy roar and shifting of gears. Margaret and Helen simultaneously burst into laughter.

"You want to count something like *that!*" said Margaret. With a self-satisfied chuckle, she added, "But now I just say, 'Oh, there's a red truck' and I don't have to count it."

Helen nudged Margaret affectionately. "But now you've got *me* doing it!" The truck pulled ahead and passed them.

They rode in silence for awhile. Margaret leaned against the window, watching the fields roll past. Then she turned to Helen and said, "Oh, this memory! Do you think I'll ever get it back?"

Before Helen could frame an answer, a red minivan passed them and Margaret announced cheerfully, "There's *another* one."

A half hour later, they turned in at the faded red mailbox and drove up the gravel drive between two stands of Norway spruce that hid the old farm house.

When it came into view, Margaret said, wonderingly, "That's not *my* house, is it?" She stared at it as if it had floated down from the clouds.

"Yes, it is, Sis. Barb comes and keeps it up so nicely," said Helen. For a moment Helen had a qualm. Early in her illness, Margaret had, mercifully, forgotten all about her thirty-eight year marriage to the man who had blighted her entire adulthood. Helen hoped—was pretty sure—that not even the sight of her old house would bring back recollections of him, but there was always the chance. "See how well your perennials are growing? I think you passed your green thumb onto my daughter."

"It's very pretty!"

Helen felt a pang of guilt. Sooner or later the house would have to be sold.

When they opened the car doors, the heat took their breath away.

"Oh, my goodness!" said Margaret. "What is it? What's the matter? Why is it so hot?"

"Just an early heat wave. I wish it could have been a nicer day for you, Margaret, I'm sorry. I don't suppose you want to walk around the garden just a little?"

Margaret said, "Well . . . all right."

But after a minute or two, Margaret's quiet distress in the heat made Helen bring her inside. Thankfully, Barb had thought to leave the air conditioning running, though it wasn't quite a match for the sun pounding against the row of tall, south-facing windows. Even with the windows shut up and the curtains drawn, the house seemed close and uninviting.

"I'm sorry," Helen apologized again. "I'd hoped we could walk down through the meadow today, the way we used to."

She drew the curtains open. "Isn't it a pretty view, Sis?" she said. Margaret came over, and the two looked across the meadow to the river valley and the hazy green line of hills beyond. A single white barn sat like a pearl in the convergence of two distant slopes. Helen and Margaret, for some minutes, stood shoulder to shoulder.

Helen was at a loss now, how to occupy Margaret. She so wanted this outing to be a pleasure for her. She had told Cal, "I know Margaret will enjoy pulling weeds in her garden and taking that path to the river. And maybe after this she'll be willing to come out with me more often." Now they could only stare out at the view, and Helen wondered if Margaret even recognized what she was seeing.

Margaret sat down on the sofa, her long fingers limp and empty-looking on the faded cushions.

"What is it we're doing here?" she asked Helen, who still stood by the window looking around the room a little desperately.

"Well," replied Helen, "we're just paying a visit to your house."

Margaret cast uncertain glances over the room—at the bookshelves and the easy chairs—as if she weren't exactly sure who they belonged to.

"Is there anything you'd like to do while we're here?"

Helen asked this, not knowing what else to say. She apologized again for the weather and then suggested they fix lunch, though it was too early to eat.

Margaret, as usual, had little appetite. Helen put most of the food back in containers in the refrigerator. Then she led the way to the living room again, and the two of them sat facing each other.

"What are we doing now?" said Margaret, looking embarrassed not to know.

"Just spending time together," replied Helen. It was only 11:30.

Helen scanned the titles in the bookcase and thought about how she and Margaret had once lost track of time in discussions of books they'd both enjoyed. When they were children, Margaret, the older, had often read aloud to Helen.

"Remember the *Babar* books and your wonderful elephant voices?" Helen said.

"Oh . . . yes, I think so."

Helen searched the shelves. Maybe this was something Margaret would enjoy, looking at their childhood books together. But the books had long ago been handed on to Helen's children and there were none left on the shelves.

Helen's eyes rested on a framed painting Margaret had done a long time ago of sunlit hollyhocks along a weathered fence. She took it down and put it in her sister's lap. "That painting you did is one of my favorites, Sis. I just love it."

Margaret frowned at it. "I painted that? I don't remember doing it at all."

Helen gestured to other paintings of Margaret's on the walls, and Margaret got up from the sofa to examine them.

She said, "Well, they're pretty *good*, if I do say so myself."

"Oh, my, yes!" exclaimed Helen. "You're such a good artist, Margaret. That probably explains why Wayne is so artistic. He got it from his aunt."

Margaret tapped her cheek pensively and gazed at the pictures with interest. "I haven't painted for a long time, though, have I?" she asked.

"No, you haven't."

21

"I wonder why not?"

Helen paused before answering. "Oh . . . I'm not sure. Why do you think?"

"Well," Margaret said vaguely, "how would I do it?"

"I've set that table up in your apartment, Margaret. There are brushes and paints and paper—everything ready to go, if you decide to try again. It's all there."

"Well, I think I'm going to *do* that when I get back."

Helen got up and put her arm around Margaret's shoulders. "Margaret! How about doing some painting *now?*"

Margaret's shoulders stiffened. "Well, I don't know," she said.

"Or, not *painting,* but just playing with colors and patterns, you know. It doesn't have to be realistic looking. I'll bet you'd enjoy it. I'll do it *with* you."

"I'm not sure . . . "

Helen heard, but decided to ignore, the anxiety in her sister's voice.

"If you're not enjoying it, we can just stop," she said brightly, and went upstairs to find the box of Margaret's old art supplies.

When she came downstairs, Margaret was back on the sofa again, biting nervously on a thumbnail. Helen led her to the dining room table and sat down beside her. From the box she drew out a dozen or so colored pencils, crayons and chalks and a tablet of drawing paper, from which she tore sheets for Margaret and herself.

"All right, now. Why don't we choose some colors and just see what happens?" she said, sounding to herself like the grade school teacher she had been for so many years. "We used to do this when we were kids, remember? You showed me how to fool around with the colors? I was never an artist like you, but it was still a lot of fun!" To encourage her sister, she picked up a blue colored pencil and drew several diagonal streaks across her own sheet.

Margaret watched her for some seconds before hesitantly choosing a green pencil and scratching two or three thin, wobbly lines in one corner of her paper. The lines looked huddled there, afraid of the large white space that was left empty. Margaret peered at what she had drawn and held the pencil with uncertainty in the air. Helen, randomly applying new color to her own blue streaks, watched her sister's struggle out of the corner of her eye.

After several tries, Margaret put her pencil down. "I don't know what I'm doing!" she said, tremulously.

Sweat broke out in Helen's armpits. "Oh, it doesn't have to be anything in *particular!*" she said. Her voice cracked with heartiness. "We're just *playing*." Margaret's humiliation was shrinking her in her chair. Her head bowed forward as if her thin neck were too weak to hold it up. Still, obediently, she took up her pencil again, pinching it at an awkward angle between her thumb and forefinger as if it were some modern, unfamiliar implement. Painstakingly, she added a few more meager lines to her paper.

Helen was passing her pencil compulsively back and forth over her own drawing. Never claiming artistic ability of her own, now she cringed at the difference between Margaret's feeble scratches and the colorful abstract shapes she herself had drawn without even trying. "Oh, mercy," she thought, "how can I stop this?"

All at once she became aware of a change in the room. At first she only sensed it. Then she realized the room had darkened. Helen looked past Margaret through the windows and stood up, almost knocking over her chair.

"My goodness, Margaret!" she exclaimed. "Will you look at that!" Margaret turned to see.

In the clear blue sky, a single enormous black cloud, perfectly flat underneath but growing monumentally high up into the air, was moving toward them, all of a piece, like something out of a fairy tale. A fantastic floating mountain. It was already close and low enough to give the illusion that it might skim the roof of the house, enveloping the chimney and the surrounding treetops.

Margaret laid down her pencil. "Oh!" she cried. "Isn't that wonderful!"

"Amazing!"

They hurried out the front door and into the yard in time to see the cloud just emerging over the peak of the roof. A fresh breeze bathed their faces. It seemed the temperature had dropped ten or fifteen degrees since they'd come in from the garden, earlier.

Margaret tipped her head and raised her arms to the sky. "Oh, you wonderful cloud!" she said. "I've never seen anything like you before." Turning her radiant face on Helen, she said, "I'm sure I'd remember if I'd seen something like this!"

Neither of them took a step to go back inside. They could hardly take their eyes off the cloud, it was so dense and black, and it moved with such simmering energy. Helen half expected to hear deep, rolling music accompanying it.

The silence with which it moved hypnotized them. They stopped speaking, not to miss a moment.

Margaret's eyes were full of joy, her face tilted toward the cloud, as if nothing else in the world mattered, as if—who knew?—she might be lifted right up into it and carried off to exotic lands. Helen put her arm around Margaret and hugged her, pressing her lips to the thin cheek and thick white hair curling around her temple.

Helen and Margaret stood in the yard for a long time after the cloud floated past. They watched it roll above the pasture and across the road, topping the telephone poles, then across the harrowed bean field, casting everything in shadow as it passed, and on into the distance until it slowly disappeared like a ship over the horizon. Only after it was gone did it occur to Helen that she should have been afraid.

Cottony white clouds had begun to appear everywhere, and the air was cool enough for a walk. Helen reached for Margaret's hand and together they took the path through the meadow to the river.

Along the way, Margaret discovered a number of treasures with which she filled her pockets—a small fossil, a blue jay feather, an opalescent river clam-shell. In a patch of grass she stooped down and plucked a four-leaf clover.

"Margaret!" cried Helen. "How in the world did you see that four-leaf clover amongst all those others?"

"I don't know," Margaret replied.

"I could no more find a four-leaf clover than fly! You are a wonder!"

"Here." Margaret held it out. "You take it. I can always find another one."

Helen hesitated. "Well, thank you . . . I will," she said. "But you hold it for me. I know I'd be sure to drop it."

Margaret sheltered the clover in her cupped hand all the way back up the hill to the house.

They took a nap after the walk. Margaret fell asleep immediately, but Helen lay beside her, staring at the ceiling, and tried to think of things they might do together that evening. She thought of all the ways her wonderful big sister used to entertain her as a child. How Margaret would fold and glue colored paper into tiny animals, which she would hide around the house and yard, each standing on a square of paper containing a clue in verse as to the whereabouts of the next creature. Helen would run about, chasing down the little treasures, which she collected in a menagerie on the shelf over her bed.

> *Bunny doesn't like the cold,*
> *but she will dare it*
> *to find a carrot.*

And there in the vegetable drawer of the refrigerator would be a paper rabbit, its tail a piece of cotton torn from a Q-tip. Helen would snatch it up triumphantly, as Margaret applauded. What a heaven Margaret had made of Helen's otherwise mundane childhood. And now, to see her so helpless, dull, and unoccupied, it was more than she could bear. Silently she cried, Oh Sis, come back, come back to me. I miss you so.

That evening, after they ate their leftovers for dinner, Margaret's eyes fell on the treasures she had brought back from the trip to the river—the fossil, the feather and the clam-shell. Helen had already tucked the four-leaf clover into her billfold to protect it, but the other finds lay on the sideboard. Margaret picked them up and wandered around the room with them.

"What do I do with these?" she said. "Am I supposed to keep them?" She stood in the center of the room holding the objects in the palm of her outstretched hand as if the room itself might help her solve this puzzling dilemma. Helen looked around and noticed a dusty basket full of stones and shells. The basket had been decorating a corner by the south windows for so many years Helen had stopped seeing it. She carried the basket to the dining room table. "Oh come look," she said, and Margaret followed her over.

"You could add them to this collection," Helen said. "Look at all these unusual things you've found. Just like art work, aren't they?"

She pulled two chairs up and began to take the objects out of the basket to study them. Margaret set her things on the table and sat down. Together, they brushed the dust off the basket's contents, one at a time: stones, shells, seed pods and driftwood, fragments of old brick, weathered glass, and pottery. Helen marveled at each item, holding it to the light, and admiring its shape or color or texture before putting it into Margaret's hand. Repeatedly, Margaret remarked, "Now where do you suppose I got that one?"

"On one of your walks, I guess. You've always loved natural things so much," said Helen. She had come to take this for granted about her sister, but she had never paid close enough attention to the astonishing quantity and fineness of Margaret's treasures, taken altogether.

When the basket had been emptied and its contents restored, Margaret placed her afternoon's finds on top of the pile with some care, sitting back afterward to admire the effect. Then Helen noticed next to the fireplace a second basket holding another collection. She brought it to the table, too, and when she and Margaret finished going through that basket, there were still others—large and small, upstairs and downstairs—all full of natural objects that Margaret had spotted with her unerring eye over a lifetime. The sisters stayed at the dining room table examining and admiring each item until they had gone through every basket in the house. The last one held rocks in recognizable forms: people, animals, geometric shapes.

Margaret held up a river-worn piece of shale, pitted in four places. "Is it a stone?" she asked.

"Yes, but it's so much like a face, isn't it?"

"Eyes, nose, mouth." Margaret touched each feature with her fingertip and set the stone gently on the table. "I'll put you right here," she said to it, then picked up a flat piece of shale with a protrusion at one side. "This poor guy has an awfully big nose for such a weak chin!" She clucked sympathetically and laid it next to the first stone, aligning their lower edges.

Helen was elated. Maybe Margaret would retain at least some impression of this happy evening and want to come out with her again. They could work together in the garden. Helen would buy them each a pair of those red cotton gardening gloves Margaret used to be so fond of. They would work side by side, weeding and watering.

Helen had set the mantle clock when they arrived, and now it bonged the hour. It was ten P.M. Their hands were gray with dust, and Helen's neck was stiff from bending to the light. They got up from the dining room table. The floor around them was covered with baskets. Helen picked up the heaviest one to put it back in its place, but Margaret took it away from her. "*You* shouldn't do that! I'm older than you, don't forget." Then, misinterpreting the look of self-reproach that appeared on Helen's face, she said, uncertainly, "I am, aren't I?"

"Of course you are!" Helen said. "Yes, you're right, of course you're older." She transferred the heavy basket to her sister's hands and watched her stoop to set it carefully on the tile by the woodstove.

After they replaced all the baskets, they put out the lights and went up to bed. On the staircase, Helen stopped and touched Margaret's elbow. "That was fun, wasn't it?"

Margaret turned to look at her. "What was?" she said.

Helen blinked. "Looking through your baskets of stones and things."

With a little thrill in her voice, Margaret said, "That was so much fun, Helen." Then more wistfully, "I don't think anyone has ever looked at those baskets with me before." Following her sister up the stairs, Helen pressed one hand tightly to her mouth and the other against her chest to suppress an impulse to weep out loud. She drew several deep breaths. When she could speak, she said, "Well, it was fun for me, too, Sis! Thank you for such an enjoyable evening."

In the middle of the night Helen woke in the old double bed they were sharing.

"Hello?" Margaret was saying. "Hello?"

Helen took her hand. "Yes, Sis, I'm here. It's Helen. What do you need?"

"Will I be home soon?" Margaret said in the darkness.

Helen tried to make out her face silhouetted by the nightlight. It looked hazy, almost indistinguishable from the pattern behind it on the faded wallpaper. She squeezed Margaret's hand. The bones were as fragile as a bird's. Enclosing the long, thin fingers in both of hers, she could only say, "Yes, Sis, you'll be home in the morning."

JULY

✽

i.

CAL HADN'T REMEMBERED that the poison ivy was why Helen had given up her walk. If he had, he would have done something about it sooner.

"That's why I don't take that path down through the ravine anymore," Helen reminded him, "since that one section's gotten so overgrown with the ivy in the last two or three years." She could catch it just by breathing the same air. And he knew that if she couldn't make her way past that overgrown part, she couldn't follow the old horse trail she liked to walk on so well.

"We ought to put weed killer on it," she told him, but it wasn't something he could bring himself to do. Wayne had criticized him for years about pesticides, and after half a lifetime of using them on his crops, he had to admit that the untimely deaths by cancer of too many farmers around there had brought him to Wayne's way of thinking.

It was worth the risk, he decided, to dig the poison ivy up by its roots, vine by vine, and next year, if necessary, do it again until he'd got it all. It was a big job, he knew, and he had to be careful on two counts—his back and hip and his own allergy to the plant himself, not as bad as hers was, but he'd had a nasty rash a time or two, and the plants were wily. They'd fool you into thinking they were innocent hawthorn shoots. You had to know what you were looking at.

"I'll get it out of there for you," he said to Helen. And she said, "Don't, Cal. You'd better leave it alone."

"You just have to take the right precautions," he told her. "You just

31

have to use your head." He would wear those old suede work gloves that were worn out enough to be sacrificed when the job was done, and that long-sleeved shirt he'd painted more than a few sheds and fences in. He could put on his ancient cracked leather boots and rinse them off later with a bucket of hot water and detergent.

It took him over two hours to do the job. By the time he finished, his right hip and low back ached pretty bad with all that stooping and bending. He knew he should have divided the work over a couple, three days, not go asking for trouble, but once you started yanking up weeds, it was addictive.

When he was finished digging the ivy, he took a long stick and tamped the tangled vines down inside two hefty garbage bags. Well, now, he thought, what do I do with these? You couldn't leave them lying around. The sticky juice that causes all the trouble was persistent, practically immortal.

He wondered if he could dump it with the county. But he couldn't remember if they still burned waste over there. You wouldn't want someone breathing the smoke from that. A person's lungs could blister inside and swell up like the stomach of a goat that's grazed on grass too long, and that could be the end of you.

Maybe the best thing would be to bury the bags way down at the bottom of the ravine, pinch them tight shut around the neck with twist ties so the darn poisonous things couldn't climb out and sprout up again. But to bury them, he'd have to lug them way down to the bottom of that steep hill, with his hip bothering him and his back and shoulder aching, and then have to dig a big hole, cutting through roots. It just didn't seem manageable.

He leaned against the pickup truck and considered the bags sitting on the gravel in the driveway. It was a hot July day, but not humid, thank God—he felt the humidity more lately than he used to. Or had it always bothered him? Suddenly he couldn't remember if it had or hadn't. It seemed like it hadn't, but how could you forget something like that about yourself? He was getting old.

A brisk dry breeze sneaked its way under the cuffs of his old paint shirt and puffed out the sleeves. The air carried the sweet molasses-like smell of tree sap laid on the road to keep the dust down and the pungent, exhilarating scent of sage bushes that grew around the clothesline poles. A couple of sheets were billowing on the line like sails, pushed by a steady southeast breeze.

Well, he thought, maybe I'll burn the bags myself—pick an isolated open spot well away from habitation, pour a little kerosene on them, stand upwind, throw a match and let the bags melt down while the weeds burn to ash. He knew just the place for it, an empty stretch at the corner of land where his neighbor once kept a mobile home. He could set the bags on the old concrete slab it had stood on. His neighbor's house and his own house were a good mile away, and there was nothing northwest of them, downwind, but a scrappy patch of timber and a bean field.

Cal threw the bags in the back of the pickup, gingerly drew off the gloves and threw them on the truck bed. He grabbed a can of kerosene and a box of fireplace matches from the garage and put them in too. Helen came to the kitchen window as he drove around the side of the house and waved at him. He drove the mile or so past the bend in the road where the old trailer used to be and continued on to his neighbor's, just curious to see if anyone was home—not that they'd care what he had in mind to do, they were easy-going generous people, the Millers. Neither of their vehicles was in the drive, but it was a workday, of course. Wednesday. Or Thursday maybe. You didn't need to remember the day of the week when you didn't have a regular schedule to keep anymore.

He backed out of their drive, drove back to the bend, and pulled onto the shoulder. After he got out, he went around the truck bed and carefully slid his hands into the gloves. Then he took the bags out, crossed down and up the drainage ditch and scanned the open area for the best place to set the bags down. There wasn't as much of that old concrete left as he'd remembered, just pieces showing through the weeds, but he dropped the bags next to each other onto a moderately big chunk of rubble. He removed one glove and held a finger up to test the wind. Sure enough, it was still blowing steady from the southeast. Some distance away, a stand of willows in the bottom of a dry watershed trailed their weeping branches toward the northwest, and well beyond that, all the way to the horizon, an ocean of soybean plants rippled and bent in the same direction.

One-handed, he opened the neck of the bags, slipped off the second glove and dropped them both in. He squirted some kerosene inside, and then sprinkled some on the plastic and a little more on the concrete underneath.

Just to be safe, he took off his glasses and tied his big cotton handkerchief around his nose and mouth before replacing the glasses and pulling his seed cap well down over his forehead.

He stood back and lit a couple of the fireplace matches, got them going good in the shelter of his body before tossing them at the two bundles. One of the matches went out, but the other one landed square on top of a bag, where it flared up. The bag started to melt right away. He threw several more matches on the bags before backing off to stand at a safe distance over by the ditch. Pretty soon he could see vines and leaves showing through. It was gratifying to see that they'd caught, too, and the whole shebang was crackling away as tidy as you please, sending nice controlled little columns of black and white smoke off away from him without so much as a scent of burning in his nostrils. He untied the handkerchief from around his face, lifted his cap and mopped his brow.

The sun was scorching out here in the open with no shade trees or any water, just a hot burning blue sky and the silence of the empty road deepened by the soft crooning of two mourning doves perched along the telephone wires.

Cal watched the poison ivy flare up orange and crackling as the black plastic of the garbage bags curled and melted away like arm hair held to a match flame. He used to do reckless things like that as a kid. He loved a fire, especially a bonfire. Plenty of downed trees and old lumber around a farm to build one up, on a winter's night. Nothing like it to hypnotize you into a quiet state like you were some long ago prairie tribesman.

The bags were melted by now and the poison ivy gave off a shower of dancing ashes and sparks and a shimmer of heat, blue at the core. In a few more minutes it was burned completely down. Climbing stiffly back across the ditch—his hip and back still giving him trouble—he returned the can of kerosene to the trunk, took out a plastic bucket and a long-handled spade and scooped up some road gravel to carry back so he could throw it on top just to be sure.

But when he came nearer to the pile of ashes, he saw that sparks had jumped to the other side of the slab, where they had started up a small irregular line of flames in the low, dry grass adjoining. There had been a long dry spell, and there was a fair amount of brown weeds about. He reached for the bucket. The thin row of flames began to spread out. He tossed the gravel at it, which smothered some of the fire, but stirred up sparks as well.

Cal went back and scraped some more dirt and gravel off the road, groaning at his stiffness when he bent to lift the shovel full of rock. When had he stopped being able to spend a morning shoveling rock or dirt without suffering later? All the work he used to do without even thinking—feeling only good and tired at the end of the day—had become like the work of that Sisyphus in the myth. One by one, he'd had to rent out plots of his land because farming them was beyond him, until there was no land left for him to work.

He imagined if Tom had lived. The boy would be in the prime of his life now, and together they would have bought more land instead of renting or selling off their heritage. And now, with the economy the way it was, what would become of him and Helen as their meager investments lost value? And what if one or both of them got sick or disabled? Wayne wouldn't care for them and Barb had her family to look out for. He saw himself stuck in a wheelchair or becoming like Helen's sister, and the thought terrified him.

The second load of gravel smothered more of the little line of runaway flames. This secondary fire was close to the ground, only an inch or so wide and two or three yards long. It wasn't much of a blaze and he started to tromp on it to stamp it out. There was a pleasure in that, in spite of the twinges of pain in his hip. The low flames extinguished under his boots and he continued down the line systematically crushing them. Then he went over to check on the pile of ash where the poison ivy had burned down and saw there was yet a slim wisp of smoke. Leaning out of its range, he stamped out this last vestige of the fire and said to himself out loud, "That's got her."

The job finished, he picked up his bucket and with a feeling of satisfaction headed back toward the truck. Before crossing the ditch, however, he took one last glance over his shoulder and, to his surprise, saw that the second fire had somehow revived itself, veering off toward a cluster of nettles that was rustling dryly in the wind. Cal felt a small stir of fear under his ribs. He set down the pail and hurried over to the burning weeds. He brought his foot down hard several times, fetching a flash of pain in his hip and down his leg. The low flames licked around the soles of his boots, though he couldn't feel any heat through the thick leather.

Then he noticed that another spot of renegade flame had flared up on a stalk of last year's golden rod, off to his left. "For Christ's sake," Cal muttered, stepping quickly over to kick out the new flames, but the goldenrod was a couple of feet tall, and he was nervous about setting his pant legs ablaze. He decided smothering it would be safer.

I should have just gone ahead and put weed killer on the poison ivy, he thought as he limped back to the road for more gravel. The sweat was dripping into his eyebrows by now, and his throat was as dry as the dust on the road. His wife had said, "Just use weed killer." But no, he'd gone on about how pesticides weren't all that selective—whatever the advertising on the box claimed—and before you knew it, you'd end up with a hillside of buttercups and sunflowers hanging their heads and giving up the ghost. Where had he come up with all that foolishness? It had been his son talking through him. And why in the world did he listen to the opinion of a man who'd turned his back on farming from the day he'd first been asked what he wanted to be when he grew up: "Not a farmer." That's just how he'd put it. In the negative. Where was he now, when this job for his mother needed to be done, and his old man was getting up in age and could have used some help?

The bucket of gravel slowed the new fire considerably, giving him time to attend once more to another line of flames moving slowly but steadily across the open land toward the ancient stubble of downed trees in the direction of Millers' bean field. It struck him then that Miller had let weeds grow tall in that field before he sprayed three weeks ago, and those dried, dead weeds would be lying there between the rows. If sparks were carried in amongst them, Miller's bean crop would be a goner.

Cal ran up and down the line of flames, trying to keep them in check. As he finished stomping down one part and moved on to the next, the first stretch kindled up again and seemed to spark off more little side fires. "Oh Lord," he thought. "What've I gotten myself into?" He wondered why he hadn't called over to the landfill to find out if they burned waste or not. He should have yelled for Helen to make the call, but he had felt foolish standing there in his protective get up. She'd given him a look when he walked down towards the ravine in it. It was easy to see she didn't trust him to know what he was about these days, like she once did.

The joints in his knees were beginning to swell from the effort of repeatedly raising and stomping his foot on the weeds. His left leg was fatiguing, but if he switched to his right leg, that troublesome hip complained in a big way.

A ground squirrel poked its head from a hole nearby, sniffed the air, and with a frightened eye on Cal, made a dash for the road.

Cal stumbled on a clod of earth and cursed at the shooting pains in his body. He stopped for a moment to think what to do. Pressing a hand on his chest where his heart was beating rapidly, he considered getting back in the truck and racing home to call the fire department, but by the time they arrived all the way out here from town, the fire would likely have reached his neighbors' soybeans.

He tore off his long-sleeved shirt and his undershirt, both drenched with his sweat, and he returned to the fire to slap the shirts against the burning weeds. He made a little headway, but it was slow going. Then he remembered an old blanket behind the truck seat, and he limped back up the ditch again, threw open the door of the truck and pulled the blanket out.

Panting heavily, he hurried back as fast as he could—he was hobbling now—and threw the blanket over the burning goldenrod, kicking at it frantically until the crackle of fire went silent and the smell of hot polyester was strong in his nostrils. Then he whacked the singed blanket across the grass on the widening band of blackened ground while stamping up and down on it in his leather boots. But he still couldn't make enough progress.

Sooner or later a car was bound to come along. It might be the only hope of getting this thing stopped. Momentarily, he did think he heard a car, and his heart hammered, though the sound turned out to be the faint roar of a downshifting semi truck on the interstate. In all likelihood if someone came along it would be Helen driving out to look for him. If it was anyone else, well, he'd just swallow his pride and flag them down, though he might tell them he'd happened on the fire instead of caused it. Two people could probably beat the flames out pretty quick. But if it was his wife, oh, he felt sick at the thought of her finding him in this fix—a dumb boy's mistake, like forgetting to unload the rifle before putting it up, or driving a baseball through a window, or building a fire in the fireplace with the flue closed. His dad would have tanned his behind 'til he was black and blue for pulling a stunt like this. What grown man with a jot of sense would start a fire using kerosene in a windy field during a dry spell?

He looked at the black scorch moving relentlessly across the land in an ever-deepening and widening rectangle, and just for a moment it occurred to him to run. He could jump into the truck and drive away. He was sorely tempted, but he trudged back to the road instead, picked up the shovel where it lay in the truck bed and returned to the fire, skirting around the end of the line of flames and coming up the other side of it to dig a fire break.

Sweat, mingled with smoke, stung his eyes. With each push of the shovel the muscles in his chest seemed to close around his heart. He could imagine a moment of constriction when he crumpled and fell to the hard ground and the low line of flames inched toward him. He saw himself lying there in just his old baggy pants and cracked boots and clutching the sagging pectorals and sparse white hair of his bare chest. He imagined the line of fire stopping for a moment in disbelief at the sight of him, like an army halting in the middle of a battle to behold a vision of something comical and unexpected, a donkey in a straw hat, maybe, pulling a driverless cart.

But he kept on turning over the soil at a speed he didn't think himself capable of, with the hot wind on his face drawing the row of flames toward him. Panic gripped him when he looked back to check the little progress he had made and realized that instead of just turning the dirt over, he should have been tossing it back onto the flames. He tried doing this with the next shovelful, but by now the motion of thrusting the heavy shovel blade out in front of him was too much. It sent knives of pain stabbing through his shoulder, and he felt angry.

If he'd had a little help—if he didn't have to do every goddamn thing alone—there would have been two heads to think it through instead of one. That's how it was supposed to be. Even after he was married and had kids of his own, he had never let his dad—as aggravating as the old man was—take on a two-man project alone.

He took some deep breaths and tried to calm himself, to think rationally. It was then that he noticed the cistern. He must have seen that cistern lid a thousand times poking out of the weeds amidst the rubble—seen it, but not really seen it, as he came around the bend on his way into town. It was the first thing he should have noticed when that little fire began to get out of hand.

What a lunkhead he was if there'd been water at his fingertips and he'd never even thought to look because he was so addled he just stomped around on that grass fire like some big old dancing bear with no brain. The thing was out of control now. Could he afford the time to go back and pry off the three-inch thick concrete cover and get a rope from the truck to tie to the bucket? And what if the cistern had gone dry?

With a desperate eye on the line of flames and the little spontaneous blazes here and there, he staggered over the uneven ground, dragging the shovel after him. He picked up the bucket and took it and the shovel to the cistern.

Having wedged the shovel blade into a crevice under the rim of the heavy concrete lid, he leaned with his whole weight on the end of the shovel handle and by inches slid the cover off. He was so intent on getting this job done, he was almost numb to his pain by now.

He peered down the hole and with sudden hope saw the dark shape of his head reflected against sky. When he threw in a rock, he felt a jolt of relief at the clean-sounding plunk that suggested deep water. Now with a little more energy to his step, he made the trip back to the truck where he hauled out a tangle of old rope piled behind the wheel well.

Back at the cistern, he tied the rope around the bucket handle and lowered it in. It hit water. He gave it a moment to tip and fill. With thoughts of a permanently ruined shoulder and aggravated hip, he braced the sole of one boot against the concrete edge and pulled up the full bucket. The sight of water splashing over the sides elated him, clearing his mind a little. He got the idea to unfasten the rope from the pail and re-tie it to the blanket. He dropped it into the well and brought it up soaked. Then with the handle of the heavy pail clutched in one hand and the dripping blanket around his shoulders, he staggered back to the fire.

There was a gratifying hiss of steam as he threw water sparingly along one section of flames and awkwardly flung the sodden blanket over another. He looked back and saw that his fire break had, for the moment, stymied the first stretch of fire, which was flickering and darting indecisively, as if making up its mind what to do next.

Heartened, he grabbed up the blanket and the empty pail and returned to the cistern, where he plunged them in again. It took four more trips to quench the flames and douse their smoldering remains.

When he'd thrown the last bucketful of water, he stood listening at the edge of the fire line for the whine and pop of sparks exploding, the low mutter of flames drawing in oxygen, but there was no sound. The sun beat down on the silent field. Even the drone of insects had fallen still.

Pain and exhaustion caught up with him. He looked dazedly across the charred land and couldn't believe the fire was dead. To the southeast, the air shimmered with heat. To the northwest a haze of smoke hung over the field. Staring at it, he almost expected to see the field spontaneously combust, to see flame leap out everywhere from the blackened grass and move down the hill toward the bean field like whirling demons. But the fire was truly out.

He stood panting for some minutes. His heart drummed against his ribs, and his throat was so dry he couldn't swallow. Intense pain was gathering in his body. He could feel it starting to spread up and down his back and legs and shoulders and arms and hip, even into his hands, that had held the shovel. A thousand little spasms quivered under his skin.

He thought, I've got to get home while I can, and he walked unevenly back across the burned ground, dragging the shovel and blanket behind, his trembling legs hardly able to carry him. When he got to the cistern to collect the rope, he stopped and stared at it, dismayed.

He saw that he would have to replace the cover. For some seconds he gazed at it dully. It didn't seem possible that he could lift the thing again. But you couldn't leave a cistern uncapped for a kid to fall into.

He had a sudden memory of the time he and Helen had beat the woods looking for six-year-old Barb, who had failed to show up for lunch one Saturday. He had stopped in his tracks, cold with terror, remembering having left their cistern lid ajar. Without a word to Helen, he left the path and took the shortest route through the woods, crashing through brambles and leaping over fallen logs until, racing around the side of the barn he saw the little girl on tiptoe pinning doll clothes on the clothesline. Tears had come into his eyes and he couldn't answer when she looked up and said, soberly and proudly, "I'm doing laundry, Daddy."

Groaning as he wedged the shovel blade under the lid and pressed down on the handle for a second time, he took a great breath, closed his eyes and pushed. The concrete lid shifted and tilted on the point of the blade. With all his strength he pushed on the handle and felt the lid tilt forward and slide towards the center. When he had no strength to slide it any farther, it lay on top of the cistern with just a rodent-sized gap left. That was the best he could do. If a field mouse smelled water and fell in, so be it.

Even after he got back behind the wheel and started to pull away, he kept looking over his shoulder to be sure another fire hadn't rekindled. He imagined it breaking out as soon as he drove back around the bend in the road. He would be dreaming all night, he thought, about fires he couldn't put out.

Cal was pretty sure Helen hadn't seen him standing with the bags in the driveway before he'd left. It was a good thing, because he didn't have the presence of mind after the wildfire to think what he would tell her if she asked what he had done with them.

Luckily she was out back when he got home, and didn't hear the truck pull in. He managed to get into the house and wash off the sweat and soot before she came upstairs. In the shower his arms trembled and his legs felt as if they would collapse under him. The spray needled his sunburned back and chest. He positioned the shower head so the cool water would soothe his fiery right hip. When he finished showering, he lay down on the bed and closed his eyes.

"Well," Helen said later that night, "I thank you for pulling out all that poison ivy for me, but I'd rather you'd not have done it and gotten yourself in this condition." He'd told her he had buried the poison ivy down in the ravine and then taken a drive into town.

In the morning he was in so much pain that she drove him in to the doctor. Sciatic pains shot down his right leg. If Helen knew about it, she'd start insisting on that hip surgery or some other "intervention," as they liked to call it these days. But any intervention would involve more out-of-pocket doctor visits. They hadn't been able to afford the Medicare supplement. After fifty years of farming and putting kids through college, it had come to this—he hadn't been able to save enough to pay his own medical bills.

When they came to the bend in the road where he'd burned the poison ivy, Helen slowed the car. "My goodness!" she said. "Looks like Millers had a pretty good-sized grass fire down here. See that?" She pointed at the scorched field and shook her head. "I'll bet somebody threw a cigarette out a car window. People ought to be more careful this time of year. Millers are lucky they didn't lose their beans."

He felt queasy wondering how many times he would have to pass the place before he could stand to look at it. He leaned back and gazed at the road with half-shut eyes, exhausted. Thinking of Helen's sister, the way he was headed these days, it wouldn't be all that long before he would come around that bend in the road, feel ashamed of himself, and have no idea why.

ii.

It started as a very small theft. Not technically a theft at all, from Helen's standpoint. She had only wanted her sister to have something pretty to look at.

Margaret had been lying on top of her made up bed day after day, fully clothed down to her shoes and stockings. She lay on the bedspread and apologized every time Helen came to visit. "I'm sleeping my life away," she complained, but she wouldn't leave her room, except to go to meals when an aide came to remind her, and even this she did hesitantly.

Helen tried to coax her sister out. "Won't you go for a walk with me, Margaret? The air is so fresh today."

"No," Margaret said, her eyebrows tilting in a distressed little frown, "No, I just don't think I'd better."

Helen sat on the edge of her sister's bed and took her hand. "Don't you feel well?"

Margaret raised herself up on her elbows. She looked vaguely down toward her feet in the tidy pair of lace-up flats she always wore. "I think I feel all right."

"Not dizzy or anything like that?"

"No, I don't think so," she said, making an effort at a reassuring smile. After a moment she said, "I don't remember *why* I can't go out, but I know there's a reason."

"Well, maybe you're thinking that you shouldn't go out *alone*, Margaret . . . Maybe *that's* what you're thinking of."

"Because I would get lost?" she said glancing up briefly at her sister's face, then away.

"Well . . ." Helen didn't like to say, *Yes, you might get lost*, to her older sister, who had always been the one to lead them, delightfully, down paths of fun and invention. ". . . Only because you might get a little *disoriented*—because of your memory problem, you know—and have a hard time getting back to the building."

Margaret picked listlessly at the cuticle of her thumbnail. "I'm sorry for being such a deadbeat," she said.

A pair of cardinals swooped down onto the pole feeder outside the picture window, scattering a flock of sparrows who had been pecking single-mindedly at the fallen seeds in the flowers underneath. Helen had installed the feeder outside the big window and planted a few impatiens flowers she had bought at the supermarket. The ground was hard to turn over—bare, dry soil, sparsely covered in weeds, and riddled with chunks of concrete and gravel left from the building's construction.

There had been no landscaping on the back side of the new, one-story facility on the outskirts of town, and the contractor had not run plumbing for a spigot in back. Helen had to haul milk jugs of water around the side of the building to water the flowers. These few she had planted in the shade of a scraggly bush were wilting in the summer sun.

"Do you want to lie down with me for awhile?" Margaret said.

"All right," said Helen, and she lay down close beside her sister on the single bed.

She pointed to the painting on the wall. "I love this picture you did, Margaret. Your old garden. Such beautiful colors."

Margaret reached for her bifocals where they lay on her chest, attached around her neck by a string. She peered at the painting. "Did I do that?" she said, marveling.

Margaret had been the only one in the family with artistic ability, yet anytime Helen had tried her hand at a painting or drawing, no matter how commonplace or uninspired, Margaret had praised it to the skies. "You could be an artist, Helen!" she always exclaimed.

When Helen left, after having supper with Margaret and staying to watch television with her, it was getting dark, a crescent moon just rising over the parking lot. Helen stood and watched it for a minute before getting in her car. Margaret never got to see the moon coming up now, or going down. Her room was on the north side of the building.

Helen almost went back inside then. She couldn't stand to think of her sister lying there on her bed alone in the dark, deprived, for all the endless nights and days ahead of her, of the moonrises and sunsets and other delights of nature that had given her such happy times ever since she was a little girl.

"Oh my poor Margaret," Helen said aloud in the parking lot. And she pulled a tissue from her pocket and cried quietly into it for a few minutes before heading back to the farm.

Margaret's assisted living residence, Oakridge Manor, was just off Oakwood Parkway, a new street that had been cut into a stretch of flat farmland on the north edge of their small town. In spring, the bare bulldozed land had been sodded and sprayed for weeds, so that by July there was an expanse of grass on either side of the street. Along the parkway, foundations and outer walls of condominiums had gone up almost overnight and then been left unfinished, with the downturn of the economy. Spindly, shoulder-high trees, widely-spaced and anchored by outsized metal poles and rubber tubing, dotted the landscape.

The only spots of color, Helen noticed as she drove down the otherwise barren parkway the next day, were little groups of yellow flowers growing here and there in the grass at the edge of the street. She recognized them as yellow coneflower—a wildflower that often grew on roadsides around there. Its trailing sun-ray petals beamed among the prairie grasses and wildflowers that had been introduced in the last few years along the interstate to keep the topsoil from eroding.

Helen slowed as she passed each cluster of yellow blooms along the curb, distributed randomly, it seemed, every block or so. Had someone planted them or had they just come up by themselves?

Yellow coneflowers, it occurred to her, would make a nice cover for that bare ground outside Margaret's window. A sunny splash of color, they wouldn't need much watering once they took hold. Certainly they never got watered on the interstate, and look how they thrived there. They might spread and keep on flowering through August. Margaret would like that.

The next day Helen went to the local nursery and asked if she could buy potted yellow coneflower plants, but they were sold out, and in July, it was too late to expect the flowers to grow from seed. Helen left the store disappointed.

Now that she noticed the coneflower blossoms, they were on her mind every time she drove on the mile-long parkway to and from her sister's. She counted ten small clusters of them. Five on the south side of the street and five on the north, butter yellow blooms stirring in the breeze like sunny spectators cheering the cars along. She didn't see any of it growing in the grass away from the parkway up toward the development sites. The flowers grew only in these irregularly spaced patches along the curbs.

At night in bed beside her sleeping husband, Helen got to thinking about the yellow coneflowers. Evidently they were growing there by accident like a weed, the seeds carried on the wind maybe, and lodged in cracks between the street and the grass. Was there any reason not to dig up one clump of it and transplant it outside Margaret's window? She had once dug up a bit of chamomile growing wild near their farm in the ditch along the county road, and it had transplanted nicely.

On a Friday morning, Helen drove down Oakwood Parkway with a small wheelbarrow, plastic water jugs, a spade and a plastic tub in her car. She wondered how it might look if she stopped right on the parkway and got out and dug up a plant. How deeply coneflower roots went, she had no idea—whether it would be a job of a minute or of five. Well, it might look strange, but if she pulled the car right up close to the patch of flowers, maybe it would be hard for someone to see what she was doing. There was no traffic at the moment. At ten A.M. most people were already at work.

Dressed in her Keds, an old pair of culottes and a sleeveless blouse, she got out, took the spade and tub from the trunk and set to it.

Getting the flowers out, she had to dig into the thick, stubborn grass

47

around it in order to keep from cutting into the roots and to bring up enough dirt. A minute went by. Seeing a vehicle up ahead, she slid her shovel down between her car and the curb. A man in an SUV slowed and came alongside her.

"Need help?" he said, pointing to her raised trunk lid. "Got a flat?"

"Oh no," she called back, cheerily. "I'm fine, thanks."

The man drove on. Helen closed the trunk and returned hastily to her digging.

Finally the roots, in a large clod of earth, came loose, and she lifted the whole thing out and set it gently into the waiting tub. The flowers looked beautiful, ten or twelve blossoms, the long petals trailing from their brown centers. She took a moment to pass her hands lightly over the delicate blooms and smell their meadow fragrance before hurrying them to the trunk of her car. She threw the shovel in, and just as another vehicle, a block distant, was pulling to a stop sign on the side street, she slammed the trunk lid shut, jumped in her car and drove away. The whole thing had taken only about five minutes. She had considered asking Cal to help her, but she wasn't quite sure if he would approve, and now she was glad she had gone ahead and done it by herself.

Helen tapped on Margaret's window.

"Margaret! It's Helen!" she shouted through the glass. "Come see what I've got."

After a considerable wait, she saw Margaret appear at the window, her white hair disheveled and flattened on one side where it had been pressed into the pillow. Helen held up the tub of coneflowers.

"I'll come in, and you tell me where you want me to plant them."

She hurried around to the front of the building, punched in the security code, and strode down the hall to Margaret's room. Her sister was still staring out.

"Look," said Margaret. "There's something so unusual out there. What is it?"

"It's a tub of flowers, Margaret. I thought we could plant them. Do you want to come around and help me put them in?"

Margaret stepped back from the window.

"Oh, I don't think I should. Not yet. Maybe later, when I'm more myself."

"Well, then, you tell me where to put the flowers."

Tentatively Margaret put her face to the glass. "Look at these yellow flowers. Aren't they beautiful? Where did we get them, now?"

"I brought them for us to plant. It's called yellow coneflower or some people call it prairie coneflower."

"That rings a bell. I believe I've heard of it."

"Now, where would you like them?"

Margaret chose a spot just to the left of the bird feeder and close to the sparse patch of impatiens.

"I'll just go out and plant them," Helen said, and hurried back out and around the building. The flowers were drooping from the shock of being uprooted, and she wanted to put them in the earth immediately and give them a prodigious drink of water from the water jugs in the wheelbarrow she had pushed from the parking lot.

When the coneflowers were planted and Helen had returned to the room, she and Margaret stood at the window admiring them. On the stubbly plot, the yellow flowers, stirred by a breeze, looked luxuriant above the red impatiens.

Margaret said, "My goodness, that's just as pretty as can be. I'm so lucky to have this view, aren't I?"

"It's thanks to your artistic eye, Margaret. I would have just stuck them down any old where."

"Well, thank you." said Margaret.

An hour later, when they came back to the room from lunch, instead of lying down on her bed, Margaret, passing the window, stopped to gaze out. She pointed at the flowers.

"I always enjoy that patch of yellow flowers so much," she said. "Look how nicely they're coming in, and I planted them from seed."

Helen agreed that Margaret had done her usual good job. Margaret said, "I apologize for the state of the rest of my garden, though. Everything got eaten by the crickets. Is that what they're called? Crickets?"

"Grasshoppers, you mean?"

"Yes, that's it. Grasshoppers. It about broke my heart to watch them gobble everything up. If I could just get out . . . But I'm not sure where I've put my garden tools."

Helen took her hand and squeezed it.

"I know where they are. Why don't I bring them to you next time, and we'll do a little planting together."

"All right. Would you enjoy that?" said Margaret.

Helen hugged her. "Oh yes! I'd enjoy it so much."

As Helen drove along the parkway toward home, she looked for the place where she had dug up the flowers. She almost passed it, it was such a small patch of dirt. Unless you were looking carefully, you wouldn't notice anything had been growing there at all.

She thought, it won't hurt to take a few more of them.

Imagining Margaret in her red gardening gloves, on her knees with a trowel in hand, Helen eagerly dug up more coneflowers from the parkway early on Sunday morning, when people were either sleeping or getting ready for church. She dug the flowers from both sides of the parkway this time, several blocks apart, so the gaps wouldn't be obvious. She hadn't asked herself why she was taking these precautions if what she was doing wasn't stealing. She only thought that, to some people, it might *look* like stealing, and in a small town you had to be somewhat concerned about appearances.

Only two cars passed while she was going about her work, both of them bearing out-of-county license plates. The air was cool, there was still dew on the grass, and the exercise felt good. At one point, she looked up to hear the sound of power mowers nearby. Close to the abandoned condominiums, young shirtless boys were riding mowers in and out around the little trees. They called to each other periodically, but took no notice of her. She dug up four groups of flowers this time, having brought three tubs to carry them in.

Helen pointed to the new flowers in their tubs outside Margaret's window.

"They're waiting for us to come out and put them in, Margaret." She opened the old canvas bag Margaret had always kept her gardening things in. "See here? I've brought your gloves and your floppy hat."

Margaret took the articles out and turned them over in her hands.

"Isn't that funny? They don't look familiar."

Helen guided Margaret down the hall to the front door of the facility. She tapped in the security code to open the door, but suddenly Margaret turned and took several steps away.

"Now, where is it we're going?" she asked, glancing, bewildered, at two women in wheelchairs flanking the entrance to the dining room.

"Just around the building to plant those flowers I brought."

Margaret seemed to sink into herself a little.

"I hope you won't blame me, Helen, but I think I'll save it for another day."

"Oh really, Margaret?" Helen tried to keep the pleading out of her voice. "Are you sure? You might enjoy it out in the fresh air."

"I'm sorry, but you go on without me. I won't mind a bit."

Helen led Margaret back to her room. At the door, a little behind her, Helen was dismayed at how slumped her sister's shoulders had become, once so straight, and how small it made her look, as if she were shrinking away. Helen could hardly bear it, and for a minute after they entered the room, she couldn't trust her voice.

When Helen went around the building to put in the new flowers, she saw that the first group of coneflowers she'd planted were drooping a bit. It hadn't rained for some time, and though she'd watered every other day from her milk jugs, the sun had baked the ground pretty hard.

Margaret had said, "I do love these sweet yellow flowers. They're looking kind of gloomy, though. I'm not being a very good mother to them, I'm afraid. But when I'm myself again, I'll get out there and give them some attention."

That night, Helen heard on the news that a thunderstorm was due to blow through some time Tuesday morning. She had been thinking about getting the rest of those coneflowers—so far, no one had seemed to take any notice of her transplanting activity at all—and it occurred to her that newly transplanted flowers needed a lot of watering at first, especially wildflowers like these. If she brought over the last five bunches and got them in before the storm, they and the other flowers would get a thorough soaking when it rained, and might start to really take hold.

This time—Monday night—she did the job around dusk. It was just light enough to see what she was doing, too dark to be obvious to anyone else, and sufficiently late so most people were home from work already.

Wearing a dark purple sweat suit, Helen drove along the parkway with a flashlight, stopping at intervals to lean out first the driver's window, then the passenger's and shine the light along the curbs to locate all the remaining clumps. Digging out the tenth and final cluster, she was tired but deeply gratified when she nested the third tub beside the other two in the trunk.

Margaret was sound asleep when Helen dug the holes and put in the last of the flowers by moonlight. It was nine-thirty P.M. She wished Margaret could have instructed her on this last planting, but it would have startled her to be wakened, and the flowers had to get in before the morning rain came.

She wasn't able to get over to Oakridge Manor until Wednesday. That morning she was eager to see how the flowers looked. There had been a good, steady twelve-hour downpour, and she was quite proud of herself for getting the thing done in time.

At breakfast, Cal chuckled over the *Dunlop County Sentinel*.
"Listen to this," he said. *"'Flower-loving Thief Steals Street Decorations'."*
Helen put down her cup of coffee.

*"'The Dunlop County Sheriff's office is looking into the disappearance
of $400 worth of floral landscaping stolen some time last week from
along the new Oakwood Parkway on the north edge of town. Sheriff
Eldon McCoy said, 'We have no idea who could have done it.' Town
Council member Nancy Bannister, returned from visiting her daughter's
family in California, was the first to notice the plants' disappearance.
'There are patches of dirt up and down the street where someone came
along and just dug up those flowers,' she said. 'Who would do a selfish
thing like that?' Ms. Bannister was the member of the Council committee whose idea it was to beautify the road with the yellow blooms, called
prairie coneflowers. 'We had only a small budget for landscaping,' she
said, 'and I thought it would look pretty to plant them here and there
along the street in a natural way, as if they had just grown up there
serendipitously.'"*

Cal laid down the paper and snorted.
"'Serendipitously!'" he quoted. "Who in blazes uses a word like
'serendipitously'!"

Helen felt slightly sick. Her breakfast sat like lead in her stomach.
For over forty years, she had taught school in Dunlop. Both their
extended families lived in the area.

"Long-Time Teacher, Charged With Stealing Parkway Flowers." She
could picture the headline.

She wondered if she ought to tell Cal about it and ask him what
to do. He would be sure to find the situation funny. But it didn't feel
like a laughing matter to her. Stealing money from the town was
what she had done, or might as well have. How Cal's cronies in town
would rib him about it! Worse, they might say nothing at all, just keep
a conspicuous silence when her name came up.

Someone at Oakridge Manor might already have noticed the flowers outside Margaret's window, seen the article in the paper, and put two and two together. The staff, the director and head cook were from out of the county, but several of the young girls who served and cleaned were local high school kids hired for the summer. One had been a pupil of Helen's at the grade school before she retired. They came into the rooms in pairs, chattering while they vacuumed and stripped beds. Would they notice what she had planted outside of Margaret's window? And how much attention did they pay to what was in the local paper? Very little, she hoped. But all it would take was one exceptional, observant young woman. Margaret's room was due to be cleaned on Friday.

On her way to the nursing home, it struck her how bare the parkway looked, now that those spots of color were all gone. How could she not have realized what a big difference those few little clumps of flowers made?

When she walked through the Oakridge Manor lobby after breakfast, there was the usual contingent of on-lookers clustered in wheelchairs near the front door. They seemed to be staring at her in disapproval. She couldn't tell, though. Half the time they wore that look when she'd done nothing to deserve it. She greeted them with a brave smile and walked back to Margaret's room.

"I do believe I've gotten my green thumb back!" exclaimed Margaret. "Just see how my garden is filling out! It makes me smile every day just to look at it." Helen stared at the blanket of yellow flowers, their slick green leaves shiny after the rain. Even the red impatiens had perked up. "I'll give you some to transplant, Helen," said Margaret. "Oh, but I forgot, you've never been all that keen on flower planting, have you?"

"Yes, you remember! I don't have your artistic eye."

"But your vegetable gardens are always just glorious, Helen. And I can transplant the flowers for you, if you like."

For a moment Helen forgot her worries in the hope that this time

Margaret might really leave her room and even go out to the farm to do a bit of gardening.

"Today, you mean?" Helen said.

"Oh." Margaret got that uncertain look on her face. "Well . . . no . . . I think I'm not supposed to go out quite yet. I'm sorry. But as soon as I feel more myself, I'll do it for you. " She frowned. "*What* was it I was going to do for you?"

"Transplant flowers."

Margaret got a distant look in her eyes.

"I don't suppose I can expect it to go away, can I?"

"Your garden?" Helen said.

"The memory problem."

"Oh. Well, it's not impossible . . . If they can find some treatment or medicine for it." Helen turned and gazed abstractedly at Margaret's bed, which for once did not bear her imprint.

Margaret gave Helen a worried look. "Helen, you seem kind of weighed down." She took her by the elbow and brought her closer to the window. "Just look at my flowers out there. That'll cheer you up. I chose them with you in mind because I know how partial you are to yellow. I can't think for a moment what they're called, though."

"Yellow coneflowers."

Helen thought to herself: I guess I have to dig them up and put them back.

Margaret said, "It won't be long before they spread all over, like a meadow!"

No, Helen thought, there's no way I can put them back.

"Look there," said Margaret. "Those flowers brought a little old bumblebee out of bed this morning!"

But—Helen wondered—if the coneflowers on the parkway were replaced, how could anyone say Margaret's flowers were stolen?

High atop the steep verge, Helen stood looking down at cars going by on the interstate. Her own car was parked behind her on the frontage road. A half moon was slipping in and out of the clouds. She wore her purple sweat suit again and carried six nested plastic tubs. Under her arm was a long-handled spade.

She couldn't bring herself to tell Cal about this, even if he had been in shape to help her with it. As far as he knew, she was spending the evening with Margaret and would be back late.

She would have to pace herself, work fast, but not too fast. No one was likely to come by here now, out in the country between interstate exits at nine o'clock at night. She would have to save most of her strength for the second part of the job—putting the flowers into the original spots on the parkway, if she could find them in the dark, and watering them—with the much greater chance of getting caught.

She waded a foot or so into the thick grasses covering the hillside until she came to the large patch of coneflowers she had spied from her car when she had gone searching earlier that day. Stepping down on the shovel blade, she pressed it into the earth. She would have to dig them out in ten separate bunches so she could transplant them quickly in the other place, and she had to bring up lots of earth along with them because the roots here would go deeper.

At first she found herself trembling a little and had to calm down before she could continue digging. She filled one tub, then two, and stopped to rest her back, remembering her husband's back and shoulder and hip troubles and how, at her age, it could take just one stupid mistake to be disabled by pain for the rest of your life. She straightened and stretched and took several long breaths.

Below on the interstate, the traffic was thinning out. A silent squad car raced by at top speed, causing the few drivers on the road to slow momentarily to a snail's pace. Helen's heart beat faster at the sight of the sheriff's car, but it sped on, and quickly its taillights reduced to pricks of light and disappeared.

She returned to her digging, but the bending and stooping were beginning to make themselves felt, and she despaired of having the stamina to re-plant these flowers on the parkway that night. Still, she pushed on, and finally the last tub was full. She put it heavily down on the front seat of her car. The other tubs took up the back seat and trunk.

Resting her forehead against the steering wheel for a moment, she considered whether she was up to the next task. But she could see no alternative. It was almost a sure thing that if she didn't do this tonight, she would be discovered and accused, and even though she had an excuse for her actions that some in town might find forgivable, she knew there were others with elderly sisters and grandfathers and mothers, who would condemn the notion of running out and stealing things off public property for any reason.

She turned the key in the ignition, drove onto the interstate, and took the next exit into town.

By the time she got to the parkway it was ten-thirty. The moon had moved permanently under the clouds. There were no street lights in this new section. She felt protected by the darkness, but it was hard to locate the bare patches she was looking for. Finally, after some minutes' driving up and down, she spotted the first one. She got out of the car and, after taking some flowers from the tub on the front seat, nervously jabbed the shovel a few times into the moist earth, then crouched by the curb and set the flowers in with a trowel.

The noise of her digging masked the sound of the squad car pulling up quietly on the smooth new pavement and stopping behind her vehicle with its lights off. She didn't look up until she heard a car door slam.

The sheriff's deputy strolled slowly around her car and came to stand a few yards from her with his thumbs sticking into his gun belt.

Robbie Peterson. She had taught him in the fifth grade, a big aggressive boy, always in trouble over some mischief or act of destruction. She'd had to send him to the principal's office more than a few times.

With all the paraphernalia hanging off him, he looked like a man ready to go into combat. She thought to herself, Well, as they say on TV, 'It's payback time'.

She stood up.

"Mrs. Earlywine," the deputy said.

"Robbie."

There was a silence as he pulled a flashlight from the back of his belt and shone it on the tub full of flowers, then at the shovel on the ground, and over to the newly planted flowers at the curb. Nodding toward them, he turned the light on her, clutching the trowel in her hand, and said, "How many more of these were you planning to put in?"

"I *thought* that was your car up there on that frontage road."

He took a step toward her in the dark. She heard the creak of leather and the sound of his handcuffs clinking against his belt buckle.

"Did you know that taking flowers from an interstate highway is a federal offense?"

"No," she said. "I guess I didn't."

"I would of thought a teacher would know that," he said, rubbing the nighttime stubble on his chin. Then he said, "You need a hand here?"

He pulled the squad car out of sight on a side street, then got in her car and drove while she sat in the passenger side searching the curbs with a flashlight. "Here," she said, and he stopped.

While they planted they didn't talk. With a few efficient thrusts and twists of the shovel, Robbie prepared the holes and received each clodful of flowers that Helen lifted carefully out of its tub. He knelt down to place the flowers into the holes, then stood and tamped the earth in around them with the sole of his boot. Finally, he bent and poured water from a gallon jug Helen handed to him. Only once did he make conversation. "Stealing flowers off the interstate don't carry as high a penalty as stealing a town sign or an exit marker," he mused.

"But," he added, reminiscently, "it's probably higher than for making a U-ey across the median or mooning someone from your car."

When he was putting the last bunch of flowers into the last hole, he said, "Well, don't steal no more of these, Mrs. Earlywine. Crime don't pay, you know."

She said, "Robbie, I'm just as embarrassed as I can be. I'm just sick about it." He hadn't asked her why she took the flowers, and she didn't want to make excuses for herself.

He put the shovel and the tub into her trunk for her and drove back to the squad car, where he got out.

"Well, thank you, Robbie," she said as she slid over into the driver's seat. The two cars were side by side, facing opposite directions. "I hope no one's been trying to get ahold of you."

Robbie tapped a small electronic device clipped to the front of his shirt. "If they had of, they would have called." Then he looked at her and said, "You remember what you wrote on my drawing that one time? That picture I drew of my uncle's rebuilt '69 Cobra GT 500? I couldn't draw worth a nickel, but that wasn't too bad of a picture. You remember what you wrote on it?"

"I'm not sure I do," Helen said.

"You wrote, '*You could be an artist, Robbie.*' Remember that?"

"Oh, I believe I do remember that."

"'*You could be an artist, Robbie.*'" He gave a small, self-conscious chuckle and shrugged. "That's what you wrote. You must of been thinking of someone else, though."

"No, I'm sure I had *you* in mind."

"Okay," he said.

As he turned left onto Oakwood, he made a little salute out the window. Helen pulled into a drive, backed out, took a left onto the parkway and drove home.

OCTOBER

i.

"NANCY BANNISTER'S GOT another damn bug in her ear," said Cal, tossing the *Dunlop County Sentinel* on the kitchen counter next to where Helen was peeling beets.

"What's that?" she said.

He picked up the paper and read it to her.

At Wednesday's Town Council meeting, ideas were discussed for bolstering Dunlop's flagging economy. One idea receiving preliminary support was Councilwoman Nancy Bannister's proposal to create a corn maze on a local farm property to draw tourists to the area. 'Labyrinths of corn are doing well all over the state,' says Ms. Bannister.

"'Labyrinths of corn'!" Cal snorted, slapping the paper down again. "I suppose she'll stick Kyle Branson's five-legged heifer in there and call it a minotaur."

"Well," said Helen, rinsing the red off her fingers, "I've heard that that corn maze over in Dyersville took in a bundle last summer."

"Sure," said Cal, "because they're driving in busloads of Japanese to that so-called Field of Dreams they got there. Running around the bases, looking for Kevin Coster to come out of a corn row."

"Costner," said Helen. She dried her hands on her apron. "You never know, though. Nancy has a good idea now and then."

"Yeah. You watch how fast she'll have a billboard up on the interstate: Visit the Labyrinth of Corn. See the Minotaur. Stay in comfort at Bannister's B & B."

"You can't put billboards on the interstate."

"On the roof of our barn, then, with flashing arrows."

That afternoon Helen got the call while Cal was in Dunlop at the chiropractor.

"Helen, the Council's come up with a terrific plan!" said Nancy, bypassing, as usual, a salutation in her hurry to get to the soul of the matter.

"How are you, Nancy? How was your visit with your daughter's family?" said Helen.

"Oh, just terrific! Stevie Jr. 's taking violin *and* piano *and* drums, and Kathy is all-state center this year, back and forth to tournament games, and they've got Tracy on the debate team practicing for regionals. My daughter can just hardly keep up with it all. I told her, Ginnie, you let Steve chauffeur them around for a week and you come back to Iowa with me for some rest and relaxation. Say, Helen, listen—"

"I expect that *would* be restful for her."

"If she'd just take me up on it!" Nancy clucked ruefully. "But, say, Helen, we've got an idea here that I think could get Dunlop back on its feet and really turn us into a center of tourism—bring back jobs, give the teens a reason to stay. We're just so close to I-35, you know, it's a shame we're missing the chance to bring in some of that traffic between Minneapolis and Kansas City."

"You're talking about the corn maze?"

"Did you read about it in the paper? Oh, my goodness, I've just gotten so many nice calls from people since that notice came out. *Everyone's* behind it. People are offering to put up money and volunteer time. But the thing is, we need to figure out a real good site for it."

"Who's putting up money?" said Helen, glancing out the window at the barn and thinking that the roof needed re-shingling.

"Oh, a few town businesses. But the thing is—"

"So how would that work? Would it be a public project or a private business or what?"

"Well, now that still needs to be decided yet, but before that happens what we'd like to do is to have a real specific plan ready to present. Now I believe somebody mentioned that you and Cal have a little fallow pasture next to your house bordering on County Road R37. About two miles off the interstate, isn't it? Exit 133, I think they said?"

"It's not fallow. There's a tenant raising alfalfa for hay on it."

"So it hasn't been planted in corn for awhile? Because, of course, that would be a big plus. How many acres is it?"

"I can't remember exactly. The land got divided up. You'd have to ask Cal about it."

"Oh, I see. Well, I don't suppose Cal happens to be there right at the moment?"

"No, he's in town."

"Maybe I could catch him. Where was he going to be?"

"I'd better have him call you, Nancy, when he gets back."

"That's fine, Helen. Just have him leave a message on my machine if I'm out, or better yet, have him give me a buzz on my cell phone." She gave Helen the number.

Cal wasn't in the best of moods when he returned from the chiropractor and heard about the call.

"I leave here with a pain in the back and come back to a pain in the neck."

"She wants to put the corn maze in Kyle's hay field," Helen said.

They were silent for a second or two. They never talked about the memory hovering over that field.

Heaving a sigh that came all the way up from his hip and lower five vertebrae, Cal eased himself into his recliner and lay with eyes closed. For a moment his knees and feet splayed outward like an old broken-spine book until the pain in his hip drew his legs together. Helen sat down next to him and patted his hand.

"How was your treatment?" she asked.

"Punched 'em and crunched 'em."

"Did it make you feel any better?"

"I don't know. Maybe." He opened his eyes. "Who did they think was going to plant the damn corn maze if they did put it in our field?"

"Nancy didn't say, but I suppose anyone could plant it."

"It wouldn't be me."

"No, it wouldn't have to be."

"I've done my time."

"Yes, you have."

"Anyway, that piece is Kyle's to work. He needs the hay."

"He probably wouldn't want to give it up."

"She'll have to talk to Kyle."

The phone rang.

"I'm asleep!" said Cal.

"No, you're not," said Helen. She handed him the phone and started for the kitchen.

"Say, Cal," said Nancy, "I was just talking to Helen about our corn maze idea, and we were discussing that little section of land you've got there along Route 37. Did she mention our thoughts about that?"

Cal called Helen back. "Say, Helen, what was that thought you and Nancy had about Kyle's twenty-three acres?"

Helen rolled her eyes.

"Well, actually," Nancy interjected, "Helen wasn't just sure the land was available—it's twenty-three acres, is it? That would just be a perfect size!"

Cal smacked himself on the forehead. "Maybe it's less than that— I'd have to check the rental agreement. It could be fifteen."

When Cal hung up, Nancy Bannister had talked him into coming with Helen to an "ad hoc" planning meeting—a brainstorming session, she called it.

"We're supposed to bring our 'thinking caps'," he told Helen.

ii.

Cal knew exactly how the corn maze meeting would go. Nancy Bannister, who somehow had a key to every public building in Dunlop, would arrive at the library early enough to get the coffee maker going, spread lemon bars on a platter, fan out a pile of child-size napkins in alternating colors, and commandeer the chair at the head of the table.

Garland Spong, president of the Dunlop Farmers and Merchants Credit Union, would show up seconds too late to grab the seat of power and would beetle his brows at Nancy as he filled his coffee cup—a real ceramic one since Nancy Bannister would sooner serve coffee in dog bowls than degrade the environment or cheapen a table arrangement with Styrofoam. The chair at the other end of the table could have done for a competing seat of authority except for the ceiling fan that hung by a thread directly over it like the sword of Damocles. No one ever sat there if they could help it.

George Massey, Dunlop's current presiding mayor, would amble in, still wearing his pharmacist's white jacket, and spend some time piling lemon bars on a napkin before lowering his spreading haunches onto a chair. George would spend the meeting taking side roads off the point until no one could remember where the original thought had been going, and Garland Spong—Mr. Devil's Advocate—would counter anything anyone suggested, regardless of his actual opinion.

When Cal and Helen arrived, their fellow civic leaders were confirming all of Cal's predictions, and, following the mandatory chit chat, Nancy called the meeting to order. Cal consigned his tetchy spine and aching hip to one of the uncompromising wooden library chairs and emitted a doleful sigh. Helen touched his arm. She had pulled a small pillow from her tote bag and pushed it at him, out of sight under the table, but he shook his head, and she put it back in her bag.

Nancy stood up.

"I know our Mayor will forgive me for taking charge tonight—"
George looked up absently on hearing his title mentioned.

Forgive her, my eye, thought Cal. As if George would notice.

Everyone in town with at least half their marbles had to do one or more terms as mayor. It was like tithing or serving on church committees. You couldn't expect to sit back and reap the benefits and then shirk your duty. When a farmer retired, it wasn't long before he or his wife pulled the short straw and had to do a stint. It was probably the reason farmers worked until their bodies wore out, knowing that sitting through a thousand contentious meetings was as bad for your back as a thousand hours on a tractor seat. Worse. At least on your tractor you could listen to the radio. In his opinion, it was a good thing when middle-aged women started getting into politics. Their backs were in better shape and their well-padded fannies could take anything a metal folding chair could dish out. Bannister, now, *she* didn't mind taking her turn when she had the time. She'd done, how many? Four stints? Maybe five. Willingly. Everyone in town would have gladly handed her the job of Mayor For Life, with all her boosterish ideas—bringing back the soda fountain and adding "wifi"—whatever the hell that was—at Massey's drug store—things to stop Dunlop's youth from flowing out of town like water from a tap left open. But Nancy needed her freedom every few years, she said, to take off and travel, God knew where.

"Is that all right with you, Cal?"

Cal sat up a little and brought his mind back to the proceedings. "What was that?"

"I thought, since I'm the one who had the crazy idea, I'd help us get going by laying out some thoughts that I've been hearing from people around the county. However, I'm only going to play the role of facilitator." She sat down.

"Play *like*," Cal whispered to Helen.

She rapped him on the knee.

"Because, really, we want a full hearing of peoples' thoughts and concerns. There are no bad ideas," Nancy added. She paused to glance at the round library clock on the wall, which was loudly ticking away on battery power. "We're expecting one more person, but he seems to have gotten delayed, so—Oh, here he is!"

Deputy Sheriff Robbie Peterson, out of uniform except for his black troopers' boots, loped into the room, his thumbs in the pockets of his low-slung jeans. He spit a wad of tobacco into the wastebasket before taking a seat opposite Garland Spong. Once seated, he crossed an ankle over a knee and leaned back so far in his chair that the legs creaked dangerously. Cal wondered how in hell Nancy Bannister had managed to strong-arm Robbie Peterson into coming to the meeting and for what reason. Robbie wasn't exactly the most civic-minded or reliable of Dunlop's citizens.

"Won't you take some coffee and refreshments before we get started, Robbie?" Nancy held the plate of sweets out to him along with a napkin. Robbie picked up three lemon bars in his bare fingers.

"No thanks," he said, to Nancy's offer of coffee. "I've had so much caffeine today I'm pissing brown," he said.

"Well," said Nancy brightly, "why don't we get started then." She took a sheaf of papers from her "Bannister's B & B" tote bag. A picture of her Victorian house was stenciled on the canvas. "I've done a kind of informal survey, and—"

"Now shouldn't we have a written agenda of the order of business?"

Here we go, thought Cal. Spong's going to have us here all night, objecting to every trivial thing. But no, Cal had forgotten Nancy Bannister's unique aptitude for squelching Spong's automatic naysaying.

"Yes, that's a terrific idea, Garland," she enthused, "but I thought this should be kind of a *casual* brainstorming session. Just a chance for us to put our thinking caps on and let our thoughts flow." She took a tablet and pen from her bag and handed them down the table to Helen. "Would you do us a great favor and play the role of recorder, Helen? You've got that wonderful Palmer handwriting. I will regret to the day I die that penmanship went out of fashion just at the time I started high school." Helen, with a glance at Cal, who raised an eyebrow in return, picked up the pen. "But feel free to chime in, too, Helen. And

I'll type up the notes later on my laptop and distribute them to you all. That should satisfy you, Garland, I think?"

Spong opened his mouth, but Nancy forged ahead before he could contradict her.

"Now, as I said, I've been doing a kind of informal survey around the county and I'm finding huge enthusiasm for our idea of a corn maze."

Cal raised his hand. "Who do we mean by *our*?"

"Well, now, Garland and George here have shown a great deal of interest, and Robbie has an idea or two about it, and I think, Helen, when you and I were talking on the phone—"

"I didn't say one way or the other, Nancy. I'd like to hear some more particulars."

"Exactly. Just why we're here. So, why don't I start by throwing out some of the suggestions we've had, and you can all put in your two cents."

George Massey got up and made a show of tiptoeing over to the refreshment platter. He loaded up his napkin again and gave Nancy the okay sign. "Would you give my wife the recipe for these?" he whispered.

"Glad to," Nancy whispered back, handing around her stack of printouts. "So, I've made copies for you all of these graphs, which show the earnings of corn maze enterprises in the state, and you'll see that those that are close to an interstate highway exit bring in the most revenue. Now notice that—"

"Strictly speaking, these are not graphs. These are tables."

"You're so right, Garland, thank you." She winked at the others. "This is why we're glad to have a banker on our committee, to keep us honest."

Cal turned to Helen. "Is this a committee? I didn't agree to be on a committee."

"No, of course not, Cal," said Nancy. "Don't mind me. I've been on so darned many committees this last year that I took my niece and nephew to McDonald's the other day and almost called them to order. No, we're just a little ad hoc group."

"Ad hoc . . . *what?*" said Cal.

Helen kicked him. "You know very well what ad hoc means," she whispered. Cal shut his mouth.

"So, as you see, the first … *table* shows the range of net income of these corn maze projects after three years of operation—anywhere from $20,000 to as high as $75,000, and if you look at the other table, there's a direct, positive relationship between revenue and proximity to the interstate. Now Cal's and Helen's twenty-three acres that border County Road R37 are only two miles off Exit 133, and ideally situated for—"

"I think that's 2.2 miles off the exit," interrupted Spong, smiling at Nancy severely.

"Right again, Garland. I know you bankers don't hold with rounding. As well you shouldn't. Who knows how far off calculations can end up if you round every figure. So. At 2.2 miles—"

"You know, I remember when R37 only went up as far as Baxter's place. Before they built up that berm to keep it from flooding," said the mayor, reflectively, speaking with his mouth full.

"Before my time, I'm afraid," said Nancy briskly. "So with ten acres for the maze itself and another thirteen for the rest of the park, it's possible to bring in considerable revenue, which could go for all kinds of town and county improvements. As well as the additional income tourism would bring to our local businesses—our gas station, our café, our motel, our pharmacy—"

"Our Bannister's B & B," mouthed Cal to Helen.

"More people with a bit more cash to bank." She smiled at Spong. "To say nothing of the volunteer and summer job opportunities for our senior citizens and young people."

Robbie had taken out a pocket knife and was scraping dusty flakes of dried mud onto the linoleum from the bottom of his boots.

"Robbie, do you want to say a few words about your idea for the young people?"

Robbie put his knife down. "Give 'em jobs selling stuff at the concession stands, hauling out the customers that get lost or get heat stroke—"

"Oh now, I don't think there would be any problems with heat stroke," broke in Nancy. "One of the concessions we thought of was to sell that flavored bottled water that's so popular now. Also inexpensive broad brimmed straw hats with the Dunlop Labyrinth logo on them. Maybe hand-held fans printed with advertising for local businesses—"

"'Dunlop Labyrinth'!" protested Cal. "We haven't okayed it and it already has a name?"

"Oh that's just a working name until we make up our minds."

Garland Spong set his cup down hard on the table and his coffee splashed on the printout, causing the ink to run. "People aren't going to know what a labyrinth is. It sounds like some kind of highway construction detour."

"I remember studying about the minotaur in high school," reminisced the mayor. "Maybe we could put a minotaur in it."

"A minotaur is a mythical animal, George," said Cal.

"I mean something out of paper maché or … I guess that wouldn't hold up in the rain, would it? But maybe someone could slap it together out of scrap metal, or—"

"These details can be worked out later. In fact, maybe, since there's this dispute about the word labyrinth, we could have a name-the-maze fundraiser—get everyone in town involved. I thought of The A-mazing Maiz Maze, as a name for it." She wrote it out on her notebook and passed it around. "Cal," she said, "that word, "maiz," is the Spanish word for corn, spelled m-a-i-z, the Spanish way, with no 'e' on the end." Cal thought, all the years I've been in agriculture she doesn't think I know what maiz is?

Helen said, "The Spanish word isn't pronounced with a long "a" the way it is in "maze." It has two syllables: "mah-ees."

"Oh, really?" Nancy sounded put out. Cal smiled. Helen hadn't been a school teacher for nothing, even if the damned Bush administration had ended Spanish classes for these little country school districts.

Cal couldn't help adding, "Is there a reason for a hyphen in the middle of a word that doesn't have a hyphen? Is A-mazing like that beauty salon that calls itself L'Belle?"

"Well, I think the name can be discussed later," said Nancy, "We're just brainstorming here, and remember there are no bad ideas when you brainstorm. Anyway, the first question is still where to put the maze."

"Liability could be prohibitive."

"I'm so glad you brought that up, Garland. If you'll turn over the second sheet, you'll see some insurance estimates, which show that the profit margin is still well above costs, including insurance and infrastructure—"

Infrastructure! thought Cal. Where the hell does she think she is, Afghanistan?

"—Parking, a road into the site, concession stands, port-o-potties, maybe an area for tossing horseshoes, a pen for a petting zoo—"

"Petting zoo? Now that's asking for trouble."

"Well, Garland, Robbie here had the great idea of putting the teens to work supervising the petting zoo, and also setting up an observation post in the middle of the maze to monitor people's progress. Robbie personally offered to train the teenagers."

Cal turned to Robbie, "Twisted your arm, did she?"

"Goodness no! He came up with that idea himself, didn't you Robbie?"

Robbie was idly making little dents in the table with the tip of his blade, and didn't reply.

Cal wrote in the margin of his printout, *Wrenched that arm up behind his back and gave it a good half turn*, which he passed to Helen. Helen wrote back, *Robbie Peterson never does a thing he doesn't want to do.*

"Robbie has become such a good role model for our young people! We've had him down at 4H and Junior Jaycees sharing the mistakes he made when he was their age and how having a goal and sticking with it turned him right around."

His goal now, thought Cal was to get the Charger up to 140 on the interstate without blowing a gasket. That siren was his best buddy.

Cal felt himself getting agitated about this corn maze idea. He could see it now. At night, teenagers high on pot and booze and meth in the field, taking turns as lookout on the "observation post." Bottles, syringes, and condoms swept up every morning and no one to call when the music got so loud you could hear it up at the house.

Then, before he could banish it, the image of twenty-year-old Tommy gripped Cal's heart. That good-humored expression, that open, what-you-see-is-what-you-get face. Tommy had probably had a beer or two in high school, but he'd enjoyed life too much to turn to alcohol as an escape, to use up his young days hung over or "wasted" or whatever they called it. Wasted. Cal's throat constricted and he had to clamp down on his jaw to keep it from trembling.

Why the hell were they all going on about this? Didn't everybody know about that field? Was it possible they had forgotten what happened there? He wished he could ask Helen that question, but he couldn't, and the reason was simple. He knew without any doubt that if he said one word to her about that day or about anything related to Tommy and that field, he would start bawling. This, after twenty-six years. And maybe it was stupid or foolish, but he knew what kind of sounds would come out of him once he got started, and he couldn't stand the thought of breaking down to that extreme in front of her or in front of anybody. That's just the way it was, and that's the way it had to be.

"—close to an exit or area of high population density," Nancy was saying. "Now of course Dunlop County isn't anywhere near a large metropolitan area—"

Cal couldn't help himself, he felt suddenly so angry. "Nancy, you got something against the word 'city'?"

She stopped for a moment and cocked her head. Her lips came together in a bland, close-mouthed smile.

"Oh, Cal, you're such a kidder, sometimes your jokes just go right over my head. So anyway—"

"What about Miller's piece?" said Helen. "It's a lot closer to the exit."

"Well, now, we thought about Miller's, but it's *too* close to the interstate. The trucks are just deafening." Nancy leaned forward eagerly. "You know, what would really bring the community together would be a contest to decide the design theme. Something unique. That maze over by Duran was laid out as a full body portrait of all four Beatles one year and the University of Iowa sports mascot another year—Herby the Hawk."

"*Herky*," said Garland, indignantly.

"Oh yes, Herky! The winner of the contest could get a season pass to both the maze and the haunted cornfield."

Cal sat forward. He felt the blood rise to his face.

Helen said, "What do you mean by haunted corn field?"

"Oh, they do this in October when the corn stalks in the maze are dry and brown. It's very popular. There are sound effects. The teens dress up in ghoulish costumes and lead people through, with bats and ghosts jumping out at you and these zombies and vampires that are all the rage now." She clapped her hands. "Say, I just thought of this! We could get a couple of handsome senior boys to dress like the vampires in that Twilight movie the girls are so smitten by."

"You know, my granddaughter glued posters of that Twilight boy on every wall of her room. Her mother didn't say one thing to her about it even though they'd just had that bedroom painted." George shifted his wide buttocks on the narrow chair. "They indulge 'em these days like we never did. We would have had her tear those things down and re-paint the room herself. But we keep our mouths shut.

It doesn't do to interfere. Now, to me, that Twilight boy looks like a girl," he said, irrelevantly.

Cal felt like something hadn't settled right in his stomach. At the same time, he had the urge to take his coffee cup and throw it in George Massey's face. He whispered to Helen, "I can't sit here anymore. I'll meet you outside." She put a restraining hand on his arm.

"Cal already told you, Nancy," she said, "that those twenty-three acres aren't available. Kyle and Millie Branson are renting it to grow alfalfa for their cows."

"I understand their rental agreement is up for renewal this year, and—"

"Understand that from who?" Cal snapped.

"Millie and I were having a chat the other day and—"

"You've been hounding Millie Branson about the land?" Cal's voice was rising. Helen squeezed his wrist.

"Of course not. I wouldn't dream of it. No, Millie and I happened to run into each other on the square, and she said she and Kyle were thinking of selling their herd. It's getting a little too much for him, and they aren't really making money on it."

First I've heard of it, thought Cal, angrily, but he didn't want to admit it.

"So when I mentioned the corn maze idea, and how you could earn enough on the sale of the land to make up for whatever you were getting from Kyle, why she thought Kyle would be glad to give up the land for a project like that."

"I'll be damned," said Cal. He pulled his wrist out of Helen's grasp and walked out of the room.

There was a silence as everyone stared at the door he had left by and listened to the sounds of Cal's footsteps diminishing down the hall, then the pneumatic front door clunking open and shut.

Helen thought, That security door was Nancy's idea. Who did she think was going to break into a tiny library full of romance and detective paperbacks and a cash drawer full of dimes and quarters? Not all of Nancy's ideas made sense.

Helen stood up, too.

"Excuse me," she said. Robbie Peterson pulled his outstretched legs back as she edged by him. She hadn't seen Robbie since he'd helped her plant those flowers, and she felt a little fluttery at the thought that he might bring up the subject in front of the others after she left. He winked at her and made a zipping motion across his lips as she passed. She nodded slightly, casting a quick glance at Nancy Bannister to see if she had noticed. Nancy never missed anything.

No sooner had Helen opened the outer door than Nancy was there beside her on the sidewalk. Helen frowned and scanned the square for Cal. He had already crossed the street and was walking around to the back of the courthouse, where the truck was parked. He would wait there for her, she knew.

"Nancy," she said. "Cal and I cannot go along with this corn maze scheme. We can't sell that land."

"Was it the Haunted Cornfield part that made Cal uncomfortable?"

Helen stared at her. For a moment she didn't know what to say. Then she took a step away from Nancy so she could look her square in the face.

"Don't you understand what that field means to Cal . . . to us?"

Nancy nodded solemnly. "Of course I do, Helen. No one has forgotten. And everyone knows that Cal's been carrying it for twenty-some years without once opening his mouth about it. If you had to find out from Cal, you would never know Tom existed."

Helen blinked. She was so taken aback she stuttered.

"When . . . when . . . when you lose a child like that, twenty-six years is nothing. It could be yesterday."

"I know that, Helen. But you've been able to grieve about it openly. Tom is not a taboo subject with you. You can mention his name at the supermarket and at church. But Cal, he's carrying around that death as if he died himself, and that field reminds him of it every day, sitting right there by your house and yard."

Nancy put her hand on Helen's arm, and Helen's eyes welled up with tears.

"Helen, I think the corn maze will be good for everybody, but you know who it will benefit most? Cal. Because once that field is transformed, it won't torture him anymore. Little by little it will become a different thing altogether, and Cal can start remembering his son in other ways."

Choking on her tears, Helen said, "Well, I don't know."

"Just you two take your time to think it over and let us know what you decide."

Nancy went back into the library, and Helen took the long way around the courthouse to get control of herself. She walked past shops on the square that had stood empty for months, their plate glass windows dusty, their shelves holding a scattering of cardboard boxes. The gothic courthouse tower, enclosed in scaffolding for over a year now, waited for county funds to finish the renovation. Dunlop used to be a bustling, pretty town, but it was fading in these times. Nancy was right. Something was needed to revive it.

When she came up to the truck, Cal was sitting sideways in the driver's seat, his feet on the running board, the door open. He was chewing on one side of his lower lip, a sure sign he was embarrassed. He could have told everyone his back was bothering him and he was going to take a stroll to get the kinks out. But just walking out like that, with no excuse, he'd exposed himself.

She got in without saying anything. He moved to start up the truck, but she put a hand over his before he could turn the key.

"Cal," she said. "You never say a word about it. You've driven down that drive for twenty-six years and never turned your eyes toward that field. It was Nancy talking about a haunted cornfield that sent you out the door, wasn't it? She said that word "haunted." And I have to say, I believe you are haunted by that field."

Her heart was racing a little. His emotions were so untouchable.

He stared straight ahead.

"Well . . . " he said, after awhile, not looking at her, "aren't you?"

"Yes, I am. I don't forget. But when I got used to talking about it, it took away some of the pain. And I go out there sometimes and weed the volunteer thistles and the—"

"Well, I don't go in for flower picking."

She felt suddenly as if her patience was at an end.

"Do you want to move to town, Cal? Would that make it easier— not to have to see that field every day and remember?"

"No. I don't want to move to town. What would I do in town?" Then he turned to her and said, almost humbly, "Do *you*?"

"No. I've always lived in the country. I like living in the country. But I hate to see that expression on your face when you drive out past that field or walk down to the mailbox."

"What expression? I wasn't aware I had any expression."

"That's right. Your face gets as blank as a blackboard—every bit of expression erased. And it stays that way until you're well up the road to town."

"Well, I didn't realize you were studying me so close," Cal said and turned the key in the ignition. "From now on I'll mug like a monkey."

She shook her head. What shame had there ever been in grieving openly and expressing your regrets for a dead child? And what were wives and husbands for but to give comfort to each other in such times? She used to have her sister to turn to, and now her daughter, since Barb was grown. But who did Cal have to relieve his feelings with? Me, she thought. Me. But I might as well be a stranger when it comes to his grief.

She thought about the funeral, and how Cal, and Wayne, too, had sat at either end of the pew, both stony faced when everyone else was weeping. Well, she supposed she couldn't blame Cal. He got it from his own father, and unlike that grim, mean-spirited old man, at least Cal had a sense of humor, even if it was always so sarcastic.

"Not grieving takes a lot of your energy, Cal. And it doesn't help you remember Tom happily. All you feel is useless regret."

He flared up, almost shouting. "How do you know what I feel?"

"I know by what you never say."

"What do I have to regret about?" The engine was running, but Cal didn't put the truck in gear.

"You have nothing to regret, but you do anyway. Everyone knows not to say a word to you about Tommy."

Cal slammed his hand on the steering wheel.

"That's Nancy Bannister, isn't it?" he shouted. "Babbling away in your ear with her book psychology. Dr. Bannister's advice to the bereaved." He hit the steering wheel again, accidentally sounding the horn. "That woman will do anything to get her way." He pulled out of the parking space and drove out to the county road. They drove along in silence for a mile.

"Cal," Helen finally said. "Don't be like Garland. Don't argue just to be contrary. Don't be against something only because it's Nancy proposing it."

"A haunted cornfield!" He wrenched the steering wheel to the right and pulled over. Through the open windows came the sound of wind rustling the dry weeds in the ditch.

"Well, the maze, then."

"Fine. The corn maze. Let the woman steam roll over Spong and Massey and that juvenile delinquent deputy sheriff. It's a goofy idea, but I've got nothing against it except the location. I'm damned, though, if I'm going to have some teen-age kid in white make-up jumping out of the cornstalks with his hair spiked up to look like its standing on end, playing Lightning Boy or Voltage Boy or—"

"That will not happen."

"Oh, yes it will. If Nancy Bannister thinks it'd be therapeutic to get Cal Earlywine to look at that field when he goes out to pick up his mail. That's *her* idea, isn't it? And you bought it. She could talk the pointed hat off the Pope's head."

The fact was, he was right. Nancy had convinced her. Everyone knew that Cal had been carrying his grief for all these years without opening his mouth about it, just like those war veterans who could never utter a word about their experiences. Of course people would gossip. You had to expect that in a small community. If he could have shared his feelings with his own wife, it would have been easier for both of them—not to let Tom go but to take some happiness from the memories of him, miss him together. She didn't much like crying either, but there were times when you had to do it or you'd turn dead inside. Sometimes that was how Cal seemed to her. For a long, long time she had been living with someone dead inside, for all his sarcasm and kidding. He didn't used to be like that. Before Tom's death there was a lightness to him. His humor had been silly and whimsical. When he kidded, his deadpan face betrayed the boyish laughter that would come next.

She recalled his old habit of entering a room and introducing himself to the kids as if he were a stranger—what they called "Dad's How D'You Dos."

"How do you do, young lady." He would grasp Barb's little hand in his big one and shake it solemnly. "You don't know me, but I'm a very close friend of your mother's." Barb would start to giggle. "Are you by any chance the 1976 Dunlop Consolidated Schools Second Grade Spelling Bee Champion I've heard so much about? Honored to meet you." More giggling.

"Oh, Daddy, you know who I am."

Or "How do you do," to Wayne, "you don't know me, but I was wondering, are you the Wayne Earlywine who recently rescued his terrified mother from a bat in the kitchen with a single swipe of a broom? I just wanted to shake your hand." Even aloof Wayne, though he rolled his eyes, couldn't help cracking a smile.

Cal was a different man in those days, before Tom's death. Nancy was right about the field. Even if her motives weren't pure, she was right.

iii.

Helen was glad for an excuse to get out of the house and visit Margaret. After last night's "ad hoc" meeting, Cal was particularly grumpy and sarcastic.

"I'm going to go have lunch at Oakridge Manor," she told him. "There are leftovers in the fridge you can heat up."

Cal grunted. He was lying in his recliner. He'd had a restless night, and his face was grayish as if his hip and back were especially bothering him. He had always rested from his day's work in that old Naugahyde recliner, but it seemed like he was in it all the time now. She wasn't sure how much was due to pain, since she could never get a straight answer from him as to how serious it was. Often when she came home after being away, she'd find him standing in the middle of the living room or kitchen, but once, accidentally steadying herself with a hand on the recliner, she found the old Naugahyde warm to the touch and realized he'd just gotten up on hearing her come through the door.

Today she felt a little guilty for leaving and for feeling this creeping sense of impatience. She stopped and patted his shoulder before she left.

The public areas and corridors of Oakridge Manor were adorned with pictures of peasant cottages and romantic landscapes of the type you could buy at the Ben Franklin store. The lounge was furnished with plush, overstuffed sofas and chairs that were hard to get out of. As soon as she walked through the entrance, she was hit with the reek of plug-in air fresheners that clung to her skin and clothes. The relatives of prospective residents, taking the tour, always exclaimed, "Oh, isn't it pretty!"

A man named Norman sometimes sat at Margaret's table in the Oakridge dining room. His daughter told Helen, "Dad's a little bit smitten with your sister."

Can you be 'a little bit' smitten? Helen wondered. She was glad of it, though. She liked Norman—a short, broad-chested man with a rose red complexion—not the unhealthy ruddiness of an alcoholic, but a robust, blushing red that brought out the powder-blue of his eyes. Paint brush bristles filled his nostrils, and his thick lower lashes hung, wet-looking, on his cheeks like a child's just out of the pool.

Helen arranged with Norman's daughter to have him regularly seated next to Margaret at meals. Although he had Alzheimer's, too—much less advanced than Margaret's—he hadn't forgotten the little courtesies. He passed her the salt and pepper before seasoning his own food, filled her water glass from the pitcher, offered her his dessert. Helen sat back and watched the show. She hoped Norman's attentions pleased Margaret. It was hard to tell.

Norman wasn't a talker—not like Harold, another resident who also appeared to have a crush on Margaret and sat down at her table whenever he could. Harold was not losing his memory as Margaret and Norman were. Quite the opposite. Helen had to tune Harold out when he went off on one of his rambling exhibitions of knowledge: "It's sure too bad about these Israelis and Palestinians. You know when it got started, it got started in Biblical times. There was Abraham, and he was married to Sarah. But they were childless. See, she was in her '80s and she couldn't get pregnant. So she allowed her husband to take up with that Palestinian lady . . . I can't remember her name. My son-in-law was telling me about it just this morning, but I forget her name. Anyway, she had two children. And then Sarah, she got pregnant. And she had a child. And that's where the trouble began between the two sides . . ."

Norman acknowledged the story politely with, "Is that a fact." Margaret gazed absently past the two of them without comment.

* * *

"Norman's a good guy, don't you think?" Helen had once asked Margaret when they returned to her room after dinner.

Margaret frowned. "Now, who is he?"

"The man we were eating dinner with—the man with the red cheeks."

"Oh, yes," said Margaret, unconvincingly. "And what about him?"

"He has a little crush on you. His daughter told me so."

"Oh I doubt that." Margaret gazed at the steam that had made a design on the outside of the window like a range of mountain peaks. She touched the glass. "Isn't this pretty? And so cold!"

Helen had rather hoped the news of an admirer would give Margaret a boost, but apparently she was indifferent to it. Certainly she had good reasons to distrust a courting man. That devil husband of hers, Jim McIntyre, who had spent every day of their married life crushing her self confidence, had praised her to the skies right up until the ring was on her finger. Then he beat her down with words, which left scars and bruises worse than any fists could have made. When he finally dropped dead of a heart attack, Margaret sat on her davenport for four days before emerging, like a mouse caught in a box trap, hovering uncertainly at the threshold after the door is lifted. Then, she rushed out into the world, taking long, luxurious walks on her beloved country lanes, marveling at every stone and seedpod underfoot, every tree, every bird. She learned to drive and began painting and playing the piano again. For two years, before the illness began to whittle her away, she had her freedom back.

Jim McIntyre. How could the man have had such an ordinary name? The name was so hateful to Helen that it left a little stain on all the other Jims she knew—harmless, innocent men. As poor as Margaret's memory was now (she could no longer recall her husband, thank goodness) she must, Helen was sure, retain some gut memory of the man's abuse, and have no interest in repeating the experience.

Still, Helen was encouraged when Margaret smiled at Norman's aphorisms. To his daughter's anxious question "Dad, do you know what day it is today?" Norman replied, "The days don't matter as long as they keep coming."

Norman was at the table when Helen walked Margaret into the dining room. He put down his fork and gazed up at Margaret with his big blue eyes as full of devotion as an old yellow lab's.

"Not very nice of me to start without you," he said.

"Oh no," said Margaret. "You go ahead."

"Cherry pie for dessert today." He handed them the bread basket and butter plate before lifting his fork again.

"Are you fond of pie, Norman?" Helen asked.

"Yessir! I could win a pie-eating contest." Norman paused to search for a fleeting memory. "I think maybe I *did* one time. Must be how I got myself in this shape." He patted his thickened midsection.

They ate in friendly silence. Harold the Talker's daughter had taken him out that day. Margaret likes Norman's quietness at the table, Helen thought. It must be soothing to her with all the noise around them—the clatter of dishes being stacked, the kitchen door constantly slamming as the aides go in and out, a server shouting at a hard-of-hearing resident: "DO YOU WANT A SECOND HELP-ING, MABEL, OR ARE YOU THROUGH? . . . MABEL! FIN-ISHED? OR A SECOND HELPING? . . . MORE FOOD OR NOT, MABEL?"

"Goodness!" said Margaret, not looking up.

Margaret barely touched her food.

"Wouldn't you like to eat some of this meatloaf, Sis?" Helen had cut it into bite size pieces for her.

"Do I have to?" Margaret stared down at the food with what looked like dismay.

How could she answer that? Was she her sister's jailer? Her tor-menter? Who had the right to make her eat? If she told her she had to, Margaret would take those little bites, grimacing with each swallow. She would do it even if she had no appetite, even if eating might give her pain, even if under all her confusion what she wanted was for death to come soon and starving was the only way to make it happen. She would eat because she never wanted to contradict, disappoint, or draw anyone's disapproval down on herself.

When the pie came, Norman said, "This pie is all right, but nobody could make pie like my wife could."

Helen was touched that he still remembered his wife. "She was a good cook?"

"Best cook in the county. I was a lucky man." His eyes filled with tears, and Helen reached over and squeezed his hand.

"What was her name?" she asked, immediately regretting the question when she saw him hesitate.

Just then an aide carrying plates passed their table and said, "How are you doing today, Norman?"

"Oh pretty good." The two tears dropped onto his napkin. "Well," he said and smiled up at her, "maybe not pretty, but good."

When they got back to Margaret's room, Helen asked for a song, and Margaret obediently sat down at the upright piano that Helen had arranged to move to her apartment from her house. Margaret had taught herself to play by ear from a book, long before she was married. She had been so proud of learning chord progressions so she could play in any key, just simple, unsophisticated tunes, old stand-bys, all with the same bouncy rhythm. She had never become what you'd call fluent at the piano; she stammered over the notes every few bars. Not that Helen was any expert on music herself.

Margaret didn't seem to care about her mistakes. She had loved playing the piano and could have spent hours completely lost in the pleasure of it if her husband hadn't locked the piano lid and pocketed the key.

"I can't stand those infernal pauses she makes!" he announced to everyone around the table at Christmas dinner that first year after they were married. "It sets my teeth on edge." He sang a verse of "Silent Night," butchering the song with stammers and hesitations. Then he held up the key to the piano lid. "This is Maggot's Christmas present to me." And he laughed that laugh that made Margaret go red and clutch her throat. That key was the first thing Helen went looking for while Margaret sat on her davenport those four days after they'd stuck the evil man in the ground.

It was funny how fast Margaret took up piano again after so many years, and how she could still play in spite of her memory loss. She couldn't remember the first part of a sentence she herself had just uttered, but she could still play those choppy chords—no better and no worse than ever. All you had to do was mention a tune and she'd start in. Sometimes she'd play the song three or four times in a row, stopping once in a while to ask, "Have I already played this?"

Helen sat in the rocker behind her and sang along. Those wrong notes and hesitations were kind of irritating, she had to admit, if you were trying to sing to them. Sometimes just out of the blue for a few awful moments, Margaret's bad playing would strike Helen as terribly funny. She had to take deep breaths and concentrate on something else to keep from laughing and was glad Margaret's back was to her. But then, watching that dainty back and shoulders bent over the keyboard, the elbows making little flourishes as Margaret's fingers trembled over the notes before pounding out the chords, Helen felt her throat constrict and her eyes fill and she thought she couldn't bear the pain.

Every ten minutes or so, Margaret turned around, realized that Helen was behind her, and exclaimed, "Why, Helen, whenever did you get here?"

She knew that as soon as she got up to go, Margaret would stop playing and go back to lying on the bed. The aides reported she never played unless someone prompted her and stayed to listen. Helen wondered if she could engineer visits to Margaret's room from Norman now and then. He would appreciate the fact that she could play at all and not carp about a few hesitations and misplayed notes. Maybe she would mention the idea to his daughter. But would Margaret like it? It was so hard to know what would make her happy.

As always, Helen felt sad and guilty leaving Margaret alone and with nothing to do after her visit. On her way back to the farm she thought for the thousandth time, uselessly, what a shame Margaret had been unwilling to leave her husband. He had refused to let her have children. Helen suspected, though Margaret never said, that she'd been coerced into an abortion—maybe more than one. Now Helen was just about all the family Margaret had.

With Cal's parents and Tom gone, only Cal's brothers were still alive, but they were a taciturn bunch, not at all sociable. And of course Wayne stayed away as much as possible. Thank goodness Barb and her kind, generous husband and their kids had settled nearby, just twenty miles the other side of Dunlop. But Barb couldn't be expected to visit her aunt more than once every couple of weeks. She had her hands full. By rights Helen thought she should spend every day with her sister, but today she had Cal to think of, and she was worried about having left him in such a blue mood and probably in pain. She was sure it was his hip that was causing him the most trouble. She could tell by the way he walked. Garland Spong's wife had walked that way before her hip surgery.

As she rounded the bend in the road past Miller's place, she saw, standing with its head hanging over the fence, that sad-eyed old quarter horse the Millers kept for their grandchildren to ride and she suddenly felt a terrible pity for Cal, almost as if his grief had poured into her and she could feel its deep, penetrating ache. Or was it her own ache? She pictured Tommy on a horse years ago, his little bare legs dangling on either side of the saddle, his eyes as round as an owl's. Cal stood beside him holding onto one of his bare feet.

NOVEMBER

i.

HELEN DIDN'T SAY anything further to him about the corn maze, and a week had gone by without Nancy Bannister calling to raise the subject again, but Cal knew Nancy would just be biding her time.

Driving into town for a haircut, he thought about the cars they had owned over the years and how he balked the first time they were talked into buying a car with an automatic transmission. How were you going to downshift on an icy hill with an automatic? With a stick shift, *you* drove the car, not the other way around like some useless grandee letting the car do all the work.

Now, he wondered, if things went on the way they were, whether he would even be able to drive the five-mile trip to town. Since that grass fire fiasco he had trouble every time he braked, and with continual pressure on the gas pedal, he felt the twinge especially in his right hip and the corresponding ache down his leg. He guessed he had to be thankful they'd invented automatic transmissions and cruise control, because now he *was* that useless grandee.

At the barbershop, the corn maze idea was brought up and talked about as if it was a done deal.

"I don't know about putting Robbie Peterson in charge of the summer help, though," said the barber, Baldy.

"Didn't he get arrested for stealing the Dunlop exit sign off the interstate?" George Massey was waiting his turn, the *Sentinel* crossword puzzle open on his lap.

"When he was sixteen. He used to cut up pretty good."

"*Used to!* You wonder if he's *always* on urgent county business when he takes that cruiser up to ninety on the interstate." George shook his head. "Nancy Bannister defends him. Says *she* used to cut up when she was that age."

"Yeah, I'll bet. Shoplifted a tea cup out of Aunt Fanny's Bric-a-Brac and Collectibles."

Both men laughed. "Still," said Baldy, "if this corn maze'll bring in business, I'm all for it. I don't know about the name, though. She wants to call it the A-mazing Maiz Maze."

"Amazing Maiz Maze?"

"No. *A*-mazing. To rhyme with 'hay.' She likes all those 'a' sounds. *Assonance*, she calls it."

"Hm. *Assonance*." George shook his head. "Then there was the time Robbie mooned the sheriff from the back seat of Ron Hoyt's father's convertible," he added.

"Bannister's so set on getting it," Baldy told Cal, "I expect you'll get top dollar for the land. Six thousand to eight thousand an acre."

George did the math in the margin of his crossword puzzle. "A hundred eighty-four thousand. Buy a lot of hair cuts with that." He winked at Baldy.

Cal said nothing. The thought of profiting by the sale of that field disgusted him. It was one thing to rent the land for a crop, but for a carny show? It was more than he could stomach. When Baldy swung him around to approve the back of his head, he just nodded, got up to pay and left without a word to either of them.

Coming home, as he drove through the gate, he slowed down and deliberately turned his head to face the field. A rabbit leapt across the stubble, zigzagging away from the fence toward the creek on the far side.

Thanksgiving wasn't here yet and it had already snowed, warmed up and frozen, the temperature dropping into the teens, leaving patches of ice between the rows. Cal wondered at the agility of the rabbit, how it could move so fast without once slipping.

Cal stopped the car, turned off the engine, and rolled down the window. He took in the whole field. The pale late afternoon sun mottled the stubble with shadows and caught the bronze in the rabbit's fur. There was no wind, no sound. The field wasn't unfamiliar, something he had never glanced at, like Helen claimed. But then, in a way, it was.

The ravine, the fence along the driveway, the road, and the stand of sentinel-like pines way off by the creek all enclosed the field, made it a thing by itself. He was aware of discomfort in his neck from turning his head to look at it—a stiffness which was not one of his usual complaints. He pivoted his head back and forth for a few seconds before turning again to look.

What was he supposed to feel? He waited for some emotion to define itself.

It didn't seem as if he felt anything. Just the strangeness of this framed piece of land, so separate, and a wish that the field wasn't there anymore. Maybe it would have been better if, instead of renting it out, he'd let it revert to meadow. It would be overgrown with volunteer willows and pines and honey locusts by now. You wouldn't look at a meadow full of trees and think of your boy being the tallest thing out there.

Cal's heart started to pound. He looked away, then forced himself to look again. The field was like something out of a goddamned fairy tale—a strange, solitary rectangle of ground like a land under an evil enchantment. Ground zero. And where was his vanished boy? Where was he?

Cal rolled up the window and drove on to the house. His neck was stiff and his hands shook.

Helen went out that evening to pick up Barb and take her to visit Margaret. Cal thought about the reaction he'd had to the field that afternoon and said to himself, Okay, you get back on the horse.

93

He put on his wool watch cap and old greasy, down-filled parka. He sat on the bench in the mud room and laced up his deep-treaded work boots and drew on the fur-lined gloves Barb had given him last Christmas. It was about fifteen degrees out and the wind had picked up. He grabbed a flashlight and went out the back door. As he came around the house, a blast of wind hit him in the face, making his eyes water. Not the best time to be stumbling over icy ruts in the dark, with his hip giving him grief every inch of the way.

Was he doing something foolish again like when he'd started a grass fire out of sheer stupidity? He stopped and thought about turning back. If he fell on the ice and broke his hip, he could freeze to death before Helen got home and figured out where he was. But he couldn't do this thing when Helen was around, and now that he was out here, he wanted to get it done.

The gravel on the driveway was slick. He had to stick close to the fence where there was traction on the snow-covered weeds. Halfway down the drive he entered the field by way of the opening that Kyle Branson drove his tractor through.

Once into the field there was nothing to hold on to, and he shone his flashlight ahead of him to catch glints of ice. The wind was biting. Already his toes and fingers were feeling the cold. He pulled his parka hood down over his forehead and blinked the water from his eyes. He should have put on the safety helmet he wore for welding. Strange thought. It flashed into his mind how he had thrown the helmet off before running out of the shed on that day.

He limped on, turning sideways to the wind. Once he slipped, flailed his arms wildly and caught himself. He went on more cautiously after that, one foot in front of the other until he figured he was about at the center of the field.

He switched off the flashlight. Okay, he thought. I'm here. It might be the exact spot, or not. It doesn't matter. I'm here.

He stood with his back to the north wind, facing the invisible horizon where the distant squall had spawned that lightning bolt, that bolt out of the blue. The night was black now, Dunlop too far away and too small to reflect even a hazy glow on the dark sky.

He waited. The wind beat against his back and rustled the few straggling stalks of alfalfa remaining in the field. 'Not grieving takes a lot of your energy' she said. Okay then. Grieve away. Let 'er loose. He closed his eyes and tried to bring back a picture of Tommy on that tractor.

But he couldn't seem to hold the image of Tommy that had made him tremble earlier that afternoon. It kept slipping out of his mind like a fish you tried to catch with your bare hands. Other thoughts crowded into his mind. Strangely, it was Wayne he thought about, and the fancy lure Wayne had sent him for his birthday last summer after their outing on the lake. What did the note say? "Happy Birthday, Dad, from one middle-aged coot to one old coot. Catch yourself a big old bass for me."

The card was in Wayne's own handwriting. Wayne hadn't given him a birthday present since he was a child. All he'd ever sent since then was cards, and then only after he'd gotten married and JoAnna wrote the message, collaring Wayne to tack on his signature.

At the time, that birthday gift kind of got to him. He felt almost choked up and turned away. But when Helen exclaimed over it, he said something sarcastic like, "Will wonders never cease?" He expected Wayne to come for Labor Day after sending him a gift like that, but he didn't, and probably had other plans for Thanksgiving and Christmas—Helen hadn't been able to pin him down yet—and it occurred to Cal that maybe Wayne's birthday gift hadn't been a friendly gesture but had meant to mock him.

Out of nowhere, Cal remembered them all walking down the hill from the cemetery after Tommy's funeral, and Wayne getting in his car, already re-packed for him to head back to New Mexico right from the cemetery. There was no suggestion that he might stay a while and help out. Nothing. Hardly even a proper good-bye. Helen and Barb had to hug him through the car window. What was that but his goddamned selfishness? Did it occur to him that Cal would have to go and put that corn in by himself after what had happened? Although as it turned out, his neighbors, without his knowing it, had quietly done it for him.

Cal balled his fingers up together to warm them inside his gloves, and his toes squirmed around in his boots. The wind made his eyes water, and the tears froze on his cheeks. His nose was completely numb.

Was there any point in standing out here in the middle of this freezing, cursed field? Not grieving might take a lot of his energy, but he felt less like bawling at this moment than he ever had in his life. What he felt like doing was driving up to Minneapolis and shoving Wayne against a wall and punching the breath out of him. That would take him down off his high horse—Mr. Art for Art's Sake, always turning up his nose at small town ways, laughing at the little craft shows that the local churches put on to raise money, applying the word 'tacky' and 'commercial' to just about everything but his own murky, depressing dabbings on canvas. Like he wasn't always trying to sell the damn things.

What Wayne would have to say about Nancy Bannister's corn maze and her *asso*nance, Cal could just imagine. The A-mazing Maiz Maze. It wouldn't matter one iota to Wayne where the thing was located. He would only be disgusted with the concept. Tacky. Commercial. Yeah, it would be commercial all right. Probably make more money in one season than Wayne had made his whole life trying to sell those pictures of his. A tacky circus on the land that one day would have belonged to him. That would give him a royal pain in the ass—Nancy Bannister's *asso*nance.

Cal gave up trying to conjure up thoughts of Tommy. He turned north into the wind and stumbled across the rutted field back to the house.

ii.

Helen was astonished that night as they were getting ready for bed and Cal said, almost as an afterthought, "If Bannister wants the damn field and Kyle agrees to give it up, let her have it. I don't care one way or the other."

His back was turned to her. He slipped the straps of his overalls off, let them fall to the floor, and stepped out of them, not bending down to pick them up and lay them neatly over the chair as he used to. She picked them up for him. It hurt him to bend down, she knew. He unbuttoned his flannel shirt and hung it on a hook in the closet, still facing away from her.

"What changed your mind?" She had to ask.

"She'll just keep after us until she gets her way. If she was a mosquito, I'd swat her, but she's not, so I figure we might as well save ourselves the bother."

This did not ring true. He would no more cave in to Nancy Bannister's persistence than put on a cowboy shirt and perform at a karaoke bar. Maybe he had taken to heart that talk she'd had with him after the Council meeting. Maybe he saw the sense in it after all.

"Well, I think you're probably right," she said, to put herself on his side and to help him save face. If he just would *face* her. But he turned the light out and got into bed, and she couldn't gauge from his expression what he was feeling.

After a silence, he said, "You can call her and tell her."

She gave his arm a pinch. "You tell her yourself!"

"And get roped into putting on horns and wearing a minotaur costume?"

"Now, you know you won't have to do a thing once they own the land—the city or the county or whatever she has in mind."

"Time will tell."

She handed him the extra pillow, and he turned onto his left side and maneuvered the pillow between his knees.

She lay a hand on his shoulder. While he was in an accommodating mood, she decided to bring up the subject of his hip.

"Cal, you've got to see someone about that hip."

There was a silence.

"Who am I going to see? That doctor in town didn't know beans."

"He suggested that you see a specialist."

"Chiropractor's good enough. He got me pretty much squared away on the rotator cuff and the back strain."

"Yes, he did. But this hip problem may not be a chiropractic thing. How long has it been bothering you? Since way last Spring. Even before that. And it seems like it's getting worse and worse no matter how many trips you take to the chiropractor."

He turned toward her a little and said over his shoulder, "Well, what's a doctor going to do?"

"Take X-rays. See if you need surgery."

He turned back. "Oh yeah. Cut me open, stick a rod down my leg and send me home with half a dozen hospital infections."

"Cal, I know at least four people who got new hips and it changed their lives. Marian Spong says it's like a miracle. She wished she'd done it years ago."

"We don't have that kind of money."

"Between Medicare and her supplement, she didn't have to pay a penny."

"We don't *have* the supplement. We couldn't afford it"

"Well, Medicare would pay all the hospital costs. We can tighten our belts and pay for the out-of pocket visits. We know how to economize." She knew better than to remind him that the sale of the land would give them a cushion.

"Barn needs a new roof and—"

"It can wait. Your health is more important."

"I'd be out of commission for months after—"

"Six weeks, that's all! And anyway,"—she hated to say it so baldly,

but facts were facts and he needed to face them—"you're out of commission *now*."

She felt him shift away from her. Was he just plain scared? Or
couldn't he admit to a weakness? She couldn't figure it out, and she had
lost patience with it. She imagined how Margaret's admirer, Norman,
might have received the same suggestion from the wife whose cooking
made him a "lucky man"— 'Well, it couldn't make it worse,' he would
have said, 'and they give you them pain drugs, so if it puts you out of
your misery permanently, at least you'll go with a smile on your face.'

She tapped Cal's shoulder. "Cal, I'm not taking no for an answer.
I'm calling to get an appointment for you to see a hip specialist at the
University Hospital in Iowa City. At least you can find out what the
problem is. You can decide what to do about it after."

He snorted. "And you don't follow their advice, they blackball you
so Medicare won't cover anything else they claim is related to the
problem, which from their point of view will be everything. You get
a boil on your butt, they won't pay to lance it 'cause you turned down
a hundred thousand dollar hip replacement."

"Forty-seven thousand."

"Forty-seven thousand?! That's what Spong's wife's cost?"

"As I said, she paid nothing out-of-pocket."

"Except for the sky high supplement premiums she pays every
month. It's a scam any way you look at it."

"Be that as it may, I'm calling Marian Spong to get her doctor's
number tomorrow."

"If you call Marian, everyone in town will be talking about Cal
Earlywine's bad hip."

"Well, let them."

He had nothing to say to that. And by his silence, she knew he had
capitulated. Maybe he was relieved.

iii

On Saturday, when Helen left to do some Christmas shopping in town and look in on her sister, Cal put aside his *Farm and Home* magazine, but continued to lie in the recliner. There was nothing on television he cared to watch. Barb had bought him a book to read—something about farm life in Iowa during the Depression. It was supposed to be uplifting, how everybody helped, even the little kids, and nothing was wasted and everything was made from scratch. He'd leafed through it, but he was never a reader. Helen was the reader. She had a school teacher's mind, her memory as sharp as ever. She learned how to use a computer just like that when Barb bought her one and showed her how. She did their taxes on it and the bookkeeping.

That computer screen gave Cal a head-ache. He didn't see how she could concentrate enough to do anything on it. But he wasn't going to chalk his inability up to old age. It was too easy to blame everything on that. The fact was he had never been comfortable with strings of words on the printed page.

If he had something to fix, assemble, re-make or re-tool, that was something else. Except now it couldn't be anything too heavy to heft onto his work bench. And he couldn't work on it if he had to stoop or bend very far in any direction. And it couldn't be anything that oper-ated with some kind of computer chip in it, which left old kitchen appliances that he could fix, and a few of his grandkids' simpler toys.

Of course it wasn't as if Helen couldn't fix things. There were plenty of times when he'd been too busy to get to something she needed done, and she'd gone ahead and done it—caulked around the windows, got up on a ladder and cleaned out the gutters, such things. She couldn't do anything with motor vehicles or farm machinery, though. But then he couldn't either, now. He couldn't get down un-derneath a car to save his life. He had to take it into town for some kid to work on.

He eased himself out of the recliner and thought about what he could do that wouldn't bother his hip too much. He put on a coat and went outside to see what might need doing in the yard or the house exterior. From the driveway, he looked back at the good old traditional four-square house—three stories, white with green trim. It was solidly built back in the twenties, but the paint was starting to crack and flake. It seemed like he'd just finished painting it, but that was—what? Twelve years ago? A hell of a hard job, especially those dormers. He'd felt his age even then. Today he couldn't do it himself, and it would cost an arm and a leg to pay someone, with labor and materials so much higher. He supposed with the sale of the field they'd have a chunk of money to fix things up. Better than investing it, when nothing was earning. But still, you had to conserve every penny. You never knew what was around the corner. Something like what Margaret had could drain you dry.

He limped back into the house and wandered into the kitchen, remembering that the knobs on the kitchen cabinets and drawers were loose. He got a Phillips screw driver out of the utility drawer. It wouldn't be that hard to tighten the eye level cabinet knobs without bending, and it occurred to him that the height of Helen's office chair could be adjusted, so he could get at the low drawers that way. He wheeled the chair into the kitchen, sat down, and cranked it to its lowest position. He still had to bend forward a little, and it gave him a twinge, but it wasn't too bad, and he could roll the chair along the linoleum from one drawer to the next before standing up to do the higher knobs. There were twenty-eight knobs altogether, every single one of them loose. The ones she used most often were practically hanging out of their screw holes. It was very satisfying to give the screw that final turn and feel the knob move firmly into place.

When Helen got home, Cal waited for her to notice the knobs. He sat upright in his recliner with Barb's gift book open in his lap and listened as she took off her boots, put her coat away and went upstairs to get her slippers. He didn't hear her come down the stairs, her slippers too quiet on the stair carpet. But then there was the shuffle of feet on the kitchen linoleum, the refrigerator door opening and closing, a creak, and finally, the exclamation of surprise.

"Cal!" she called. He got up out of his chair. She was standing by the sink, opening a cupboard. "Why, Cal, did you tighten all these knobs?"

"No," he said. "Must have been a poltergeist."

"It's poltergeists that *loosened* them," she said. She pulled open drawers and cupboards and closed them again. She shook her head and put her hands on her hips. "Isn't it funny how such a small thing as a tight cupboard knob can give you such a lift? I don't know why I put off doing it for so long."

"You were busy."

"Well, thank you. It makes the whole kitchen feel more efficient somehow."

He didn't tell her he'd had to pull her office chair in to do the job. Still, he felt a lift, too, and he sat down at the kitchen table while she took out the fixings for a slow-cooking pot roast with vegetables. Barb and her family were coming over for dinner.

"How was Margaret?" he asked.

"No worse, I guess." She took her apron from the hook inside the broom closet. "I just wish she'd *do* something. She lies there all day. She won't even walk with me around the building for some fresh air. I don't know if she's depressed or just scared to go anywhere because everything is unfamiliar and confusing. She must be so bored."

"Well, you're doing what you can. You can lead a horse to water . . ."

She nodded. "I know. But it's just so unfair. She was held down by that man for thirty-eight years, and now only two years after she found herself, she lost herself again." She took out a knife and opened up a bag of carrots. "If he weren't dead already, I could murder the man for all the stress he gave her. I know it's not the cause, but they do say stress is a factor in that disease."

Cal didn't like to hear that. He had plenty of stress himself. She shook her head and stood staring at the carrots for a moment. Cal thought she looked close to tears. "Want me to cut up them carrots for ya?" He winked at her. She raised a schoolteacher eyebrow at him. He corrected himself primly, "What I intended to say, of course, is 'Would you care for me to cut up *those* carrots for you?' "

She pushed the knife and cutting board at him and got another set for herself. They sat at the table cutting up vegetables together, not talking. He wondered if she still had things to say to him about the corn maze. But he wasn't ready to discuss it again. He turned on the radio for the Car Guys show. It amused him to second guess their diagnoses. The afternoon passed, and his hip and other aches and pains felt a little better.

The following week, Barb and Gordon and the kids came over for Thanksgiving. Helen had looked forward to it, and it turned out to be a pleasant evening for everyone, though Helen felt a pang at the absence of Margaret, who had apologetically refused to come. After dinner she set up the card table in the living room and had several games of Scrabble with Barb's thirteen-year-old, Cindy. "The Word Wizards," Cal called them. In the basement, Gordon took on the two little boys at ping pong, and Cal sat at the kitchen table with Barb for serious hands of poker, playing for nickels.

While Cindy took her time weighing her options on the Scrabble board, Helen cocked an ear toward the kitchen, listening to Cal's and Barb's banter about their poker faces and getting rich off each other. It was a good sign that Cal was tolerating an upright kitchen chair for so long without lapsing into the silence which meant he was enduring pain. And it was nice to see father and daughter enjoying each other's company, just the two of them.

Even though Barb, like Wayne, looked so much like Cal—had his round face, his dark hair and sturdy body—she had none of his personality. When she felt things, she let you know straight out and then let the feelings go. She was an optimist. There wasn't a brooding or sarcastic bone in her body.

There was a saying that boys marry their mothers and girls marry their fathers, but except for being a hard worker, Barb's husband was nothing like Cal. Gordon was sunny and generous and forgiving. His only fault was that he over extended himself. He was on half a dozen planning boards and gave up what little free time he had to help out friends and relatives. He was gentle and sensitive with all three children and shared the child rearing responsibilities willingly. Gordon was, it just occurred to Helen, a lot like Tommy. Funny how she had never thought of that before. Barb hadn't married her father but her brother.

Helen heard a clattering of something on the kitchen floor and laughter. She leaned back in her chair to peer through the doorway. The cat, Ornery, had jumped on the table, knocked the piles of nickels off and sprawled out on the cards Cal had laid down.

"That's what she thinks of your two threes, Dad." Barb spread her winning cards out and scooped up the coins from the floor.

"Damn cat." Cal stroked the back of its neck and it leaned into his hand. "Ornery, you're the worst cat in the world, you know that? Bad through and through."

Barb said, "It's a good thing that cat doesn't speak English. You'd give her a complex."

"Deal the cat in. We'll see if she does any better than I've been doing." He scratched the cat between the ears. "Yes, you're a bad, bad animal, and you know it." Ornery's eyes closed and she smiled that indulgent cat smile.

From the basement came the tock tock of the ball on the ping pong table and bursts of triumph from the little boys when they got a ball past their father.

Helen got up and left Cindy to her deliberations in order to stoke the fire. Gordon had brought in several big piles of logs from the stack by the barn and filled the wood box when they first arrived. Cal didn't seem to mind. Carrying two or three logs at a time was the best he could manage these days, and he didn't say so, but she knew he was leery of slipping on the ice.

* * *

After Thanksgiving Helen had two calls to make—one to the doctor's office and one to Nancy Bannister. The soonest they could get Cal in to see Marian Spong's hip doctor was March 8th. Cal was predictably outraged.

"Four months! Jesus Christ! Who does he think he is, the President of the United States?"

If he was disappointed, that must mean he had let himself feel some hope.

When she called Nancy and told her that Cal was willing to sell the land, Nancy's voice warbled with glee.

"Just as soon as you and Cal have a minute, Helen, let's talk about price so we can get the loan papers drawn up."

iv.

Within a week it was a done deal. Cal made it clear he didn't want anything to do with the negotiations. Helen could handle it. She was good at that kind of thing. He said nothing in Garland Spong's office at the Farmers and Merchants Credit Union when he and Helen put their signatures on half a dozen documents agreeing on $7,000 an acre. Before Cal could quite take it in, the field was no longer his.

He didn't know what he felt. He guessed he felt kind of blank. Helen tiptoed around him that afternoon and evening, proposing all kinds of distractions—a game of Parcheesi, a Cyclones game on TV together (she was never much interested in basketball), or a visit to Barb's. They ended up watching the game. He sat in the recliner, she on the sofa. Mostly he felt tired and wished there was some drug he could take to put him out like Rip Van Winkle until March, when he would visit the doctor and *maybe*—probably not, but just maybe— wake to a new possibility of life after pain. As to the field, even if it wasn't his anymore, it still sat there looking ordinary like a Civil War battlefield with nothing left of the blood that was shed.

V.

"Now that we have the right place for it, we can go full steam ahead," Nancy had said in the parking lot after the sale was finished. "There's scads of things to do way before planting season gets here. Seven P.M. on Tuesday night good for you, Helen? And Cal, too, of course?"

Cal didn't answer, and Helen said, "We'd better count Cal out. He's pretty busy," but she would try to make it.

This time, Nancy's son-in-law, Steve, was at the meeting. He was a computer whiz, according to Nancy, and could plot out the maze digitally, but she'd let *him* explain how it was done.

The son-in-law, visiting from California with Nancy's daughter and grandkids, had brought his laptop to the meeting. He sat at the head of the table. Garland, George and Robbie stood around him, staring over his shoulder at the various grid images on the screen that appeared and transformed with the movement of his finger on the mousepad.

"This is how they designed the maze over at Duran last year," Nancy told Helen, who had arrived a little late. "Only they had to hire a company to do it and got charged an arm and a leg. Steve's offered to do it for free, bless his heart."

"You plug in your parameters," Steve was saying, "and lay the whole thing out mathematically on a grid." The three men leaned in closer. "The program will automatically translate it into square feet or hectares or whatever your measurement is. You can plug in your rows any way you want them."

Robbie said, "What games you got installed on that laptop?"

"Well," objected Garland, "that's impressive, but I don't know that we're going to get the manpower to put in twenty-three acres right at the peak of planting season."

"Thank you for looking on the practical side, Garland," said Nancy. "The maze itself will only cover ten acres. I think I've talked Kyle into helping out." She turned to Helen hopefully. "I suppose Cal is not in a position to do some planting. Correct me if I'm wrong, Helen."

"No. He won't be involved."

"Well, Robbie's got some boys lined up to do the mowing after the corn starts to come up."

George was admiring the case the laptop came in. "That's pretty handy. Did it come with the computer or did you have to buy it separately?"

Nancy put her finger to her lips to gently shush George, who didn't—as he never did—seem to take offense. He was used to being shushed by his wife. "We have to decide just as soon as possible on the maze image so Steve can plot it all out."

While Steve got up from the computer to help himself to coffee and a lemon bar, Robbie ventured a fingertip onto the mouse pad and moved it toward a game icon on the desktop.

"You got UFO2 Extraterrestrials installed on here?"

Nancy tapped the back of Robbie's hand smartly with a pen. She was holding a clipboard now and settled into Steve's place, ready to get down to business.

"So we've had several suggestions for the design. Robbie, I know you've been pushing for a Harley Davidson image, but would you believe it, it was done in 2007 on a farm in Tipton. I saw an aerial photo on the internet. It made a very nice maze, though. Very intricate. So you were on the right track, Robbie."

George said, "My granddaughter told me to suggest a picture of that Twilight vampire boy."

"Now that's a thought," said Nancy. "But you know, something came to me in the middle of the night last week. One of those inspirations you have when your mind is in a receptive state." She paused significantly. Garland frowned—his forehead and eyebrows gearing up before any idea could race past his automatic objection. Helen saw this and felt weary. How had she let Nancy talk her into serving on a committee once again?

"I think the maze should be a corn row," said Nancy. She sat back, her lips pressed together impishly.

"I thought it *was* a corn row. A *bunch* of corn rows," expostulated Garland. "What else *would* you plant that would grow tall enough? Elephant grass?"

"Elephant grass?" George looked puzzled. "I think that only grows in Asian countries like Vietnam. Or maybe Africa?"

"You want the image itself to be of a corn row?"

"Exactly, Helen. Wouldn't that be original? The A-mazing Maiz Maze would be a corn row!" Nancy exclaimed, jubilantly. "Think how complex it would be. Stalks, leaves curving over, roots. Cul de sacs in the shape of ears of corn. From the air it would be really pretty."

"Who's going to see it from the air?" Garland objected.

"Well, we'd get someone to fly over and take a picture for the brochure."

"Huh?" George wasn't getting it. Robbie either.

"It can be done," said Steve. Nancy had apparently settled it with him beforehand.

"How would that work? It doesn't make sense." Garland was shaking his head. "A picture of a corn row made out of corn rows?"

"A wonderful celebration of corn, right here in the corn state —Iowa!"

"I *know* where we live," Garland said, irritably. "Anyway, we can't call it The A-mazing Maiz Maze." Garland had crossed his arms over his chest.

"Whyever not?"

"Because those people with the maze over in Princeton, Iowa already used it."

"Well, how did they spell it? Ours would be *A-mazing* with a hyphen and *maiz* without the *e*."

"What happened to that naming contest you wanted to hold? Wasn't there going to be a community vote?"

That went out the window, thought Helen, the minute Nancy sat up in bed inspired. Helen held her tongue, though. An A-mazing Maiz Maze was fine with her, and she was relieved to know there would be no boy vampire image or anything of that sort to set Cal off again. In fact, she found herself rather liking the idea of the corn row design. There was something artistic about it. She thought of Grant Wood and Marvin Cone—that school of Iowa artists who appreciated the contours and colors of their rural state—the deep, black rows of earth, the cylindrical hay bales dotting hillsides, the gullies and stands of trees along the watersheds. Wayne would like Nancy's idea. He would enjoy the humor and the whimsy of it. And the art, if it was designed well.

"My son Wayne might do the initial drawing," she said impulsively. "He's an artist." She felt a little boastful and foolish for saying it. Of course everyone knew her son was an artist.

"Oh, Helen, that's just a great idea!" Nancy clapped her hands.

"He would want a commission," Helen thought to add. How close she had come to selling him short!

Steve had reclaimed his laptop from Robbie, shut it down, and closed the cover. "Just have him photoshop and send me the drawing and I'll digitize it," he said.

"Well . . . " Helen began to back pedal. Maybe she was wrong. Maybe Wayne would hate the idea or wouldn't have time, "I'm not sure he'll agree."

"Oh he'll agree," said Nancy. "Do you want me to ask him?"

"So how was the meeting?" Carl was standing looking out the patio window into the darkness when she got back from town. "A-*mazing*?"

"Pretty much what you'd expect. Nancy's son-in-law is going to lay out the maze design on his computer."

"When is Nancy going to hold her big contest?"

"She isn't. She's settled on the A-mazing Maiz Maze."

"What? No one else had their thinking cap on?"

"It's going to be a picture of a corn row."

Cal turned from the window. "A *corn* row?"

"To go with the name—A-mazing maiz maze."

"She thinks this is going to attract people?"

"Maybe it will."

"Huh. So, no contest."

"No contest."

She didn't mention that she had volunteered Wayne. It was late, and she was tired.

vi.

Helen put off calling Wayne. She guessed he might see the cornfield in the same light Cal did—forbidden ground. She would have to work up a little courage before talking to him. So instead, she washed and pressed a homemade lap quilt she had found cheap at the re-sale store to keep Margaret's knees warm when she sat in her rocker to look out the window at the bird feeder.

She had seen Margaret just yesterday, but already had an urge to go again, at lunchtime so she could gently encourage her to eat more. She was getting so thin. And Norman would be there. He might like the extra company, since his daughter worked all day.

Margaret and Norman were already at the table when she arrived, with no sign, thankfully, of Harold the nonstop talker. Norman had just returned from a trip with his daughter to the Meskwaki casino at Tama.

"How'd you make out at the slots, Norman?" called an aide, walking past with a coffee pitcher.

"Well, I don't think I took any of their money," he said philosophically.

Margaret was even quieter than usual and ate only a few bites of steamed carrots.

"The food is pretty bad here," she whispered in Helen's ear.

"I can bring you anything you'd like, Margaret. What do you have a craving for?" Helen pulled out a little tablet from her purse, ready to make a list.

"Oh no, don't go to the trouble. I'm not very hungry anyway."

"How about some homemade tuna salad with horseradish? You always liked that."

"No, no, I'm fine." Margaret pushed her plate away and stood up.

"Finished?" said Norman. His mouth drooped and his bushy eyebrows tilted upward in disappointment. "Don't want dessert? You can have my portion."

Margaret smiled vaguely and shook her head. Helen felt sorry for him. He never remembered Margaret's name, but whenever they were together, he seemed to light up. "That gal with the big brown eyes," he called her, and told his daughter he had a girlfriend at the home, though he couldn't recall exactly who it was until he saw Margaret again at meals.

"I'd like to hear about your trip to the casino sometime, Norman," Helen said. His face brightened.

"As good as throwing quarters in a wishing well." He drew his arm back in a tossing gesture and almost knocked the dishes off a tray that an aide was carrying by.

The aide said over her shoulder teasingly, "Norman, you lookin' for trouble?"

"No," he called after her. "I *know* where *you're* at."

Helen smiled and touched his arm. "You're so quick," she said. "How do you think up these come-backs?"

"Oh," he ducked his head, reddening with pleasure, "I'm the slow one in my family. You should hear my brother. I'll bring him over. You'll see."

Helen knew for a fact that his brother was dead.

She had forgotten about her sister. While she was chatting with Norman, Margaret had gotten up and wandered away. Quickly Helen excused herself and found Margaret staring at the place where the two wings of the building branched off from each other.

"Where do I go now?" Margaret said.

"Let's go to your room. This way." Helen guided her by her elbow. "Maybe you'd give me a little piano music."

"Well, if you'd like."

She and Margaret walked slowly down the hall, giving Margaret time to study names on the doors and the decorations the relatives and staff had put up for Christmas.

"'Struve'," she said. "What does that mean?"

"It's someone's last name. The person who lives in that apartment."

"What an odd name. 'Struve.' It seems like it should mean something, but I don't know what."

Norman came up alongside them with a slice of pie on a paper plate.

"I'm saving it for later," he told them. To Margaret he said, "But you can have it if you want it." Margaret smiled politely and shook her head. He continued down the hall. He was wearing the wide red suspenders his daughter had given him. He wore them every day.

"Aren't those red what-do-you-call-'ems striking?" said Margaret.

"You like them? His suspenders? You should tell him."

"Well . . . maybe I will sometime." That was her way of never coming right out and saying no. She still had all her old instincts to protect other people from contradictions or unpleasantness, Helen thought. She had always been like that, even before her husband made it a necessity for survival. What a pity she was spoiled now for someone like Norman. To Helen, the man was a bright spot in any day.

On her way home, Helen thought about Cal and wondered how he would react if he were stuck in Norman's place. Not cheerfully, that was for sure. If he got this dreadful disease, he would be one of those people whose more unpleasant personality traits emerged with a vengeance. No red suspenders for him. He wouldn't be caught dead in them.

"Am I supposed to *know* you?" she could hear him saying in that sarcastic tone.

Norman was a generous, humble man. Whatever pettiness he may have possessed in the past—if he'd possessed any at all—the illness had sifted out, leaving his basic goodness intact. She found him restful. Too bad Margaret didn't feel the same.

DECEMBER

i.

SNOW HAD DRIFTED UP to a half foot outside the double-glazed patio door. Barb's family visited again, and left the house warm, friendly and peaceful after they departed. Helen thought tonight would be a good time to mention her idea to Cal about Wayne drawing the corn maze design. When everyone left and the two of them were sitting down to a cup of cocoa before bed, she brought it up.

Cal didn't take it as well as she had hoped.

"Wayne!" he sneered.

"Why not?"

"Well, for one thing I don't think anyone will understand a corn row that looks like a four-year-old dropped a handful of pickup sticks."

"What are you talking about?"

"You forgetting that show he had up there in Minneapolis? Every picture was as unlike its title as humanly possible. That exploding orange thing he called 'Silence'—about as silent as an Iraqi IED."

"Wayne is perfectly capable of drawing realistically when he chooses to. He graduated from a four-year art school with high grades."

"Well, you'd never know it. Anyway, why would he want to help out? You couldn't get him down here if you told him you'd broke both your arms. He'd just say, What's wrong with using your feet? *If* he said anything at all." Cal took his half-drunk cup to the sink and poured the rest of the cocoa down the drain.

Helen sat there feeling utterly exasperated. The cat jumped up on the table again, and she pushed it off. She kept silent for a minute or two while Cal, perhaps to make up for his display of temper, rinsed out his cup and put it in the dishwasher.

She said, "Well, I'm going to ask him. I'll tell him we want something realistic, and see if the job appeals to him. If it doesn't, so be it. Nancy's idea actually sounded kind of pretty to me. I think Wayne would like it."

Cal slapped a dishrag over a place on the counter where he'd splashed some cocoa. "You're going to tell him where this *A*-mazing maze will be located?"

"Of course."

"Well, good luck."

Cal left the kitchen without another word and tramped heavily up the stairs to bed. Helen stayed downstairs for half an hour or so tidying up.

When she finally joined Cal, he was lying on his back with his hands behind his head. She took a breath. She'd made up her mind to have it out.

"Cal, why are you always so hard on Wayne?" Cal withdrew his hands and folded them across his chest.

"How am I hard on him? I'm not hard on him. He's hard on me."

"You've been hard on him since he was a child."

He turned to look at her sidelong. "Are you saying it's my fault he is the way he is?"

"What way is he?"

"Drifting. Doesn't give a damn about family. Plays around instead of getting a real job."

Helen shook her head. "Why do you keep saying that? He doesn't play around. He's aimed to be an artist since he was a child and worked hard to make it happen. And he's a good husband and a good stepdad to Jake. He's loyal to his family."

"Which family? He was never loyal to *our* family."

"Just because he never wanted to farm? He isn't the same as Tommy. He was *never* going to take that place. Even before Tom was born, that was not the right place for Wayne."

Cal turned over and set his back to her. "You don't know what you're talking about. I've been *soft* on Wayne. You know what my Dad would have done to me if I'd acted like Wayne did as a kid? I'd have gotten the strap on the bottoms of my feet. Enough to make me limp for days. And I'd still have to get my chores done and walk two miles to school on swollen feet."

"Cal, your Dad was a brutal bully, which you are not, thank goodness."

"My Dad was way too hard on us kids, but I didn't turn into a selfish wimp like Wayne. I knew the duty I had to my parents. The only thing I've ever asked of Wayne is that he lend a hand and show an interest. But he won't. He has a grudge against me and always has. Even when he was a little kid. He wouldn't let me pick him up or show him a thing."

"He wouldn't let *me* pick him up either. He was born prickly as a cactus and stubborn and independent." She wanted to say *Who does he remind you of?* Cal kept his back to her and after a while pretended to sleep, but she knew what his real snore sounded like. She pushed his shoulder. "Cal. When Tommy came along, you quit loving Wayne." The fake snoring stopped and there was an ominous silence. Immediately Helen regretted what she'd said. She hadn't meant to. And she knew as soon as she said it, it wasn't even true. She rested her hand on his shoulder. "I'm sorry," she said. "I know you love him. But you stopped *showing* love for him." Cal pushed her hand off and rolled over to face her.

"God damn it, I fed him and clothed him and worked eighteen-hour days to give him a secure home. I even helped send him to that so-called art school. What did you expect me to do, go around saying 'love ya' every time he walked out the door? *Love* ya,' " Cal simpered, " '*love* ya'.'" You want me to say '*miss* ya' on the rare occasions he lowers himself to call? 'Gee, Wayne, we *miss* ya. Come on home occasionally, but only if it's convenient for you. Bye, bye. *Love* ya. *Miss* ya!' "

"All *right!*"

She lay awake wishing she could take back her harsh words. He didn't need the aggravation now when he was feeling so diminished, so useless, and always in pain. But if they didn't deal with this now, when? She had waited too long already. She'd had to stick up for Wayne over and over when Wayne was a child. But after Tom died she'd just given up confronting Cal about it. It was so clear how despairing he was, and Wayne's disappearing made it easier to lay off him about his surviving son. Then Tom became a taboo subject for Cal, and Wayne did, too, except to criticize him.

She could see why Cal had been frustrated by Wayne from the get go. Wayne's Terrible Twos were indeed terrible. Every word out of his mouth was no. The fact that anyone would try to control him put his back up. With Cal it was always do this, do that, because I say so. And Wayne would defy, defy, defy. She tried to teach Cal the art of manipulation. Just say, Wayne, which do you want, a bath or a wipe down, bathtub or washcloth? Give the boy a choice and he'd cooperate. But Cal rejected such compromises on principle. Wayne should simply do as he was told. What difference does it make, she'd argue, if the goal is to get him cleaned up? The goal, according to Cal, was to get him to respect his parents. Sometimes Helen thought Cal himself was in his own Terrible Twos.

Tommy's Terrible Two's were more like *Me* Too's. "Time for a bath?" would have Tommy trying with his little hands to turn on the hot and cold water taps, and Cal saying, "That's right, that's right. Good boy," none of which was lost on Wayne. Helen could see how he resented Tommy's good nature and the rewards it brought him. He'd turn the taps back off just to frustrate his brother, putting Cal, not Tom into a rage. Cal would pick Wayne up squirming, and banish him from the bathroom, locking the door against him, and Wayne would kick the door—for no reason, according to Cal, but sheer cussedness.

Still, she had to give Cal credit for never hitting Wayne or any of the kids. Cal's father had beaten his boys at the least provocation, while Helen's parents had never even spanked, and she wondered, when she and Cal were first married, if she would have to stand firm against the practice. But it had never been necessary. Even when Wayne got so stubborn or mouthed off at him, Cal never raised a hand against him. She guessed he had made a pledge to himself after what he'd been through. Once, at the county fair, they had seen a father whack his son hard on the side of the head because the boy had scampered away for a minute to look at the farm animals. After hitting him, the man had taken the little boy by the shoulders and almost shaken his head off, yelling, "*Shame* on you!" In two strides, Cal was in the man's face. "Shame on *you*! he exclaimed. Startled, the man released the boy, and Cal walked back to Helen with fire in his eyes.

She thought about poor Barb, who had loved Tom so much. For a while after Tom's death, Barb kind of got lost in the shuffle. Thank goodness she had the sense to marry a sweet, kind man. It was almost a miracle that Barb was getting along so happily in spite of all the old family tensions.

Well, she hated to add to Cal's burdens, but she *was* going to ask Wayne to do the drawing. She was pretty sure it would please him to be asked, even when he heard where the maze was going to be planted.

In the middle of the night Helen woke from a vivid dream. It was a brilliant sunny day. She was at some kind of training place for race horses. There were several tall thoroughbreds grazing in a pasture, one so black it was almost purple, another a deep rust red color and a third a rich chocolate brown. The sunlight gave their coats a silken sheen. Only a dilapidated old split-rail fence separated her from them. She put out her hand, hoping they would come over so she could stroke their velvet noses, but they were cropping grass and didn't notice her.

She became aware that Norman was by her side. He put one foot on a lower rail of the fence and it broke in two. She wondered if the horses could somehow squeeze under the broken place and run off. "I wasn't paying attention," Norman apologized, "because I was thinking about you." He put his arm around her shoulder and pressed his cheek to hers. Their lips were almost touching. He said, "I remember *your* name. You're Helen." She felt as young and romantic as a teenager.

After she woke, she lay in bed re-experiencing his cheek against hers, the closeness of their lips, his bicep hard against her back, and the firm grasp of his big hand on her upper arm, making her feel light and dainty. She re-lived the moment in the dream for as long as she could before it began to fade and she fell back to sleep

In the morning the dream stayed with her as Cal got out of bed stiffly and hobbled into the bathroom. It always took him a few minutes to get the kinks out, as he put it, but lately he was limping more and more. She felt a mixture of irritation and pity, remembering how strong he was once, but how he had sometimes worked himself unnecessarily and failed to ask for help when help was available.

He didn't seem too interested in sex since he had been having so much hip pain. And it probably didn't help that on the rare occasions he did turn to her in bed and things got started, she couldn't keep herself from asking, "Does this hurt? Does this hurt?"

It was funny how some things lodged in her memory about their sex life, even after decades. She remembered how, on a Saturday morning, several months after Barb was born, she got up to get dressed, feeling insecure about the loose belly flesh that persisted. She put on a robe to hide it. Cal got up and took her hand. "How do you do, Ma'am. Would you be that Helen whose beauty started a war?" Before she could protest, he drew her robe open and ogled her up and down. "*Oh* yeah. I can see what all the fighting was about." She tried to close the robe and push him away. "Oh, Cal, you don't mean it," she said. "The hell I don't!" And he slipped the robe off her shoulders and led her to the bed, where he swooped her into his arms and kissed her all over.

ii.

She had meant to give Wayne a call that night, preferably from the phone upstairs while Cal was watching a basketball game on TV. Not that it was secret. She told Cal, "I'm going to give Wayne a jingle and ask him if he would be interested in drawing the design for the corn maze," and Cal hadn't argued with her. But she would rather not have Cal listening to her end of the conversation in case Wayne asked something she would have to respond to that might set Cal off.

Now, on top of the accusation she made that Cal didn't love his own son and on top of that dream about Norman, she was worried that asking Wayne to draw the maze was disloyal to Cal. All day it was on her mind, and she dreaded Nancy Bannister's calling to badger her about it.

She stayed at home for lunch the next few days and ate with Cal through silent meals. Sitting across the table from him, the word that came to her was "gloomy." He was a gloomy man, there was no getting around it. His sense of humor had turned sarcastic so long ago that—except for the night he and Barb played poker—she couldn't remember when she had last heard him laugh with simple pleasure.

What would it have been like, she wondered, to have married someone a little sentimental, a little humble? Someone with a rosy view of the world, forgiving of others, not so stubborn? It simply wasn't fair, though, to compare Cal with Norman. What about the Cal who was her companion before Tom died?

Closing the curtains on the patio doors, she remembered how, years ago, she told Cal she wished the living room weren't so dark. It was just a thought. But the next week Cal had taken out the door to the patio and replaced it with big glass sliding ones that let in all that sunshine, and then he finished it off so nice you'd never know they hadn't always been there. What must it be like for him to be so limited now? He had always worked hard, and now he could hardly work.

* * *

The call came a week after the last meeting. Cal answered it.

"Her Majesty, for you," he said, handing the phone to her, not bothering to put his hand over the mouthpiece.

She frowned at him. "Don't be rude," she whispered. She took the phone. "Hello?" she said, with false enthusiasm.

"Hi, Helen. It's Nancy."

"Oh, Nancy. How are you?"

"Just great!"

Her daughter and son-in-law were still visiting, Nancy said, but were going back tomorrow, and she thought she'd check in about the corn maze design. "What did Wayne have to say about it?"

Helen hedged. "I'm not sure he'll have the time."

"For a simple sketch of a corn row? Oh, I'll bet he could knock that off in five minutes, he's so talented." As far as Helen knew, Nancy had never seen any of Wayne's art work. "Unfortunately no one in my family has that artistic bent. You're lucky. I envy you."

"Well, I haven't asked him yet."

"Would you like me to call him and explain the concept?" This was the second time she had made the offer, and Helen wouldn't put it past her to nose out his phone number in Minneapolis and call him even without her say so.

"No, no. That's not necessary. I'm planning on calling him this weekend anyway. I'll mention it to him then."

"That's excellent, Helen. The sooner the better. And just let me know as soon as you know. Steve is raring to go on that digital formatting."

"You won't be planting until May. Is there such a hurry?"

"Once we're sure of the actual design, there's a whole slew of publicity to plan, licenses from the state, insurance applications, getting commitments from volunteers and staff. There's a lot of red tape. You can't start too early."

"You haven't talked to Wayne?" Cal asked when she hung up.

"Well, no. I'd tell you if I had."

"What's standing in your way?"

She looked at him. Was he trying to provoke an argument over it? But no, he was looking over her shoulder instead of straight at her. He seemed to be making some kind of concession.

"Nothing," she said. "I'm going to call him this weekend." Cal nodded.

The more Cal thought about Helen's claim that he didn't love his son, the more it nagged at him. He made mental lists of all the things he'd done for Wayne, from getting up to soothe him in the middle of the night after a nightmare to sending him to that expensive Kansas City Art Institute after he graduated from high school.

He put up with Wayne's sulks and attended meetings with his teachers after an exhausting day of mending fences or harvesting winter wheat. Damn it, he had treated the boys fairly, given them generous allowances—more for Wayne because he was older.

It was true he enjoyed Tom's company better than Wayne's but who wouldn't? Wayne made himself so unlikeable. Even at school he was a loner. Everyone loved Tommy. There were dozens of girls hanging around making google eyes at him, all the more because he was a gentleman. He treated them with respect, like he did his mother. Wayne always looked down on the local girls. Got himself a battered up used car and drove to Des Moines or Minneapolis to go out with city girls and spend the night with them.

Wayne could have been kinder to Helen, too, considering how lenient she was toward him. But for her to say he didn't love Wayne? Of course he loved him. What was love supposed to be between father and son? Not something mushy and talky. You showed it by feeding and clothing the boy and pushing him toward a decent future.

Cal thought about the talks he and Tommy had when they worked together in the barn, sometimes past Tom's bedtime. Nothing especially personal. Just the weather and what needed doing around the property. Sometimes they'd be silent, watching a bald eagle with its great straight wings stretched out as it soared low, heading for the river. They grinned and shook their heads after those sightings. "The national bird," Tommy said, "and around here you get to see it more often than on a dollar bill."

Cal's eyes filled with tears. So, okay his love for Tommy was mushy. And there'd been a lot of talking between them that had never taken place between him and Wayne. He probably shouldn't have given up on Wayne so early in his life. But what more could he have done? Wayne seemed to prefer to go his own way, even as a child. And now it was like they lived in different countries with an ocean separating them.

Limping down to the mailbox, Cal recalled that moment last spring, literally that instant, when he thought irrationally that Wayne had been struck by lightning in the boat while they were fishing. He had instinctively lunged forward to grab Wayne's shirt. Why? To save him from falling out of the boat? Or just to hold on to him and somehow prevent his sharing Tom's fate. Maybe that proved he loved him. But he couldn't tell Helen about it.

iii.

Helen made small talk with Wayne's wife before asking to speak with him. JoAnna was a self-employed tax accountant, and December was a slack time of year. Helen mentioned that she enjoyed learning how to do their taxes with a computer program.

JoAnna laughed. "I use one too, naturally, but I hope not everyone is as smart as you, Helen. I'd go out of business."

She put Wayne on.

"How are you all doing?" Helen asked. It was safer to open the conversation this way than to inquire about his work. He was always on a deadline, getting art ready to submit to competitions, but he must have gotten a lot of rejections because she seldom heard anything more about it afterwards. Whether she asked or avoided asking, he could get defensive either way. Sometimes in their phone conversations she thought Wayne acted as if he could see Cal standing over her shoulder, judging him.

The stepson Jake was doing okay, Wayne said. Getting A's in Shop and Phys Ed, C's in everything else. He had a hard time sitting in classes. Wayne could relate.

"Well, honey," she said, "I've got a favor to ask you, and just say no if you're too busy." She put a smile on her face, even though he couldn't see it, and blurted out her whole speech in one breath. "Dunlop bought that piece of land Kyle Branson rents from us. They're going to put a corn maze on it, and we volunteered you to draw the design for it."

"Say, what? A corn maze?"

"To bring in some tourism and earn money for the town."

There was a pause. "On the piece by the driveway?"

She found herself stuttering. "To . . . to . . . uh . . . because it's just off the county road and close to the interstate without being too—"

"What does *he* think of this idea?" It was never a good sign when Wayne referred to his father as "he".

"Well, at first your dad didn't think much of it, but he did come around."

"Grudgingly, no doubt."

"He wasn't too enthusiastic, no. But Nancy Bannister—you remember her—?"

"Who could forget?"

"Nancy put together figures showing it could make the town a pretty decent income over time, and of course they offered a fair sum for the land. So Cal agreed to it."

"Got hornswoggled by the Bannister, did he?" Helen didn't answer. "Or was it because even Calvin Earlywine has his price?" His voice was bitter.

"Wayne, your Dad doesn't care about the money."

"*Something* must have convinced him."

"*I* liked Nancy's idea."

"Oh." His voice had softened.

Helen cleared her throat.

"Anyway, we volunteered you to draw the design for it." The little lie had slipped out before she could catch herself.

"You and *Dad*?"

"Well, *I* did. Cal wasn't at the meeting."

"Ah."

"And really, if you're too busy, it's fine. But it would only need to be a simple pen and ink sketch," Helen hurried on, "of a corn row. And the town would pay you a commission, of course. I'm not sure how big it would be, but—"

"A corn row? Are you talking about a picture of a corn row made from corn rows?"

"Yes, exactly. The roots and tassles and leaves could overlap just like in a real corn row, to make the cross walks, or not, so they'd come to dead-ends, and the ears of corn could be cul-de-sacs—"

"Yeah, Mom, I get it. People walk around in it, get lost, and find their way out." His voice was dry. She wondered if the request insulted him, if it implied that drawing for corn mazes was the best he could do.

"I know it's a commercial kind of thing, honey, but, you know, as soon as Nancy proposed the idea of a corn row, I could picture it. Kind of simple and pretty and natural, and I thought you would do justice to it."

"Hnh." Wayne was silent for a few moments. "How do you figure it's going to look pretty if it's a maze? Who's going to see it when they're in it?"

"Oh. Well, they'd take a photo of it from the air for a brochure, and, I suppose, they'd feature the original drawing on the brochure, too, and maybe something about the artist—'original design by Wayne Earlywine,' something like that. Nancy wants to sell T-shirts with the picture on it—" Here, again, she'd said a silly, possibly insulting thing, as if that kind of publicity would do Wayne any good. Maybe he'd think it was cheapening.

But Wayne said, "You told Dad you were going to ask me to draw it?"

"Yes."

"What did he have to say about that?"

Helen sighed. "Honey, I wish you wouldn't always ask me to speak for your father. Ask him yourself."

"Which means he laughed at the idea."

"No, he didn't—"

"I'll draw it. When do you need it?"

When she got off the phone, she wasn't sure if she should feel happy or disturbed about Wayne's agreeing so quickly. He hadn't said much about the location of the maze, but then he wouldn't. He was like Cal that way.

She went downstairs and found Cal dozing in his recliner, the cat asleep on his lap. She decided to wait until he woke up to tell him about Wayne's decision. It was a crisp, clear day with the sun shining on three inches of new snow. She put on her boots, bundled up and left the house. The snow crunched under her feet as she walked past the wood lot toward the river. It was slippery making her way down the steep path into the ravine. She clambered over and detoured around the new deadfall that had come down during a recent ice storm.

It brought back the walks they used to take as a family along the horse trail that went for miles beside the sleepy river under the shade of old sycamores and cottonwoods. All the neighbors agreed it was okay for each other to ignore the sagging, rusty barbed wire and No Trespassing Or Hunting signs that marked property boundaries. It had been a neighborly time, those days before Tom's death. Afterward, Cal hardly ever accepted help from neighbors. Why, she wasn't sure. Because he didn't want anyone commiserating with him about the loss of Tom's help? Or because he wanted to show he could manage without it? He would give but not take, and maybe people unconsciously stopped asking him to give, since they weren't allowed to reciprocate. Little by little some of that sense of neighborliness got lost along the way.

But before that, there was the family, walking together, Barb riding on Cal's shoulders, the little boys running on ahead. She and Cal talked about the land as they walked, how they might put in an orchard or dam up the creek and make a swimming pond. He would take her hand in his thick calloused one and they'd swing them, like kids—not something he would do in town, of course, but it showed that private affection that was always there between them.

Halfway down the path now, she came to the trunk of the old black oak with the burl growth protruding from it like a great pile of shriveled potatoes. What was left of the oak had managed to remain standing due to its sheer bulk. The tree had stood there since the children were little, all the heavy branches now fallen and rotted away. How fascinated the kids had been by that gnarly burl, which grew in size along with them, over the years.

She recalled how Wayne had said the burl was the tree's brains, and if you put your ear to it, you could hear what the tree was thinking. How many times had Wayne raced down to the tree, Tommy running to keep up on his shorter legs. Wayne would press his ear against the burl and translate for him. "I can't hear it!" protested Tommy, pressing his ear, too. "You will," Wayne reassured him, "when you're old enough."

Sometimes when she and Cal walked to the river, they would come across sculptures that Wayne, with Tommy as his helper, made out of branches, giant sycamore leaves as big as elephant ears, mushrooms, bits of fur and feathers, all tied together by vines. The sculptures hung from tree limbs or peeked from the crevices of fallen logs.

Once, she and Cal found what looked like a little grotto made from a tube of stripped birch bark set upright into the ground. The boys had found a cluster of four-leaf clovers and run up to the barn for two pieces of broken window glass, between which Wayne had pressed the clovers flat and set the glass on the ground inside the birch bark tube. Wayne called it the Church of Good Luck.

By the time Barb would have been old enough to join in, it was too late. Cal had started to take Tommy with him into the barn and fields. Wayne tacitly fired Tommy as his sidekick and from then on roamed the woods alone.

Somewhere Helen had photos of those early art collaborations, pictures of the two boys standing beside their sculptures and cutting up for the camera in that period when they were still pals.

The day after her phone call, Helen received Wayne's corn row drawing as a jpeg attachment to an e-mail. When she opened the attachment and saw what he had done, she let out a cry, "Oh my goodness!" which brought Cal into her office. Together they looked at the drawing in silence. Cal took his reading glasses out of his pocket and put them on.

"Damn!" he said, and after a moment, in a gruff voice, "What'd he do, take a photograph?"

"Of course not. This is winter. Look at the colors."

The green leaves drooped and curled gracefully, just as they would on a calm, windless day. The stalks were crowned by tawny tassels. A tangle of brown roots intertwined at the bottom of the row, almost hiding a single, mottled-gray field mouse. Each stalk held fat ears of July-ripe corn streaming bright yellow silks, and at the top of one tassel—bending it with its slight weight—a red-winged blackbird perched, its head cocked to the sky as if it were singing.

Helen felt a lump in her throat. She looked up at Cal, who was leaning over her to get a closer look. For once he had nothing sarcastic to say. She waited.

He said, "Well, the boy can draw, all right. He can draw."

"It's lovely!" Helen exploded. "He drew that in one day! One day!"

"Well, I'd hope after four years of art school he could draw a corn row."

"Cal, it's exceptional, and you know it."

Cal nodded and kept nodding as if he were undoing a great deal of head shaking, years of it.

Finally he said, "I wouldn't mind having something like *that* on our wall."

Helen instantly clicked the print button and the drawing slowly emerged from the printer. It was a pale replica of what was on the screen. Cal frowned.

"It's not the same. Did the computer pretty it up?"

"No, no. Not at all. This is just a cheap printer, and you also need photo quality paper. I'll forward the drawing to Nancy. She's got everything up-to-date." Helen typed in Nancy's e-mail address and forwarded the drawing while Cal watched.

He continued to stare at the print out. "I'll be damned," he said. "I'll be damned."

From seeming to avoid mentioning the corn maze, Cal now seemed preoccupied with it.

"How the hell are they going to turn out a design like that from corn stalks?" he asked, the next morning.

Helen had fixed his favorite breakfast of eggs with fried potatoes and onions and her homemade sourdough toast with jam. She had felt celebratory, and his belligerent tone exasperated her.

"Nancy already explained how it works. They sow the whole field in tight rows and when the plants come up to about a foot high, they mow in the design."

"Well, that's a waste of good seed. And how're they going to keep ten acres of weeds down? Bannister going to put on her pink gardening gloves and get down on her hands and knees and pull 'em herself?"

Helen re-filled his coffee cup, accidentally spilling some into his saucer. She didn't wipe it up.

"Well," she said, "I suppose they'll have to spray."

"Oh ho! What did Mr. Clean Environment have to say about that?"

"Wayne didn't ask about it."

"And you knew better than to tell him." She ignored the comment. "Is Bannister still bent on calling the thing "The A-mazing Maiz Maze" and risking a lawsuit for trademark infringement?"

"What would *you* call it then?"

Cal frowned and laid his fork down. After a moment, he said, "I don't know. But something . . . more dignified, respectful."

His use of the word took her by surprise. Respectful of Tom's lost life? Or of Wayne's talent. Maybe both. She went to the stove and picked up the skillet. There were a few potatoes left, and she scooped them onto his plate.

"Don't you want these?" he said.

"You finish them." She sat back down. "I think you should 'put your thinking cap on' and find a better name. Then see if you can change Nancy's mind, now that it's made up."

"Last time she had us putting on our thinking caps they got snatched off our heads before we got in any thinking."

"I guess you'll just have to go head-to-head with her bare-headed."

Cal laughed. "I'd need a football helmet."

iv.

Unconsciously, she looked for Norman when she arrived at the Center at noon on Monday and felt a twinge of disappointment to see Margaret at the table with only Mabel, and the garrulous Harold bending their unattending ears. But then as salad was being served, Norman showed up.

He sat down next to Helen, and she found she was very aware of him, and of the irony—that she would have this little crush on a man—even someone with such glowing cheeks and sky blue eyes and sweet disposition— who couldn't, in fact, remember her name and soon wouldn't remember his own.

A niggle of guilt unsettled her stomach. How often had she been coming to have lunch at Oakridge and leaving Cal on his own, with Margaret as an excuse? Her own sister, whom she loved dearly, an excuse? An excuse to get away from her husband and be around a more likeable man?

She searched her heart. Was this what brought her here so often? No. She could honestly say that she didn't come to see Norman. She came because she felt more pity for her sister than she did for her husband. Maybe that was worse. Norman just made the pain of watching Margaret suffer and deteriorate a little less unbearable. That was all.

v.

Wayne was vague about bringing JoAnna and Jake for Christmas when Helen invited them. Then, a week before the twenty-fifth, a package came in the mail, containing gift-wrapped computer games for Barb's kids and a "Fun for All Ages" game for the whole family. The card was in JoAnna's handwriting except for Wayne's signature scrawled next to hers under the word "Love."

"Well, that about says it. If they were coming, JoAnna wouldn't have had to spring for the postage," was all Cal said about it. Helen knew he was hurt. She couldn't help feeling hurt, herself, and a little resentful. Did Wayne's feud with his father always have to spill over on her, too?

JANUARY
2011

i.

AFTER NEW YEAR'S, Wayne had another opening at a gallery. He had mentioned it to Barb, who told Helen, who talked about the possibility of going up for it. Wayne's framed corn maze design would be part of the show.

Cal dreaded the trip, anticipating the stress that all the sitting and standing would put on his hip and back. After three hours in the car, they would probably be expected to go to a restaurant before the gallery reception—one of those restaurants where you wait for half an hour before they even seat you and another quarter of an hour to take your order.

After eating, there would be an hour or more of standing around in front of the paintings with an aching hip, pretending to be impressed and making small talk with a bunch of strangers he had nothing in common with. Then a night on a hard, unforgiving motel bed and waking stiff and achy in the morning, barely able to walk to the bathroom, only to face another three-hour ride back.

It had come to a pretty pass when his body was failing him to the extent he dreaded even a short jaunt to the twin cities. If he refused to go, though, he would have to say why, or be thought disloyal and unloving toward Wayne. That's what Helen thought. She'd let that cat out of the bag, and he wasn't going to give her any reason to think she was right. But if Wayne hadn't been willing to get himself home for Christmas, why the hell was he expected to drag himself up to Minneapolis?

* * *

"You're sure you're up to it?" Helen looked him up and down as if she could see his joint pain through his clothes.

"I'm up to it," he replied curtly.

"Wayne will be happy to see you."

I'll bet, thought Cal.

They arrived at the small gallery to a packed room of people. She had had a few words with Cal beforehand and thought Cal was going to behave himself this time. At first his conversation with Wayne had gone as well as could be expected.

"They going to pay you?" Cal asked.

"A percentage, if they sell anything."

"Oh, a commission deal. What's your cut?"

Wayne began to look belligerent. "Forty percent."

"Forty percent? That's a sweet deal for them—you do all the work."

"They have to hang it and do all the promotion and pay the rent on the gallery and insure the art."

"I guess that's fair."

But Helen could tell Cal was embarrassed about the formal way he was dressed. She had miscalculated and asked him to wear a suit and tie. Most of the crowd was dressed informally. Embarrassed and defiant, he trotted out his display of deliberately butchered grammar. To a group contemplating one of Wayne's paintings, Cal said, loudly, "My son done some damn good art there. Them pictures ought to bring a pretty price." The group turned as one to look at him with blank expressions, which only spurred him on. "Say, any of you got some chaw on you?"

Helen grabbed his arm and furiously steered him out the door. On the street, she said, "You stop that right now! Are you trying to shame your son here in front of everyone he knows?"

Cal got that stubborn look in his eyes. "I'm just teasing like I always do. Anyway, *you're* the one got me into this monkey suit."

He went back inside and said to the group of strangers who still stood discussing the painting, "You always got to watch your language being married to a school teacher. She don't allow no double negatives and such."

Helen supposed this was his way of making up for his tomfoolery, and that he imagined they got the joke. Fortunately, Wayne had wandered off to another part of the room during the whole episode and didn't hear any of it.

Later, when she stood with Wayne in front of his framed picture of the corn row, she said, "Your dad really liked your design."

"How would you be able to tell?"

"Well, when he saw it, he said, 'Damn!'"

"'Damn?'"

"His very words."

"Well, damn."

"You see?"

Wayne looked over at the refreshment table where Cal was eating a cracker spread with cream cheese. "I guess he liked it because it wasn't 'something his kid could have drawn.'"

Helen laughed. "Except his kid *did* draw it." She touched Wayne's elbow. "He's never been crazy about abstract art. He doesn't understand it."

"You don't have to understand it."

"But he doesn't understand that you don't have to understand it."

She had come back from that trip with a familiar longing to get away to somewhere utterly foreign and grand, to somewhere that Cal would not be interested in accompanying her.

After New Year's, Nancy Bannister reserved the high school cafeteria for a video showing of her Christmas trip to Costa Rica. It was advertised in the *Dunlop Sentinel* as a fundraiser—"Donations welcome. All proceeds to go to the A-Mazing Maiz Maze project."

Helen and Cal ran into her at the supermarket in Dunlop the day before the event. Her shopping cart was loaded with the ingredients for the production of lemon bars on a mass scale.

"I hope to see you there!" she sang out. She had treated her son and daughter and their families to the Costa Rica trip. "My husband would have loved it, bless him," she said.

Almost before she was out of earshot, Cal mumbled, "The Merry Widow wasted no time enjoying her husband's blessed money. She's pretty well-fixed now."

"I'm sure he wanted it that way," said Helen, sharply. "They did a lot of traveling together."

Helen went to Nancy's show alone, Cal declining on grounds that he had already seen enough footage of the Bannister grandchildren. There was a nice turnout, and Nancy's son-in-law had edited the film well. Watching scenes of white sand beaches, glowing sunrises and sunsets, fish swimming in and out of colorful coral, lush jungles with monkeys swinging and parrots flying through the treetops, Helen imagined how it would feel to be able to just take off for some such exotic place, without money worries or having either to drag along an unwilling partner or leave him behind all alone, not to mention abandoning a dependent, disabled sister.

She sat in her folding chair for a few minutes before going up to thank Nancy afterwards. It was silly to feel envious. Nancy had lost her well-loved husband only two years ago. And all the rest of her family lived far away on the east and west coasts. But the film, at the same time that it had entranced Helen, gave her a feeling of hopelessness.

When she went up to compliment Nancy on her presentation, her envy turned almost bitter at Nancy's announcement that she had won a trip to France, all expenses paid, "in a raffle at a B & B convention."

"Well, congratulations," Helen said forcing a smile. "How lucky." Nancy had already been to France twice.

Helen never spoke about it, but she had always wondered what it would be like to escape, if only for a little while, the confines of the community she grew up in. She had taught her students about the great seats of religion and literature, art, architecture and politics, of the tragic wars and the sorrowful and evocative locales commemorating youth who had fallen on foreign ground. But there had never been money or the opportunity to travel to such places. During school vacations Cal needed her to help with the farming since Tommy died and Wayne long ago decided to make himself unavailable.

Apart from a few teachers conferences and a wedding in Montana, she had seldom traveled farther than Kansas City, for Wayne's art school graduation, or Minneapolis on those rare occasions when Wayne let slip to Barb that he had a show. That was it. And now, her prospect of ever getting away looked as dim as ever.

ii.

Helen had two sets of books and budgets to keep track of—hers and Cal's and, as her sister's trustee, Margaret's.

None of it looked good. She and Cal received their social security, and she had her pension from the Dunlop County school system, such as it was. They had never been able to invest much—the farm economy always so up and down. They had put away some in the years Cal moonlighted (or daylighted, since he worked at Pioneer Seed during the day and plowed by tractor headlight at night during the lean times). Still, none of it was earning any interest to speak of now, and the principal would go just so far. The same went for this big chunk from the sale of the field. It was a puzzle where to put the money. All their neighbors were suffering the economic slump. She hoped their renters wouldn't give up their contracts.

Margaret inherited her husband's retirement account when he died and some extra investments, but these, too, had earned little since the downturn. What would happen if Margaret lived long enough to run out of money?

Helen imagined caring for both Cal and Margaret at home. Cal's hip problem was disabling him more and more. She would care for her husband and sister, of course, as long as her own health held up, but she felt bleak at the prospect.

And now it was time to think seriously about selling Margaret's house. Every time she thought about it, she felt undecided. This was a terrible time to sell real estate. Meanwhile, the house was sucking money from Margaret's reserves. Taxes were low, but upkeep was high and would keep increasing. The acreage had to be mown and the driveway plowed, the roof would need replacing soon and the house re-painting. The furnace was old.

More worrisome was the idea of selling the house and all its belongings out from under her sister without her informed consent. It didn't seem right, even though the last time she had persuaded Margaret to come out there for an overnight visit, Margaret found the house unfamiliar, and now, just eight months later, she no longer recognized it in photographs.

Helen asked Barb to come out to the house on a weekend and look things over with her. She felt guilty asking her. Barb was so busy with her full-time job, her three kids to care for and a husband she had to snatch time to see. But Helen couldn't face it alone, and Barb had such good common sense.

The man who plowed the drive had turned on the heat and opened the water pipes. When they came in, a faint rotten egg smell met them. The water in the toilets had evaporated, letting sewer gas into the house. They flushed the toilets and cracked some windows, and the smell dissipated. Otherwise, things were as they had been on that last Memorial Day when Helen and Margaret had sifted through her collections of found objects.

Once at the house, Helen hardly knew where to begin. She sat down on the sofa at a loss and looked to Barb, who was walking around surveying the living room.

"What do we *do* with all these things?" Helen said, feeling an equal measure of guilt and relief at this reversal of mother-daughter roles.

"Well," Barb stopped to study one of Margaret's paintings. "I think we should think of who in the family might want what, toss everything else that can't be sold or given to charity, then hire an auction house to come in and deal with the rest. We won't have to do anything. They just come in and pack it up."

Helen was distracted for a moment by the remembrance of that evil man's having tossed a huge stack of Margaret's sketches and unframed paintings into a trash bin, saying they took up too much space. Helen had happened to come over the next day, even though the man was always trying to estrange her from Margaret by discouraging such visits, making Margaret a little furtive when they were together.

That time, she told Helen outright and with tears in her eyes what her husband had done, and Helen marched to the garage, pulled all the drawings out of the bin and locked them in the trunk of her car. She wasn't sure what she would do with them either—her walls were already covered with Margaret's and Wayne's art work—but she took them home and stacked them up in the storage area under the eaves. There they still sat, gathering mouse droppings. But Helen couldn't stand to think of them relegated to a trash bin again.

"We could see if Wayne wants any of her art," Barb suggested. "And donate some to the bank and the library. Maybe the Des Moines Art Center would take some. And you know, all the state buildings in Iowa have to spend at least half of one percent of their budget on art. We could offer some for free. They'd probably be glad not to have to pay."

They turned their attention to the books. The evil man had never been a reader, so all the books were Margaret's. They could call a book dealer to buy the lot. But what about the art and painting books? They had been so precious to Margaret. Helen had already brought the large coffee table art book over to Oakridge Manor, and Margaret had sometimes enjoyed leafing through it if Helen sat with her and encouraged her. "My, these are lovely," Margaret had said. Then, hesitantly, "*I* didn't paint these, did I?" "No, Sis," said Helen, "but you've painted many just as good, in my opinion," and once again she pointed out the drawings that decorated the wall of the two rooms where Margaret spent all her days.

Barb began leafing through the well-worn art books on the shelves. "Wayne might be interested in these, too."

Helen went upstairs and opened the clothes closet. She was glad she and Margaret had gotten rid of every vestige of that man's clothing after he died. Helen made sure not even a hat or a belt or a pair of his shoes was left anywhere in the house. After they had stuffed the clothes into garbage bags and dumped them off at the Goodwill, Margaret had said, "He's really gone, now, isn't he?" and Helen had thought hard about whether there was a trace of grief or guilt or regret in that statement, but couldn't hear any. Her sister was finally free, not just legally, but in her heart and mind, too.

Margaret's own clothes, the best ones, were mostly at Oakridge Manor. What was left could go to Goodwill.

"Oh Mom!" Barb cried from down in the living room.

Helen ran downstairs. Barb was standing at the bookshelf with a large folio-sized drawing instruction book open in her hands.

"Come here, and look at what she's written."

Helen put on her reading glasses and turned on a light. The day was overcast, and it was dark even when they had thrown back the curtains.

Barb put the open book in Helen's hands, and immediately Helen recognized Margaret's small, slanted handwriting almost like calligraphy, filling the margins and spaces between paragraphs. She turned a leaf and saw that the white spaces of the next pages, too, were covered in writing.

At random, she read,

> *He came home today and asked me*
> *why I'd read the paper before he'd seen it,*

after he'd told me not to.
You never put the second section
neatly inside the first can't you
see how annoying that is does everything
you do have to be an implicit no to my
needs are you two years old shall I call you
Terrible Twos?

After a while I stopped listening to him.
I was thinking that I didn't have to read
the newspaper in the morning. It was
a reasonable request. I have better
things to do while he's away, for example,
I might spend the day tearing the newspaper
into little bits and pile them on the dining room
table, lay out Scotch tape and his
reading glasses for him. Wouldn't that be a
considerate and wifely thing to do?
Not as if I were only two?

Helen pressed the open book to her breast. She closed her eyes. Tears were coming, and she didn't want to cry in front of Barb.

"It's like a diary?" Barb asked, gently. Helen nodded. "I didn't see any dates." Now the tears were rolling down Helen's cheeks. Barb came over and silently put an arm around her shoulders. "Poor Aunt Margaret," she said.

After a while, when she had composed herself, Helen looked at the book again. She leafed through the pages and saw that every one contained that close-written script as well as little drawings, and that the writings were poems—some rhyming, some free verse. When she and Barb examined the other art books, they were all the same—filled up with Margaret's most private thoughts, in verse form.

Barb said, "Maybe we should write the number on the flyleaf of each book in the order they're in on the shelf. She might have written them in that order instead of dating them."

But should they even read them? Did they have the right? Margaret had so clearly used the art books to hide her thoughts from her husband.

"If he had found a blank notebook or journal book in the house, he'd have read it in a minute," she told Barb," but she must have known he didn't have the imagination to think of looking in the margins of an art book." Was she herself violating her sister's privacy now? Margaret was still alive, still keeping her secrets, and didn't she have a right to them?

But Helen and Barb numbered the books, boxed them up, and put them in Helen's car. She could decide later whether or not to read them.

Then they set about starting the house inventory. It took the good part of three weekends to finish the job before the furnishings and other belongings were ready for the auctioneer to come whenever Helen could make up her mind to go ahead with the sale of the house.

Helen stored the art books on the floor of the clothes closet in Barb's old room. But every time she passed the door to the room, the books seemed to call to her—*Your sister may be dwindling away, but her true self still lives here. You think you know her, but maybe you don't. She didn't write herself down for no one ever to read.*

iii.

Helen asked Cal if he would like to go with her to visit Margaret, knowing he'd give some excuse not to.

It annoyed her that he so seldom accompanied her. With all that time on his hands, you'd think it would be a diversion for him. But then he and Margaret had never hit it off very well. Cal took Margaret's shyness for coldness toward him. Maybe he was right. She had always been kind of standoffish with Cal. It was probably just a spilling over onto Cal of her wariness of men after having been treated so badly by her husband. And now that she had lost so much of her memory, more often than not she didn't recognize Cal. Still, it would be a support to Helen if he would make the effort occasionally.

Annoyed as she was by this indifference of Cal's, she was also a little glad not to have him around when she and Margaret sat with Norman for dinner. Cal would probably put a damper on Norman's good cheer. This, she felt, as she drove into town faster than she should have, would be intolerable, and she hardly saw the snow-covered fields and barns she drove past, as she imagined a fight with Cal over something she thought he would say about Norman on their way home.

"Didn't you say that good ol' boy had a crush on Margaret?" she imagined him saying. "Looks to me like its nursing home cooking he's got a thing for. He may have lost his marbles, but he hasn't forgotten how to shovel in the mashed potatoes." Cal had lost his appetite lately and dropped a few pounds. No reason for him to be smug about it, though. But who says he *was* smug about it? Here she was, pinning crimes on him he hadn't even committed. What on earth possessed her to be so negative toward him?

When she pulled into the parking lot, she skidded on an icy spot and told herself to for heavens sakes quit making mountains out of molehills.

After Helen left, Cal felt guilty. He should have gone with her to give her some moral support, he knew. It was a heartbreaker to have her older sister in such a state. She had almost worshipped Margaret when they were kids—admired that creativity, which Helen claimed not to have herself. But look at how much more sensible and practical Helen was. She wasn't the one who stuck herself with a selfish bully. At least he hoped he wasn't that kind of man. He probably wasn't as smart as Helen though, or not smart in the ways she was smart. And these days he didn't have Helen's perfect memory and good health.

147

That was another reason he didn't like visiting Helen's sister and got out of it whenever he could. It scared the bejeezus out of him. Every time he couldn't remember a name or a phone number or some incident from their past that was clear as a bell in Helen's memory, that fear hit him in the solar plexus, and he imagined himself in the next room over from Margaret's at Oakridge Manor, Helen dutifully visiting the both of them.

He looked through the patio doors at the ravine and remembered the poison ivy incident last fall—how he'd seemed to forget all the good sense he'd been taught about the toxic weed and about winds and avoiding wild fires and just plunged in like an impulsive boy whose brain hadn't had a chance yet to lay down the experience that turns you into an adult.

But maybe there was another explanation for his forgetfulness. Maybe it had to do with putting away certain memories. Repression, they called it. He'd heard something about that on television. Once you repressed a memory, the repression generalized to other things associated with it. There was no doubt that he shuttled away thoughts about Tommy's death that crept into his head on a regular basis, and Helen was probably right, he'd even pushed away the happy memories of Tommy. That was a big chunk of his past. But the memories weren't erased, not scoured out of his brain as Margaret's were. They popped up at odd moments complete with sounds and sights and smells. It was mostly smells that did it. The smell of that baby shampoo Barb used on her kids when they were little. It used to take him back in an instant to three-year-old Tommy standing naked and dripping in the bathtub with his arms at his sides like a little soldier, waiting to be wrapped in a towel and lifted out.

When this kind of memory came up, he said to himself, "Put it away before you get emotional." He had to admit he did that, and wasn't that the crime Helen—and that meddling, power-hungry Bannister—had accused him of? So maybe it was all that repression that accounted for his lousy memory. Better than the alternative, anyway.

iv.

Helen felt obliged, even if Margaret wouldn't understand, to explain the necessity of selling her house, and to get some kind of permission. Cal reminded her that she could sell it and Margaret would never know. This was true, but somehow she would feel sneaky about it.

She had almost made up her mind to put the house on the market in spring when people were in the mood to look for homes. Maybe some couple who worked in Ames or Des Moines but liked the idea of living in the country would take a shine to the old place, see themselves on the porch swing looking out across the meadow and woodlot and watersheds. They might find the long commute relaxing before and after a day's work. She would call a realtor to sell it, though she hated to pay the commission, knowing they were likely to get so little for it anyway.

She was thinking of these things when she entered the Oakridge Manor dining room just as lunch was starting. Mylar balloons were swaying on the table where Norman and his daughter sat. Margaret's chair, as Helen knew it would be, was empty. She would have to try to coax her out.

Helen stopped to say hello.

"What's the occasion?" she asked.

"It's Dad's birthday. There'll be birthday cake for dessert. I hope you'll stay for it." In a loud, emphatic voice, the daughter added, "You'd like that, wouldn't you, Dad?"

Helen found the balloons childish and distasteful. When the serving girls brought the cake in, they would put a party hat on Norman's head. She imagined how Cal would react to such a thing if he were in Norman's shoes. But Norman never seemed to take offense, even when his daughter spoke to him as if he were a two-year-old.

"You're eighty years old today!" the daughter exclaimed, clapping her hands with exaggerated enthusiasm.

"I am? Well, I'll be!"

"I would never have guessed you were eighty," said Helen. "I would have pegged you for sixty-five or seventy." No harm in flattering him a little.

"It's my schoolgirl complexion," Norman quipped. Helen thought, it's true. The roses in his cheeks and youthful brightness of his blue eyes put the lie to his knotty, work-worn farmer's hands and old man's stoop.

"How does it feel to celebrate your eightieth birthday, Norman?" Helen asked.

He winked at her. "I don't mind, as long as they keep coming."

Keep those birthdays coming. That was Norman's outlook. Never mind if sixteen-year-old aides put a paper hat on your head and adjusted the elastic band under your chin for you. What did it matter? Everything was good. He spent much of his day in the lounge and wasn't particular who he conversed with. He never seemed to judge anyone except—philosophically— himself.

Helen resisted giving Norman's shoulders a squeeze.

"Isn't there another lady?" Norman asked Helen, a little plaintively. He admired Margaret so, and must have an image of her in his mind, yet he never remembered her name.

"I expect she'll be along soon. I'm just going to her room to get her." She would do her darnedest to bring him the birthday present he would most love: the 'other lady'.

But Margaret would not come to lunch. Lately she had grown quietly resistant about being led to the dining room for meals. If someone didn't bring her a tray in her room, she wouldn't eat. Even if they did bring her a tray, she often left the food untouched.

Today Helen ended up bringing a tray to her after much unsuccessful wheedling.

"Are you sure you don't want to go to the dining room? It's Norman's birthday, and I know he'd be tickled to have you there. He enjoys your company so much."

Margaret bit her lower lip and tilted her head with that little frown which indicated chagrin at her own confusion. "Norman," she said.

Helen could have kicked herself. "He's just a guy here that you don't know very well." She saw the chagrin pass as the topic floated out of Margaret's consciousness.

She ate only sweets off the tray—Jello and the birthday cake with ice cream. It was a symptom—Helen had read—this craving for sweets. Before the illness struck her, Margaret had never craved them.

How long, Helen wondered, as she watched Margaret savor the sugary treats, before she walked through that door and got a blank stare. How long before even the word "sister" lost its meaning? She had to be ready for it, know it to be inevitable, not be anguished when it came.

"Sis," Helen began, sitting on the piano bench, having settled Margaret in the rocker. They were looking out the window at the bleak January landscape cheered only by chickadees and purple finches at the pole feeder, fluttering and edging each other out to grab seed, dart away and flit back for more. "Since you're not living in your old house now, and it's just sitting there unoccupied, I thought it would be a good idea to sell it and put the money away for when you need it."

"My house?" Margaret stared out at the birds for a moment. Then she turned to Helen and said, "I'm sorry, but I don't seem to remember it very well. Is it a pretty house?"

Helen hadn't expected this question. If she said it was pretty, would Margaret say she wanted to hold on to it? But she had to tell her the truth.

"Yes, it is pretty. It's an old-fashioned house in the country. It's got tall windows and porches and a nice view. But it's starting to need repairs."

Margaret shook her head. "I just can't picture it."

"I'll show you." Helen got up and brought out one of the photo albums she had put together to help jog Margaret's memories. She opened it to the page of house pictures, which she had shown Margaret so many times.

"That's a pretty house. Whose is it?"

"It's yours, Margaret."

"Mine? Really?" She squinted at it and put on the glasses that hung around her neck.

"But you don't go there much anymore. So what do you think about our selling it?"

"I suppose that would be fine," Margaret said vaguely. The album lay open in her lap, but she stopped looking at it and took off her glasses. "Are my things in my house?"

"Yes, your things are still there."

"Do I have books?"

Books. Helen felt a pang of guilt.

"Yes, several shelves of books. Were there … any in particular you wanted?"

Suddenly Margaret's face turned a little sly. She seemed to be suppressing a smile.

"I did a very clever thing," she said.

"What was that?"

"You won't tell him, will you?"

"Your husband?" Margaret nodded. "No, I would never tell him. What did you do?" Helen held her breath.

Margaret narrowed her eyes, searching a hazy past. "I'm not sure what you mean."

"You said you did a very clever thing. Do you remember what it was?"

Margaret shook her head slowly. "I said a clever thing?"

"You said you *did* a clever thing. Something about your books?"

"I wonder where my books are. I wish I had them."

"Would you like me to bring your books to you?"

She didn't answer. Instead, she heaved a sigh. The decision seemed more than she could cope with.

"Whatever you think," she said. And Helen recognized the statement as Margaret's cover for having lost the thread of the conversation.

* * *

Should she allow herself to read Margaret's diaries? She decided to feel Margaret out on the subject, in hopes that her response would give a true and definitive answer.

On her next visit, she led Margaret to the rocking chair by the window and set a book of Impressionists on her lap. The low winter sun streamed in, illuminating Monet's *Woman with a Parasol,* which illustrated the cover.

"Those colors are pretty, aren't they?" said Margaret. "What is that green thing?" She pointed.

"It's a parasol. An umbrella."

"Oh. Is it upside down?"

"No, I don't believe so." Already this wasn't going well. Helen cleared her throat. "This is one of your art books, Sis. It has pictures by famous artists in it. The Impressionists."

"How nice of you to bring it. Is it a gift?"

"No, it already belongs to you." Margaret made no move to open the book. Helen opened it for her and leafed through a few pages. "You have quite a few books like this."

"I do?" Margaret squinted at the open page then awkwardly between thumb and forefinger took hold of a corner and turned to the next page and the next, seemingly to please Helen, rather than to study the pictures. Helen felt a bit like a guest who has brought an inappropriate hostess gift, which the hostess is making a polite effort to appreciate.

"Sis, do you remember that you kept a diary for many years?"

"Did I? Oh, I don't think so."

"You wrote it in the margins of your art books."

"My, what a strange thing to do."

"See here? There's your writing." Margaret put her glasses on and brought her face close to the page. "I noticed it when I was preparing your house to sell—"

Margaret let the book fall back in her lap and turned to Helen. "You shouldn't have to do that. I'll do it myself when I'm feeling better."

"It's already done, Sis. No trouble."

"Well, thank you."

"So I found these diaries." Helen pointed again to the writing in the margins. "You've written them all in verse. Isn't that remarkable? Would you like me to bring the rest of them over so you can read them? Or . . . I could read some to you, if you don't think they're too private."

"Read *what* now?"

"These diaries here."

"These are diaries?"

"You kept them in the margins for many years."

"Did I? I can't imagine they'd be very interesting. What did I write?"

"Well, I didn't want to read them without your permission."

"Oh, I don't care. If you'd enjoy it, go ahead."

"You're sure?"

Margaret's face got that blank look. She had forgotten again what they were talking about.

"Oh yes, I'm sure."

Could this, by any stretch of the imagination be called 'informed consent'? Helen took the book home again and returned it to the closet.

Some days later, she went irresistibly back to the diaries. She felt drawn to them like any child forbidden to snoop in a drawer or a cupboard. But it wasn't just snooping and wasn't just to understand what made Margaret stay with her husband or to find out whether some happiness had been left to her. It was the only way she knew of having Margaret back, whole. Her gentle personality was still intact, but that creative mind, that intellect was lost now, and though Helen had no choice but to accept that a disease had robbed her of it, she didn't think that one coldly manipulative man, no matter how determined he had been to do so, could have crushed Margaret's creativity before the disease struck her.

* * *

Many of the early entries were like the one she had come across about the newspaper—sly rants about his cruel, bullying nature, alternating with wistful praise of the natural world around her.

Squirrels in the attic
reach the eaves by scurrying up the tree,
leave their droppings on the attic floor.
He sees them through the kitchen window,
grabs his pellet gun and rushes out the door.
They'll gnaw the wiring, cause a fire, says he.
I know I'm wrong to tap the glass and make them flee,
But he is wrong to shoot them with such glee.

In the third book, among the poems written when Helen and Cal had been married and had their children, she found this:

Two boulders side by side,
have dammed the hurrying stream
to form a placid pool wherein
the children swim before they
leap like fish into the whirling eddy.
I would be a golden carp
content to glide forever in the
pool they've made together
from their love, immutable and steady.

FEBRUARY

i.

THERE WAS NO QUESTION, his hip hurt like the dickens all the time
now. He had sciatic pain down his right leg, too, that electric shock
kind of pain, especially when he walked down stairs. Between the hip
and the leg, and sometimes his low back if he twisted a certain way, he
was like the Princess and the Pea. At night in bed he had to keep turning from side to side and adjusting a pillow between his legs. Lying on
his back was no good. In minutes his lumbar region started to ache.

He was thankful Helen was a heavy sleeper. She had no idea how
bad it had gotten. But he was limping all the time now and he couldn't
hide that from her. He said it was just stiffness, but she looked skepti-
cal. His father's voice mocked him whenever he inadvertently gasped
at the sharp pain that shot through his hip. *"Goddamn sissy! Lucky for
the army, you were too young for one war and too old for the other. You would
have washed out as a soldier."*

His dad could out-stoic any of them—Cal and his brothers—even
when he was old and practically dying. Cal thought of all the times
the old man kept working alongside them when it was so cold they
couldn't feel their fingers. He remembered the excruciating ache after
his dad finally let them go into the house and his fingers started to thaw.
It was probably one reason why his hands were so stiff today. That,
and having to do so much heavy work alone. Who could say exactly
what caused what? But Wayne's refusing to pitch in sure hadn't helped.

Now he had another month to go before his doctor's appointment.
Helen was probably right to have kept after him about it. But would

it be worth the trouble and expense? These doctors got you into the hospital and one thing led to another until you left more banged up than when you went in.

He had definitely taken a turn for the worse after the poison ivy and grass fire incident last fall, though. He wished he could go back in time and undo that act of stupidity. It seemed like before that happened, his aches and pains had come and gone, but afterwards they were pretty much constant, especially the hip. He had done that to himself, and when he went to see this hip doctor, he would probably have to confess it. All that kind of information would be necessary for a diagnosis.

The plastic texture of the Naugahyde recliner against the skin of his hands and wrists had become an irritant, the chair too familiar, too disappointing in the false relief it gave him whenever he sank into its puffy synthetic cushions and let the mechanism slowly lower his back and raise his legs. Within a few minutes, the relief gave way to the same old aches and pains. Yet he stuck to the chair, somehow believing that if he stayed in it long enough, that fleeting comfort would return. It was as if he and the recliner were in a mostly miserable marriage sustained only by the smallest glimmers of friendliness—joined 'til death parted them, which he sometimes wished would happen sooner than later.

It was 2:30 on an especially nice afternoon, unseasonably warm for February—fifty degrees, blue sky, no wind. He decided it was time for him to take his butt off the damned recliner, push through the pain and get something done. He cast around in his mind for some task he could handle, and it came to him that now would be the time to go to the barn and tag things he didn't need anymore and could be sold.

The cat, Ornery, trotted along ahead of him, like a puppy. Her arrival sent the few feral cats and kittens that had survived the winter into their hideouts in the wood pile and crevices in the stone foundation. Inside, the barn smelled damp, and Cal looked up to see daylight coming through a hole near the peak of the roof. He had put off re-roofing too long, had only gotten the worst places patched. He stood inside the doorway and surveyed the equipment that sat dusty and colorless like artifacts in an unvisited, small-town museum.

There was his eight-row field cultivator and his planter, a chisel plow, two tractors—all at least fifteen to twenty years old. Hardly anybody would want them now, even though he'd kept them functional. A sprayer no one would buy—so old and small. His John Deere 445 riding tractor mower—already twelve years old and prone to stalling out. It needed to be replaced, but what would a comparable mower cost today? More than he wanted to pay.

Ornery had jumped onto a tractor seat and was licking the dust off her paws. That cat was ten years old—a pretty good age for a cat—but she could still leap straight up onto the kitchen table, and she still kept the house free of mice. You'd never know she'd started out in life as one of those bony, flea-bitten feral kittens, a little tamer than the rest. Maybe it was her calm disposition that accounted for her health and longevity. She was ornery only in her stubborn insistence on jumping into the middle of things. He could learn something from her.

Cal rubbed her forehead and massaged the back of her neck to make her purr. The sound, along with the soft coo of a mourning dove somewhere up in the hayloft soothed him, and he turned his attention to his dad's stuff—the much older implements stored behind the newer machinery. There was the old spike tooth harrow for leveling the ground and ripping weeds. His dad used to pull it behind a horse before Cal helped him change the hitch to work with a tractor. Farmers had stopped using harrows when herbicides came in. It was an antique now. There might be some buyers for antique farm equipment.

Cal wandered down the center of the barn, looking into the stalls and cribs. Maybe some antique buyer would want his old hand corn sheller. He remembered cranking the handle and feeding ears in through the hole, the grain falling into the basket. But that was when they'd kept chickens to feed. Now there were these huge chicken operations with facilities that cost hundreds of thousands of dollars. His chicken waterer would be useless, too.

161

He considered the old hand tools he had thrown together in a crate, thinking the longer he held on to them the more they'd be worth. But now that he thought about it, he remembered that antiques weren't as popular these days as they once were. Helen had tried to sell her grandmother's cane rocker in pretty good condition, and an antique dealer in Des Moines had told her he had more rockers than he knew what to do with. They were too small, he said. People had gotten bigger, and the seats and backs were too hard. If people didn't want rockers, who would want old corn shellers and hand drills and such? When Cal pawed through the tools, he saw that all of them were thick with rust.

He continued to limp around the barn considering the tools that he had been using on a regular basis up until lately when it seemed no job was minor enough for him to tackle. There was a wire stretcher and post hole auger for making fences. With the coming of those giant cattle and hog confinement lots, he and his neighbors had sold off their livestock, so he didn't consider fence mending urgent anymore, but maybe someone could get some use out of them. When he surveyed his shop tools, though, he couldn't imagine giving any of them up. His tap and die set and his drill press and that whole set of bits—you never knew when you might need such things. Those log chains for pulling something out of the mud, too, they never lost their use.

He thought of the loft and rafters high above at the roof peak. The old hay fork and track should have been pulled out long ago when he didn't need to store hay bales anymore. They would have to stay put until someday when the farm was sold and the barn torn down.

He had come out to the barn to tag items for sale, but now it seemed an overwhelming job. Too many decisions to make with no one to help him think it through. And how would he go about selling the stuff that he *could* bring himself to part with? There wasn't enough inventory for a sale here at home, and if he sold it at a consignment auction, how would he load and haul the equipment there? Of course his neighbors would pitch in if he asked them, but he would never be able to reciprocate.

Maybe he could get hold of one of those guys—what did they call them? It was a common word he'd heard a hundred times. Not an auctioneer. These guys who came to your place, paid you a lump sum, hauled the stuff away for you and sold it at a profit to various dealers they knew. He wouldn't get much, but it would be something anyway. How could he look up one of these outfits in the yellow pages, though, if he couldn't even remember what to call them? It scared the hell out of him to forget familiar things like this. Helen might know, but it would be embarrassing to have to ask her.

Suddenly he felt exhausted. He had been standing too long and his hip was nagging at him. The cat's head was twisted sideways, as she licked the fur on her shoulder, and Cal envied her flexibility. He sat down on a bench next to the stick welder—a piece of equipment that might fetch a decent price. He gazed at the red metal box.

What was it he had been welding when the lightning bolt blasted the air with its tremendous sound and light so brilliant even through the dark glass of the helmet he was wearing, which hung now by its fraying strap from a nail in the wall? A disk. It was a disk he'd been welding. A stress crack in the tongue. Tom could have welded it easily. And they had seen that line of squalls, that little bit of lightning way off in the distance. Why in the world had he let Tom go out into that field? Couldn't he have done it himself? Or waited. Just waited. So what if they lost the whole crop? So what? It wouldn't have made a difference one way or another. With Tom alive they would have made up the loss somehow. Why the hell had he let him do it?

Had he always been that dumb, like his father said? *"Cal's got no more sense than a bucket of mud."* Had he sacrificed his only boy to his own stupidity?

He heard himself think it—*his only boy*. What made him think such a thing? What kind of father was he? Just as bad as his own dad, who

163

treated him and his brothers as if they were machine parts and turned his older sons so bitter that they never came within spitting distance of him once they were grown. A father who exploited the one boy who didn't leave—himself, Cal, who did his duty, waiting hopelessly to be respected for it. And here he was, telling himself he'd had only one boy.

It was true that he had favored Tom over Wayne ever since Tom was born. He'd tried not to, though. For a long time he had given Wayne every chance to work with him, to take the privileged status of an older child, but Wayne just wasn't interested. It was like he belonged to a different family or no family at all. Whose fault was that?

Cal stared at dust motes moving languidly in the shaft of light from a window. All the work he had done in this barn over the years, work which had seemed purposeful, necessary, even creative, now seemed to have been labor just to mark time. He might as well have been punching a clock for some heartless corporation, for all it amounted to. The only thing anyone valued about this place, where he'd raised a family and grown food for other people's consumption, was twenty-three acres about to be turned into a tacky amusement park. Twenty-three acres which, somewhere in its center, still held some miniscule genetic remnant of his son. A few cells blasted off that freckled skin and buried in the soil by the force of a million volts.

Cal began to cry. He covered his face with his hands and tried to stifle his sobs, but they came out of his throat more and more high pitched, scary and shrill in his own ears even though muffled by the vastness of the old barn structure and its softened wood. "Stop it!" a part of his brain was yelling at him. "Stop it. Quit your blubbering!" But he couldn't stop. He wailed and wailed, and pretty soon the wailing sounded almost like shrieks, and he tried to control himself. He bent forward to cut off his air. A sudden soft weight on his shoulder made him jerk up and choke back the sounds he had been making. He almost couldn't take his hands away from his face, horrified at Helen's catching him this way.

Ornery balanced on his shoulder, her long bushy tail curling across his chest. She nudged his temple with her forehead and jumped into his lap.

"Goddamn," he said, thankfully, "goddamn," and took his big handkerchief out of his pocket and blew his nose.

I came out to the barn to get something done, he told himself, and I'm not going to leave until I do it.

From a work bench he took up a dusty old clipboard with yellowed sheets of paper and a pencil attached by a string and limped around making lists. He would inventory all of it. Everything. Then later, when his brain wasn't so addled, he'd cross out the things he decided to keep.

It took half the afternoon. His shoulders and wrists and fingers ached from holding the clipboard and pencil. He'd had to stop a bunch of times to sharpen the pencil with his pocketknife. In the end, his hands were black, and his back and hip had turned fiery with pain from the work of pulling things out of boxes and extracting others from piles and drawers. But he got the job done.

By this time, Ornery was sprawled on her back in a shaft of low sunlight coming through the doorway. He tickled her belly with the toe of his boot rather than make the effort to bend down and pet her. The cat stretched extravagantly, rolled over, got to her feet in one smooth movement and followed Cal back to the house.

He showed Helen the inventory list that evening at dinner.

"Well, it looks like there's a lot of good stuff here," she said. "What do you think you can part with?"

She didn't appreciate just how little there was of monetary value, and he was glad she didn't.

Barb and Gordon and the kids came over later, and Helen showed them the list. Cal thought his son-in-law might detect how pitiful the inventory was, and he said, "We can't get much for any of it, I know, but something's better then nothing."

165

Thirteen-year-old Cindy looked up from the crossword puzzle she was helping her brothers with. "Sure you can, Grandpa. Put it on Craig's List."

"Oh," Cal waved the idea aside, "I don't know about all that internet goings on."

"Yeah!" piped up Gordon, Jr. "You can sell anything on the internet. For big money, too."

"It's easy, Grandpa." Cindy took out her pink cell phone. "I'll come over and take pictures of your merchandise and upload them to an account for you." He knew the phone had some kind of camera device in it.

Barb winked at Cal. "She's very enterprising. Just put it in her hands. She'll have that barn cleared out in no time."

Cal frowned. "What's the catch? What do you end up paying?"

"Nothing!" exclaimed Cindy. "There's no catch. It's a free service. I've sold a bunch of things that way. You set the price. People buy your stuff and come and pick it up."

Cal looked at Helen. She raised her eyebrows, apparently just as surprised as he was. This internet idea was the best news he'd had in a very long time. And maybe he should feel foolish to have it delivered by a child, but by god she was *his* grandchild.

ii.

Helen and Cal together pulled out the antique tools from the big wooden crate, wiped away the oil and dust, soaked some of the rust off, and laid the implements on a tarp on the barn floor. It took several days, Helen doing whatever required stooping and bending.

She said, "Why don't you try to sell the antiques first and hold off on anything you think you might use, in case you get a new hip and can get around better?"

"Optimistic, aren't you?" he said, gloomily.

"Don't be an Eeyore." She had teased him with this nickname before, but her tone was testy now, and he could see she was annoyed with him.

"Are you getting cold?" she asked, more kindly.

"No. Why? Are *you* cold?"

"No, I'm fine."

The temperature was in the thirties, and his hip was aching and getting stiffer the longer they were out there but now that they had started, he wanted to get the job done. He was still nervous about the possibility of surgery, but he felt a little reckless with his hip, knowing that it might be replaced soon like a worn brake lining.

On the weekend, Barb dropped Cindy and the boys off at the farm so that Cindy could take pictures of the tools for sale. Barb and Helen drove into town to visit Margaret and do errands. The boys mostly scampered around, clambering up on anything of the right height to jump off while Cindy lined up her shots.

"Don't you need a flash for that thing?" Cal asked. He couldn't see how a decent picture could come out of something the size of a lottery ticket.

"No, Grandpa. Light adjustment is built in. See?" On the little screen was the picture she had just taken, the colors and contrast clear and crisp.

"I'll be damned."

Cindy pointed to a hand drill on the tarp. "What's this for, Grandpa?"

"For drilling holes in wood." It cheered Cal to take her hand and lay it on top of the knob, the pale brown wood smooth as velvet. He wrapped her other hand around the wooden handle and showed her how to crank a hole into a pine plank.

"Cool!" she said.

The boys wanted to get in on the act, and he let her show them.

"Drills are all electric now," he said.

"I like this way better."

Gordon, Jr. declared, "Me, too."

"Me, too," chimed in Mason.

And Cal had to hold himself back from returning the drill and all the other old tools to their crate.

"You're going to get a lot for these things," Cindy said, confidently.

She probably didn't know what she was talking about, but it gave him a boost to hear her appreciate his old relics and maybe she was right. She was smart and practical like her mother and like Helen and even Helen's mother, a whole line of women who got things done with a minimum of fuss. Watching his granddaughter at work, he felt a sudden sweep of affection for his wife.

When Barb and Helen got back, Cindy set up a Craig's List account on Helen's computer and uploaded the photos.

"You first get contacted through the website, and then if you think the buyer is okay and you like the price they offer, you can make an appointment for them to come and see the merchandise. Have them bring cash, though, no checks."

"What about serial killers and drug dealers coming down my driveway?"

"Oh Grandpa, everybody buys and sells this way. It's perfectly safe." She added, in the voice of her mother, "Just use good sense."

iii.

All week Helen argued with herself about Margaret's art book diaries. Just because someone's mind is gone doesn't mean you can go prying without their permission into the mind they used to have. How would she feel if Margaret—or Cal or her kids—read something private of hers if she'd lost her memory, too?

But then, she didn't really have any documents of that sort. No letters or secret thoughts meant only for her own eyes. Of course she had saved the four or five love letters from Cal when they were dating and he had gone to Iowa State University in Ames to chaperone a 4-H group. But these were pretty tame, as love letters went.

Barb had asked if he had ever written any, and she showed them to her, not even bothering to ask Cal if he'd mind, for what was there to be embarrassed about in such sentiments as these?

> …The kids are behaving pretty well considering they're sixteen and full of beans. They're learning about animal husbandry from these Ag profs, who turn out to know more than I'd have given them credit for. Well, I better sign off, honey. I sure miss you. I'll be glad when the month is over and I can see your smiling face again.
>
> Love,
> Cal
>
> P.S. Hope you don't get any ideas about bestowing those smiles on anyone else while I'm gone.

She and Barb laughed together about that last line.

"Dad used the word 'bestow'?"

"Probably trying to impress me. I was already teaching school."

"And *did* you bestow your smiles on anyone else?"

"Your dad had nothing to worry about. I was smitten with him."

"What made you smitten?"

"It was his sense of humor. I knew I'd never marry a man who couldn't make me laugh."

They were both quiet after she said this. Helen wondered if Barb, too, thought about how Cal's sense of humor had turned sour after Tom's death.

Barb didn't ask if she had read the rest of Margaret's diaries, and Helen didn't mention them, but she kept thinking about those books in the closet.

* * *

Norman was watching television in the lounge along with a contingent of people slumped sideways in wheelchairs or sunk into the oversized and overstuffed armchairs flanked by walkers.

Helen took a detour to say hello, and he gazed up at her with his habitual look of happy surprise. By now he didn't connect her with Margaret if they weren't actually together, but the smile that lifted his rosy cheeks said, Well, I'll be darned, you're a sight for sore eyes. This, in fact, was his most recent stock greeting, and it seemed such a generous thing to say that it warmed her, even though she knew he repeated it to everyone who approached him.

"Take a load off," he invited her and started to rise, as there were no empty seats in the lounge. She perched on the fat arm of the upright Lazy Boy instead.

"What are you watching, Norman?" On the big screen television was an old black and white western, a posse on horseback riding through a canyon in what seemed like fast motion.

"I can't quite make it out," Norman replied. "I left my glasses somewhere. But it's interesting."

His glasses case was sticking out of his breast pocket. Helen did something that surprised her. She pulled it from his pocket as familiarly as if he had been her husband, and touched his sleeve.

"Are these your glasses?" She took them out of the case and put them in his hand.

He chuckled. "I'd lose my head if it wasn't screwed on tight," he said. Then he held the glasses out to her. "Pardon my manners. Would you like to use these?"

"Thanks," she said, tapping her own glasses, "but I'm wearing my own."

Norman shook his head. "I guess you don't need two sets," he said, "unless you want to see twice as good." He laughed at his joke. Then he put on the glasses, which made his big spaniel eyes look even bigger. The glasses case fell down into the space between his thigh and the chair arm. Helen fished it out and put it back in his pocket.

"Well," she said, "I'd best get going. I'm here to visit my sister Margaret."

His face lit up again. "She's a ringer!" he said, surprising her. How this memory business came and went!

"Yes, she sure is." Helen reluctantly got up off the arm of the chair, patted his shoulder, and left him to his galloping posse.

As she sat in the rocker half-listening to Margaret's ever more eccentric piano playing, she thought about the diaries and wondered if they might reveal why Margaret insisted on staying with that man when there was nothing to keep her—no children, no financial dependency—their parents had stipulated in their will that her inheritance could not be shared or given over to him.

Of course Helen had read the popular articles and several books explaining how and why abusive and controlling men (it was mostly men) gradually undermined the self confidence of women who already had low self-esteem. And Margaret, even as a child, had certainly been shy and insecure despite her artistic talents, her beauty and sweetness. Yet, knowing all that, Helen had found it maddeningly irrational of Margaret to excuse and put up with the man's behavior and refuse the support and protection Helen offered with her whole heart if only Margaret would leave him. How many times had she told her that she could come and live with her and Cal and the kids if she was afraid of being alone or afraid of her husband's wrath. Cal would have put up with none of the man's bullying. Those books about abuse—she had offered them to Margaret, but she had refused them on the grounds that if her husband found them his feelings would be hurt.

Maybe there was something in the diaries that would reassure Helen that her sister's life hadn't been entirely tragic—something pleasureful that made her life, in spite of the man's sabotage, more than just bearable.

On Sunday evening, when Cal was napping in his recliner, Helen went up to the guest bedroom and dragged books out of the closet. The art book labeled #1 was on top. She had only dipped into it randomly before. Now it seemed best to begin at the beginning. She hesitated. What if Cal woke and came upstairs, to find her at this shameful occupation? But she would hear him as soon as he set foot on the creaking old staircase, and with his bad hip, it would take him a while to get himself to the top. She would have plenty of time to push the books back in the closet. No, it was unlikely that he would catch her at it. But why did it seem like such a crime?

The diary started with the words,

> *I made my bed*
> *And now I lie.*
> *Day and night I lie,*
> *I lie I lie.*

That was her first entry. How long into the marriage had she written it? Days? Months?

> *I cannot blame the man*
> *When vanity said him yes,*
> *While sanity warned me no.*
> *I tried to tell me so.*
> *A hypocrite, I can't admit to it,*
> *Not loving him, you see*
> *But only the image of myself*
> *That he held up to me.*
> *I cannot blame the man.*
> *I blame my vanity.*

He had flattered her when he courted her, and made her think he loved the things about her that she surely prized in herself. The artistic talent, her natural whimsy, the free spirit that she had shown only in the security of her family. As soon as they were married he disdained all of it.

Helen was surprised to see this insight expressed in poetry. She flipped through the pages, skimming bits and pieces of the writing. In wonderment she realized that every single diary entry was a poem. There would be hundreds and hundreds of them, apparently written down as she thought of them, just flowing from the pen or pencil with only a few erasures, crossings out, or revisions. And scattered throughout the writings there were little pen and ink sketches, sometimes filled in with colored pencil. Birds, animals, and flowers mostly, but here and there a humorous drawing of herself—Margaret kneeling in her garden, nose-to-nose with a hummingbird, so close both of them were cross-eyed. Her house, with her husband's car in the garage, being sucked into the eye of a tornado, she standing in the yard looking up at it, her arms folded matter-of-factly. A little sketch of Helen and Cal and the three children standing as if for a formal photograph in a cloud of bright yellow, edged with pink.

There were thirteen books in all. If this first book was any indication, Margaret had written sometimes three, four, or more poems in the white spaces of each page. If you figured two to three hundred pages per book—Helen did the math in her head—Margaret had completed some 11,000 poems, not to mention all the little sketches. It was the output of an Emily Dickinson or a Walt Whitman. Not just a diary but a memoir in drawings and verse. Helen couldn't judge if the poems were any good. She herself couldn't have written a poem to save her life. No, she was no judge. They were probably very uneven. But that didn't matter, did it? Margaret wrote to get her feelings off her chest.

> *He acts as if we are in a competition*
> *yet I do not compete with him.*
> *He must point out my every error*
> *Can't sleep, or eat, or leave the*
> *house til I'm aware of*

my childish laughable failure
in giving the name of airplane to what
"anyone with sense" would call
an aircraft. Whereas what I
need to know is this:
What do I do with my anger?

Helen had to put the book down. She could feel her face reddening. Tears of fury filled her eyes and dropped onto the page. For thirty-eight years her dear Margaret had put up with this. It was unthinkable.

She heard Cal's foot on the staircase. Quickly she returned the books to the closet. Maybe she should stop reading there. It was too upsetting, too revealing.

She went out into the hall. "Do you need anything?" she called down to him.

He looked up at her. His eyes, underlined with deep pouches, seemed so weary.

"I'm coming up for the bottle of Tylenol." He was going to climb all those stairs for something she could easily get for him. Stubborn.

"I'll bring it down to you, Cal." It came out sharply, and now she tried to think of something softening to mitigate the sharpness. "I'm coming down anyway," she said in a lighter tone. But it was too late. Her first tone was the one he registered, and nothing would stop him now from dragging himself up the stairs.

"I'll get it," he replied. And rather than stand there and watch the painful spectacle of him limping up one stair at a time, clutching the rail, she said, "Okay then," and came downstairs more slowly than she normally would so as not to call attention to her relative spryness.

iv.

These days, seeing her grandchildren playing in the barn always brought up layers of nostalgia—for Wayne and Tommy and Barb when they were little, the younger trotting after the next older, Wayne out ahead, following his fanciful visions. It brought up nostalgia for her own childhood, too—her father coming home from the war when she was five and Margaret seven, sweet memories of her parents caressing each others' cheeks, and holding hands across the breakfast table. Her mother had managed the farm the whole time he was gone. How did she do that? He told her many times how much he appreciated it.

Helen and Margaret had loved to touch their father's uniform and medals and the gleaming sword he took off an SS officer after the liberation. There was a long white scar across their father's forehead. He had just removed his helmet to wipe the sweat from his brow when a bullet whizzed past, stripping off a line of skin. "It burned like the dickens!" he told them. An eighth of an inch closer and it would have cracked his skull. The story made them shiver, and they loved it.

If their father was traumatized by his experiences, they never knew it. He was gentle and easy-going his whole life, a homebody, never happier than when he came in from the fields, collapsed on the sofa after a wash, and let his girls climb all over him.

Margaret had been happy and active inside the family, but timid and unsure outside of it. She was born as shy as a fawn, their mother told Helen in later years. Even when she was five or six years old, she clung to her mother and hated strangers to look at her. If they went into town, Margaret spent the whole time with her face in her mother's skirts. "Whereas *you*," her mother said to Helen, "You were the one to skip ahead and talk to everyone you met. Like night and day, the two of you." But Helen thought, more like two sides of a coin, the coin being their inseparableness. Whatever Margaret did, Helen imitated. Without her, Helen's childhood would have been devoid of fantasy.

Looking out the window toward the open barn door, at the grandsons scrambling around on the tractor and Cindy just inside talking soberly to Cal like one adult to another, she was overcome again with the urge to read more of her sister's inner life. She went quietly upstairs to the closet.

The diary entries weren't all preoccupied with the husband's cruelties. One after another of Margaret's poems mused about oddities and surprises in the natural world that must have distracted her from her anger and fear and given her comfort during those grim decades.

> *Floribunda roses*
> *furred with autumn frost*
> *and pink as babies' cheeks.*

> *Twilight's flame-red clouds,*
> *embers beneath the smoke*
> *of thunderheads.*

> *Twin firs lean*
> *one to the other*
> *quivering needles*
> *gesturing arms.*
> *Old women*
> *sidelined at a dance*
> *earnestly conversing.*

One poem brought back to Helen the bittersweet trip to Margaret's home last year, when they laid out her stones and shells on the dining room table.

> *You bit of shale*
> *with double chin,*
> *winking eye,*
> *crooked grin.*

Rock face, shall I
let you tumble on
in Ice Age dreams and
stony recollection?
Or reach in and pluck you
from the rushing stream
to add to my collection?

Helen smiled. Her sister had chosen to collect that bit of personified shale.

But some of Margaret's poetic observations struck Helen as thinly disguised metaphors for her isolation and fear.

The copper rooster
atop the weather van
shifting, shifting.

Cold fall day
with gale so fierce
it sleets leaves.

And then in Book #3, Helen came across something she wished she hadn't.

How the heart persists
without answer.
Refuses to desist
though it beats in
only one romancer.

Helen set the book down in her lap. Who was the romancer? Could this poem mean that Margaret thought her husband had undergone a change of heart and was now wooing her, and it was too late, she had turned cold? She found this impossible to believe. She had never seen a shred of evidence that the man had ever been anything but snide and belittling. There had been no romancing whatsoever, she was sure of it. So it must have meant that over time Margaret, in her isolation and dependency, had grown to feel an abject love for him. The prisoner's desire for the jailer's approval, the slave's admiration for the master. It was horrible to think of. But the more of such poems she came across, the more she had to admit it.

> *Waxing crescent moon,*
> *back turned to a*
> *pinprick star,*
> *contemplates the universe,*
> *unaware of her hopeless*
> *glimmer of regard.*

Helen remembered a time early in Margaret's marriage when she tried to convince her to leave the man. "But if he doesn't love me," Margaret said, "why is he so jealous?" When Helen explained how jealousy had nothing to do with love, Margaret seemed to grow vague and to stop listening.

Helen put the diaries away again. For now, this was all she could stand. The man was dead and couldn't undermine her sister anymore, but he was also out of reach of the lacerating words Helen would like to have cut him with. She pictured herself denouncing him in front of all the people at his workplace, where he was thought to be the nicest, most generous of men. "He'd do anything for you, give you the shirt off his back." She would run down a list of his atrocities—calling her brilliant, lovely sister "Maggot," throwing her paintings in the trash, locking up her beloved piano, making her feel guilty and furtive any time she communicated with her family.

The thought that Margaret may have grown to love and admire this man was almost more than Helen could bear.

When Cal came in from the barn, some of her disgust rubbed off on him, just because he was a man, she supposed. Before she could catch herself, she said, "I guess you expect dinner to be on the table already." He looked at her, bewildered.

V.

Within days the e-mails were arriving from buyers asking if they could come take a look at the antiques, some even inquiring about other old implements he didn't have. Initially, Cal wasn't sure what to do about these responses. Most of them gave a phone number, and after some hesitation he made the calls.

The first one was a young-sounding woman with a matter-of-fact voice like his granddaughter's. She and her husband had bought some acres in the country and wanted to raise their own food the old-fashioned way. They planned to have an organic truck garden and some chickens and goats. On a small scale they would sell some of their produce to local restaurants. She was interested in the chicken waterer. They lived in the next county over—could they come by that afternoon? She sounded all right, so he said yes, and then felt nervous. No telling if her story was true.

Helen was home when the young couple's old truck rattled down the driveway, and she called to him where he was sitting at the kitchen table reading the newspaper.

After the couple drove their truck to the barn, they walked up to the house hand-in-hand. They were probably in their late twenties, both very tall and healthy-looking.

Cal limped out to the barn with them. The young woman said, "Look what a nice old post and beam barn it is," and he saw it through their eyes, solid, and worn by history, the paint faded to a soft, pinkish red.

Timidly, they asked if they could climb to the loft just to look around, out of curiosity, and he led them painfully up the wooden stairs. The great loft held the smells of dusty grain and hay and old pine beams. It was chilly, but peaceful and quiet except for the flutter of doves and the faint scrabble of mice, which made Ornery, who had followed them up, crouch and twitch her tail.

Downstairs again, he showed them the chicken waterer and the implements spread on the tarp. They held up one item after another, running their hands over each with a kind of reverence. The woman exclaimed over the corn grinder. She knew what it was, and she called out to her husband, "Oh look, Erik, isn't this great? We could use this to make chicken feed. It's in perfect condition!"

Cal stood by feeling rather proud, but once again had the urge to put everything back and say he'd changed his mind. The objects, it now seemed to him, had the pricelessness he had assigned to them when he was a boy.

The young couple found other things to their liking, too, and when they finished looking, they put the corn grinder, the chicken waterer and some miscellaneous tools in the back of their pick-up, lifting and carrying together the heavy, bulky items with coordinated precision like a team of experienced movers. A man and woman attuned to each other, he thought. He liked imagining their using these old implements everyday, as if fifty years had not gone by and the past could be given back to you, after all.

They gave him one hundred and seventy-five dollars for this haul— the asking price he had come to after Cindy had done some research on the internet to see what antique dealers were getting for such things. He was astonished at how such information could pop up with a few clicks of the mouse.

Before the couple got back in their truck, they asked about his tractor and eight-row planter.

"I don't know if I want to sell any of that stuff yet," he said. "Check back with me in a few months if you're still interested." Helen had put the idea in his head that he might be able to get back to work again if he had a new hip. Maybe he'd do a little truck farming himself.

The young man and woman waved out the windows as they turned their pick-up around. Watching them drive away, he thought, if only Tom had lived to get married and have kids, they could have built a one-story Mom and Pop house on the property for him and Helen, and Tom and his family could have had the four-square. In the big house the grandkids would be sliding down the bannister, playing hide and seek in the attic.

Like these two young people, Tom and his wife would have started out healthy and optimistic the way he and Helen had, and for Tom's family things would have turned out okay with his dad there to help him farm. He would gladly have handed over land to Tom right from the get-go, not hanging onto it as his own father had, even after he was too old to care for it properly. He would never have made Tom take up the slack for him, in addition to his family responsibilities.

But where was Wayne in this picture? he asked himself, guiltily. For the first time, it struck him that Tom's death may have kept Wayne from ever getting close to the family, although it should have been the other way around.

Helen came out and stood beside him. He handed her the cash.

"Don't spend it all in one place," he said, nudging her in the ribs.

She counted out the bills and whistled. "Not bad, Calvin Early-wine." She peeled off two fives and handed them to him. "Your commission. Buy yourself socks before I throw those holey old stinkers of yours away."

He put a hand on her shoulder and leaned on her slightly as he limped back to the house.

More people called, and the next buyer was an antiques dealer from West Des Moines. She and her husband had a sideline in antique tools, she told him on the phone.

She was a woman about his age, who slid easily out of her SUV, carrying a book under her arm. He went out to greet her.

"Have any trouble finding the place?"

"Not at all. Your directions were quite specific," she said. "Shall we see what you've got?"

She walked briskly ahead of him toward the barn until, looking back, she must have noticed his limp and slowed down to allow him to keep pace. In the barn, she looked without expression at the tools laid on the tarp. Silently, she picked them up one by one, scrutinizing each with an expert eye before putting it down, and occasionally consulting the book she was carrying, some kind of catalogue with prices. Cal stood at a distance, suddenly dreading her saying, "I'm sorry. There's nothing here I could sell," dreading rejection of his father's tools.

Instead, she offered him $200 for everything, including his dad's old ball peen hammer with a loose head. It was less than what he and Cindy had priced them for, but it wasn't a bad offer. After all, she had to make her profit and pay her overhead. She probably put out a lot for gas, too, driving around the countryside. He felt grateful, and now he was ashamed that he couldn't help her load the tools into her vehicle because he just couldn't bend down.

She dismissed his apology. "Oh, that's all right. Nothing heavy here. I'll bring the car around and back it into the barn. I can load these items in a minute." Which she did, but not before she counted out the $200 in twenties into his hand.

"Well, thank you," Cal said. "I'm glad to see there's a market for these old things."

"Oh yes. There'll always be someone who appreciates an old plane or an old wooden feed bucket, even if they just want to use them as a bread board or marigold planter. There's a lot of family restaurants, too, that use old tools for wall décor." The thought made Cal smile. Serve the old man right, he thought, to have his precious ball peen hammer hanging on the wall of a pancake house.

The successful sale of his father's tools raised Cal's spirits, and now he began to count the days until his doctor appointment. It seemed to hold out some hope for change, and he imagined a different future.

The field was sold and all of his other cultivable land was rented. There was just the orchard left, a swath that gave them access to the river, and the plot for Helen's vegetable garden. She wasn't much for flower planting. There were just the peonies by the house, and along the fence the hollyhocks that came up every year since he could remember. They took care of themselves. But tilling the big vegetable garden was work. Last summer it had been a struggle and he'd thought he would never be able to do it again. Their son-in-law would have volunteered, but that was the last thing Barb needed—her overextended husband squeezing in one more good deed into his crammed schedule. Helen was capable of running the tiller, of course, but it was heavy work— what if she put her back out and they were both out of commission? Besides, he had always done it. It was the kind of thing the husband did for the wife. Yes, he would do it for her this summer, if all went well.

MARCH–APRIL

i.

EARLY ON THE MORNING of March 8th, Helen drove Cal to the University of Iowa Hospitals and Clinics in Iowa City for his appointment with the hip doctor.

"When you go," Barb had told them, "look for Wayne's painting."

"What painting?" Helen asked.

"Oh, he sold one to the hospital. The hospital's full of art work."

"First I heard of it," Cal said sourly. "Which one is it? The corn row one?"

No, she thought it was something more abstract. Well, at least he got paid, Cal thought, and then put it out of his mind.

His sleep was even more disturbed than usual the night before the trip. He finally got up around two A.M., ran a bath, and lay in the warm water for half an hour, but then he had trouble getting himself out of the tub without the pain stabbing his hip, and by the time he had gotten onto his knees and grasped the wobbly towel rack and hoisted himself up, the bath had no longer done him any good.

The car ride to Iowa City didn't help matters.

"Why the hell do they make cars with seats that force your knees up?" he complained to Helen, who was driving. "I guess the ones who design these things, they're fresh out of engineering school, twenty-two years old with joints like rubber." He put his seatback down as far as it would go, but that seemed to put a different kind of pressure on his hip.

The drive seemed endless. Then there was the walk down one long corridor after another in the giant hospital complex. He was starting to perspire.

"Shall I get you a wheelchair?" Helen had spotted a bank of them at an entrance. The very thought of being pushed by his wife in a wheel chair was as mortifying as if he had to walk down the corridor in a dress. He shook his head without speaking and limped on.

At the clinic, when even sitting on one of the hard chairs would have been a relief, he had to stand in line at the desk to be registered on a computer. When it finally came his turn, the clerk—a cheerful thirtyish woman wearing a low cut blouse and apparently unconscious of the spectacle her cleavage made—kept him for forty minutes answering questions that were nobody's business. "Do you use illegal drugs? Do you smoke? Does your disability affect your sexual activity? Are you depressed? Do you ever have thoughts of suicide? Do you have trouble sleeping?" Of *course* I have trouble sleeping, he wanted to say, and what do *you* think it's like to try to have sex when you have grinding hip pain? But he suspected the questions as having some deeper implication related to depression and suicide, so he said, No, he didn't have trouble sleeping and his sex life was fine.

When she was finally through with him, there was another trek, this time to X-ray, where he was brought into a cubicle to take off his clothes and put on hospital scrubs because his own pants had a metal zipper and there were metal buttons on the patch pockets of his shirt.

In the X-ray waiting room a television tuned to FOX news was attached to the wall too high to change the channel without pulling a chair over and standing on it. On the screen, a woman rigged up to look like a Barbie doll was shouting down the opinions of a "guest" who had accused the channel of biased coverage. Five minutes of this was followed by seven commercials.

"Good God," Cal said.

"Just ignore it." Helen pulled a mini-cribbage board from her purse.

"How about some cribbage to pass the time?" But he couldn't. At home he enjoyed the game, but here he felt too tense.

What if they found that his hip problem couldn't be fixed, and he would have to put up with it for the rest of his life? Or his hip pain was due to some untreatable cancer? That suicide question didn't seem so out in left field now.

Two chirpy young women who appeared to be no older than his granddaughter and spoke in sentences that all sounded like questions brought him into the X-ray room, where he was made to lie on a metal table with only a thin pad cushioning his bones. The room was chilly.

"Are you comfortable?" asked one of the young women. "I'm sorry it's so cold, but we'll have you out of here in a jiffy."

Suspended from the ceiling, the X-ray machine hung over him like something from a science fiction movie. He pictured it seething with silent electrons, ready at the flip of a switch to invade his body with lethal radiation.

"If you would bend your knee and turn a little more on your side. Good. And hold that, please."

He had thought there would be just one X-ray, but they put him through three positions, each time leaving the room and standing behind glass while the electrons did their work. He thought of the Chernobyl meltdown and all that radioactivity killing trees and destroying animals' thyroid glands.

"After they fix my hip," he said to Helen when he finally changed back into his clothes and emerged, "I'll probably have to come back for more X rays to treat the tumors caused by all these X-rays."

She laid a hand on his. "They perform this surgery all the time. They know what they're doing."

He felt like a hypochondriac then and shut up.

They were sent to the clinic waiting room to wait for the results of the X-rays. Another TV was tuned to FOX News, and the volume was up high enough to make Cal plug his ears at the sound surge when a barrage of commercials came on—the last one asking, *"Do health issues limit your mobility? Call the Scooter Store today!"* Just what he wanted to hear.

After another hour, a nurse brought them to the examining room, where she took his height, weight and blood pressure.

"One hundred sixty over one hundred. A bit on the high side," she told him.

"Your blood pressure would be high, too, if you'd been watching FOX news all morning."

She laughed. "Yes, they're talking about changing to the Disney channel for that very reason."

She logged into a computer, asked about medications, and then left him and Helen to wait for the resident to come in. Helen suggested he sit on the ergonomic office chair, but he took one of the others. By this time, he was in so much pain a chair was beside the point.

At last a resident came in with a medical student in tow and brought Cal's X-rays up on the computer screen.

There it was. His right hip socket, the bones thinner than he imagined, almost dainty-looking. And in black and white, the unmistakable deterioration of the hip joint. The resident circled it with his finger. There was practically nothing left of it, just bone on bone.

He had Cal lie on the table and move his leg around—"Does this hurt? How about this? On a scale from one to ten?"—and stand up and walk a few steps away to check his gait. He left then, the student trotting behind, writing notes on a clipboard, and there was chitchat outside the closed door, too low to hear what they were saying about his hip.

After another interminable wait, the great hip doctor himself popped in, shook Cal's hand, introduced himself, and said, "Your hip looks like it needs to be replaced. See the secretary to schedule the surgery" and popped out again. He was in the room for probably thirty seconds. Cal wouldn't have been able to identify him in a lineup.

"Well," Helen said, "now we know. That's a relief."

And, strangely, after all these hours, these weeks, these months, it *was* a relief. He felt a weight lifted off him. The surgery and recovery would be miserable, but afterward, soon, he might be his old self— his young self—again. He might be well enough to till that garden. Six weeks, the recovery period was supposed to be. In six weeks you could drive a car and get back to normal activities. For a moment he felt almost like crying. He looked at Helen and felt a deep sense of gratitude. What would he do without her?

"You were right," he said, and let her put her arm under his elbow to support him as he limped out of the examining room, "as always."

At the front desk the secretary already had Cal's report in hand.

"Scheduling hip surgery?" she asked brightly. He nodded. She clackety clacked on her computer for some seconds, and then, squinting at her screen, said, "The earliest we can get you in is Thursday, July 12th. Will that work for you?"

He thought he couldn't have heard her right.

"*July* 12th?"

"Yes, on a Thursday."

"Four *months* from now?"

"Or if you can't do it then, the next opening would be in September."

He felt like someone had sneaked up behind him and shoved him to his knees. He couldn't speak. He just shook his head. The woman said, "September then?"

"No, no." Helen stepped forward. "He'll take the July opening."

The clerk handed Helen a thick information packet. She and Cal were silent as they left the clinic.

"Christ, what a place," he said, pulling his elbow away from Helen's hand as they walked down the corridor, every step like a knife in his hip.

They had put him on a cancellation waiting list, but weren't very encouraging about it. "You never know," Helen said, "maybe someone will cancel soon and you can get right in."

"When pigs shit blue," he said. "By then I'll be a goddamn cripple and you'll have to haul me back here on a stretcher." What in the hell had given him the idea that once they diagnosed you they'd whisk you right in, and what was he going to *do* with himself for four more months? Seeing it right there in black and white on an X-ray, they should know that he wasn't just a whiner and complainer who shirked his duties out of laziness or an unwillingness to work past a little discomfort. How stupid of him to think someone would look at those X-rays and say, My god, how have you stayed on your feet this long?

Squeezed in on the elevator with an anesthetized man on a gurney and two orderlies, he said to Helen, "That arrogant son of a bitch shakes my hand, and is out the damn door without ever even looking me in the eye."

When they stepped off the elevator, Helen said, "I wish you would not curse every other word. It's jarring to the ear."

"Well, excuse my French," Cal retorted. "What I meant to say was, My goodness mercy me, what do you suppose that blankety blank so-and-so earns for thirty seconds of his time?"

Resentment flared up in Helen, and she immediately chided herself for it. There was no clearer indication of how severe Cal's hip pain had been all these months than this anger he was expressing now. She knew that. He was disappointed. Of course he was. He had finally begun to believe that it wouldn't be much longer before he would get some relief and be out and about at last.

She should have questioned Marian Spong in more detail about the whole process, or asked the scheduler, when she first called, especially after she learned how long it would take just to get the clinic appointment. It had never occurred to her there would be *another* four months to wait.

But why did he have to act as if it were *her* fault? She had nagged him until she was at her wits end just to get him to see a doctor. It was *his* hip, not hers. *He* could have asked some questions. Let him sulk, then. She was not going to take any more responsibility for that Eeyore personality of his. Glass half empty, that fit him to a T.

She heaved a sigh, thinking of four more months of this attitude to look forward to. Well, she would be supportive, but she would not blame herself. And she would stop trying to read his mind. If he refused to tell her how he felt, so be it. She had her own stress to deal with—Margaret slipping away from her, choosing not to eat. Was that just part of her forgetfulness, or was Margaret ready to let go? How could she let her sister starve herself to death? But what reason was there for her to stay alive?

They'd had no lunch and it was 4:30. The hospital cafeteria could get them in and out quickest, so they went there.

The food wasn't as bad as she had expected. And the cafeteria, she noticed, was full of art. There were paintings on every wall, and not the mass-produced kind, but original art by professional artists. Come to think of it, there had been paintings on the clinic walls and in X-ray and all along the corridors. She remembered that Barb had said Wayne sold a painting to the hospital.

"You should see it while you're there," she told them.

Helen thought, Wayne can never bring himself to call us about these things, but he always tells Barb. He must know she'll pass the word on to us. Barb once said, "I think he doesn't call you because if Dad answers the phone, he'll have to talk to him. Maybe now you've got your cell phone, he'll call you more often." But that would only make his calls into a private thing, and Helen didn't encourage it. Well, at least Wayne had Barb to be close to, now that they were grown up.

She looked around the hospital cafeteria and wondered where Wayne's painting was.

At the next table a group of people in scrubs and shower caps were drinking coffee. She leaned over and asked, "Say, do you happen to know if there's a list or catalogue of the art in the hospital?"

They referred her to the information desk, which she and Cal would have to pass anyway on their way out the main entrance. The elderly volunteer at the desk was determined to give them more help than Helen wanted, with Cal starting to look pale from pain and fatigue. "Never mind," she said when the woman started to put in a call to the art curator's office. "We'll look into it another time."

"No trouble. It's not quite 5:00. I'll just see if they're still there—oh, you're in luck!" said the woman. "Say, I've got a lady here," she said into the phone, "asking about listings of the art we've got in the hospital—" She turned back to Helen. "Did you have anything particular you were looking for or—"

"Just a painting by our son. But we'll come back another time."

"Oh, your son! That's wonderful! What's his name?"

"Wayne Earlywine, but really—"

"His name is Wayne Earlywine," the woman said into the phone. She smiled at them. "He's just going to look it up for you. It won't take a minute."

There was a long wait, and Helen thought, why in the world did I bring this up now of all times?" She glanced at Cal, who was leaning with his two hands on the counter, a pose that took some pressure off his hip.

"I'm afraid we'll have to—" she began, but the woman held up a finger.

"Elevator D?" She wrote it on a slip of paper for them, looking pleased. "Just go back there where you see the coffee kiosk, take a left, and go down the corridor a little ways. It's hanging on the wall next to Elevator D."

Helen thanked her and stood with the paper in her hand, momentarily at a loss. It would be odd and ungrateful to walk out the door now in front of this woman, but sometimes you just had to do what was necessary.

She said to Cal, "Well, we need to get you home. You look all in. There'll be a chance to see it another time." The last thing he would want to do, even if he felt well, was look at one of Wayne's far-out paintings.

But Cal said, curtly, "I'm fine," and he limped slowly toward the coffee kiosk.

Well, she thought, if he felt he had to tough it out, she wasn't going to contradict him, but my goodness, it was painful to watch.

It was a big painting, maybe four by three feet. His son had taken the canvas and covered it with black paint. That was it. A black canvas. A hell of a lot of wasted paint, Cal thought. It was the kind of painting that made him mad as a hornet. State taxes paid for it! He glanced at the title. "Variation #3." What in the Sam Hill did that mean? Had he done *three* versions of this so-called picture, this travesty, from an artist who was capable of drawing a simple cornrow and making it a thing of beauty?

Cal stared at the thick black paint, and then stepped in for a closer look. Oh, so it wasn't *only* black. Great. Under the top edge of the frame there was an almost invisible horizontal line of metallic blue. So Wayne knew how to draw a straight line. More power to him. Probably Variation #1 had a purple line and Variation #2 a lime green one. Maybe there were variations 4 through 10, working their way through a paint color chart.

Then he noticed that if you looked hard, right in the middle there was an irregular diagonal slash of darker black against the black background. And a couple—no three—no *four* smaller ones, criss-crossing it, as if scattered on top of each other like forest deadfall. He stared at them. They came in and out of focus. It was hard to see the darker slashes in this light. His middle range vision wasn't so hot. His bifocals were no help.

He squinted. And then he saw it. The finest silver line, a thread maybe a tenth of a millimeter, so fine it was hard to imagine you could apply it with a paint brush. Still, how had he not immediately seen it against the black background, a straight line like the blue one, but traveling from the upper right corner to the center of the black slashes. And he thought, Well, I'm not stupid. I see what this is. The blue, the silver streak, the scattered black figures. He gave it his own title: "Out of the Blue." And he understood why there would be variations. There were so many ways of thinking about it. In his own mind, there had been a hundred, a thousand variations. What surprised him was that in this painting Wayne had put everyone in there. Those five slashes. All together on that field of black. Wayne had not left himself out.

He didn't look at Helen. He could feel her turning toward him, probably waiting for him to say something. Well, let *her* say it. Let her say, "You see? Wayne was deeply affected by Tom's death too." That's how she would put it 'Deeply affected.' Well, if Wayne was deeply affected, why didn't he ever say so? And he thought, *Why didn't you?* Was his own silence on the subject selfish? Had he kept silent for his own sake, not Tom's, not his family's? Was running Wayne down any way to honor Tom? Especially because Wayne maybe loved Tom after all? Cal stared into the black on black pile of slashes. Which slash was Wayne?

ii.

The Monday after they got back, Helen drove Cal into town to see the dentist while she dropped in on her sister. Cal looked forward to getting his teeth cleaned because the dentist had a state-of-the-art zero gravity chair that could be adjusted every which way until pressure on all the parts that hurt a person was relieved. He routinely fell asleep in the chair, and had to be nudged to keep his mouth open even when the dentist used the drill,

"Where can I buy one of these chairs?" he asked. But it turned out the chair wasn't state-of-the-art after all. The design had already been changed, for the worse.

"I guess I'll just have to up my candy intake and grow more cavities and an abscess or two so I can get some decent sleep," he said and closed his eyes again.

Helen brought Margaret a bouquet of bluebells and lilies-of-the-valley that were growing along the fence. Nice April flowers. The lilies-of-the-valley brought back the smell of childhood, when she and Margaret took bouquets to their mother. Now, as then, the bluebells drooped quickly, but the lilies-of-the-valley stayed fresh and gave off their delicate fragrance.

She held them up to Margaret's nose, forgetting that the Alzheimer's had taken away her sense of smell, even of something so strong and so familiar. Margaret frowned and shook her head.

"I don't think these flowers have any smell at all, do they?" Before Helen could answer, Margaret said, "My sister might know. We could ask her."

A little gasp escaped Helen before she could hold it back. She turned from Margaret to set the vase of flowers on the bedside table. She told herself, don't cry, you knew it would come, this is not a surprise. She took several breaths, but still could not turn back.

Then Margaret said, "Sis, did you have a long drive?"

Helen wiped her eyes with her sleeve and turned to Margaret, smiling. "Why no. I just drove the few miles from the farm."

"Oh," said Margaret. "Weren't you in California?"

Today, after she visited Margaret, she stopped by the lounge area and sat with Norman for awhile before picking up Cal.

"This here's where they've got me posted," he joked. "to keep an eye on that clock there, make sure the second hand keeps moving."

Norman's daughter arrived a minute later and exclaimed, with the pleasure of a mother whose child's guests had all shown up for his birthday party, "Oh, how nice! You've got company, Dad," and kissed her father on the cheek. "Are you and Mrs. Earlywine having a nice chat?"

"Well," he said, "*I'm* having a nice chat with *her*. You'd have to ask her if she's having a nice chat with me."

"Very nice," said Helen, but got up to go. Even though the daughter was happy to see her father occupied, Helen wondered if she might consider Helen's attentions to her father odd. She wondered about it herself.

Cal talked about the dentist's chair on the drive back, going on and on about the economics of planned obsolescence and how nothing of any quality had been produced since the 1960's and if their old appliances broke down beyond repair, they might as well go back to Stone Age technology for all the good they'd get out of anything they bought new.

She half listened, growing more annoyed with him. Finally she said, "Margaret didn't know me today."

"She didn't?"

"Just for a few seconds she didn't."

"Hm," he said. "Well, you knew it was bound to happen. She hasn't known *me* for five or six months."

"I suppose."

She herself didn't seem to know him at this moment. Who was he? Had there ever been a time when he saw into *her* heart as she saw into his everyday? If she pulled over and started to cry, he would pat her awkwardly and in silence, and he would hope she would pull herself together quickly, which is what she would have to do. For the next day, he would do a few helpful things around the house, but nothing would be said about any of it. And why? Because he could not stand to show his own feelings, unless it was anger or irritation. *He* refused to be comforted, so he darned well wasn't going to say the words that might comfort *her*.

She stared at the road unwinding ahead as they approached the turnoff to the farm. There were no other cars on the road, but she drove slowly, feeling unreal, not herself. There was no one now. She was orphaned. No one left to turn to for comfort. Wayne was as closed off and self absorbed as if he had never stopped being a teenager. Barb was compassionate, but Helen would never burden her daughter in that way. And now Margaret, the gentle and tender one, the unconditionally loving one, the one who could even express what she felt in poetry, Margaret was lost to her, too.

After Cal settled into his recliner for a nap, Helen put on her old shoes and took a walk down through the ravine to the horse trail. The trees were fuzzed with green and the path spotted with spring growth. Snow drops still bloomed here and there. When she reached the bottom of the ravine and started along the horse trail beside the river, a rabbit hopped onto the path. It didn't dart into the weeds as she approached but stayed some yards ahead as if it meant to lead her somewhere.

Soft sunlight shone through the greening branches. When she stopped walking it became hushed, and the air pleasantly warm. Not warm enough to shuck off a sweater, but warm as if the air was taking care of you.

It was a pity Cal's hip didn't allow him to take the steep path that led down here. He would like the silence and the soothing air. Especially since it was he who had rid the path of poison ivy last fall. He did it for her, and probably sacrificed his hip in the process. She bit her lip. Stubborn man. Well, it was too bad he couldn't join her as he used to. But it was nice to be by herself, feeling dreamy the way she had as a child with her hand in Margaret's and Margaret saying, "Shhh, listen to the ants marching." And she, Helen, could hear them.

iii.

On the morning of April twenty-third, early, Cal heard the sounds of vehicles pulling in off the road and into the field. From the living room window, he could see Nancy Bannister tripping up the drive toward the house, a basket in her hand and eager as a terrier carrying a freshly dispatched squirrel.

"Bannister's coming. Put your thinking cap on," he warned Helen. They went outside to meet her. "What's this?" he said. "The Welcome Wagon? You're a little late. We've been in this house for forty-eight years."

Nancy laughed merrily. "Oh Cal, you're such a card!" She held the basket out to Helen. The handle was decorated with a complicated yellow bow. "This is just a little token of everyone's appreciation to you two for making the A-mazing Maiz Maze a reality. We've fixed the grand opening for Saturday, July 16th." They all three turned to listen as another vehicle pulled in from the road. "The people from that outfit that plots out the design in the field are here, and then next week we'll be planting. And the best part—it really brings tears to my eyes—" Her eyes were, in fact, glistening, and she pulled a white handkerchief from her pocket to dab at them. "—is how everybody has just pitched right in, donating time and supplies and equipment and ideas. I'm just as proud as I can be of our community. Really, our only *major* expense is the cost of hiring this company to do the actual layout of the thing on the ground." She took a deliberate pause here. "That's a big ticket item."

Cal shook his head. How does the woman come up with expressions like 'big ticket item'? Where does she think she is? Wal-Mart's board room? Nancy pulled out contents of the basket and held them up to show Helen—two T-shirts neatly folded and bearing Wayne's design across the chest, some decals of the design, a laminated *Dunlop County Sentinel* article with the headline, "Local Man Designs Maze," a small front door wreath made of miniature multi-colored cobs of Indian corn, and a bouquet of silk sunflowers.

It wasn't hard to see where she was going with all this. She had the nerve to try to shame them into donating money now that they'd got that check for the field. Well, he and Helen were on fixed incomes. The barn and the house needed new paint and roofs, and the old man needed a new hip.

He let the pause draw itself out, let Nancy's innocent expression grow strained.

"That sounds like a big ticket item, all right," he said. He lowered his voice conspiratorially. "I'll bet you could get some spies to see how this outfit works this maze layout thing. Then pay Robbie Peterson's high school crew to do the work next year."

Nancy's eyes narrowed as if she might be considering the suggestion.

"Well," she said, turning back to look down the drive. "The Credit Union gave us a very reasonable interest rate on the loan—we can thank Garland for that," she said, pointedly, "—and we should be able to pay it all back by the end of three seasons if we do as well as we expect to." She gave them a rather sour smile. "Nice seeing you both," she said, and walked back down the drive, in what seemed like a hurry.

"I think she took to my idea. No need to round up spies when she can do it herself."

Helen laughed. "Next year she'll have her own company: All Phases of Corn Mazes."

"'It Pays to Buy a Bannister Maze'."

Helen took his arm. "Let's go down and see what they're up to." But he said, no, he thought he'd stay out of it.

He watched her follow Nancy down the drive, thinking that she probably assumed he didn't want to come because of Tom. And maybe it was partly that, but mostly he didn't want to admit that the walk just to the end of the drive was too much for him. No way was he going to ask his wife to drive him in the car the length of two city blocks. He imagined what Nancy Bannister would make of that. *Poor old man, the town should take up a collection, a little something toward buying Cal a state-of-the-art wheelchair that rides smoothly on gravel.* She'd manage to get it at cost from The Scooter Store.

He continued to watch the two women, one walking determinedly, the other meandering along, raising her face to look at the few white clouds sailing in the blue spring sky. He felt utterly useless.

MAY–JUNE

i.

MARGARET NEVER LEFT her room now. Meal trays were brought to her, but she nibbled only at the desserts. She spent most of her time sleeping or sitting in the rocker staring out the window. When Helen visited, she could no longer persuade Margaret to play the piano. They lay side by side on the bed and, for lack of anything else to do, watched television.

Sitcoms or movies or news bewildered Margaret. Only two kinds of programs kept her attention—pro golf and right-wing talk shows. Lying next to her, Helen tried to analyze the reasons for these preferences and decided it was because both were easy to follow without benefit of memory. A golf ball made a pleasant arc through the air and landed somewhere. "Good shot," Margaret would say encouragingly, no matter where the ball ended up. On the talk shows, people sat around on easy chairs and yelled. Margaret didn't have a clue what they were yelling about, but at least she understood what was going on—people were mad at each other. Given how intimidated Margaret had always been at disapproval or anger, Helen guessed her preference for the Bill O'Reilly show and others of its ilk indicated how desperate her need was simply to grasp *something*. Or maybe she enjoyed these shows because for so many years she had not allowed herself to speak her own mind and she got a thrill watching others do it.

Helen sometimes thought if she had to watch one more man in a sun visor squint across a green, or one more mean-spirited bigot interrupt his so-called guest, she would start yelling, too. For Margaret's sake, she endured it.

"Anything good on TV tonight?" Cal would quip from his recliner when she came home. She picked up the newspaper's TV section and swatted him with it.

On a sunny day in late May, two weeks after the last possibility of frost, Helen loaded her wheelbarrow into the truck with jugs of water, a shovel and trowel, and drove into town for her afternoon visit. She stopped first at the garden center and picked out colorful annuals— orange and red and pink impatiens and blue salvia in containers and packets of zinnia seeds. She bought some perennials, too—purple coneflowers, black-eyed Susans and statice—which would bloom through the summer along with the yellow coneflowers. The coneflowers, she noticed, had spread since last summer and were greening up nicely.

She considered the potted perennials as the cashier rang them up. She thought, next summer another elderly person would likely be enjoying them through Margaret's picture window. By then, Helen would probably have moved the single bed out and the rocker and the piano and TV and the small closet full of clothes Margaret had seldom worn. She would have cleaned off and thrown away the bits of lint, paper clips, scraps of Kleenex, buttons, bobbie pins and other detritus that Margaret picked up off the floor and arranged in little piles on the dresser or along the window ledge, not knowing what else to do with them. The garden would continue to flourish in its sunlit spot. Although maybe not. If there was no one to lug water by hand, it would wither and become overgrown with weeds.

Before going into the building, Helen pushed the laden wheelbarrow around to the back and spent an hour sowing the seeds and planting the container flowers, putting the impatiens against the building where they would be in shade. She filled the pole feeder with seed and poured water into the bright blue ceramic bird bath that sat on the ground. Then she watered everything and pushed the much lighter wheelbarrow back to the truck.

When she entered Margaret's room, sweaty from her exertions, Margaret was lying on her bed as usual. She was wearing her blouse inside out, but Helen didn't mention it.

Margaret conjured up a wan smile. "Are we supposed to do something today?" she asked vaguely.

Helen got her up long enough to walk her over to the window for a look at the new additions to the garden.

"How pretty," Margaret said, but then turned back toward the bed. "I think I'll lie down for a bit, if you don't mind."

Helen felt a twinge of impatience and disappointment. Really, was her little garden scene worth the effort? She went into Margaret's bathroom, washed the dirt off her hands, wet a washcloth, and wiped the sweat from her face and neck. Then she lay down next to her sister and picked up the remote. "Interested in watching some golf?"

"That would be nice," Margaret said.

ii.

The new corn for the maze started to come up. Cal could see it from the upstairs bedroom window. In a few weeks it was as dense as a green carpet, the rows planted so close together.

On a Saturday, the volunteers—teenage boys with tattoos scattered over their shirtless chests, and wires in their ears leading from gadgets in their jeans pockets—rode in on the donated mowers and started mowing the paths marked by little red flags. Robbie Peterson sat on the fence in a T-shirt and cutoffs, spitting Red Man and "supervising."

Helen was in town shopping. Cal had intended to stay away from the project in all its phases. Whenever he heard the distant drone of vehicles entering at that end of the drive and parking along the fence, he went out back and found something to do in the yard. With the electric pruner blocking out whatever sounds came from what was going on in the field, he could stand long enough to prune back the honeysuckle that blocked the view across the ravine. But he couldn't stop the memories that kept popping into his head.

While he and Helen had been making Tom's funeral arrangements and holding the visitation, Kyle Branson and some of his neighbors had quietly come over and put in the corn for him. He came back from the funeral home and saw it had been done, under a clear blue sky without a sign of bad weather on any horizon, and he felt a deep anger toward his neighbors, which he couldn't account for. His muttered thanks to them at the funeral was, he knew, ungracious, but he could hardly even get out the words.

And then, the following spring, he went into that damned field and planted corn again by himself so that by the third year, when he rented it to Kyle and Millie, no one would put together that grief was the reason he was steering clear of the land. The truth was that the planting that second year had about killed him. There was no problem with weather, but as soon as he had gotten on the tractor, his heart started palpitating and pounded so hard he could feel it shaking his whole torso. When he was almost finished, he started to feel weak in all his limbs and short of breath. Fortunately, he turned off the ignition and got down from the tractor, because the next thing he knew he was lying on his side on the ground, his cheek in the dirt, without a clue how he'd gotten there. It took him some seconds to understand that he'd fainted.

He lay there and waited for awhile until he felt sure his heartbeat was close to normal, and then he got back on the tractor and finished the job. He never said anything to Helen about it or to a doctor. At harvest time it wasn't quite so bad, but he told himself that that was the last time he would set foot in that field.

So he had intended to keep away from all the comings and goings of the corn maze construction, but that afternoon, when the mowing started, from an upstairs window he saw Robbie Peterson idly looking on with his usual disregard for his own assigned duties. Knowing that Robbie and his charges hadn't even been born when Tom died,

Cal felt pretty sure he could master his emotions long enough to see how Wayne's little sketch would translate on such a large scale. He limped slowly down the drive.

Robbie raised his chin at him and spit an arc of tobacco juice into the dirt. "Hey, Mr. Earlywine."

"How's it going, Robbie?"

Robbie shaded his eyes and gazed off at the boys as if to evaluate their work.

"Pretty good. Should be done in a couple days."

The two of them watched the mowing for a while. Cal felt a kind of tug in his heart and became vaguely aware that it was because of the tattoos on those teenaged boys. How could they deliberately do that to their young, unblemished skin? What had their parents felt when their sons first came home with chests and backs and shoulders permanently disfigured after all their efforts to protect their children's bodies from harm?

Cal shook off these thoughts and came through the gate to move in for a closer look at the progress of the maze. Robbie stopped him.

"You don't want to trample the plants, Mr. Earlywine. They're put in pretty close together. Mrs. Bannister says to walk only between the flags, where the corn'll be mowed down anyway." He slid off the fence. "I'll take you around to the entrance." Cal followed behind so Robbie wouldn't see his limp. They entered a narrow path that had already been mown through the twelve-inch-high corn. "This here's where you go into the maze."

"How come it's so narrow?"

"It's the stick."

Cal stopped walking. "What stick?"

"The stick for the Cream Wiener."

"What are you talking about? Cream Wiener?"

Robbie gazed past Cal with that guilty-innocent look he'd always gotten in his eyes since childhood when he sensed someone was about to give him a dressing down.

209

"Mrs. Bannister added a Cream Wiener entrance." When Cal didn't say anything, Robbie added, "For the little kids. To get 'em pumped about coming into the maze. They all go for Cream Wieners-on-a-Stick. There'll be a Cream Wiener stand outside the entrance and one at the exit. Cream Wiener people gave big bucks to the project."

Cal looked off to where the narrow path widened; the wiener section, apparently. Without standing on something tall, it was hard to see the whole picture.

"What the hell happened to the corn row design?"

Robbie jerked his head toward the bare-chested boys. "They'll start mowing that tomorrow. This here is just the way into it."

Cal said, "That damn woman!" and started limping off along the path after the mowers. "Hey!" he yelled. "Hey!" But they couldn't hear him over the sound of the machines, and didn't notice him until he flagged them down with an emphatic slashing gesture across his throat. They turned off the mowers and waited.

"No more mowing today!" he yelled.

"How come?" one asked.

The other said, "Do we get paid for the full four hours?"

"You'll have to take that up with Bannister." Cal turned on his heel and limped back, treading on the slender plants that had been felled along the path.

"Don't let anyone mow until I say so," he told Robbie, who was loping along beside him.

"What am I s'posed to tell Mrs. Bannister?"

"You don't have to tell her anything. *I'll* tell her." Cal left Robbie standing at the bottom of the Cream Wiener path chewing on his Red Man.

Nancy Bannister insisted on another ad hoc meeting to discuss the matter.

"I hear what you're saying, Cal," she said on the phone, "and I think you should have a chance to air your objections so others can weigh in. Don't you think that's the fair thing to do?"

"By others, you mean *you*?"

She ignored the question. "The sooner the better. How about tomorrow evening? I'll get hold of Garland and George and Robbie, and you can let Helen know." It was rare for Nancy to let an edge creep into her voice, but Cal heard one now. Before he could answer, she said, "Thanks for bringing it to my attention" and virtually hung up on him.

Okay, he thought. You're on.

"Cream Wieners-on-a-Stick are an institution in Dunlop County," Nancy began. She was thoroughly ensconced in the leader's chair at the head of the table. On a doily-covered silver platter in front of her, a pile of lemon bars sat ready to be passed around like sacramental wafers. When the platter came to him, Cal pushed it to his left without taking one.

"Everybody loves Cream Wieners," she continued. "They even serve them in Dunlop County school cafeterias. The kids can't get enough of them."

"Now that's a bad idea," said Garland, meticulously lining up three lemon bars on his paper napkin. "Aren't the schools trying to cut down on fatty foods? Think what's in those things—creamed corn mixed with mostly offal—beef and pork. Animal fat, salt, sugar, binders, preservatives—"

"They're pretty tasty, though. I wouldn't call them 'awful'."

"*Offal*, George. O-f-f-a-l. Intestines, organs, and whatnot."

"Really?" George frowned. "Well, I wish you hadn't told me." He raised his eyes to the ceiling, reminiscing. "I remember the first time I ever had a Cream Wiener. It was at the Dunlop County Fair. I thought I'd died and gone to heaven. Ate four of 'em in a row, one right after the other. My wife had three." He hesitated. "No, what am I thinking? That was my son who had three. My wife couldn't risk it at that time because she'd just got the diabetes diagnosis and had to be careful of food that—"

"At *any* rate," Nancy interrupted, more testily than Cal had ever heard her, which gave him considerable satisfaction. He leaned casually back in his chair with his hands in his lap and gazed at her steadily as she made her pitch. "The local Cream Wiener franchise was kind enough to pledge the cash to build the observation post and to buy the gravel for the drive from the road into the parking area."

"Mrs. Bannister don't like to pay for nothin' she can get for free," pitched in Robbie, admiringly.

"With what strings attached?" Garland demanded. Cal wanted to jump in here, too, but held his tongue. He could count on Garland's naysaying as long as he himself didn't give Garland anything to counter. Let the banker do the work.

"Not really strings," said Nancy. "My, it's warm in here." She got up and opened a window to let in some air. "I hate for the town to pay for a.c. so early in the summer." She then spent a minute unnecessarily bringing the coffee pot and cups from the counter to the table. She's thinking what to say about 'strings', thought Cal. When she had poured coffee for Garland and George (Robbie, Helen and Cal declining), she smiled in that way she had of showing her teeth and dropping her jaw like a panting fox, and Cal knew she would defend her idea as if it was a threatened cub.

"As far as strings," she said, "It was *my* idea to have the entrance to the maze be in the shape of their product—a straight narrow path to represent the stick, wide enough for a wheel chair, then the wider path for the wiener itself, which would narrow again at the top, where people would emerge into the maze. *They* brought up the wheelchairs— they're a very sensitive company. The whole idea was to attract the kids, who love Cream Wieners and would think it fun to be inside one."

"And that's it? No other strings attached?" Garland looked around the table, nodding at no one in particular as if to show he wasn't one to be hoodwinked.

"As I said, the entrance wasn't something they brought up. But of course they want something substantial for their money and we agreed that there be a Cream Wiener stand outside the entrance and the exit. It fits the entire corn motif."

Cal raised an eyebrow. *Motif* he mouthed to Helen.

"There will be the premium sweet corn on the cob and caramel corn stands, the cornhusk "maiz maidens" stand, and other corn-related concessions, a stand for T-shirts with the full color maze design on the front—"

"I believe they're actually called Cream Weenies," mused the mayor.

"Only children call them that," countered Garland sternly. "The brand name is Cream Wiener."

"Cal," said Nancy sweetly, smiling her vixen smile, "I'm not sure I understand your objection."

"Well," said Cal, "maybe I heard you wrong when you saw the drawing for the maze design, but I could swear I heard you say it was . . . how did you put it? 'Elegant', I think you said. Or maybe you said 'classy'. How do you figure a piece of junk food on a stick goes together with that 'elegant' maze design?"

"It's just the *entrance* to the maze, Cal, not the maze itself. And it fits the corn theme. Cream Wieners are made with creamed corn."

"Creamed corn is the secret ingredient," said George, dreamily eyeing the plate now emptied of lemon bars, as if he might find a Cream Wiener on it and repeat that ecstatic first taste experience so many years ago.

"I *live* on the damn things." Until now, Robbie hadn't contributed anything to the discussion. He had been idly picking at a frayed hole on the front of his T-shirt, revealing more and more bare belly. "Cream Wieners taste great and they're cheap."

"Well, why don't we just call the maze "Pig-Guts-on-a-Stick" or "Pig-Guts-on-a-Stick with Corn."

"Now, Cal, there's no need to be sarcastic."

"What? I'm just 'brainstorming' here. There are no bad ideas."

Garland rapped his fingers reflectively on the table. "Well, you can't expect a business to donate money without getting something back." To Cal's chagrin, Garland appeared to be reversing his original objection to strings being attached. Now it was four to two.

Nancy said, "I think we should take a straw poll."

He thought fast. It would be a risk. It could backfire and he'd have to swallow the travesty that the Cream Wiener would make of Wayne's design. He could just imagine what Wayne would have to say about it. But after a quick glance at Helen, Cal turned to Nancy and said, "I don't know. Maybe business is business. You gotta lay down cow shit to make something grow."

Nancy beamed and threw her hands up. Cal thought she was going to applaud. "I wouldn't have put it in such salty language, Cal," she said, chuckling, "but you've said it very well."

Cal held his breath and sneaked a look at Garland. He saw the banker frown and puff out his cheeks like a blow fish. He'd taken the bait.

"No," Garland said, "business is not without principles. Or standards. You always have to have standards."

Gotcha, thought Cal. He stood up. "So let's have the straw poll," he said. "Everyone in favor of the Cream Wiener entrance raise your hand."

Nancy, George and Robbie raised theirs. Garland appeared to be thinking. He was rapping on the table again, but then his fingers fell silent and he left his hand where it was.

Three to three.

Nancy sat back, still smiling. She looked earnestly from one person to another. "We've heard from those against it—Helen, I assume you're making the same argument as Cal?" Helen nodded. "But maybe we could hear a little more from those in favor of it. Robbie, would you like to tell us more about your opinion?"

Robbie removed his finger from the hole in his T-shirt and tipped back in his chair. "Yeah," he said, "I think it's a great idea. For one thing, every teenager in Dunlop County would pay the seven dollars just to say they came through the Cream Wiener." He grinned. "The official food of the senior prom. Good for a whole lot of laughs." Nancy's smile became fixed. "Cream . . . Wiener," Robbie said to her, pointedly. "Your kids grew up here. You probably made that connection?"

iii.

On a rainy, unseasonably cold June morning, Helen was staring out the patio windows, feeling flat and dull. Cal hadn't come downstairs yet, after a night of tossing and turning. The telephone rang.

"Good morning, Helen! It's Nancy." Her voice sounded a little breathless. "I have a request and I won't take no for an answer!"

When had she ever? Helen sat down on the sofa.

"You might have to. What is it?" That Cream Wiener business had been put to rest. So what now?

"How would you like to come with me to France in August? All expenses paid!"

Helen didn't reply. In the silence, she wondered if Nancy was speaking metaphorically, as she often did. Maybe she had a new maze idea—Climb the Eiffel Tower of Corn! View the Maze from Above!

"What do you mean?"

"Remember I told you I'd won a trip to France? Two tickets, all-expenses paid, ten-days. What do you think of that?"

"Oh yes. I'd forgotten. Well, that's wonderful. Now, how did you win them?"

"I was at the BABOA Conference in Cleveland, and I put in my five dollars and won the grand prize in the raffle!"

"BABOA?"

"Bed and Breakfast Operators of America. *Paris, France*! With side trips, Helen. What do you say?"

"You're asking *me* to come with you?"

"Absolutely."

"But Nancy—you have kids and grandkids who would want to go."

"To be honest, of course I did think of them first, but I've taken all of them to France before, and this summer they're just so busy. Alice and Steve are involved with a startup business right now. It wouldn't be a good time for them to be away, and their kids will be at music camp. My son and his family on the East Coast are in the process of selling their home, so—"

"But why—"

"So I thought of you, Helen, because of that wonderful program you gave for the seniors—what, five years ago, was it? About the Renaissance—"

"That was just something I worked up from a little reading I did, and notes from when I subbed at the high school. In fact, *you* asked me to do the program."

"And wasn't it a success!"

She had rather enjoyed putting it together. Nancy saw to it there was a decent crowd, and for several weeks afterward people told her it had "opened their eyes."

"Well, thank you for thinking of me, Nancy, but—"

"I'm sure a trip to France wouldn't exactly be Cal's cup of tea, but I assume he wouldn't object to *you* going for just a short time."

Helen stood up and gazed out at the woods. She curled the telephone cord in and out of her fingers. Cal was moving around upstairs, and she hoped he wouldn't come down yet.

"I doubt if it would work out, but . . . when would it be?"

"From August twelfth to August twenty-second. Just ten days."

A stone-like weight filled the space under her sternum. She pressed her hand to it.

"Cal will be recovering from his hip surgery then. I couldn't possibly leave him."

"When's the surgery? July fourteenth, didn't you say?" She hadn't said, but Nancy knew everything. "You know, the recovery period is about six weeks total. They get them up walking the very next day. After four weeks, they're almost as good as new. By six weeks they can drive again."

"That's if everything goes well."

"Let's see, August twelfth would be . . ." She paused to calculate. "the end of the fourth week—"

"I couldn't leave him stuck at home while he couldn't drive."

"Of course not. But I'll bet you anything your daughter would be happy to look in on him once a day. Have some quality time with just her dad—"

"No, no, that wouldn't be possible. She and Gordon have a camping trip in the Colorado Rockies planned for August. You have to reserve those camping spaces months ahead of time. They never get a chance to get away, all of them together, with Gordon working so many hours—" Now she'd done it. Nancy would be telling everyone it was a pity Gordon was such a workaholic.

"Well, what about Wayne? He substitute teaches, if I'm not mistaken, so he wouldn't be working in August. I'll bet he'd be glad to come down and help you out with Cal for ten days." Helen almost snorted. "They don't see so much of each other, do they?"

You know they don't, and you know why.

"I wouldn't think of asking him. He spends his summer on his art work."

"That's portable, though, isn't it? He could bring an easel, set it up in his old room—"

Helen had had enough.

"I thank you very much, Nancy. It sounds wonderful. But it's just out of the question. On top of everything else, I've got my sister to think about."

"Poor Margaret." Nancy's voice lowered to a sympathetic tone. "I can understand why you've seemed melancholy lately. You've had a lot on your plate." *Did* she seem melancholy? "Well, keep it in mind, Helen. Where there's a will, there's a way. And it might do you a world of good to go off on a little adventure. Paris, Chartres, the chateaux of the Loire Valley. I think you'd make a great traveling companion. I don't like traveling alone. It takes the fun out of it. But I won't look for anyone else just yet."

When Helen hung up, she went into the kitchen to start the coffee. The floor overhead creaked. Cal was in the bathroom now. She should call up the stairs to see what he wanted for breakfast, but she stood at the sink, unconsciously filling the coffee pot with water until it flowed over and she had to pour some out.

Since childhood, she had wanted to travel, from all the books she had read—*The Island of Adventure* with those double sets of English twins exploring tunnels beneath the cathedral island of Mont St. Michel; *Alice's Adventures in Wonderland* and *Through the Looking Glass*, Dickens.

She put two slices of bread in the toaster.

She knew of those Loire Valley chateaux. She had seen them in a book about France. Fairy tale castles surrounded by moats, or built astride reflecting pools. Hundreds of rooms, grand staircases, turrets, mullioned windows, gargoyles, statuary, vast green lawns. And the Louvre in Paris. The greatest art collection in the world. How Margaret would love it. Her poor Margaret.

She jumped at the ping of the toaster. She had forgotten to take the butter out of the refrigerator and had to press it on the toast in chunks, tearing the bread apart.

JULY

i.

THEY HAD TO MAKE another trip to Iowa City for a teaching session about what to do the night before surgery, what to expect after the operation, and so on—all information covered in the packet they had been given four months before.

"Do they think I'm illiterate? They could have saved their breath and saved us a trip," Cal grumbled.

There had been plenty in the packet about all the things that could go wrong—blood clots in the leg, lungs or hip; urinary infection; difference in leg length; the possibility of dislocating the new hip and having to re-do the surgery with less chance of success. Now he had to hear these horrors repeated as he signed various forms releasing the hospital and its personnel from liability.

"Why don't they just tell you if you come out of it alive or only half maimed, you should thank your lucky stars?"

Helen made no comment. She took notes at the consultations, but otherwise didn't seem to have much to say.

On the Fourth of July, ten days before his hip surgery, Helen convinced him to go into Dunlop for the festivities. He wasn't much in the mood.

"We're staying for the parade, and that's it," he told her. "No hanging around 'til next Tuesday chitchatting with half the town and their Aunt Heloise from Boise."

The pain in his hip probably wasn't significantly worse than it was a month ago, but now that he was so near his surgery it seemed almost intolerable. His idleness made it harder to bear, he knew, and that was the only reason he agreed to go with her. The sight of Dunlop's five Shriners making fools of themselves in fezzes and kiddie cars might take his mind off himself. A Republican presidential hopeful would be riding in the parade, which might be good for a laugh. The man was scheduled to talk for no more than ten minutes at the picnic later that day. Even the Republicans on the Fourth of July Committee were good and sick of the hot air that had been filling the state of Iowa before the caucuses next January. Cal thought of his father and grandfather, old New Deal Democrats, who would have come out just to spit tobacco juice at the man's feet.

Helen found a spot on the sidewalk right in front of the courthouse on the square. She dropped him off with the chairs and a cooler of sodas, and drove away to park the car. It was 11:00 A.M. and the sun was already high and broiling. Cal put on his old seed cap with the extra long brim, settled himself into one of the chairs and took a cold root beer from the cooler.

The Dunlop County Consolidated Schools high school marching band was warming up two blocks away—a dozen brass instruments blaring dissonant notes, woodwinds tootling their scales, a bass drum thudding, and cymbals crashing at random. It took him back to his children's high school days, when each one took up a musical instrument for awhile, got in a year with the marching band, and then gave it up, none of them particularly musical. Cal looked forward to the marching band part of the parade, though. Something about a group of young people stepping smartly in unison to a lively drum beat and swelling music put a catch in his throat. He gazed down Main Street hoping the parade would start soon.

"Trading in the old hip, I hear." Garland Spong stopped on his way to the seat he had procured for himself and his wife in the shade of the courthouse portico. He stood looking down at Cal with the sun behind him so that Cal had to crane his neck and shade his eyes to look up at him. Garland shook his head gravely.

"When you going in?"

"Thursday the fourteenth. Just a two or three-day stay."

"A Thursday? You can forget a three-day stay. They won't dismiss you on a Saturday. Doctors' golf day. You won't get out of there 'til the Monday, is my guess. Too bad. The longer you stay in there, your chance of getting an infection rises exponentially."

Exponentially. Leave it to a banker to throw that in.

"I hope you don't run into the trouble Marian here got into with *her* hip —" he tilted his head toward his wife, who was gandering around to see who had turned out for the parade. "Picked up a serious infection from the surgery. They had to take out the new hip and put in a—" He turned to his wife. "what did they call that thing they stuck in your hip for your infection?"

"A spacer," she said.

"A spacer. They stuck it in the empty socket to dispense the medication until the infection was gone and they could redo the hip." He nudged his wife, who was waving at a friend across the way. "You were in a nursing home how long?"

"Three weeks."

A *nursing* home. This was the woman who Helen had told him was so happy with her surgery. Cal pictured himself in a cramped double room, unable to get up, lying next to some agitated man with dementia. He might ring and ring for someone to bring a bed pan or take it out from under him, but no one would come.

"But your hip is okay now?" Cal couldn't resist asking Marian.

"Yes," she said. "I'm very—"

Garland interrupted her. "Well, she's up and about as you can see. But—" he added ominously, "who knows how long *that* will last?"

"Excuse me a minute," his wife said, and crossed the street to speak to her friend. Was that a limp Cal saw? It seemed like she was limping.

"You've got to be very careful not to pick up an infection when you have invasive surgery," Spong said.

And how was he supposed to do *that*? What could *he* do about it, short of not having the surgery at all, and at this point, was that an option? You're damned if you do and damned if you don't.

By the time Helen joined him, he wished he had never come into town today.

"I thought you said—" he started to accuse, but stopped himself.

"Said what?"

"Never mind." No point blaming her. Anyway, he should consider the source. If Garland Spong was reminded that the earth orbited around the sun, he'd say, "Yeah, but who knows how long *that* will last?"

In the distance the band had struck up a Sousa march and the first of the parade came into view a block away—the color guard carrying flags and just behind them George Massey, the mayor, and his wife, George nodding and craning his neck back and forth dreamily like a benign camel. Next came the Chamber of Commerce employees, four abreast in red blazers, throwing candy to the children, who scrambled out from the curbs to grab it. Behind them was the volunteer fire squad hanging off the big pumper, then several convertibles from the Chrysler dealership with contest winners waving from the back seats—Class of 2011 Prom Queen and King, Miss Dunlop County, 4-H blue ribbon winners. Cal took out a root beer for Helen and opened another one for himself. The presidential hopeful, with a big stiff grin on his mug, waved from a 1955 Chevy Bel Air festooned with red, white and blue bunting. His vintage Banlon shirt was dark in the armpits.

Following the sheriff's car, Robbie Peterson in full cop regalia rode his Harley classic Road King, revving it with deafening flatulence.

Nancy Bannister, dressed in a nineteenth century period costume with leg-'o-mutton sleeves, waved gaily and tooted the horn at Cal and Helen from a Tin Lizzie. Mounted between the head lamps was one of her signature made-to-order wreaths ($20–$75), decorated with dried flowers, pine cones, fluffy bows and other gew gaws. A sign draped across the car door said in bold letters:

BANNISTER'S BED AND BREAKFAST
OLD-STYLE HOSPITALITY

Right behind her, kids hobbled past, dressed as ears of corn, with openings for arms and feet and slits for eyes. Nancy had gotten the Methodist Quilters' Circle to sew the costumes. Two older children brought up the rear, struggling to hold high a banner:

GRAND OPENING OF DUNLOP'S
A-MAZING MAIZ MAZE
SATURDAY, JULY 16TH
FUN FOR ALL AGES!!

Twelve more days. Well, at least his surgery gave him a good excuse for missing the "Grand Opening." Bannister had once mentioned the idea of him and Helen cutting a ribbon or some foolishness as that. She'd tried to rope Wayne into coming, but he refused. At least he had that much sense.

Helen took a flyer one of the kids was passing out. It had a map to the maze park and hours of operation. Cal took it from her. Wayne's corn row decorated the top of the page. Even though the colors looked somewhat washed out on the cheap paper, the drawing was still something to be proud of.

But Cal couldn't enjoy the parade. The paunchy Shriners didn't amuse him now, as they rode their putt-putt cars in circles, did tricks on three wheelers, and blew their horns, old men biding their time in foolishness until they were too obese and too disabled to squeeze themselves into those little cars or maneuver them. Had Marian Spong been limping? He looked back to the courthouse portico. The Spongs were sitting now. She had a glum expression on her face, but maybe that was just from putting up with Garland for forty years.

The high school band had finished the Sousa piece and was marching up the street now. The solemn, rhythmic beat of their footsteps made his heart race a little. The band leader in a tall furred hat, marching backward ahead of them, stopped and blew her whistle twice, raised her baton, and signaled. "God Bless America" streamed out of the oboes and the trombones and the piccolos. All up and down the sidewalks people sang along, the bass drums punctuating each phrase. *Stand beside her (pum), and guide her (pum).*

On the phrase *To the oceans, white with foam*, tears pricked Cal's eyes. He wasn't particularly patriotic—not in the "my country right or wrong" sense of the word—but the song peeled back layers of his life to better days. Days when he was young and healthy and full of hope. He glanced at Helen. She was openly wiping her eyes. He wished he could do the same. He was tired of always buttoning down his nostalgia, his fear, his grief, his guilt. It wore him out.

Helen put an arm around him and leaned her head on his shoulder. He took her hand. A tear dropped on it, and he hoped she would think it was hers.

ii.

They would be gone to Iowa City for the surgery, and Helen was afraid Margaret would have forgotten her completely by the time they got back. With every other sentence, Helen called Margaret "Sis" to forestall those awful lack-of-recognition moments. As it was, there were more and more lapses.

"Sis," she said on the Wednesday afternoon before the Thursday surgery, "Cal and I have to go in to Iowa City tomorrow. He'll be in the hospital having his hip replaced. We'll be gone for three or four days." Too late, she realized this was much too much information for one utterance.

"Oh?" Margaret looked bemused. She was sitting on the side of the bed. "Will you be bringing home a baby?" She had registered the word "hospital."

"No, a new hip for Cal. His old hip hurts him."

"Like an old car."

Helen laughed. "Yes, he's trading in the hip for a new model."

A tray of congealing food sat on the piano bench next to the rocking chair.

"Didn't you eat anything, Sis?"

Margaret looked at the tray. "Is that mine?"

"Your lunch."

"I didn't cook that, did I?"

"No."

"Oh, that's good. It would be strange if I cooked it and didn't remember doing it. I wonder about my memory these days. It doesn't seem quite right." Margaret cocked her head inquisitively. "Are you a specialist?"

"What do you mean?"

"Something to do with . . ." She lost her train of thought. Probably she meant a memory specialist. "Oh, I can't think what I was going to say. My sister will know. Can you ask her?"

What could she say but yes.

Margaret lay back on the bed and stared at the ceiling. Helen wondered whether, if she lay down beside her, Margaret would think a stranger was being presumptuous.

"Shall I lie down, too, Sis?"

"If you like. But it might be boring for you."

Today it wasn't just boring, it was excruciating. Helen watched the hands of the wall clock move and thought about how long she must lie there to satisfy her own conscience. Did Margaret even notice when she was gone? Did she wonder where her sister was or when she would come next? What went through her mind during those long hours she was alone? Was it just blank, or churning with fearful confusion?

Out of this dreadful boredom and desperate need to find something of the old Margaret, the authentic Margaret, Helen asked impulsively, "Do you remember Jim McIntyre, your husband?"

"My husband? Yes, I think so. Where is he?"

"He died eleven years ago."

"That's too bad." She said it with kindness, as if she were consoling someone.

"Did you love Jim?" It was the question she had been wanting the answer to for weeks.

"That's my husband?"

"Yes."

"What, again?"

"Did you love your husband?"

"Oh, yes. I'm sure I must have. Why? Is he upset about that?" Margaret propped herself up on her elbows as if she thought there was something she must do.

It was hopeless. Helen would never understand Margaret's feelings for the man. It was too late to get a real answer.

"No, he's not upset. He's dead," she said bluntly and was furious with herself for being so unfeeling.

But Margaret said, "When is the funeral? Should I be there?"

Helen treated herself to a chocolate milk shake at Massey's drugstore. Tomorrow Cal would face surgery. She might be gone as long as five days and when they returned she would be busy helping with his recovery, with less time to devote to Margaret. Her sister's mind would just shrink and become a husk of itself. Their relationship as sisters would be ended.

The milkshake did nothing to comfort her. It was just something cold sliding down her throat. She barely tasted it.

As she turned into the driveway, she looked over at the activity in the field. Cream Wiener and other concession stands had been brought in on a flat bed truck and were being unloaded. A large tent lay flat in the grass. Young shirtless boys were pounding tent stakes at the corners and assembling poles. Nancy Bannister, in jeans, a frilly blouse and a wide-brimmed straw hat was giving directions to men delivering porta-potties. She waved at Helen briefly and flashed a bright smile before returning her attention to the task at hand.

At home Helen pulled out the box and started reading the diary again. There were more nature poems, and then more of those poisonous verses:

> *Foolish me*
> *To love so hopelessly.*
> *Cold comfort,*
> *but comfort still*
> *upon his finest qualities*
> *to dwell.*

There were many others like this. It seemed to be a period in which Margaret was almost obsessed. What happened to the earlier, angry Margaret, who would have ripped the man's newspaper to shreds, and watched with satisfaction as his house and car were consumed by a tornado? Helen felt betrayed. How could Margaret give her love to someone who tried to estrange her from her own sister, from her parents, from herself?

But then her anger dissolved when she came across a poem written in blue ink over a background of hand-drawn pastel garden flowers.

> *My zinnia sister*
> *my orange and yellow*
> *and red and white*
> *and pink dear.*
> *My sister of every hue*

except blue.
My sister cheer.
My purple sage,
My coneflower, coral bell sister
My black-eyed Sue,
Perennial sister,
  without you near
  what would I do?

Helen hugged the book to her chest. Aloud, she cried, "Oh Margaret, Margaret, I tried, I tried …" Tears choked off the rest of her words.

Through the blurring tears she looked for more, anything to bring them back together. Toward the end of book #3 it was given to her, but not as she expected.

They claw and clutch
  the air.
But he's not there.
His innocence and
  sweetness out of reach.
No one, nothing to beseech.
He never will be given back.
Oh, how will they not
  disappear
  into this gaping lack?
How find a bridge with span
  enough to cross
  the abyss of their
  eternal loss?

She read it again and again. At the funeral, Margaret had written a poetic little eulogy in praise of Tommy, which Helen had put away among mementoes of him. But Margaret had never shared *this*.

"Cal!" Helen called down to him and started toward the stairs, the open book clutched to her. But she stopped. No, not right before his surgery. Later, maybe. This was not the time.

iii.

Helen called up Barb. "I know you're busy, honey, but if you get a chance, could you pay a visit to your Aunt Margaret while we're gone?" Helen felt guilty asking.

"Of course, Mom. Don't worry. I'll bring the kids over, too."

"Oh, I expect it would be unsettling for them."

"Well, I'll bring Cindy, anyway. She's matter-of-fact about the whole thing. She just treats Aunt Margaret as if everything was normal."

After Helen hung up the phone, she fixed herself and Cal a light dinner of sandwiches and salad. From midnight on, he wouldn't be able to eat anything until the operation was over. They waited nervously for the hospital to call and tell them what time the surgery was scheduled for. It was already seven P.M. and they hadn't heard yet. Cal gloomily predicted it would be postponed at the last minute.

"The surgeon probably got himself into a golf tournament."

But the call came, and they were told to arrive at the hospital at six the next morning. They set two alarm clocks. Neither Cal nor Helen slept much, and both were fully awake by three A.M.

They put Ornery out of the house before locking up. Barb would come by everyday to feed and water her in the barn.

The lock on the gate to their driveway had rusted and fallen off long ago. Cal said, "You watch. Cars are going to confuse this with the maze entrance and come in and chew up our drive."

"I'm sure the maze entrance will be well marked."

"It rains, we're going to have ruts a foot deep."

Helen felt anxious when they got on the interstate in the dark. The lights of oncoming semi-trucks were blinding. She was grateful when the sky began to lighten, but then she put the visor down and squinted against the rising sun. Her eyes didn't adjust as fast as they used to.

Cal was silent, morose, probably apprehensive, she thought. Picking up on his mood, she imagined a truck careening out of control, or a deer leaping out in front of them, the jamming of brakes, the car sliding sideways across the lanes, death coming to both of them before they could take advantage of this chance for Cal to have a pain-free life again.

It was a relief when they exited the interstate and drove the silent, early morning streets of Iowa City to the hospital complex. Cal seemed to come out of a trance and clothe himself in full curmudgeonly armor again, ready to do battle, any battle, no matter the absence of enemies. "Valet parking! Well, whoop-de-doo!" he commented as Helen handed over the keys to the parking attendant.

"It's cheaper than paying by the hour," she retorted. "Nothing fancy about it."

"It won't be so cheap when you have to tip the guy twenty percent to get your car out of hock."

Helen walked a little ahead, finding the elevator and the corridors to the Day of Surgery Room. Then it was all taken out of her hands, and she followed behind Cal as he was ushered into a curtained cubicle, asked to undress and put on a hospital gown. His blood pressure, temperature and weight were recorded. He peed into a cup. A nurse had him lie down on a gurney and she inserted an IV. The anesthesiologist and an aide came in soon afterwards to roll Cal away to the operating room.

Helen pressed Cal's hand as he was leaving. Already his eyes had a vague, sleepy look from the pre-surgery sedative. He didn't smile at her, and she leaned over and kissed his lips, with the sudden fear that this could be the last time she would see him alive.

Don't be silly, Don't be silly, she repeated to herself as she went off to the waiting room.

* * *

The last thing he remembered was lying on a warm pad and having a warm blanket laid on him. There was a big bright light overhead and people—many people—moving back and forth. A woman with a kind face put a hand on his shoulder and said in a far away voice, "How are you doing?" Next to her was a circular table saw. He thought, I've got something like that in the barn.

He came to slowly. Noises around him seemed muffled at first, as if a television were on in another room. He turned his head and saw Helen sitting beside him, smiling, and he noticed that several parts of him were hooked up to monitors.

Helen said, "How do you feel, honey?"

He thought about the question and drew a breath to speak when the agony hit him. Pain like fire, like a searing, steel torture device being driven into him. *My God, I made a terrible mistake. It hurts worse than ever.*

"Like hell," he croaked. His voice didn't sound like his own.

She stood up. "Remember, they said some people have a lot of pain at first."

He hardly heard her. All he could think of was, why did I let her talk me into it? How could I have been so stupid?

The anesthesiologist came into the room and said, heartily, "Are you feeling awake, Mr. Earlywine? Ready to go to your room?"

Cal nodded bleakly.

Aides wheeled him past doors and along corridors into a small private room and slid him from the gurney to the bed. It was a quick and gentle transfer, but Cal couldn't control a shout. He heard the nurse say to Helen, "We'll get him on the morphine pump now." The nurse leaned over Cal and guided his hand to a button on a gadget clipped to the bed sheet. "When you feel pain, just press the button. It's fixed so you can't overdose."

Morphine! Christ, now they were going to turn him into a drug addict. Could he hold out against it?

To Helen, the nurse said, "And get him to drink as much water as possible to keep the fluids moving through. We want to reduce the risk of infection. We'll remove the catheter tonight."

Catheter?

His mouth was so dry he could barely swallow. "Honey," Helen said, "would you like some water now?" He nodded, and she filled a paper cup from a pitcher on the bedside table, put a straw in it, and cranked the head of the bed up. She held the straw to his lips. I'm not a baby, he thought. I can hold a goddamn cup. But his hand was shaking from pain. He drank and asked for another.

Fluid was being pumped into him from a bag hanging off a stand next to the bed. Clipped to a finger was a flat, pinching, clothespin affair. A beeping monitor lit up with ominous flashing numbers, and a blood pressure cuff squeezed the heck out of his arm every three minutes.

Some time that evening, a nurse came in and drew a curtain around the bed. She told Helen, "If you wouldn't mind stepping outside for just a moment? I'm going to remove his catheter." Helen disappeared behind the curtain.

"Mr. Earlywine," she said in a loud voice, "I'm going to take the catheter out now. We want to get you urinating normally as soon as possible."

She snapped on gloves, and in a moment he felt the sting of alcohol, and she was fiddling with him down there. He gritted his teeth against a sharp burning sensation in his penis. When did they put the thing in? he wondered, and imagined the damage that could be done by shoving things in and out of such a sensitive organ.

The nurse pushed the curtains open and Helen reappeared. "All done," the nurse said. "Just press the call button if you need me." She squeaked out on rubber-soled shoes.

"Are you okay, honey?"

Okay? What in the hell was okay under these circumstances? No, he was not okay. And probably never would be again. A band of muscles in his low back was screaming, and he tried to pull the leg up on his good side to take some pressure off. Pain shot through his right hip and groin. He lay there panting and trying not to meet Helen's eye. She was leaning over the bedrail with a hand on his arm, her lips bunched up the way they did when she was worried.

He didn't want her there. He didn't want her to see his helplessness or notice his hopelessness either. Not now, when he was too demoralized to hide them.

"You want to go find me a newspaper?" he said.

"A newspaper! You feel like reading? I can turn on the television for you. There should be a remote here somewhere." She cast her eyes about the bed and the bed table.

"No, just a newspaper."

"Well, sure, if that's what you want. I'll go down to the gift shop and get one. Do you want more water before I go?" He did. He had never felt so thirsty in his life. He sucked down two cups of water through the bent straw before she left.

Almost as soon as she was gone, he had an urgent need to pee. He turned his head to see a blue urinal in a cellophane wrapper on the bed table. It might have been sitting in the next county for all the good it would do him. He couldn't reach it lying on his back, and he couldn't turn to get himself closer. Even if he could have gotten hold of it, he would have had to bend at the waist to get it into position. He knew without even trying that the pain of bending would be excruciating. He was going to have to call for help.

He lay there contemplating this necessity as his bladder seemed to fill up like a balloon about to burst. He recalled the snappy, matter-of-fact way the nurse had removed the catheter. Better someone impersonal like that than his own wife answering his call of nature. He pressed the call button and took deep breaths to prevent the release of urine. He waited for what seemed like five, ten minutes, but no one came. Contracting his sphincter muscles jacked up the agony in his hip and groin. He rang again, twice. Another five minutes went by and still no one came. He rang and rang, keeping his finger on the button.

Where, he wondered, was Helen? The gift shop was a pretty long distance from orthopedics, and today's papers were probably sold out at this hour. Maybe she got the car out of hock and drove to a convenience store to find one. Why had he asked for a newspaper in the first place? What a ridiculous request.

Then he thought maybe Helen had found a newspaper and was down in the cafeteria reading it over a cup of coffee. This struck him as very funny. The old man has to piss like a race horse, and she's reading Dear Abby in *The Iowa City Press Citizen*.

Dear Abby, My husband is an ungrateful old coot who doesn't listen to me even though I've never steered him wrong. He insisted I go off and buy him a newspaper, and now he's holding his water, about to burst, when he could be comfortably watching TV, as I suggested. What should I do with a guy like this?—Had It in Iowa City.
Dear Had It, Make him wait for his newspaper. He'll learn.

Cal started laughing. He heard his pain say, "Don't laugh. That hurts like hell," but it spoke without conviction, and at that moment he let his sphincter relax and the feeling of warmth spreading under him was second in bliss only to the relief of his bladder deflating.

Just then Helen returned with a newspaper under her arm.

"You got here just in time for the show," he said. "I pissed my bed. I guess you'll have to potty train me when we get back."

"What?!" She lifted the sheet. "You didn't have time to call the nurse?"

"Oh, I called. They must all be on a Code Red or Code Orange or whatever that code is where they have to drop what they're doing and jump on someone's chest." Helen looked around for the call button.

"It's no good calling 'em. I tried. You'll have to clean me up yourself, and then just put a diaper on me." He laughed again.

"Where is the call button?"

"Right there. It's practically part of my hand now."

"Good grief, Cal. That's the morphine button you've been pushing."

The nurse bustled in. "How are we doing in here?"

"Never better," said Cal.

Helen said, "He's gone and urinated in the bed. Where is the call button?"

The nurse found it hanging from the bottom bedrail.

"I'm so sorry. I forgot to put it on his bed." She turned to Cal. "I'm sorry, Mr. Earlywine. We'll get you cleaned up in a jiffy." She went out.

Helen leaned over and kissed him. "You're a little drunk, I think."

"Yeah. You want some?"

Off and on for the rest of the day and into the evening, they had him using his breath to raise a ball inside a plastic cylinder.

"It's to prevent fluid on your lungs after the anesthesia," the nurse told him.

They had put some kind of blow-up boots on him that drove him crazy inflating and deflating, to prevent blood clots, the nurse explained, matter-of-factly. Urinary infections, fluid on the lungs, blood clots. Jesus, what else could go wrong? He held fast against pushing the morphine button again. Every time he moved and felt the shock of pain, he gritted his teeth and gave himself a talking to about drug addiction.

Helen kept asking him how he felt, hovering, pushing the spirometer and cups of water at him. He tried not to be sharp with her, but it took all his self-control not to say, accusingly, "I'm worse off than before."

iv.

The next morning, the physical therapist had him doing exercises in bed, bending his knee and straightening it, wiggling his feet—practically impossible in the inflating boots that had been startling him awake all night. Every exercise was a torment.

The physical therapist came again later in the morning to get him out of bed.

Cal said, incredulously, "No way." They had removed the morphine pump and switched him to something much less effective called Percocet.

The therapist and an aide took off the inflating boots and disconnected him from the various tubes and wires. They snapped down the bedrails and supported his legs as they pulled him to a sitting position and swung the legs over the side.

Cal shrieked.

"Wait, wait!" Helen cried. "Are you sure he should be up so soon, with the pain he's in? Shouldn't we ask the doctor?"

The physical therapist replied jauntily, "Not to worry, Mrs. Earlywine. For some patients, it's totally normal to hurt a lot at first, but the sooner he starts moving, the faster he'll heal." The aide brought a walker over.

Between them, they got Cal on his feet. He stood, clutching the arms of the walker, feeling as if he might pass out, but they had him firmly under the armpits.

"Just stand there for a minute and get your balance, Mr. Earlywine, before you take any steps." Steps! He couldn't imagine it. After a minute or so, the therapist said, "Okay! Good! Let's take it slow. The therapy room is just across the hall. Just fifteen steps away. One foot at a time. You can do it."

Helen stood at the door, pressing her lips together and clutching herself by her elbows. Well, he wasn't going to be allowed to get back in bed, so what choice was there but to move his foot forward. It took fifteen minutes to get across the hall, one minute per step, the aide jollying him along as if he were a toddler.

"Way to go, Mr. Earlywine! Only five or six more and you're there."

When he got there he thought, how in hell am I going to walk fifteen steps back?

They kidded Helen that her husband was right up there on their list of most cranky patients, a list which included, not surprisingly, athletic coaches and physicians. No one needed to tell *her*. Cal seemed determined to believe the worst about everything that was done to him or that he was asked to do.

They didn't release him until Monday. It took that long for him to show he could get himself to the bathroom, go up and down the four stair steps in the PT room, and accomplish the other required "activities of daily living."

When she asked about his level of pain, all he would say was, "Considerable."

"But better than before?"

"Different."

Of course he would be sore, said the doctor, who came in every morning at six A.M., but the pain he was experiencing was the normal pain following invasive surgery.

"Sore!" Cal said, after the doctor and his entourage trooped out. "I'd like to know how the guy would describe his own pain after someone carved him open, wrenched his muscles apart, sawed away at his joint, and shoved a steel rod into his thighbone."

"Please!" said Helen.

She wished he would take the doctor's word for the success of the surgery and trust that he would heal. So far, he'd had no complications, no infections. All the medical staff said he was doing fine. Did he expect to be instantly restored to his forty-year-old body? They'd both read the literature. None of this recovery process should be a surprise to him.

She called for the car to be driven around to the front entrance and an aide brought Cal down in a wheel chair. They pushed the car seat back as far as it would go and lay a plastic bag on it to make it easier for Cal to pivot himself. The aide propped Cal's right leg up with a pile of disposable pillows. In the trunk was a toilet seat extender with rails, a grabber for pulling on socks, a package of Ted hose, a walker, and other "geriatric equipment," as Cal called it.

"Does it feel good to be headed home?" Helen asked as they pulled onto the freeway entrance.

"Good to be out of that torture chamber."

She turned on the radio, but on AM there was only the depressing commentary of political pundits and on the FM station an aria being sung by a particularly screechy soprano. She switched it off and they rode in silence.

As they got closer to their exit, she found herself dreading the moment when they would drive up to the house and she would help him out of the car and onto the porch. Picturing it, she felt the house looming there like one of those "humane" traps with a door that drops down as soon as the mouse or squirrel or raccoon ventures inside, imprisoning the creature in a space just big enough to turn around in. Whether or when the animal got released depended on someone remembering to check the trap.

They got back around 4:00. In her preoccupation with Cal and their homecoming, she had completely forgotten about the corn maze. Pulling up to the drive, she saw that the maze parking area was about two thirds full. Pretty good for a Monday, she thought. On Saturday, cars must have been lined up along the road for quite a stretch. Of course the place had only just opened, but still, maybe Nancy was right about the enterprise. It could bring in a decent income.

The gate to their driveway was closed, and fastened onto it was a wide yellow tape with black lettering: PRIVATE PROPERTY. MAZE ENTRANCE THAT WAY with a finger pointing to the left. That had to be Nancy's doing. She thought of everything.

Helen got out, opened the gate, drove through and got out again to close it. When she got back in the car and started up the drive, Cal said, "So from now until November we have to open and close the damn gate every time we go in and out of our own driveway."

Helen thought, "There's no pleasing the man!"

Somehow, their three-story house looked smaller and shabbier than before, as if she hadn't seen it since she was a child.

She undid her seatbelt, got out, and pulled the walker from the trunk. When she brought it around and opened the driver's side door, Cal glanced at the walker before taking the hands she held out for him. He said, "I guess you got your work cut out for you now," and the hangdog look on his face reminded her what all the belly-aching and hostility had been about. Just plain old shame and fear.

A little after eight, once they had eaten dinner, Helen left Cal resting on the bed that Gordon had helped her bring downstairs from Barb's old room. Then she walked to the maze.

The low sun was still hot, the air sultry and smelling of dust and the chamomile that grew along the fence line. In the distance, she could hear the eager cries of children, cars pulling out onto the gravel road, and a faint clang from a horseshoe toss.

It seemed happily familiar and right, just what summer should be. Hot and dusty, with people out in it not noticing that particular kind of discomfort, free of burdensome layers of winter clothing and the need to hug oneself against the cold and scurry back into the confines of four walls for interminable months. Here under the blue sky was that lovely, sweaty freedom that didn't end when the sun went down.

She thought of the yard and fields sparkling with fireflies at dusk and her children scampering about, each with an outstretched hand

and an empty jam jar, how they would race back to the front porch and offer their living lanterns for her or Cal to line up on the porch rail and admire, and when it was time to go in, the ritual release, more enthralling to the children than the lanterns themselves—the unscrewing of the lids and then a fireworks of lightning bugs fleeing into the night.

She entered through the parking area and walked across the grass toward the ticket booth. It was impossible to get a fix on the center of the field now. All of Nancy's "infrastructure" confused the proportions. Tommy could have fallen on the spot where a penned lamb and kid suckled on their impassive mothers, or maybe somewhere on the ground beneath the concession tent. Not in the maze itself, she reckoned. Those ten acres lay closer to the edge of the ravine.

The teenage girl pushed her seven dollars back at her.

"Oh no, Mrs. Earlywine. Mrs. Bannister says you and Mr. Earlywine can come in free anytime." The girl stamped the back of Helen's hand with a stenciled picture of a corn cob.

"Well," said Helen, pushing the money back at her, "thank you, but I'd like to contribute at least this once." The girl looked doubtful. "You don't have to tell Mrs. Bannister. *I* certainly won't."

"But it's too late to walk the maze now. It can take an hour or more, and we'll be closing at 9:00."

"That's all right. I'll walk the maze another time. Tonight I'm just taking a look around."

She meandered among the concessions and activities in progress, watched a teenage boy competing with his father at the horse shoe toss, was momentarily tempted to buy a Cream Wiener, thought better of it and bought corn on the cob instead, hot from the steamer and dripping butter. What was more delectable than Iowa sweet corn in July?

If she wandered long enough, would she eventually hit on the spot where Tom had fallen, and simply feel it? No, no. She didn't believe in that kind of intuition or superstition. Anyway, all twenty-three acres, the whole farm, in fact, contained Tom's memory, not just the spot where he died.

He would have gotten a big kick out of the carnival atmosphere here. He would have headed straight for the maze, with his little sister in hand. She could imagine him coming back again and again, bringing friends.

And Wayne? Here and there she noticed people waving fans in front of their glistening faces, the fans that bore Wayne's pretty drawing. He would have sampled all the activities in his quick way, like a businesslike bumble bee, disdaining some, becoming absorbed in others. Probably the maze itself would have struck his fancy, but he would have insisted on walking it alone.

She and Cal would come along with the children, Cal getting off a joke or two about the tractor ride on its circular track. "Somebody slap cultivators on 'em and send them kids down to the back forty where they can do me some good." But he'd say it with that chuckle in his voice and a crinkle at the corners of his eyes, with no bitterness. They were better days, those twenty years when the kids were growing up, even if she and Cal were strapped for money and Cal still had to do double duty for that mean, ungrateful father of his.

She left the maze park and walked back up the driveway toward the house. Salmon red twilight reflected off the windows, making the house look as if it were on fire inside. She hoped Cal would be so tuckered out from the long hours of waiting to be dismissed and from the drive home and the pain drugs, that he would be asleep when she returned and would sleep through the night, for once.

He was on his back, snoring. She went upstairs and brought out Margaret's books. She had bookmarked the poem about Tom's death, and she went back to it to read it again.

. . . Oh how will they not
disappear
into this gaping lack?
How find a bridge with span
enough to cross
the abyss of their
eternal loss?

Those last lines stirred her just as much the second time. Had they found that bridge? She thought not, and something of their love and happiness together had dissipated. From there she kept reading, looking for more about Tom. She read all the little poems, cramped in their margins, until she finished the third book, but there was nothing more about Tom's death, or his life. She went on to the fourth book, which contained more nature poems interspersed with those dismaying praises of the husband.

Since some of the nature poems recorded the passing of seasons, now she could mark time, using the poem about Tom's death as the marker, and estimate when each succeeding poem was written. Those in book #4 had come several years later. One of them puzzled her. What was she to make of it?

He will always blame himself
Though he was not to blame.
This man of heart
Drives to the hilt
His blade of shame
His knife of guilt.
Yet the criminal
   was merely chance.
Only a heartless man
   takes up a blameless
   stance.

More forgiveness? More benefit of the doubt? Did she truly believe her husband blamed himself for the cruel things he did to her? That he repented? Helen had never seen the slightest sign of it. She closed the book and went downstairs to check on Cal.

V.

Cal was able to swing himself in and out of bed and slowly walk to the downstairs half bath and kitchen when he needed to. He used the walker grudgingly.

"Use it," Helen said. "I am not going to have you falling down and undoing all that work!"

She had to leave him to go into town to shop and visit Margaret, but she didn't trust him to follow doctor's orders. Was he going to do his exercises while she was gone? He would resent her asking. She couldn't even get out of him how the pain was. It seemed like his hip felt better, but he didn't want to concede any improvement. Why that should be, she couldn't fathom.

Before she left, she went to the garden and picked a bowl of raspberries for him and left it on the kitchen counter.

"Help yourself. There's plenty more on the bushes. The half and half in the fridge is still good."

He thanked her, and she left him propped up in bed reading yesterday's newspaper.

She was afraid of what she would find when she returned to Margaret after six days away. The nurse greeted her as she walked past the nurse's station, and Helen stopped to ask if Margaret had been eating since she left. As it happened, Margaret had taken a shine to rice pudding, and they were making it specially for her everyday.

"Thank you." Helen pressed the nurse's hand in gratitude.

"Yes, I think we can keep her off the care unit for another few weeks." Helen withdrew her hand. "Or even months. One thing about her, she's never any trouble." Keep her off the care unit. She would soon be dying of starvation.

Helen continued down the hall with the image of Margaret lying hollow-cheeked, mute and fearful in the nursing home bed next to some inexplicable stranger.

Helen knocked, waited a few moments, and entered, to find Margaret lying down as always, staring up at the ceiling.

"Hi Sis, it's Helen," she called out with false cheer.

Margaret slowly sat up. "My goodness, I wasn't expecting you." She frowned. "What are we doing now?"

"Nothing special. I've just come for a visit."

"Well, it's nice to see you." Margaret picked at a piece of lint on the bedspread. She had some difficulty plucking it from the fabric, and when she finally succeeded, she held the lint between her fingers and looked around the room. "Where does this go?" she asked.

"I can put it in the wastebasket for you." Helen took it from her.

"My niece was here. You just missed her," Margaret said. Barb had visited the day before, but Helen felt heartened that the visit had left an impression. "Do you know her? She's my sister's daughter. Or maybe my brother's. Isn't that funny, I can't remember which."

Where did Margaret get the idea that they'd had a brother? On the other hand, she understood that she had a niece.

Margaret lay back again.

"Are you tired, Sis?" Helen said.

"Yes, I do feel a little tired. I'm sorry, but I think I'll just take a nap, if you don't mind."

Helen sat in the rocker and watched her sister sleep. She wondered what Margaret dreamed. Did she have nightmares? But her eyelids showed no activity, and with her skin so pale and the bones of her face and wrists so prominent, her chest virtually concave, she might have been a corpse, a preview of how she would look after she starved herself to death.

It was pointless to sit and watch her sleep, but it seemed cruel to leave, knowing that when she woke up, she would find herself all alone. Helen stayed another half hour.

When she left Margaret's room, she wondered how Norman was doing. He wasn't in the lounge or the dining area. She was just considering knocking on the door to his room when she caught a glimpse of him sitting in the sun on a lounge chair in a corner of the empty courtyard. He wore a seed cap with a visor, and someone had put sunglasses on him. His face was bright red and glistening with sweat.

"Whew!" he said. "She's a scorcher today."

Helen stood over him, shading him with her body.

"Norman, maybe it's time to go inside. The sun is pretty strong."

"You said it!" He roused himself out of the chair. "But I hate to leave before the game even gets started."

"How about watching it on TV, in air conditioning?"

He flashed her a dewy smile. "I won't say no to that!"

An aide came up as Helen led Norman into the lounge. "I was just coming to get him," she said, rather too emphatically, and Helen felt a twinge of worry. How long did they leave Margaret alone? Did she ever forget where her bathroom was, and after wetting herself be left for hours in damp smelly clothes before they thought to check on her?

Nancy Bannister visited that afternoon, bearing a cornbread and ground beef casserole. By the time Helen led her into the living room, Cal had swung his legs over the side of the bed and stood up.

Nancy seemed to take in the bed, Cal, and the walker at a glance.

"How are you doing, Cal?" Her voice dripped with empathy.

"Like a chicken with its head cut off," he said.

"That's great! I knew you'd be up and about in no time." She turned to Helen. "I can only stay a minute, but I wanted to report in and give you both something to celebrate after your ordeal. We're all just thrilled with the crowds we're getting at the maze. We've had over two hundred fifty customers in just three days."

Helen said that was good news and thanked her for the food.

"Have you walked the maze yet, Helen?"

"No, I haven't had time," she said. "We just got back yesterday."

"And it'll be a while before *you* can manage it, Cal. But—" Nancy shook a finger at him. "that should be your goal, before we shut down on November 1st, to walk the whole maze without assistance. That can be the carrot you hold out in front of yourself to speed up the healing process."

"You going to have the *New York Times* there for the occasion?" he said. "That'll really speed it up."

Don't put ideas into her head, Helen thought, seeing Nancy squint at something just behind her eyes, a sure sign the seed of an idea was about to turn into a mile-high beanstalk.

"He's kidding," she said.

"By the way," Nancy turned to Helen, "I wondered if you'd changed your mind—"

"Thanks again for the treats, Nancy." Helen grabbed her elbow and eased Nancy out the door.

In an undertone and with eyebrows raised knowingly, Nancy said, "I guess Cal doesn't know about France?"

"There's nothing for him *to* know."

But after Nancy left, Helen stood on the front porch, listening to the distant sounds of traffic and voices and laughter coming from the corn maze park. Was this to be the extent of her excitement—debating with herself whether to indulge in a Cream Wiener while she watched children jumping off hay bales and pumpkins being shot from a cannon? What would it be like to walk the streets of a city where everyone spoke a foreign language and most of the buildings were older than your own country? The skies in Iowa were big, the horizons far apart, but after seventy-one years of loyalty to these particular few square miles of place, wouldn't it be all right to push those horizons even farther? Much farther?

When she went back in the house, Cal said, "Changed your mind about what?"

She looked him in the eye and said, "Just one of her improvement schemes."

vi.

He felt like a wobbly-on-its-legs, newly-dropped calf nudged close by its mother. He grumbled at Helen for checking on him all the time. She hovered near the bathroom door when he did his business on that damn heightened toilet seat like a potty chair. She took up throw rugs, floor lamps and the umbrella stand in the front hall—any obstacle he might stumble over.

She kept urging him to do the exercises—bending the leg, straightening the leg, holding a pillow between his knees—the simplest actions anyone could do without thinking, but he could only do five or ten at a time before the pain made him want to stop, and he was supposed to push on to fifteen. He had to take stairs one by one, holding onto the walker and hauling it along. And buttocks squeezes! He was damned if he would squeeze his buttocks with her watching.

Half the time, he waited until she was out of the room or out of the house before he put himself through these torturous routines. It probably wasn't fair to her, leaving her to worry whether he was doing them at all, but he couldn't take her standing by with that encouraging smile on her face.

The thing was, though, he felt that the pain had, in fact, become different from before—not so lacerating, not so fundamental. There had been plenty of temporary pains in his life, from muscle strain, broken bones, crushed fingertips, and he thought this new pain might be akin to those—the pain that augured recovery.

He didn't want to get his hopes up. The doctor had told them to keep an eye on symptoms of infection and to avoid certain movements that could pop the new hip out of its socket. He still had to wear those god-awful white TED hose to prevent blood clots. And how was he supposed to know if the pain from his exercises was good for him or a sign of overexertion?

He was sick of himself. He was a damn hypochondriac, preoccupied with the smallest bodily changes and sensations. He couldn't stop himself from thinking about what it all meant—the possibility (nothing he could count on and probably unlikely) that the hip was actually going to heal and, just maybe, be like new again. To raise that hope with Helen, though, only invited disaster.

She was out of the house and he was doing his heel slides and his knee extensions on the bed with Ornery trying to sit on his chest when the phone rang on the TV tray table next to him. From the deep breathing and exertion, his voice must have sounded husky because Wayne said, hesitantly, "Is this . . . Earlywine's?"

"Who were you trying to call? The Earlybird Diner? Check out the blue plate special?"

"It didn't sound like you. How are you?"

"Couldn't be better. S'pose you want to talk to your mother? She's not here."

"No, not necessarily. I just had a question."

Cal let his knee slide back down and wondered if Wayne was going to hit him up for money. It would be a first.

"What question?"

He heard Wayne take a breath. Or was he taking a drag off a cigarette? Did he even smoke?

"I know you're recovering from surgery, so maybe it wouldn't be convenient, but I was wondering if I could come down there for a couple of weeks in August."

What in the world? Cal was flummoxed. He didn't think he had heard right.

"Come down here? You mean you and JoAnna and Jake?" He could only guess it was about the boy. "Jake wants to hang out on a farm or something?"

"No. It would just be me." Wayne sounded apologetic. "Jake will be at camp, and JoAnna wants to go up to Alaska to visit her sister."

This made no sense. "How come you aren't going with her?" More to the point, why would he want to spend the time anywhere near his father when he could enjoy two weeks of selfish bachelorhood at home? Were he and JoAnna having problems? But if they were, the last thing Wayne would do was admit it by coming home.

"She doesn't see her sister very often. They just wanted to be together."

"Then how come you don't stay home and have the house to yourself?"

Wayne cleared his throat. He sounded nervous.

"I was thinking about that corn maze. I want to get some ideas for a series about it, take some pictures."

Variations #5–10? How would that black earth and those fallen figures get worked into it?

"You need two weeks to look at the maze and take some pictures?"

"I'd just like to spend some time getting a feel for the place, the lay of the land. I might do some sketches down in the ravine, too, I don't know."

"They don't have ravines in Minnesota?"

Wayne got his hackles up then and sounded more like the old Wayne.

"Never mind. It was just a thought. If it's not convenient—"

"I didn't say it's not convenient. I got no problem with it. You should ask your mother. She's the one who'll do the work. I'm about as useful as a sloth."

"Uh . . . Okay," Wayne said, sounding hesitant again. "Will you have her call me?"

* * *

When he hung up, Cal pushed Ornery off his chest, slid his legs carefully over the side of the bed and stood. He took a few steps to the walker, but changed his mind and kept going on his own. He walked to the downstairs bathroom and urinated, and then tried to climb some stairs without the walker to stabilize him, but when he put the foot of his bad leg onto the first tread, the leg didn't want to hold him, and he clutched the stair rail and backed down again.

He hadn't asked Wayne exactly when in August he planned to come. Would the old man still be hobbling around like a toddler when his son arrived? He walked slowly back to the living room and retrieved the walker. He climbed five stairs up with it and five down again.

Helen seemed as surprised as he was.

"He wants to come for two weeks? In August?"

"That's what he said." She frowned, and he wondered that she didn't seem happier about it. "You don't want him to come?"

"Oh, of course I do," she said. "I'm happy to have him. It's just so out of the blue. He hasn't come to stay for more than a couple of days since he got out of high school."

Helen found Nancy by the maze park animal enclosure. She was wearing pedal pushers and sunglasses, like a young girl, and throwing feed to a flock of exotic chickens.

"Oh, Helen, I'm glad we ran into each other," she said. "I was just going to give you a buzz. Say, aren't these chickens exquisite? They're on loan from a farmer in Story County. They've become a great attraction. That fluffy white one over there is called a Silkie, and the one next to it—almost purple, isn't it?—is a Maran. That's a French breed. By the way, how's Cal doing?"

"Mending." Helen kept an even tone to her voice. "Now why were you going to give me a buzz, Nancy?"

Nancy set the feed sack on the ground and rubbed the grain residue off her hands.

"Well, you know, I'm still holding onto those two tickets to France I told you about. I just can't seem to find anyone who can take time off in August. I thought I had a taker in George Massey's wife, Clarinda. She was all set to go, but then her kids told her they'd been planning a big shindig for her and George's wedding anniversary." She took a breath. "I don't suppose you've changed your mind, have you?"

Helen shook her head in disbelief.

"Nancy, I just can't imagine that you would take it on yourself to call up my son and talk him into coming down here during those ten days so you could have a travel companion. That is . . . is just . . ." She didn't have words to express her outrage and still maintain some semblance of politeness. It was so interfering, so presumptuous, so devious . . .

Nancy's jaw had dropped.

"Wayne is coming down?" Then she smiled broadly as if surprised and delighted. "That's wonderful!"

"You had no right to guilt-trip him into it!" Helen's voice rose now, why should she *try* to be polite? "Did you think I'd agree to that trip under those circumstances? Just consider what light that would put Wayne's visit in, from Cal's point of view. Wayne doesn't come down of his own free will, but so his mother can go gallivanting off to Europe without a care."

Nancy shook her head vehemently. "No, no, no! I promise I never said a word to Wayne. I wouldn't dream of it!"

"Oh, you didn't say a word. So you e-mailed him then? Or sent him a letter?"

Nancy took off her sunglasses and put a hand on Helen's arm.

"Helen, please don't think such a thing. Good heavens, no. I've had no contact with Wayne at all. I *wouldn't*."

She was looking straight into Helen's eyes with genuine consternation. Was it possible that she had nothing to do with it, that Wayne's request was just what he said it was? Or that it was even some kind of peace offering, a gesture of caring for his father, disguised so Cal would accept it? The timing seemed just too much of a coincidence. And yet, as devious and determined as Nancy could be, Helen had never known her to out-and-out lie to her face.

"You didn't ask Wayne to come here for a visit right at the time of this trip you're planning?"

"Helen, you give me a Bible. I will swear on it."

Helen didn't know what to say or what to think. And now, all of a sudden, the idea of that trip to France crept uninvited into her imagination. If Wayne was there at home, available to drive Cal into town or deal with an emergency . . . But if Cal didn't suspect Nancy of conniving Wayne into coming, he would surely think she, Helen, had talked him into it. *If you wanted to go off to France, why didn't you just say so. Go! But I won't have Wayne hanging around here babysitting me. I don't _need_ a babysitter!*

That was how he would see the whole thing, no question about it. And somehow, knowing what his reaction would be, she felt tired of it all, fed up. She'd had it up to here with these two men and their stubborn clinging to pride and grievances.

"Well," she said to Nancy, "as to that trip, I'll have to think about it."

vii.

He did his exercises diligently, pushed through the pain, and everyday woke up with a little less of it. Now she was after him to be careful and not *over*do, but he was damned if he would still be clutching a walker when Wayne arrived. And those humiliating TED hose he peeled off one day and threw in the trash.

By the end of the second week, on Friday, he could walk to the barn and back if he took it slow. When he returned to the house after this excursion, she was waiting for him, looking nervous.

"I want to talk to you about something," she said. She took off her apron absently, which seemed like a bad sign, somehow.

They sat down in the living room. He was breathing heavily from his exertions.

"Do you want a glass of water?" She rose to get it.

"I'm fine. What's this 'something'?"

She looked down at her hands before raising her eyes to meet his. Her mouth was grim. He wondered if it was to do with Margaret. Maybe she wanted his advice about whether she should let her sister stop eating entirely. But he was not the one to make that call.

She took a breath and began.

"A couple of months ago, Nancy Bannister invited me to go with her on a trip she won to France, all expenses paid. For ten days. In August." She paused.

"To France?" His first thought was, who would want to go to all that trouble?

"Of course I said no. I knew you would be recovering from surgery, you wouldn't be able to drive yourself anywhere, Barb would be in Colorado. It was out of the question." Her voice was high and breathy.

"With Nancy Bannister?!"

"I put it out of my mind right away, Cal. I didn't even think about it after that." The apron was on her lap, and she was twining the apron strings around her fingers. "But then we had that call from Wayne, and I got to thinking that if he was here . . ."

His mind was cranking slower these days, but not *that* slow.

"That Bannister is one hell of a piece of work."

She dropped the apron strings. "I don't believe Nancy put him up to it. I really don't."

"Well, I hope to hell *you* didn't get him to make up that whopper about coming down here to 'get the lay of the land.'"

"It's not a whopper. Nancy looked me straight in the eye and told me she had nothing to do with it. She said she'd swear on a Bible."

"You trust the word of a woman in league with the devil? Does she carry a Bible around in her purse for every such occasion?"

"No, Cal, really. I believe her. I think the timing is just a coincidence.

Wayne already contributed art to the maze project. Why wouldn't he get interested in it? And this happens to be a good time for him to come, when he's free and just a few weeks after it opened."

He wasn't buying it, even if she was. Wayne had listened to Bannister and decided to make the sacrifice for Helen—not for his dad, of course—that was obvious since he never once called the whole time his old man was in the hospital. Not so much as a get well card from him personally, he had JoAnna do the honors.

"And you want to take off for France while he's here."

"Not necessarily. It's just a thought."

She did want to go, that was obvious.

It gave him a funny feeling to think of it. In all their years together, they had never been apart except when she went to weekend teachers meetings, and he hadn't liked it even then. There was something dismal about the house when she was away from it overnight. He could see a person like Wayne wanting to be on his own, but not him.

"Well, go," he said. "I'm not standing in your way. If you think you can tolerate ten days of nonstop Nancy Bannister, you're a better man than I am. But Wayne is not coming here. I won't have him playing like he's being an artist when he's really a nurse maid and none too happy about it, I'm sure."

"You know, last spring, after you and Wayne went fishing on the pond, I thought the two of you were getting along a little better. He sent you those nice lures for your birthday."

"And that was the end of that. Never came for Thanksgiving or Christmas, and God forbid he'd call the old man in the hospital."

"How was the conversation with him when you thanked him for those lures?"

"What do you mean?" Cal heaved himself off the sofa and pulled his sweatshirt over his head. "It's too damned hot in here."

"Do you remember what you said and what he said when you thanked him?"

Cal folded the sweatshirt and laid it on the arm of the sofa. "Well,

I didn't exactly thank him."

"Not *exactly*? Either you thanked him or you didn't. Did you thank him?"

"No," Cal said irritably. "It slipped my mind."

"Slipped your mind? After some thirty years Wayne sends you a peace offering and you fail to thank him for it? Did you mention it at all?"

Cal went over to the wall and turned the thermostat down. "I figured you'd take care of it."

"Why would I thank him for a present he sent to you? And why would you think that would satisfy your obligation?"

Cal felt squirmy, like a kid caught skipping school. "You're the one that handles that kind of stuff," he said. He knew it sounded lame.

"What 'stuff'?"

"Christmas letters and . . . I don't know. That kind of stuff."

Now Helen was on her feet and standing with her hands on her hips. "What do Christmas letters have to do with it? Are you telling me you failed to thank Wayne for those lures, and you can't understand why he didn't come for Thanksgiving or Christmas—"

"He never in his life sent a card or made a phone call on my birthday, and then out of the blue, for God knows what reason, he gets it in his head to send the old man something. What was I supposed to say?"

"What about, 'Thanks for the lures, Wayne. I appreciate it.'"

Cal scratched his head and looked out the window toward the ravine. "I'm not sure he didn't mean it as an insult."

"An insult!" Helen came over, grabbed his arm and turned him around. He pulled his arm away.

"Some kind of jibe about the old-fashioned stuff I have in my tackle box."

Helen frowned at him. "You said yourself those lures were expensive. Wayne does not have the money to throw around on expensive insults."

"I don't know about that."

Helen walked back and flopped down on the couch. She gave him a look of disgust. "For heavens sake, Calvin Earlywine, use your common sense. If it was that hard for you to call him up and say a simple thank you, think how hard it was for him to send you a present." She shook her head. "You two are as alike as pigs in a litter. You don't just *look* alike, you're equally pig*headed*."

Cal moved over to his recliner, sat down in it and lay back. "Well," he said, "it's too late to thank him now."

"And why is that?"

"I'm not going to say, 'By the way, thank you for those lures you gave me ten months ago.'"

"What would be wrong with, 'Wayne, I'm sorry I never thanked you for the birthday present you sent me. It meant a lot to me, but I just didn't know how to say it.'"

Cal winced. "Sounds like something you'd hear on one of those soap operas."

"Well, if you want to be estranged from your son for the rest of your life, I can't stop you." She put her apron back on. "That's that then. I'll tell Nancy no. I'm not going to leave you here alone. But you're going to have to call Wayne and tell him not to come." And she walked into the kitchen to fix dinner.

He sat on the sofa listening to the sounds of bowls and pots and pans and utensils clinking and clattering, not emphatically or angrily, just as usual. The cat jumped up on his lap, and he stroked her firmly from her forehead to the base of her tail, the way she liked it. She turned on her motor and pushed against his hand. Why *hadn't* he picked up a phone and called Wayne to thank him? Helen was right to be disgusted with him. But he still couldn't bring himself to do it.

He thought about Helen going away for ten days, to a different world, across a whole ocean, in a foreign country where she would see and experience things that might change her in some way, make her restless, maybe, glad to be away from him. Or was she already restless, and that was what made her consider taking the trip, even if it meant putting up with that Bannister woman?

Nancy didn't seem to have the same grating effect on Helen that she did on him. Helen was more tolerant. And Nancy did do a lot of traveling. It was possible she might even show Helen a good time, and Helen would come back dissatisfied with her life at home, especially being married to an old codger who wasn't worth much anymore.

The cat rolled onto her back and stretched out to have her belly rubbed.

"You got nothin' to worry about, do you, Ornery, you lazy pest? No worries." Her belly fur was as silky as milkweed down. "You got nothing at all to worry about."

After a while he limped to the kitchen and stood in the doorway.

"Well, maybe you're right about Wayne," he said. "You can't read that boy's mind. I guess just because it's never happened before, it doesn't mean it *couldn't* happen. If he wants to come down—for whatever reason—let him."

She gave him a look over her shoulder.

"Anything to avoid calling him?" she said, and turned her back to him again.

"Guess so."

"Well, I won't go on the trip whether he comes or not."

"Yes, you will."

"No, I won't. It wouldn't be right."

"I dare you to. If you don't come back ready to strangle that woman, I'll beg her for that lemon bar recipe and cook you up a batch."

"You can't cook."

"That's right."

She turned around and gave him a studying gaze. "Well, as long as we're daring, if you and Wayne manage to get through ten days without giving each other visible physical injuries, I won't force you to attend an art show for a year."

"Two years. And *you* make up the excuses."

"All right. But don't lay bets in town on how many days I go before bailing on Nancy."

"What would be the point? It's a sure bet she'd have a tight hold on your return ticket."

She knew it wasn't fair dealings. She had manipulated Cal into consenting, and she didn't feel good about it. But the more she let the trip to France play on her imagination, the more excited she became. She had only traveled by plane once in her life—to a cousin's wedding in Montana. The experience was exhilarating—the dramatic, scary roar of takeoffs and landings and the story book view of towns and countryside from so far above. Even the thought of a long, fourteen hour flight thrilled her. She pictured the airplane seat carrying her through the air, literally above it all, like a moving cloud, and she, like a cloud, continually transforming as she was propelled eastward.

She called and left a message for Nancy on her cell phone and then wandered around the house for a while, waiting for Nancy to call back. Half the time she was making mental lists of clothes and toiletries she would pack and tasks at home to get done, and the other half she worried that Nancy might have found a different traveling companion since their talk at the animal enclosure.

She slipped her own cell phone in her apron pocket and went out to cut chives and pick sweet corn and tomatoes for dinner. As she stood breaking the corn cobs from their laden stalks and setting them in her basket, surrounded by the jungle of vegetables she had brought forth from seed over a season of hoeing, sowing, weeding, and watering, it hit her. She had no passport.

She stopped picking and clutched the basket to her breast in dismay. No passport.

Of course she wouldn't have one. Why would a farmer's wife who never had a chance to go anywhere need one? The trip was scheduled for August twelfth, thirteen days away. She remembered how long it took Wayne to get a passport. He was eighteen, and he swore he was going to be prepared to leave the country after Ronald Reagan got elected. He never used it, but it took many weeks to be issued. Today, with all the to-do about homeland security, it might even take months.

For a while she stood there trying to accept the disappointment. All along, the trip was not meant to be. Even without considering Cal, there was Margaret to think of. She owed it to her sister to stay near. In those ten days Margaret would have no one familiar to visit her. She might even die of malnutrition.

Helen's eyes filled with angry tears. She cried aloud and flung the basket to the ground, the corn and chives flying out and resting in the patch of heart-shaped squash leaves. "It's not fair," she cried. "Not fair!" Anger boiled up in her at Cal, at Margaret, at Wayne, at Nancy for being able to get away any time she wanted on a whim, at that tantalizing invitation, which Helen saw now as condescending. Nancy could see how limited her life was and felt sorry for her.

From her apron pocket the silly ring tone that Barb had set up for her—the opening bars of "Some enchanted evening, you will meet a stranger . . ."—made her jump. She took a breath and cleared her throat to get the weepiness out of her voice.

"Sorry, I didn't call back sooner, Helen. I've been on the other line with my daughter. What can I do for you?" Nancy sounded distracted.

Helen didn't know what to say now. She had been going to accept the offer, but what was the point? She felt embarrassed. Who but a hick farmer's wife wouldn't have a passport? Nancy must have taken it for granted that everyone had one. If only Helen had applied for it back when the proposal had first been made—just in case, why not?—she might have had it by now. But maybe the daughter had changed her mind anyway and was going to send one of the kids to France with grandma and none of it mattered.

"Well, I feel foolish," Helen said, bitterly. "I'd been thinking about taking you up on your offer, but I just now remembered I don't have a passport, so I'll have to decline. I'm sorry."

"You're taking me up on it? That's just great, Helen! I'm glad it worked out."

As always, Nancy heard what she wanted to hear. Helen felt the knife twist in her heart to have to repeat the news of this insurmountable obstacle. Emphatically, she said it again.

"I don't have a passport!"

"Helen," Nancy said dismissively, "don't you know you can get a passport online nowadays in twenty-four to forty-eight hours? It's nothing like the way it used to be. I'll come over and show you how to do it. I can come by this afternoon if it's convenient."

Helen pressed the cell phone to her ear. "What do you mean? Twenty-four to forty-eight hours? Are you sure?"

"Oh yes. This is a different era, Helen. We've got to keep up. How about if I come over around 4:00? I'll be at the maze then anyway."

Helen got down on her knees and retrieved from the squash patch the scattered chives and corn cobs. Then she picked a few tomatoes. Her hands smelled pleasantly earthy and pungent. She carried the basket of vegetables into the house and set it on the kitchen table, where it made a colorful still life.

AUGUST

i.

BARB AND GORDON and the kids were off to Colorado. Helen broke the news to Wayne that she was going to take the opportunity of his visit to go to France. All he said was, "Have to get that far away from the storms, huh?" She knew he meant the storms he anticipated between Cal and himself. She chose to ignore the remark.

Now she turned her full attention to getting ready for the trip. She would leave in eight days, and there was so much to do. She had to cook and freeze ten days' worth of meals for Cal and Wayne and make space for Wayne's things in Wayne's and Tom's old bedroom. Cal insisted that she get the spare bed out of the living room, now that he could take stairs, however slowly. She didn't argue, but imagined how easily he might take a tumble coming down.

She felt compelled to visit Margaret every day without fail to make up for the time she would be gone. Even though Margaret wouldn't notice her absence, she hated thinking of her being alone for such a long time, she was looking so fragile. But an aide had discovered that in addition to rice pudding Margaret would sometimes eat apple sauce, so Helen boiled up a big pot of it from fresh apples and brought it over to Oakridge.

At first she hesitated to tell Margaret about the upcoming trip in case it would distress her, if only in the moment of hearing it. Yet she thought it would be wrong to withhold the information.

"To France?" Margaret looked up blankly from the small bowls of pudding and applesauce she was studying on a tray table in her room. She held a spoon in her lap as if she didn't know what to do with it. "That's nice, isn't it? A good time for you."

Helen felt a pang of guilt. She touched Margaret's arm.

"I wish you could come with me."

"Now, where?"

"To France."

"Oh yes. I've never been there. Have I?"

"No, but you've always enjoyed those French Impressionist paintings. I'll see some originals while I'm in France. In museums. You remember The Louvre?"

Margaret pursed her lips with amusement.

"Well, of course. Everyone knows The Louvre."

So here at least was a topic of conversation to interest Margaret even if it ended up sending them in circles.

She brought the travel pictures Nancy had printed from the internet—chateaux in the Loire Valley, the Eiffel Tower, the Seine, Notre Dame Cathedral. Everyday they had the same discussion about the pictures, but they always seemed to spark a little interest in Margaret.

One day, Margaret let the pictures drop from her hand and turned to Helen with a look of anxiety.

"Are you leaving Cal?" she said.

Helen felt her face go red, "No, no. I'll only be gone ten days." She couldn't look Margaret in the eye. "He wouldn't want to go," she added emphatically. *Couldn't* go. She didn't like to tell Margaret she was abandoning her husband for so long while he was still recovering from surgery. Then the happy thought struck her that Margaret had remembered Cal's name for once. She clasped Margaret's little wrist, the wrist bone protruding so prominently under the skin as to make her appear no more than a dainty skeleton in a thin wrapping of silk.

"Cal and Wayne will visit you while I'm gone," she said.

"He'll miss you if you go away," Margaret said earnestly. "It would pain him."

"Oh," said Helen, hiding as best she could a sudden feeling of resentment, "he'll probably be glad to be rid of me for a little while."

"Who?"

As she thought about Margaret's comments regarding Cal, she worried that the pain her sister meant was Margaret's own isolation and helplessness. At home, Helen went once again to the diaries. She pulled all the books out, even the few she had already looked through, and fanned the pages to marvel at the pattern of tight, precise lines and little sketches that flipped past her eyes. The work of a lifetime. She tried to imagine herself accomplishing even one verse or one of these drawings. She could sweat over it for a week, and she still wouldn't be able to come up with anything close to the products of Margaret's imagination. She realized that Margaret's daily life in the home of that dreadful husband was not unremittingly grim after all. Margaret had spent her days producing her myriad of creations while the man was at work, sometimes away for several days. What pleasure it must have given her!

When Margaret was a child, she would become so absorbed in whatever fanciful endeavor swept her up, that she would have to be called repeatedly to hurry off to school or come to dinner. 'Helen, tell your sister she can finish that tomorrow,' was their mother's exasperated command. And Helen would tear Margaret away with difficulty, especially because she herself would get caught up in the wonder of what was revealing itself on the piece of paper her sister hunched over.

It was in a different light now, that Helen viewed the diaries. For the first time since starting to read this enormous outpouring, she felt unequivocally happy about it. In spite of the abuse, Margaret had done what artists had always been driven to do, what Wayne had gone head to head with Cal over. Margaret's was no more a wasted life than the life of Emily Dickinson or any of those writers she had taught in high school—Edna St. Vincent Millay, Virginia Woolf, George Eliot, those women who had suffered from shyness or depression or the social and legal restrictions on women. They always found a way to express themselves.

She read now with a sense of awe, and couldn't stop. She read until her neck ached from bending in to decipher the small, close handwriting. After a while she found herself skimming the poems, in the same way she glanced briefly at the paintings in the Nelson Art Museum when she and Cal had gone down to Kansas City for Wayne's graduation. Rooms and rooms of art, so much that it soon became too difficult to fully focus on any one painting. Scanning Margaret's poems in this way, she almost missed it, a poem that made her put her hand on her heart as she read it again.

> *She pleads for the impossible.*
> *For me to daily breathe the precious air*
> *that he has just exhaled*
> *and sit around a table where*
> *he eats and reads the paper, talks of rain.*
> *Impossible for me to feign*
> *indifference, stifle what would make them*
> *drop their knives and forks, and stare.*
> *She pleads for the unthinkable,*
> *completely unaware.*

She read it a third time. What "she" could there be in Margaret's life but her sister? What "plea" but to divorce her husband and come to live under the same roof as Helen and Cal. But to Margaret it had been "unthinkable." Unthinkable because Margaret had been in love with Cal.

Helen heard Cal moving about downstairs. He bumped into something and cursed. He was in a mood. She lay the book open on the bed, walked to the window and looked out at the honey locusts in the back yard. They had been there since before she and Cal came to live in the house. The children had loved to rattle the long, brown, sickle-shaped seed pods that fell in a circle around the base of the trees. Vicious three-inch thorns dropped off those locusts as well. They had always meant to get rid of them, but the children protested, and the trees stayed.

She sat down again and read the poem a fourth time. She could see no other interpretation. Did Cal know? Did Margaret tell him? If so, did he ever reciprocate? Her heart fluttered. She remembered all those abject poems of adoring, unrequited love—for the abusive husband, Helen had thought. It would take some doing to find those poems again, buried amongst all the others. She wished she had bookmarked them because now they were not clear in her memory. There was one about a crescent moon with its back turned to an adoring little star, and another with a heart persisting in only "one romancer." At least in the beginning, then, her love for Cal had been one-sided, but did it stay that way?

Now she recalled the poem about a man "with heart" who feels guilt. Where was it? She tore a piece of paper from a tablet on the dresser and stuck it into the page she had been reading. Then she spent another half hour doggedly leafing back through the earlier volumes, searching the cramped lines, until her eyes finally lit on it again.

> He will always blame himself
> though he was not to blame.
> This man of heart
> drives to the hilt
> a blade of shame
> a knife of guilt.
> Yet the criminal
> was merely chance.
> Only a heartless man
> assumes a blameless
> stance.

It was Cal who had the heart, unlike Margaret's heartless husband. The guilt, the shame, the mere chance—did they refer to an unexpected forbidden act of love? And the other poem—*She pleads for the unthinkable, completely unaware.* But Cal, too, was to have dropped his knife and fork and stared. Because he would have been surprised? Or exposed.

"Helen?" Cal was calling from the bottom of the stairs. She marked this second page and closed the book. She walked out into the hall and looked down.

"What?"

He must have heard the sharpness in her voice because there was a pause, and then he said, "Never mind."

It didn't seem possible for her beloved Margaret to have "seduced" Cal or vice versa—that tired old television scenario. It was ridiculous to concern herself with such an idea. Even if they had been selfish enough to betray her, which she could not imagine, they would never have had the opportunity.

But she remembered that Margaret's husband had traveled for his job, and she herself was at work during the school year. After Barb graduated from high school, no one was at the farm in the day time except Cal. Oh, but it was crazy to think such a thing. Cal never had a minute to spare in those days. He often worked a shift at the seed company, ran over to his dad's to help, came home to farm at night by tractor light, and dropped into bed exhausted.

She stood at the top of the stairs biting her thumbnail. Suddenly she felt overwhelmed with dread. She sat down on the top step and put her head in her hands. How would she bear this sick, gloomy man if he had betrayed her with her own sister? And what would happen to all the sweet memories of her childhood with Margaret? To say nothing of the daily grind—yes, she had to admit it was a grind—taking care of the two of them. And caring for them, not just *taking* care of them.

She thought of that novel she had once taught in high school—what was the name of it?—*Ethan Frome*—about a husband trapped in marriage to a mean-spirited, complaining wife. The man and his wife's niece fall hopelessly in love, and the two of them resolve to kill themselves by riding a sled down a steep hill and steering into a tree. Instead, they are both crippled, and the wife ends up caring for them for life as they become more and more embittered and demanding. The students always sympathized passionately with the star-crossed lovers.

She shook her head. *She* hadn't been a mean-spirited, complaining wife. She had loved Cal and Margaret whole-heartedly.

What would be left to count on if you couldn't travel back in memory to the good times with those you had loved for so long, the better days that lingered in your consciousness and made these hard times bearable? If those good times had only been an illusion, what then?

She lay her hands in her lap. They were inky and dusty from handling the pages of Margaret's diaries. She got up and went to the bathroom. There were smudges on her face where she had pressed her fingers to her forehead. She washed, and watched the dark soapy water become clear again as she rinsed and it flowed to the drain. A little of her composure came back.

There was absolutely no reason to suppose anything had gone on between Margaret and Cal. Everything pointed to an undeclared, one-sided love, understandable in a lonely, mistreated woman. She couldn't fault Margaret for simply loving Cal. Come to that, she herself had found Margaret's husband attractive when he was first courting her sister, before he showed his true colors. It was perfectly natural. She would stop making assumptions. There was too much to do before the trip to let this worry her. In any case, if something had gone on between them, it was long in the past. And Margaret's past—lost to her in a tangle of diseased brain matter—didn't even exist anymore.

ii.

She couldn't let it go. Never in her life had she felt a moment's jealousy. She was not that kind of person. But this! The two people most important to her apart from her children! The uncertainty had gotten hold of her and wouldn't let go no matter how often she told herself she was being absurd.

In spite of all she had to do to get ready for the trip, she felt compelled to keep going back and combing through every word of Margaret's prodigious writings to find conclusive evidence—proof—that Cal and Margaret had not engaged in a relationship. It was only that she didn't want her one extravagance—this wonderful trip to France, which she had started to look forward to like a little child—to be in any way marred by even the slightest nagging doubt.

Every spare minute she slipped up to Barb's room and pulled the goose neck lamp down close to the print and read with an eye as critical as a scholar's, searching for telltale metaphors, similes, and ambiguous references—all the more difficult because of the way it appeared, in Margaret's tiny script. Many of the poems looped sideways in circles around the four margins, while others marched vertically, shoulder-to-shoulder and head to foot. There were poems in the white spaces between paragraphs and curling around the illustrations. It was hard to tell where some poems began and others left off. And then there was the sheer volume of the work—multiple poems on every page, two to three hundred pages in each of the thirteen folio-size books.

Her eyes blurred. Her head ached. Her back became stiff, and she worried what Cal would make of her disappearing for such long periods of time upstairs. Maybe she should simply ask Cal outright. If something had gone on between them, he would not be able to lie. But if nothing had happened, he would be astonished, and she would appear more than just foolish. She would reveal herself as a certain kind of woman, one who nurtured obsessive fantasies and paranoia, one who didn't have anything better to do than conjure up slights and wounds. She was not that kind of woman. Yet she kept going back to the books. She simply had to be one *hundred* percent certain of what she was almost sure she was ninety-nine percent certain, that nothing had happened.

Eventually, backtracking, she came across the poems that had struck her earlier: "Foolish me, to love so hopelessly;" "How the heart persists without answer, refuses to desist though it beats in only one romancer." Nothing there to suggest that Cal returned Margaret's love. But nothing to say that Margaret hadn't declared it, which would have been a betrayal in itself.

The France thing was taking all his wife's attention. Between her trips to town to do last minute errands and look in on her sister, plus daily phone calls to that Bannister woman and disappearances for long spells upstairs where he supposed she was organizing clothes to pack and getting Wayne's room ready and such things, they barely had two minutes together. And when they did, she seemed distant, probably distracted by all those tasks on her list. He was sure the prospect of missing *him* was not on that list. She hardly noticed the progress he was making. He could walk halfway down the drive and back with just a cane now.

At least she had stopped getting after him about going to the corn maze. When they first returned from the hospital, she wanted to hang the handicap sticker from the rear view mirror and drive up through the parking area, right up close. But he had no stomach for making a spectacle of himself limping around the place with a walker or a cane. She didn't bother him about it anymore. That was okay. He could do without her cheerleading. It had gotten old, fast.

Still, he had to wonder why she'd given it up. Maybe she was just tired of his bellyaching, tired of being around him 24/7. The trip to France would be good for her, sure. He could understand that. And what did they say—"Absence makes the heart grow fonder"?

Or else, "Out of sight, out of mind."

While she was gone, he would make a list of the projects and chores he'd had to give up this year, pick the ones that were do-able and have them done before she got back, to surprise her. Nothing requiring a ladder, of course. He wasn't that stupid. But something like scraping and painting the fence. He'd have to do it himself, no point in counting on help. Wayne would be going through the motions of "getting a feel for the place." But he wasn't going to have his son thinking he was a lay about.

Since spring, Helen had been mowing the acreage. It was a big job, and he hated to see her doing the whole thing herself. He would take back the chore as soon as she was gone. The old riding tractor mower had a gas pedal, which would cause strain on his hip, but he could take it easy, do the job over a couple of days, making sure he stopped for frequent breaks. It wouldn't be like driving a car into town. And when she came back, she could rest from her trip. No overgrown lawn to mow.

He did his sitting knee extensions, his standing hip extensions, his buttock squeezes and wall slides, and walked up and down stairs, and the hip kept improving, no doubt about it, but she didn't seem to appreciate the fact.

It was already Monday the eighth. She had only two days to finish perusing Margaret's diaries before Wayne came on the tenth, and four days before the trip.

> *He leaves his inmost cares unsaid.*
> *Instead, binds his wounds in jokes.*
> *Stubborn. A cat who won't sit prettily*
> *on anybody's knee*
> *until it will, and only then.*
> *But that is his integrity.*
> *A fair trade for duties*
> *he fulfills with love,*

without display.
A most solid gentleman.
Salt of the earth, you bet.
What you see is what you get.

Well, this was high falutin' praise indeed, and misguided, Helen thought. Margaret hadn't had to live with that stubborn cat. But . . . 'the duties he fulfilled with love, without display' . . . yes, that was Cal. 'A most solid gentleman.' She was right about that.

Hale to the Extensor Carpi Radialis Longus,
Brachioradialis, Supinator.
I salute you, Forearm Triumvirate,
I prostrate my heart to the grandeur
of that subtle ripple
every time you lift the cat.

Another cat image, for goodness sake. But whose forearm did she salute? Her own? Margaret never had a cat.

She thought of the dense musculature of Cal's arms, hard and defined even now in old age when his skin had turned slack. A farmer's arms, capable and strong. She had relied on them for so many things. Carrying the overgrown sleeping child up to bed. Bringing enough firewood to fill the box in just one trip. Clasping her tightly to his chest, then lifting and turning her until she lay atop him, and she was never a dainty feather weight, but felt like one in his arms.

She was terrified. *Don't let this have happened. I couldn't stand it.* She pushed the book away and went to the window to look out across the ravine. How tangled it was—littered with fallen old growth trees that had finally succumbed to harsh winter winds and the rot of repeated rainfalls and lightning strikes.

Due west beyond the ravine and out of sight, Margaret lay on her single bed inside the low, tidy, tediously decorated building on the shadeless parkway of newly poured cement. This was the sister she must love unconditionally. Nothing should change that. Nothing. No matter what. And her husband, 'his inmost cares unsaid,' pushing himself recklessly, not to be seen weak in the eyes of his bitter, judgmental son. She must not let one percent of possibility sabotage her instinct, her reflex to cherish him.

In spite of this resolve, she went back to the books and didn't notice that the sun was almost down until it was so dark in the room she couldn't see to read and had to switch on the light. She had come to the beginning of the eleventh volume, two to go now, and the opening lines brought tears to her eyes.

> *Love at arm's length, or miles,*
> *unconfessed,*
> *unhallowed by a pledge*
> *or kiss,*
> *nonetheless, is its own bliss.*

In relief, she wept, for here it was, the one hundred percent certainty. *"Love . . . unconfessed."* And once she had wiped away her tears and could see to read again, she found in the very next poem, as if to confirm it, as if Margaret had anticipated Helen's fear and hurried to leave no doubt in her sister's mind:

> *I would not have him*
> *faithless, even if I could,*
> *for how so love this man*
> *were he not so good?*

Helen returned the last two books to the box. No need to read more.

iii.

The day before Wayne was due to arrive, Helen came into the living room looking serious. She sat on the sofa across from the high back chair where Cal was doing his leg lifts. She said, "Cal, I'd like you to promise me that you'll go and visit Margaret often while I'm gone. Wayne can drive you."

Cal lowered his leg and frowned.

"She won't even know me. And anyway, she never liked me much. Wayne's the one she got along with."

"It would be nice for Wayne to visit, too. It would do her good to see both of you."

"Well . . . but what do I say to her? And Wayne's not any too good with small talk."

She sat up straight on the sofa. "Cal," she said. Her voice sounded strangely formal. "You probably never knew this, but Margaret—" she hesitated "—was in love with you."

Cal snorted. "Yeah, sure she was. Like a cat's in love with fleas."

"She *was*, Cal. She had a crush on you for years."

Cal crossed his arms and eyed her skeptically. "All right, now you're pulling a Bannister on me. I'll go visit her. You don't have to flatter me."

"I'm not flattering you."

He felt baffled. What in the world was this all about? "Helen, when it came to this clodhopper farmer, your sister always had her nose in the air, too damned artistic to give me the time of day, just like her nephew. No wonder she and Wayne got along well."

"The reason she was so standoffish with you was because she didn't want you, or me, to know how she felt."

Now he got up from his chair and stood staring at her. "Where are you getting this stuff? That trip to France's got you making up fairy tales."

277

"Margaret did a little bit of writing about it. Some poems. If you read between the lines—"

"No chance. You took those lines the wrong way."

Helen stood up, too. "Well, you can believe it or not. But I think it would give her pleasure to see you. She has so little to make her happy now."

He couldn't believe it, but the fact that Helen believed it made him feel awkward. Whatever he said—denying it or going along with it—would somehow make the idea credible. It was embarrassing to think of.

He shrugged. "Well, if you want me to visit, I'll visit. But Wayne's got to come with me."

"Thank you. That would mean a lot to her." Helen started for the kitchen.

"She won't know us," he persisted. "Don't you think it would give her a scare to find two strange men at her door?"

"If you see she's upset, well then, of course, you should just leave. She'll forget you were there as soon as you're gone. But I do think it might give her a lift. To see both of you."

Cal shook his head. "You've got some imagination, that's all I can say."

"So you promise to visit her every day or so?"

"Whatever you want. I can't speak for Wayne, though. You'll have to ask him yourself." She went in to the kitchen and suddenly he called after her, "For God's sake don't tell *him* about this crush business."

Wayne would arrive between 4:00 and 5:00, he said. Cal didn't want his son to find him lounging around looking useless. Around 3:30, he limped down to the barn to see what he might attend to that didn't require stooping or bending.

Usually, he kept things in pretty good order, but this last couple years he'd let things go, tossing screws and nails together into containers every which way, wood screws in with metal screws, shingling nails mixed with other kinds. He sat down at his work bench and was about to pour all the containers out and start sorting when he looked at the job and saw it for what it was—something you'd set a kid to do, to keep him busy. Make work. His grandsons could do the job easier than he could, with their little uncalloused fingers. He didn't want to be caught at it.

He looked around for something else to do. He would have liked to weld something. That was a skilled job. There was probably something that needed welding, but he looked at his old welding rod and, although he had been required to use it on countless occasions since that day of Tommy's death, today he didn't like touching it, and he didn't want Wayne to find him with it in his hands.

He got up and stood in the barn door. Helen's garden was still looking abundant even though the peas and lettuce and spinach and some of the herbs were through. The corn was above his head, the tomatoes crowding their cages. Squash and melon vines sprawled all over the far end. Under the ground, the potatoes would be fleshing out. There were still some ripe raspberries, and the grapes were only now turning purple.

He wondered if her garden tools could use some cleaning up. She had been pretty busy the last month. Maybe he could knock off the dried mud, file off the rust and sharpen the blades. He limped over to the small garden shed that he had put up for her. He had shingled the sides with cedar shakes to make it pretty. How many years ago?

Her wheelbarrow was just outside. He went in and took a hoe and a spade and a shovel, some trowels, her digging knife and a long-handled weeder off their hooks, loaded them into the wheel barrow and wheeled them back to the barn.

As he applied a sharpening stone to the dull edge of the hoe, he thought about how they had sawed away at the damaged ends of his femur and pelvis and put the metal cup with a plastic liner in the socket, and a metal ball and post in the femur, and cemented it all together with something as good as superglue. You could make things new. Or almost new.

The hoe blade was loose where the old wood handle had worn down around the screws holding it in place. But that could be reinforced with some more screws. It would look jerry-rigged, but it would hold.

Before long, he was lost in the work and was a little startled when Helen brought Wayne through the barn door.

"*There* you are," she said.

Cal laid the hoe down. His son had put on a little more weight around the middle, and his hairline had receded somewhat since they saw him at his exhibit in January.

"How was the drive?" Cal looked at his watch. It was 5:30. "It took you a while."

"I got a late start."

Helen came in and noticed the wheelbarrow full of tools.

"What have you got there, Cal? My garden tools?"

"I thought I'd sharpen 'em up for you."

She said, loudly, for Wayne's sake, Cal thought, because Wayne was still lingering by the barn door, "Well thank you! I haven't looked after them like I should. That's very thoughtful." She glanced at Wayne and back to Cal. "Do you want to put that aside for now and come on in for supper? Wayne, you haven't eaten yet, I believe."

The three of them walked back to the house, Helen keeping Cal's slower pace, Wayne going on ahead.

Helen made small talk during supper.

"I've fixed up your room for you, Wayne. You can put your painting supplies there, or wherever they would be handy. Did you bring them in?"

"They're in the car. I'll get them later."

"How are JoAnna and Jake? What are they up to these days?"

"They're fine. Nothing special."

"And how is your painting coming along? We saw your art work at the hospital."

Wayne shifted his gaze from his plate to Helen's face and then to Cal's.

"Yeah?" he said.

"We thought it was very interesting," Helen said, brightly.

"Did 'we'?"

Helen must have realized her blunder because she turned the subject.

"That hospital is so full of art! It makes it nice to walk around the halls while you're waiting."

"How much did they pay you?" said Cal.

"Enough." Wayne turned back to his food.

On Thursday afternoon, Helen went to Oakridge for the last time before she would leave for Paris the next day.

Norman was a permanent fixture in the lounge now, either watching TV or just sitting there with a bland, pleasant smile on his face, looking at nothing in particular. Helen always introduced herself, and he always said, "Nice to meet you. Sit down and take a load off." She would sit next to him for a few minutes and ask about his health or his daughter. "She's a firecracker!" he said. Helen thought it a good description of the loud, definite woman who led her father out every weekend, rain or shine, for an adventure at the races, or a stock auction, or a Rotary Club pancake breakfast. Norman was always game for whatever she suggested and seemed as robust as ever, physically.

Today, when Helen excused herself to get up and leave him, he said, without apparent resentment, "I don't blame you. I'd leave me, too." And she could only put a hand on his shoulder and keep it there for several seconds in compensation.

* * *

Margaret was sitting on the bed, holding the small, empty dessert bowls, nested one inside the other.

"What should I do with these?" she said tremulously. "In there?" She pointed, and Helen saw globs of rice pudding and apple sauce at the bottom of the wastebasket.

"I'll take them." Helen found the empty dining tray, put the bowls on it, and set it, along with the wastebasket, in the corridor outside Margaret's door.

"Oh, thank you," Margaret said. "There are just so many things . . ." Her voice trailed off, and she cast her gaze around the room.

Impulsively, Helen sat down and enclosed her in her arms. "Margaret," she said, "I'm so glad you're my sister."

Margaret sat a little stiffly in Helen's embrace and gave her shoulder a few tentative pats. They had never been a demonstrative family, and Helen herself felt awkward, but she held Margaret close anyway and pressed her own full-fleshed cheek against Margaret's gaunt one.

"You've been such a good sister to me."

"Have I? Oh, I don't think so."

"Yes, you have, and I love you, Margaret"

"Well, I love you, too," said Margaret. She was the first to draw away.

Does she know who hugged her? Does she know me at all? Is it over now? Oh, sweet Margaret, come back. Remembering, Helen said to herself, *Come back to your zinnia sister, your sister cheer, what will she do without you near?*

For some moments she couldn't speak. She got up and busied herself straightening the cushion on the rocker and checking the thermostat. The air conditioning seemed a bit high. Then she glanced out the window and what she saw made her clap her hands.

"Oh Sis, come look!" Laughing, she helped Margaret up and led her to the window. "What do you think of that?"

Margaret came close to the glass and peered out. "It's very colorful, isn't it?" she said in her dutiful voice.

"Yes, but do you see what's in the birdbath?"

Margaret squinted. "Now, *where* is the birdbath?"

"There. Just down there." Helen pointed toward it where it sat on the ground.

"Oh my!" exclaimed Margaret. "What *is* it?"

"It's a duck! A drake. See its green feathers?"

"Oh, yes, I see. I'll be darned. What's it doing there?"

"Taking a swim, I guess."

"Well, it won't get far on that lake."

"No!"

Three other ducks, which Helen had to point out, though they were impossible to miss, were pecking the ground for seed fallen from the bird feeder. Redwing blackbirds and finches were vying for spots on the feeder as well.

"My goodness, it's a regular megangerie out there, isn't it?"

"A menagerie, yes."

As if she had used up all her energy watching the ducks, Margaret sank into the rocker and gazed silently at the scene outside.

Helen continued to stand by the window, and they watched the ducks for a long time until suddenly, as if at a pre-arranged signal, all four ducks spread their wings wide, flew into the air, circled the field in a tight formation and soared away.

Margaret put her hand to her throat. "How did they know when to go?" She looked up at Helen. "My garden is colorful. You should come and see it some time."

It was, Helen thought, a lovely scene, satisfying. By accident, sticking flowers in here and there, not concerning herself about relative heights or the clash of colors, she had created something artistic. Always, she had been too busy with her large vegetable garden to bother with the fuss of flower planting at home and all the designing that she had supposed went with it. But now she wondered if maybe next spring she would put in a few flowers on her own property. She seemed to have an eye for it after all.

A monarch butterfly fluttered past and busied itself among the impatiens, but Margaret couldn't detect it, as much as Helen tried to point it out.

She looked at her watch. There were errands to run before the stores closed. She wanted to buy two of those screens for the front and back windshields of Nancy's car so it wouldn't heat up too badly at the airport lot for the ten days it would be sitting there. She had to run to the bank to exchange some dollars for the euros George Massey had gotten in for her.

She held Margaret's hand and reminded her that she would be gone for several days. "But I'll be back soon, and Cal and Wayne will visit you. Let them know if you need anything."

"That will be nice," Margaret said noncommittally. Helen guessed she didn't know who Cal and Wayne were.

Margaret didn't get up when Helen rose to go. She seemed too weak. Her hand in Helen's was limp.

As Helen left, having bent down to kiss her good-bye, Margaret said, "Please tell your mother I said hello."

Outside in the hallway, Helen stood by Margaret's door for several minutes. Oh Margaret, she thought, this could be the last time I see you. How selfish I am to leave you now. Would you understand why I'm going? Would you forgive me? Yes. Of course she would. Helen knew that. But could she forgive herself?

No, she couldn't leave her to die alone. Helen took a breath and went back in the room. Margaret had already gotten herself out of the rocker and was curled up on the bed, her eyes closed, her breathing regular and light. Her face looked serene. Helen realized that what Margaret wanted—had wanted for a long time—was not to look at ducks or flowers, or to play the piano or talk or struggle to pretend she knew who Helen was. All she really wanted was to be allowed to sleep.

iv.

On Friday noon, right on time, Cal saw Nancy coming up in her Toyota Prius. She had lent Helen a wheeled, carry-on bag with extendable handle, which Helen packed in their bedroom the night before, along with a larger suitcase. She sure wasn't hiding her cheerfulness about the whole thing. In bed, she'd cuddled up against him and laid her arm across his chest. She even kissed his ear. He half resented it, in spite of how good it felt. Would she be so affectionate if she wasn't about to hightail it out of there and be quit of him for ten days?

But for the first time in months, he'd felt aroused. He hesitated to try anything strenuous, picturing that metal ball popping out of its socket right in the middle of the festivities. She must have figured this out, too, because the next thing he knew, she was sliding her hand down and taking hold of him. She drew her face back from his for a moment, her expression asking his permission. He gave it.

So they left each other on better terms than they had been on in months, but he still felt uneasy, watching Nancy's car pull away, Helen waving gaily out the passenger window at him and Wayne. He thought of suicide bombers sabotaging the airplane on the Chicago to Paris leg or on the return trip.

The car wasn't out of sight before Wayne had already gone into the house. Cal found him in the kitchen making a sandwich.

"Are you going to need anything this afternoon?" Wayne asked.

"Not anything I can't do for myself."

In that case, Wayne said, he was going down to the ravine. He put on boots and took his camera and a sketch pad.

After he left, Cal felt guilty about his promise to Helen. He could have asked Wayne to drive him into Dunlop to visit Margaret. But Helen had made *both* of them promise to visit—not just him. Wayne was the driver, so he had some responsibility in the matter. Probably Wayne felt like he did about it, just as happy to let it go until tomorrow.

285

Cal felt more on his own this afternoon than on any of the many afternoons or evenings Helen had gone into town and left him at home before. He took the stairs slowly and stood in the upstairs hall window looking across the ravine. Wayne was hidden somewhere down there in the thick growth. Maybe he really had come to do his art. Now that he thought about it, Wayne was the last person in the world to let himself be manipulated by Nancy Bannister. She would have met her match in him.

He remembered now how much time Wayne spent in the ravine when he was a kid. It was natural he would have an attachment to it, like his own attachment, as a boy, to the secret dammed up part of the creek he discovered on the other side of his father's woodlot where he would sometimes get away from the meanness at home. In summer, he would take off his clothes and float in the clear pool and listen to the gurgle and splash of water making its way over the frame of gnawed off saplings left by industrious beavers. Once or twice when he was very still, he saw a beaver swimming to the dam with a stick in its mouth, its dark, wet coat glistening. With its thick paws it balanced deftly on the slippery pile before it wedged the stick in and slid quietly back into the water to emerge on the bank and disappear into the woods.

He scanned the ravine again for a sign of Wayne, almost wishing he could have tagged along with him.

Around four o'clock, he walked down the drive to the mailbox. He took it slow, but still had to rest at the gate. Cars were stirring up dust, coming in and out of the maze park down the road. He hadn't ventured in yet, and neither, he realized, had Wayne. Maybe they could avoid it altogether.

There was a postcard in the box from Barb with a picture of a squirrel under a pine tree and a snow-capped mountain in the distance.

"Hi Dad and Wayne.
I guess Mom will have already left by the time you get

this. Last night we thought a bear was sniffing around our tent. Gordon bravely shone his flashlight through the mesh, ready to bop the critter if it came too close. Only a raccoon, it turned out, but a very healthy raccoon after it ate all our power bars. The morning air smells great! I'll never buy one of those stinky pine tree air "fresheners" again now that I've smelled the real thing. Hope you're having a great time together. Give Aunt Margaret our love.

xo, Barb"

Why, he wondered, had Barb turned out so "grounded," as Helen called her, so content and affectionate, while Wayne was still sullen and withdrawn? You could have expected Barb to be the lost one or the rebellious one, losing her brother at such a young age. It probably just boiled down to personality. She was a lot like her mother, while Wayne, according to Helen anyway, was just like him. "You're both as independent and stubborn and competitive as tomcats," she told him once. "The only difference is that tomcats spit and yowl, and you and Wayne go at it with sarcastic remarks."

Helen claimed he and Wayne even looked alike. He didn't used to see it, but now that Wayne was middle-aged, he was beginning to notice the resemblance. People sometimes mistook photos of Wayne, now almost fifty, for himself at the same age.

Wayne came back around six o'clock with burrs stuck to his pants and a high color in his cheeks. It had started to rain. Cal took out the casserole Helen had left thawing in the fridge and stuck it in the microwave.

"Those things sap the nutrition out of food and make the landfills radioactive," said Wayne.

"At the same time?"

Wayne just shook his head and took out a cold beer. While the food cooked, Wayne drank the beer and picked the burrs off his pant cuffs.

Cal put two plates out, and when the casserole was ready, they sat down. Cal observed that Wayne wasn't above eating the nuked dinner.

They didn't have much to say to each other while they ate, but afterwards they watched a MASH re-run together, Cal in his recliner, Wayne stretched out on the sofa. Then Wayne went up to his room, taking his camera and sketchpad with him. Cal would have liked to get a look inside the sketch pad—as close as he might get to a look inside his son's head.

That night, when he sat down on his side of the empty double bed, he consoled himself with the thought that he was sleeping better, now that pain didn't keep him awake half the night. But he wondered if it was all too late. Helen's generosity the night before was probably just guilt for being so damned eager to get away from him.

v.

Nancy showed Helen how to check in and get through airport security, and, while they sat at their gate in Des Moines, shared with Helen her philosophy of traveling.

"If there's a long delay or it looks like you're going to miss a connection, the thing to do, Helen, is put yourself in mind of your great, great grandparents. Just think of them pushing across that prairie one step at a time for weeks and weeks, through rain and snow, pulling their wagons across rivers, stopping to build fires to cook their meals. It just puts the whole thing in perspective. If there's a long delay, you can read a book cover to cover, and that gives you a real feeling of accomplishment. Or you can chat. You'd be surprised at the interesting people you meet, waiting in airports or on planes."

But there were no delays. Their flight to Chicago got off exactly on time, and in Chicago they had an hour and a half to get to their connection, with time left over to enjoy coffee and croissants and to buy a copy of *Le Monde*. "Might as well start getting in the mood,"

Nancy said. They had both taken French in college, and Latin in high school for Helen, and it was gratifying how much of the printed page they could decipher together.

On the Chicago to Paris flight, Nancy insisted that Helen sit by the window. She hadn't flown since her cousin's wedding in Montana, and she was always hearing how cramped and uncomfortable airplane seats were these days, but neither she nor Nancy was very tall, so they had plenty of legroom. She looked down at the Chicago skyscrapers passing beneath them, and then the glittering water of Lake Michigan and the big checkerboards of farmland. She had been too excited that night to sleep much, and after awhile, she dozed off, her head propped against the neck cushion Nancy had considerately brought for her. She woke an hour later completely refreshed.

Voluminous black clouds appeared below and to the south, illuminated inside by pale bursts of lightning. The captain came on the intercom and said, "Folks, we'll be flying well above the storm you can see out the port windows, but it may be a little bumpy for a brief spell, so I'm going to ask you to put your seatbelts on temporarily. Thank you for your cooperation."

It was exactly as he described it—bumpy—like taking the truck too fast down a pot-holed gravel road. But it wasn't alarming or unpleasant, and the whole time they were flying above the black clouds, the blue sky almost blinded them with sunlight, and soon they had outflown the storm.

At dinner time, the flight attendant brought trays of food in tidy compartments with packets of butter and plasticware and a choice of drinks. The food wasn't all that bad, not like she'd heard it was supposed to be. Helen and Nancy toasted with their plastic glasses of ginger ale. Everything was so very easy.

For a while after dinner, Nancy quizzed Helen on sentences from the French phrase book she'd brought. Then Helen lay her head back and watched the sky darken as they flew toward night. She had never in her life felt so relaxed and unburdened. When thoughts of Cal or

Wayne or Margaret intruded, she put the thoughts on a cloud and let them drift away.

Eventually, the overhead lights were turned off and, one by one, passengers switched on their reading lights. Helen glanced over at Nancy, who was engrossed in a crossword puzzle. She reached out and touched her arm. "Nancy," she said, "I can never thank you enough for this."

Nancy put down her puzzle book and smiled. "I knew it would be just the thing for you, Helen. I told Barb so, and she agreed with me completely." She squeezed Helen's hand and went back to her puzzle. It took a moment for it to sink in, and when it did, she felt . . . what? Not indignant—no, she couldn't be mad at Nancy now—but kind of sheepish. Once again the woman had outwitted her, overrun her. She should have known. All Nancy had had to do was to put a bug in Barb's ear and she'd be on the phone to her brother. *Mom needs this break. She seems "melancholy." Can you come? Do it for* Mom?

Helen watched Nancy whip through her puzzle as if she had a dictionary in her brain. Nancy was a decade younger than herself, but she seemed at the moment years older. Nancy, the fairy godmother. With her magic wand, she had tapped her on the shoulder, and now midnight wouldn't come for another ten days while she, Helen, would be tripping through a glorious ball in her comfortable athletic walking shoes instead of glass slippers.

She fell asleep watching the inflight movie, and woke to find that they were flying into a sunrise.

Nancy took care of everything when they got to Paris. She saw to their luggage and hailed a cab. At the quaint little three-story hotel just off the Rue de Madeleine, the manager was expecting them. A young man took charge of their bags and accompanied them up to their room on an old-fashioned elevator with a gate. Before he left, Nancy took out her purse and handed him, with utter confidence, enough euros to bring a smile and a polite *"merci beaucoup."*

The day's itinerary was to get settled and nap for a few hours, have lunch at the Café de Madeleine near the hotel, and visit the Louvre—only a brief visit today as they would spend more time there later in the week. Then they would take another nap, go to a special little restaurant Nancy knew of, and have a walk along the Seine to see the Notre Dame Cathedral lit up at night. They would go to bed early.

"It's a good idea to take it easy after a transatlantic flight," said Nancy. Helen, in a bliss of passivity, could only nod and say, "You're the captain."

vi.

"So are we going to visit Aunt Margaret at that place today?" Wayne sounded about as enthusiastic as Cal felt.

"Yeah, I guess we'd better."

There had been a steady drizzling rain all night, and the day started hazy, but the haze burned off and the air was hot and muggy.

It was 1:00. Cal had spent the morning in the barn, finishing the work he had started on Helen's tools. In Helen's garden, Wayne had done some weeding by hand while the ground was soft from the rain, and then picked whatever was ripe, per Helen's instructions, and put the produce in sealed containers in the fridge.

As his son steered the car down the long driveway, it felt strange to have him at the wheel. Wayne drove with his elbow out the window and the air conditioning off, just as Cal himself liked to do. A car was naturally a sweat box in the summer, but Cal never liked being sealed up in the cold, cut off from the country air—the smell of chamomile and alfalfa, dust and manure.

Wayne got out to open and close the gate, and after he got back in, Cal was surprised when he stopped the car by the entrance to the corn maze park instead of heading toward town.

"What's the maze like?" Wayne asked. Another car pulled around them and drove in.

"I don't know. Haven't got there yet."

"I'm going to check it out. Where's that handicap thing?"

"What do you want that for?" But Wayne reached over to the glove box, found it and hung it from the rearview mirror.

He drove in. It was Saturday, and the parking lot was already almost full. Cal noticed a lot of out-of-county plates, and even out-of-state plates. He had to admit Bannister knew how to advertise the thing. There was one handicap space left, and Wayne pulled into it.

"How long you want to stay?" Cal said. "We're supposed to get over to Dunlop."

"Just twenty minutes or so. It's not like she's expecting us."

They got out, walked to the ticket kiosk and stood in line.

At the counter, Cal said to the kid, whose face flamed with acne, "Say, I'm Cal Earlywine. This is my son, Wayne Earlywine." He felt a little foolish, but he remembered Helen's story of the free admission and thought he might as well cash in.

"Welcome to the A-mazing Maiz Maze," the kid said indifferently, holding out a hand for money.

Cal said, "This used to be my land the maze is on, and Wayne here drew the design for it."

The kid looked directly at them then, and his reaction took Cal by surprise. His eyebrows shot up and his mouth fell open. "Sorry, Mr. Earlywine, I didn't know who you were. You and your son get the VIP treatment!" He grabbed their hands, stamped the corn insignia and the date on them, and called over to a girl in the concessions tent. "Hey Katelyn, these guys are the Earlywines." He said it as if they were movie celebrities. "She'll take care of you," he told them. The girl gave a nod, left the people in her line, and started gathering things off the shelves behind her. She came out of the tent with two large twine-handled paper bags, each containing a water bottle, the wide-brimmed straw hat with Wayne's logo on the band, coupons for

Cream Wieners and corn-on-the-cob, a brochure about the maze, a lapel pin saying, "I took the Maze Challenge" and a maze map.

"Don't look at the map," she said, "unless you get seriously lost or after you've gone all the way through. It'll spoil it for you if you do. The mouse and the blackbird show you're on the right track." Wayne's corn row design was plastered on everything, even the water bottle labels. "That's an awesome design," she said, shyly, to Cal. "Everybody likes it."

Cal nodded toward Wayne. "It's *his* design. I had nothing to do with it."

"It's cool," she said to Wayne, and ran back to her customers.

The place was crowded with families, children running from one activity to another. There was a Mayan pyramid made of hay bales that kids were climbing and jumping off into a moat of sand. Nearby was a baby animal enclosure. Parents were anxiously supervising their toddlers, who held their fingertips to the mesh to touch lambs and little pot bellied pigs. With the perpetual movement of the crowds, the colors and banners and dust, Cal felt like he was on a stage set, he and Wayne playing extras. He tried to imagine this plot of land as it had looked only three months ago, but the field he had passed every day for most of his life existed no more.

"Jesus," Wayne said. "I thought it was just going to be a maze." Cal couldn't tell if Wayne was impressed or disgusted.

"The maze is over there."

Families were disappearing into the maze entrance at one end, while others emerged from the exit only a few yards away, the parents red-faced and exhausted, their children pulling on their arms and begging, "Let's go again!"

Cal put on the complimentary straw hat and sat down on a picnic table bench in the shade of a tarp rigged up over the eating area. He took a drink from the water bottle. Wayne did the same.

"Hot as blazes out here," Cal said.

In front of them, two little boys, shrieking and giggling, ran around and around a utility pole, the younger one chasing the older, until they fell together in a heap.

Wayne suddenly got up.

"I'm going to check out the maze. I'll be back." Without looking at Cal, he walked off. He didn't ask if Cal wanted to come with him, but it was obvious that Cal wasn't fit to walk the maze. Cal watched him go. Wayne left behind his bag with the map. Was he going to try to do the whole thing and leave Cal waiting there in the heat?

Cal went over to the kiosk at the maze entrance and traded a coupon for a Cream Wiener. He took it back to the bench. It tasted pretty good. The little boys had disentangled themselves and raced off somewhere. He looked around until he saw them clambering up to the top of the hay bales. The older one immediately took a spectacular leap and fell to his knees in the sand. He laughed triumphantly and got up and brushed himself off. The little brother held back at first, and then jumped, too, landing on his bottom a few inches from his brother. Their father came running over to check the younger one for broken bones, saw he was okay and let him follow the older boy up again. "Be careful," he cautioned the younger boy and stood watching with his arms across his chest.

The father stood bareheaded at his post for a while as the boys repeatedly climbed and jumped. Occasionally, he wiped sweat off his forehead with a handkerchief. His wife, with a toddler in tow, came up, and the man whistled for the boys, who took one last leap before the family headed back to the car park. Regretfully, Cal watched them go.

He was so lost in the little scene that he almost forgot he was waiting for Wayne. He looked at his watch. Wayne had been in there fifteen minutes already. What the hell, he thought, he's gotten himself lost and left his old man to bake in the heat. But just then Wayne came out the exit and waved at him with his hat. Cal was impressed. He heard the maze could take an hour.

"Pretty good time," he said when Wayne came up.

"Should be. I designed the thing."

They picked up their bags and went back to the car.

"How's your hip, Dad? Too much sitting? You want to go home and rest awhile before we go into town?"

Cal glanced at him. Wayne actually looked concerned.

"Sitting's okay. It's walking I have to take it easy with." It was the first time Wayne had asked him how he felt.

"Well, there won't be much walking at Aunt Margaret's."

Though they didn't touch, he and Wayne walked so close together down the corridor, Cal had the image of their clinging to each other. Lions and tigers and bears. He felt stupid to be so nervous about a simple visit to a relative who couldn't remember things. So what? They didn't have to stay long. It was just that he—and Wayne, too, he was sure—were out of their element, neither of them was any good at those social niceties that Helen and Barb possessed in abundance in delicate situations. And what if they got a blank stare when Margaret opened the door?

The stare was anything but blank. They had to knock several times and then wait a while longer, hearing her move about the apartment, maybe trying to find the door. But when she finally opened it, she looked at them as if a beloved, long missing and grieved for pet had finally returned. Or rather, she looked at *Wayne* that way.

Cal said, "Hi there, Margaret. We thought we'd come by for a visit."

She didn't reply or even notice him. Her eyes were fixed on his son. In a shaky, breathy voice, she said to Wayne, "Why, Cal, I didn't . . . I didn't expect you. Come in. Of course you can come in."

Wayne and Cal looked at each other uncertainly. They stepped inside the small living area. Cal said, "How are you doing, Margaret? They treating you okay here?" She seemed not to hear him or even notice him. She'd gotten so frail, she looked like a puff of wind would blow her away.

"Sit down, Cal," she said to Wayne, and looked around anxiously. "But where's Helen?"

Wayne said, "She's away on a trip."

Margaret stood with her hands at her sides, her fingers pinching the fabric of her skirt as if to prevent them from making some other gesture.

"You look . . . beautiful, Cal." Her big sunken brown eyes were fixed on Wayne's face. Cal saw Wayne raise his eyebrows and then frown. Cal couldn't avoid seeing what this was about.

"Margaret," he interjected firmly, "*I'm* Cal. This is your nephew, Wayne."

She turned to him now in confusion. "You're who? I'm sorry, but I didn't catch your name."

"I'm your brother-in-law, Calvin Earlywine. This," gesturing to Wayne, "is my son, your nephew."

She gazed at Wayne again and said, "Oh." She looked vaguely around the apartment. "I wish I had something to offer you. Let me just go to the kitchen . . ." But there was no kitchen. She studied the room and half turned toward the little bedroom and turned back, holding out her arms apologetically. And then, tentatively reaching up one hand, she touched the little bit of sideburn on Wayne's cheek. "Your hair is getting white, Cal. It looks so sweet."

Wayne flinched and backed away.

Margaret said, "I'm sorry. I shouldn't do that."

Cal, casting his eyes around the room desperately, noticed the piano and said to Margaret, "Would you give us a tune?" She looked at the piano as if seeing if for the first time.

"Oh. I don't remember the love songs anymore. What were they?" Wayne was standing closer to the door now. "Do *you* play?" she asked him. "Maybe you remember them." Then, gesturing toward Cal, she said to Wayne, "Excuse my rudeness. Who is your friend?"

Wayne said, "This is my father—"

"Your father?" She lowered her voice. "I thought someone said he died. I'm so sorry." And she stepped forward, put her thin arms around Wayne and kissed him on the lips. Wayne reared back like a skittish horse.

Cal didn't know what to do. Then Margaret drew away from Wayne and went to sit in the rocker. In a tight, anguished voice, she said, "I know Ellen should be here with us."

"You mean Helen?" Cal said. "Your sister?"

"Yes, Helen. What did I say?"

"You said 'Ellen'."

"I say such strange things these days." She spoke to Wayne again. "Cal, I'm happy to see you, but shouldn't my sister be here with us?"

Cal said, "She's in France."

"In France?!" Her eyes filled with tears of sympathy, and she said to Wayne, "Did Helen leave you?"

Cal saw that Wayne's jaw was set in that belligerent way he had when he was boiling with anger. Wayne said sternly, "Aunt Margaret, *this* is Cal. I'm his son." Margaret looked from one to the other.

"So you're Cal. And Helen is where?"

"In France, on vacation."

"Oh." Margaret considered this for a moment and said to Wayne, "At least you have your son. He's an artist, isn't he? Or do I have that wrong?" Wayne didn't answer.

Cal said, "Yes, Wayne's an artist. A pretty good one. Takes after you."

Wayne broke in. "We'd better go now."

Margaret looked stricken. She held out her hand to Wayne. He stepped forward tentatively to take it. "I guess this will be the last time I'll see you." More tears rolled down her wan cheeks. Wayne slid his hand from her grasp. Margaret closed her eyes and her chin trembled.

"I'll be outside," Wayne said, and walked out.

Cal had no idea what to do. He was afraid of what Wayne would think if he lingered. But he put a hand on Margaret's shoulder and said, "It was nice to see you, Margaret. Helen will be back soon, and I'll come by again." He could feel every bone in her emaciated shoulder. "You eating okay?"

"Oh, it doesn't matter," she said, listlessly, and leaned her head against the back of the rocker and closed her eyes.

He let himself out. Wayne was not in the hallway or the front lounge. He was sitting in the car at the wheel with the motor running. Cal got in and said, immediately, "Well, that was sure strange."

Wayne didn't reply. He gunned the engine and drove too fast out of the parking lot. At some point on the silent drive home, Cal said, "That Alzheimers is a crazy disease, all right. It gives people all kinds of unlikely notions." But Wayne just stared at the road.

Cal thought, He must think his old man and his mother's sister had been up to shenanigans. How could he convey to Wayne how wrong that idea was?

It was an easy thing to believe, when you read about all these politicians and athletes and hypocritical preachers who couldn't seem to be happy with the woman they'd chosen. But to him, when you found a woman who attracted you, and she was a good companion to boot, why stray? He'd never been seriously tempted, even before his body started giving out on him. But maybe such men—these men who traded in their wives for having committed the sin of growing old and familiar—hadn't been as lucky as he'd been. He worried about Helen, though. He'd gotten so achey and tired and gloomy these days, there wasn't much he felt like doing in bed anymore. Did she feel hurt about that?

vii.

The Louvre would have been overwhelming if Nancy had not taken Helen by the arm and led her past the most famous masterpieces where the crowd noise resounded off the tile and parquet floors and vaulted ceilings, where masses of tourists pressed close to take pictures with their cellphones. Instead, Nancy guided her into quieter rooms. Here, art students, studying the paintings intently, stood at easels or sat cross-legged on the floor with sketch pads.

Several works of art struck Helen with particular force. She stood for some time in front of Vermeers' simple paintings of daily life, especially "The Kitchen Maid," stout and tidy in her neat white cap and rolled up sleeves, going about the homely act of pouring milk into a bowl.

In a different room they encountered a Rembrandt she had never heard of—"Philosopher in Meditation"—in which an old man sat illuminated by a golden light from a window in a room full of shadows. Another figure stirred the flames of a fire, and a great spiral staircase climbed mysteriously into profound darkness. Helen stood before it transfixed. How had this image come to the painter? What must it be to have such a vision and the skill to put it down on canvas? She thought of her sister and her son, with an almost sickening sadness that Margaret would never have the opportunity to come in person and be inspired by such a marvel, and a fervent hope that Wayne, someday, would.

In still another room, Velazquez's portrait of the "Infanta Margarita" brought Helen face to face with her sister the way she had looked in photos as a three-year-old—the soft, wispy child's hair drawn off the forehead by a bow, the face turned slightly to the left, solemn eyes shyly, or perhaps sadly, gazing inward as if she were thinking of something she kept secret in her heart. Helen struggled to suppress the sob rising in her throat. Margarita. A little girl in a princess's brocaded finery. Little Margaret. Nancy had moved away for the moment, and Helen quickly took a tissue from her bag, dabbed at her eyes, and tried to get hold of her emotions.

As they were leaving the museum, passing through a series of vaulted rooms full of sculpture, Helen stopped, breathless, at the marble statue of Cupid and Psyche. The lovers stood close, the boy's head upon the girl's shoulder, the girl tenderly putting a butterfly in his hand. Their naked youthful skin looked so fresh and smooth and luminous that Helen could hardly keep from passing her hand over their smooth white curves, and she couldn't help but think of Tom's perfect twenty-year-old body and his gentleness, cut down just as if some jealous god had sent the thunderbolt to punish him for being more beautiful and beloved than he.

Now her eyes were streaming. Everywhere she looked, something moved her to tears. She put on sunglasses but couldn't hide her red nose and flushed face. Nancy seemed to take her condition in stride. She said, "It gets you awfully emotional, doesn't it?" Helen nodded, blowing her nose. "The first time I came, I tell you, Helen, I was a basket case, and I don't even know that much about art." She steered Helen out into the sunlight, where they sat for a while by the reflecting pool and watched the ebb and flow of people. Soon Helen was recovered enough to wonder at the enormous modern glass pyramid, which seemed so odd a thing to set between the magnificent wings of the ornate Renaissance palace. She wondered whether Cal, if he had come with her, would have been bored. This thought pricked her with uneasiness about what it would be like when she returned to Iowa. She thought she should call him now. It would be eight A.M. there. He would probably be up. But Wayne was a late sleeper, and she didn't want to wake him.

At the lovely little restaurant that night, Helen did something she never did at home. She drank a glass of wine. The alcohol seemed to surge down her arms, giving them a strange and pleasant feeling of weakness.

The physical effect of the alcohol dissipated with their walk along the Seine, but the wine heightened her awareness of the lights reflected on the water, illuminating the splendid façade of the cathedral, and of the slow promenade of couples, families, and solitary walkers of all races and ages and nationalities, speaking to each other in melodious foreign languages.

At the hotel, she made herself call home, but no one answered.

She had forgotten to bring Wayne's cell phone number with her. Was that an unconscious choice? It would be two P.M. in Iowa. Maybe they were in town visiting Margaret. She hoped the visit wouldn't be too uncomfortable for them.

She and Nancy turned in at ten P.M. and slept through the night. When Helen woke on Saturday, she felt excited and energetic. Jet lag, she concluded, had made her temporarily "melancholy."

Early that morning, they picked up their rental car to spend a day in the Loire Valley visiting the chateaux Chambord and Chenonceau. Nancy said, "There's one more chateau I won't tell you about. It'll be a big surprise. It'll wow you!"

Helen didn't see how anything could wow her more than the vast Chambord with its eleven towers all of different styles, its grand double-helix staircase, four hundred forty rooms, and three hundred sixty-five fireplaces.

Nor was the Chateau de Chenonceau, though smaller, any less spec-tacular, straddling a river and filled with galleries and rooms named for the royalty who had lived or visited there over the centuries. They looked at a bed in which five different queens had slept.

On the grounds, there were ancient formal gardens raised by stone embankments above the river to protect them from flooding. Primary among their attractions was a maze, which Nancy insisted they visit, though by this time Helen was ready to sit and watch the ducks swimming on the river that flowed beneath the arched piers holding up the castle.

The *labyrinthe* was a circular, shoulder-high hedge maze built of two thousand perfectly sculpted yew shrubs. At the center a small vine-covered gazebo provided shade. Helen and Nancy rested there for a few minutes.

"Isn't it something!" Nancy exclaimed. "You know, I was just think-ing there's no reason why we couldn't do the same thing in the Dunlop City Park." Helen looked at her incredulously. "On a much smaller scale, of course. But wouldn't it be fun for the families? And year round, too, because these shrubs are evergreens. The pattern is right here on the brochure. It wouldn't be a bit of trouble to copy it. 'Dunlop's Chenonceau Labyrinth.' What do you think?"

"I think it's as good as done."

They got up and finished walking the maze at a much slower pace than the many children who ran gleefully up and down the paths.

Helen thought two chateaux were plenty to absorb in one day, but Nancy said there was one more that Helen absolutely couldn't miss.

"Wait 'til you see!" said Nancy, as they walked from the car park. The Chateau de Villandry itself was quite stately and beautiful, but it was the gardens that Nancy steered her to. "I know how much you enjoy gardening, Helen. You're going to love this." As they drew near, Nancy threw out her arms. *"Voila! Fantastique, non?"*

Spread out before them was an enormous series of geometric vegetable beds framed by precisely cut hedges dotted with gazebos and fountains and trimmed trees.

"It's the most famous garden in France. And this part," Nancy read from her guidebook, "'is the *potager*. It means vegetable garden."

"My goodness. It takes vegetables to a new level," said Helen, wondering how many gardeners would have to tend such a thing.

"And this is just the tip of the iceberg! Come on, I want you to see the next part from above."

Nancy led her to an elevated walkway from which they looked down on four vast quadrants of geometrically cut hedges and flowers and maze-like paths.

"This," Nancy said, pausing for effect, "is the Garden of Love. See the hearts?" Helen saw them. "The first quadrant is the Garden of *Tender* Love," Nancy was reading again from the guidebook. "This garden consists of four perfectly shaped hearts carved out of boxwood shrubs. And the next quadrant, there," Nancy pointed, "is the Garden of *Passionate* Love." Here the hearts had lost their lobes and were planted every which way "as if in turmoil," Nancy read. "Then that part is the Garden of *Fickle* Love. Those shapes in the corners are fans to indicate 'volatility,' and between them—those ones there that look like pointed crowns—are *horns*." She raised her eyes from the book and winked at Helen. "And the last one is *Tragic* Love." Here the hedges formed sharp, jagged figures "to represent the swords of rivals!"

Nancy was quiet for a moment. Then she sighed and said, "I guess it just wouldn't be practical to try to do something like that in City Park?"

"No," said Helen firmly. "It wouldn't."

Nancy wanted them to tour the chateau, but Helen said her feet were worn out and she would wait outside for her. She found a bench in the shade and sat down, gazing out at the Gardens of Love and wondering how Wayne and Cal and Margaret were getting along without her. Since Friday, whenever she thought to call home, the time would be wrong there—the middle of the night or too early in the morning.

It would be eight A.M. in Iowa now. Would Margaret still be curled up in bed? Would she know Cal when he visited? Her secret love for him had kept her going all those years. It had been a kind of solace. Maybe it was a reason why her dreadful husband kept Margaret away from her family as much as he did. Jealous people had antennae for these things.

But what did Margaret see in Cal to make her pine for him so? Probably Cal seemed a paragon of kindness and sensitivity by contrast to that man she was married to. It was all relative.

She thought of Margaret's poem about shame, the one that had worried her so much when she read it the second time. How did it go? '*He will always blame himself.*' Something about his not being to blame. '*This man with heart ...*' does what? '*condemns himself to shame.*' Yes. '*though the criminal was only chance—*" Helen suddenly realized this poem was about Tom's death. 'The criminal was only chance'! Now she remembered something very insightful at the end of the poem: '*It is only the heartless man,*' Margaret wrote, '*who takes the blameless stance.'* A heartless man like Jim McIntyre. That was it. Cal had felt guilty about Tom for so many years because he was a man with heart—a much better way to think of him than as a bitter, sour man who couldn't let go. Of course Cal was foolish to keep blaming himself for Tom's death, but a heartless man would never have taken any guilt on himself at all.

He '*binds his wounds in jokes.'* '*Stubborn.'* '*A fair trade for the duties he fulfills with love, without display.'* '*Salt of the earth, you bet.'* '*A solid gentleman.'* All those lines came back to her now.

She imagined herself walking these sculptured paths with Cal. He would have plenty to say about the aristocrats who indulged in such extravagance. "To the guillotine with them. *Vive la revolution!*"

She missed his wise cracks. They would be a nice antidote to Nancy's energetic zeal. What if, instead of marrying Cal, she had married someone like Norman? He would have followed her lead uncomplainingly, always making little self-deprecating jokes, apologizing for his shortcomings. Comparing him to Cal, she thought she understood what Margaret didn't see in Norman.

She got up and took the path down into the Garden of Love, but at ground level it just seemed to her like a lot of severely carved shrubbery with uniform displays of flowers plotted in between. And where was a Garden of *Steady* Love? If she were the creator of it, she would plant it in chives, masses of them filling their quadrant willy nilly, poking out of the walkways.

Chives gave you greens from early spring to mid-autumn. Even after the deep freeze of winter, they always sprang back in abundance and persisted despite drought or hail or late spring frost. Yes, in her Garden of Steady Love she would plant chives, with their pale lavender flowers like clover heads. And here and there amidst the green—serendipitously!—she would plant hardy perennials—black eyed Susans, purple and yellow cone flowers, snow-on-the mountain—ordinary, reliable plants that would never let you down.

Slowly, she walked back toward the place where Nancy would be expecting to meet her. She hoped Cal and Wayne had visited Margaret, if only to see that she was being looked after properly. And she hoped Margaret would recognize Cal and be overjoyed to see him, for a few moments anyway. She had to believe that Margaret would still be there when she returned.

As far as Wayne and Cal were concerned, now that she knew that Wayne had only offered to come because Barb talked him into it, she didn't have much hope that he would reconcile with Cal in these few days. He was almost fifty. If it hadn't happened yet, it probably never would. On the other hand, you never knew. Miracles sometimes occurred.

viii.

Cal woke to the sound of a motorcycle shutting down somewhere nearby, not out on the road, but on the property. He looked at the illuminated face of the alarm clock. It was two A.M. He had turned the air conditioning off and opened the bedroom windows when he went to bed. Now he sat up and listened for other sounds beneath the scree of crickets and the breeze rustling poplar leaves next to the house.

At first he heard nothing more, and was just sinking back, half asleep, when the muffled sound of voices and laughter came across the field, and the clink of bottles. It was just as he thought. The maze had turned into a damned hotspot for drugged out, booze guzzling teenagers. He knew it. He'd told Helen. He'd told Bannister. So much for Robbie Peterson as a watch dog. Robbie had likely pulled his cruiser under some bypass or other and was smoking marijuana and reading girlie magazines by the overhead light.

Cal considered waking Wayne, but immediately thought better of it, remembering his hostile silence after their visit to Margaret. He had dropped Cal at the house and taken off in the car without saying where he was going and didn't come back until after Cal went to bed. Anyway, Wayne wouldn't give a damn about kids trashing the place. It wasn't his property. He'd never valued it.

Cal lay there wondering what he ought to do. He couldn't hike all the way down the drive, cross the park and wend his way through the maze, which was probably where the kids were, hanging out at that observation post, a logical place for teenagers to congregate. His hip would rebel before he got halfway there.

Still, he put on a T-shirt and overalls, took the stairs slowly, hanging onto the rail in the dark. Downstairs he grabbed a flashlight from the utility drawer and stepped out onto the porch. A waning moon hung in the sky shot with stars, and the air felt soft on his face.

He stood for a while, taking it in. At that moment, he wished Helen were with him. It seemed they never spent much time outdoors at night anymore. They used to come out sometimes, walk down the road, look at the stars, and listen to the nighttime sounds, the crickets, an occasional owl, sometimes a fox mewing from down in the ravine. They could do that again when she got back. Two or three more weeks, the doctor said, and he could return to normal activities. He wanted to remind her of that fact. The hip is nothing like as bad as it was, he wanted to tell her. I won't always be a drag on you. He didn't know why he had been so negative about it, even to himself, when that wasn't really what he'd felt. From the second day in the hospital, he knew he was going to get better.

The laughter and voices came out of the darkness again, and he thought he got a whiff of cigarette smoke on the breeze. The activity was definitely coming from the maze park. By god, he was going to flush them out and send them scattering like chickens.

He hobbled back inside and dug out the maze map from the paper bag. Then he took his shotgun from the cupboard in the mudroom and double checked to make sure it wasn't loaded before limping out to the barn.

He slipped the flashlight into his overalls pocket, got on the riding mower and started it up. The loud whine of the motor couldn't be helped, but if the sound scared them off, all the better. He lay the shotgun across his lap and drove out and down the drive as fast as the mower would go, not having to stop to open the gate because Wayne hadn't bothered to close it after the silent drive back from Margaret's.

When Cal got to the park, he turned in and drove across the grass toward the maze. Already his hip ached from keeping pressure on the gas pedal, so he slid his foot aside and grasping the gun barrel, pressed the stock on the pedal—kill two birds with one stone, he thought, feeling some satisfaction for having brought the gun along. In the mower's headlights, he found the maze entrance and drove in to the tunnel of ten-foot corn stalks.

He stopped to shine the flashlight on the map and tried to memorize the sequence of turns. Left, right, right left, right, left, left, left, right . . . He turned off the ignition and listened. In the breeze overhead, the tassels undulated and rustled against each other. Otherwise, there was no sound, not even the pulse of crickets. It was eerie. He had spent a good many hours throughout his life walking between rows of towering corn, but not usually at night, and never on a path so wide, almost a lane, appearing unexpectedly like in a fairy tale, to trick you into following it without knowing what might be around the next bend.

"Get the hell off this property!" he yelled into the darkness. He sounded weak and absurd to himself. There was no reply. If the kids had already run, he was pretty sure he would have seen them race away on the motorcycle as he was coming down the drive. He started the mower up again and drove forward, steering one-handed around the bends. Left, right, right, left, . . . right? Left? He stopped again to consult his map. Now he couldn't remember if he had, in fact, turned right at the next to the last bend. If not, he might be going in circles. Should he start back? No, he guessed he probably had turned right.

He drove on as fast as he thought it was feasible, steering one-handed around the bends. Then, suddenly, the front right tire sank into a rut, and the whole machine tipped forward. His heart lurched. The shotgun fell as he clutched the wheel with both hands and bucked his weight backward. The mower poised on one wheel for a moment and then with a shudder settled back and stopped. Cal's hip joint gave him a sharp stab. He sat there for a moment, his heart thumping and his body flooded with adrenaline. The machine had come so close to falling over and pinning him. Immediately, his concentration switched to the fiery feeling in his hip. Had he pulled that metal ball out of the plastic socket? God help him if he had. Very carefully he got off the mower and slowly shifted his weight from his left leg to his right. He took a step. The leg seemed to hold okay. The sharp pain was subsiding. He was sweating now in the warm, humid air.

Where the hell had the rut come from? He shone his flashlight on it and traced the track that led up to it. The kid on the motorcycle had spun a wheelie on that spot and dug the full weight of the cycle into the damp ground. Carefully, painfully, Cal got back on the mower, turned the key in the ignition, and took several tries before getting it going again. He held his breath as he inched the tilted mower back and forth, stalling the old motor several times, until he finally succeeded in backing out of the rut. He got off the machine, gingerly bent down, and picked up the gun.

Left, left, left, right . . . he crept through the turns, pressing the gun stock on the gas pedal. Both his shoulders ached from their unaccustomed exertion. He was out of shape in more parts of him than just his hip and leg. He knew now how easy it would be to tip the mower over on one of these turns and get crushed. What did it matter if there were teenagers on the property? It wasn't his anymore. These kids, whoever they were, might even be long gone and Wayne unaware in his bedroom on the back side of the house out of earshot. Jesus! Here he was again like some fool kid himself, setting off on a ridiculous mission that could jeopardize all his work to rehabilitate himself. And for what?

Then, before he knew it, there he was, just outside the clearing for the observation post. Parked in front of him, blocking his way, was the motorcycle. He shut the mower down and got off to inspect the cycle. The orange and red flames along the side, the naked woman gazing backward with a wink, the eagle insignia with thunderbolts in its talons—he should have known.

"Peterson!" he shouted, as he walked into the clearing. "What the hell are you doing there and who've you got with you?"

Two shadowy figures sat at the top of the observation post, one on the bench, the other at the edge of the platform with his arms on the rail and his legs dangling over the side. Cal shone his flashlight up into their faces. The man on the bench was Robbie. The man at the rail was Wayne. A half empty carton of beer sat at Robbie's feet. Robbie had a cigarette in one hand and held a bottle aloft with the other.

"Hey, Mr. Earlywine," said Robbie, "come on up."

Wayne said nothing.

"Come on up," Robbie said again. "Have the last of Wayne's beer."

Cal eyed the stairs. They were pretty steep. He didn't think it was a good idea to try to climb them after having stressed out his hip.

"Nah. I was just looking out for any drunken fool kids breaking their necks playing on the tower," he said, meaningfully.

Robbie said, "You'd like it up here. King of the hill!"

Out of the darkness, Wayne broke his silence to say, "He doesn't do well on stairs."

Robbie got off his bench, came down the stairs and said, "I'll give you a hand up."

Cal fended him off. Using the shotgun as a cane, he got himself up, one step at a time.

"Hey! I hope that ain't loaded," said Robbie.

"What do *you* think?" Cal reached the platform and sat breathing heavily on the far end of the bench, leaving room for Robbie.

Wayne continued to sit looking out into the darkness. "What were you planning to do with that thing?" he said.

"Give 'em a scare." Cal turned to Robbie. "What are *you* doing here?"

"I swung by to check for unauthorized vehicles in the parking lot. From the road I seen a light up over the maze. It was just Wayne's flashlight. I thought it might be kids. Or even maybe the headlights of a UFO."

Wayne said, "No UFOs around here."

"You never know. If E.T. looked down at a corn maze, he might get curious, bring her down for a closer look." Wayne snorted. "Yeah, I know. It's a long shot, but wouldn't you like to see one just once?"

There was a silence again. Robbie looked from Cal to Wayne and said, uncomfortably, "Well, I probably better get back pretty soon." He took a beer from the carton and held it up for Cal.

"No thanks," said Cal. "You take it, I don't want it." But Robbie stuck it in his hand.

"Wouldn't be good to have a beer on me if I crashed the hog."

"Wouldn't be good to have a beer *in* you if you crashed the hog."

"Too late."

Police gibberish chirped from the gadget clipped to Robbie's shoulder. Robbie said languidly, "Duty calls. See ya, Mr. Earlywine. See ya, Wayne. Nice shootin' the breeze with you."

Cal wondered what breeze the two of them had shot. Would Wayne have confided in the likes of Robbie Peterson?

Robbie took the stairs a couple at a time. Then there was the sound of him guiding the motorcycle around the lawn mower, revving the engine, and roaring away through the maze, taking the turns way too fast. In a minute Robbie was out into the park, and the roar faded to a mosquito's whine up on the road.

Without Robbie to fill the silence, Cal was at a loss how to deal with Wayne's unspoken accusation. For a minute or so, he picked at the label on the bottle he was holding. Then he cleared his throat and spoke.

"You know, maybe you wondered about that situation. Back there at your Aunt Margaret's place. I hope you don't think there was ever anything going on between us."

310

"I don't put it past anyone."

"Yeah, I can see how you'd think that if what you see on TV is anything to go by. But around here most people shy away from that kind of thing. I wouldn't ever get myself into a mess like that, with my wife's sister, or anybody else either."

"If you say so," Wayne replied, coldly.

Wayne's back was to him, and Cal wished he would turn around. "Listen, Wayne, your mother told me your aunt Margaret had a crush on me. I guess you'd call it a crush. I never knew it. I thought she looked down on me." Wayne gave no response. Cal pushed on. "I didn't believe her, but I guess from this thing today she was right."

Wayne took his arms off the rail and shifted his weight.

"When your mother comes back, you can ask her about it. Your aunt wrote poems about me, I guess, or something like that. What she saw in me, I couldn't tell you." He paused. "You know, Wayne, I've only ever loved your mother. She was always the only gal for me."

He realized he was speaking about Helen in the past, as if she were gone from his life for good. Not dead, but out of his reach, forever. He had a flash into the future, seeing his daughter dutifully calling and looking in on him to keep the old man from being lonely, bringing the grandkids over to cheer him up, until they were all in their teens and couldn't be coerced into visiting grandpa except on holidays. He saw himself shuffling around the empty house still trying to think of things to do. Even if his hip was healed, nothing would seem worth doing. He sighed.

"You know your mom wouldn't have put up with any nonsense of that kind," he said. Wayne said nothing for a moment and then Cal saw him nod slowly. "Those two sisters are the teeth on two gears. If one 'em turns, the other turns right with her, forward and reverse."

Wayne gave a little laugh. "I don't get the metaphor, Dad, but it sounds poetic anyway."

"I just mean what would hurt one would hurt the other."

Wayne nodded again. "Yeah."

"So . . . don't have any doubts."

"I don't."

"Okay."

Wayne stood up. He straightened his arms, put his hands on the rail and stretched out his back.

"I've been sitting too long," he said.

"What's the matter? You turning into an old man?"

"Something like it," Wayne said. He held the position for some time and took a deep, sighing breath when he quit and sat down again. "I'm probably getting what you got. It runs in the family."

"What are you talking about?"

"Hip problems, shoulder problems. You name it. Arthritis. Grand-dad had it, Uncle John, you. It's genetic."

"Who says Dad had it? Or John?"

"Nobody had to. Just look at how they walked. Stubborn old farts. They'd never *say* anything about it."

Cal thought about this. It was true. He hadn't paid attention, but looking back now, he knew the signs. It made him feel weak and ridiculous. In his family, *he'd* been the only man to whine about his pain, the only man to give in to it.

"What makes you think it's genetic?" he demanded. "It comes from too much work in rain and freezing weather. That'll affect your joints over time."

"Yeah, it will. Wear and tear. But some of us are more predisposed. It's a known fact, Dad. Just luck of the draw."

Luck of the draw. The idea jolted him. Helen's dad never had any signs of disability. Just like Helen. He had the constitution of a person half his age. He farmed until he moved to town at eighty-five and never had any sons to help him out. Margaret and Helen were his only kids. Luck of the draw. Nobody's fault. He shook his head. It was hard to have to see it, yet somehow it gave him a sense of relief.

He had always thought that if he'd had more help around the

farm, he wouldn't have gotten in such a fix as to need a whole new hip, not to mention all the other aches and pains he put up with. But Wayne—who never a day in his life lifted a hay bale or pulled an engine out of a tractor or dug post holes, had just now been standing here, at not quite fifty years old, trying to stretch the ache out of his hip. It occurred to him that Tommy, too, if he had grown old enough, might have suffered from it.

He himself had been sitting on this hard bench now for a good hour and wasn't feeling all that bad. He couldn't have done it two weeks ago. And he thought, why the hell should I feel weak and guilty for saving my body from running itself into the ground?

An owl hooted. Wayne got up again and walked around the bench to pee over the other side of the platform. When he came back, he stood leaning on the rail, looking across the maze. Cal's eyes were used to the dark now. He stood, too, and found he could make out the shapes of the hay bale pyramid and the concession tent in the distance. From the animal pen a goat bleated. He felt he had to say it now. When would he have a better opportunity than this one, with just the two of them, in darkness.

He said, "This circus they put down here on this field, it's almost like your brother—" He still couldn't say Tom's name. "—never existed."

Wayne said, angrily, "Jesus, Dad. What are you talking about? Tom existed in more than that one goddamn spot. He was all over this place. The kitchen, the porch, our bedroom upstairs. All over the house. You can't walk anywhere on this whole property without thinking about him. He's all over that ravine. Not just the fucking place where he got killed."

Cal felt his heart start to pound. "Yeah. I know that."

Wayne said, "When he was a little kid, like four years old, one time he climbed up into the crawl space under the eaves. He started moaning and knocking on the joists over our bedroom to pretend he was a ghost. He couldn't stop giggling about it after I hauled him out of there. He couldn't stop laughing. Whenever I'm on that upstairs landing, I can still remember his little laugh."

"You were pretty good buddies when you were kids, weren't you?" Wayne didn't answer. After a while, Cal realized Wayne *couldn't* answer. He tried to think of something to say to cover Wayne's struggle. "I guess it was natural you two would go your different ways when you started to get older. You had different interests."

Wayne spoke up then in a tight, strangled voice.

"I wasn't any use around the place. I suppose you thought it should have been me."

"Should have been you what?"

"The one to get zapped out of this world."

Cal's breath came short. His heart drummed all over his chest, so much so he thought Wayne might even be able to hear it. "No," he said. "I never thought that." He took a breath through his nose and let it out his mouth to steady himself. "I guess . . . what I always thought was . . . it should have been *me*."

"You?" Wayne sounded shocked. "Why?"

He didn't want to tell Wayne why. He had never confessed it to anyone, not even Helen. But Wayne had just given up that piece of himself, his guilt. It would be unfair to hold back his own piece. Wayne couldn't think any worse of him than he already did. He opened his mouth and it came out.

"I saw that line of squalls way off there on the horizon, and I wondered—" He put his hand over his eyes, remembering. "—I wondered if they might be dangerous. I said to Tommy, 'That storm is hanging out there. Maybe we'd better hold off for a few hours.'" Wayne made no response. There was only his breathing. "But Tommy laughed it off. He said, 'It's a clear blue sky. That's no storm, that's just a few clouds having a little tiff.' He said, 'Go on to the shed, Dad. Fix that disk. I'm going to go get this corn put in. I'm psyched up for it.'" Cal cleared his throat. "So, I let him." *People had always said it was a bolt out of the blue. But it wasn't out of the blue.* "I had the experience of forty-six years. Tom was only twenty. And I let him make that decision."

Wayne's voice sounded hushed and far away when he spoke, as if he were talking through a wall.

"Dad, if you'd ordered Tom to go to the shed, would you have waited to see what that squall would do before you went out to plant?"

Cal didn't have to think about it. "No," he said.

"You would have gone out there, then?"

"Yeah."

"With all your forty-six years of experience." Cal didn't reply. "So then, it *would* have been you."

Cal breathed a bitter laugh through his nose. "Yeah. One good thing about that—you wouldn't have had me on your back for the next twenty-six years."

Wayne cursed under his breath. "Goddamn, you think I wouldn't have felt just as bad if *you'd* got killed?"

"You felt very bad for Tom?"

"Jesus Christ, Dad!"

"Well, I never knew what you felt. You didn't exactly announce it to anyone."

"Gee, I wonder where I got *that* from?" He paused. Then he took hold of Cal's overall strap and he said, "So you've always thought *you* should have got blasted by that lightning? Left Mom and Tom and Barb high and dry? And me? And I'd be glad to get you off my back? Fuck, Dad, you *carried* me on your back. Like a damn bucking mule, but you did carry me."

Cal buried his face in his hands. Wayne stood next to him, fingering the strap. Cal felt the tug of it and thought, I can't get started. But it was out of his control. He cried. He couldn't stop. Wayne moved his arm around Cal's shoulders and tightened it, and they stood there together on the platform for a long time until Cal finally finished and wiped his nose with a crumpled handkerchief Wayne pulled from his pocket.

The sky was growing pale in the east now, and Cal felt embarrassed at what his face must look like after the crying jag. "We'd better get down from here," he said.

They climbed stiffly down the stairs. In the clearing, Cal said, "After we get some sleep, maybe we ought to grab poles and go fishing at the pond this evening. It's supposed to be cooler. And . . . say, I forgot to thank you for those lures you sent me last summer. I've got a lot of use out of 'em."

Wayne laughed. "Yeah, I'll bet." He turned to look at the riding mower. "So, Dad, who gets to ride this thing back?"

viii.

Her cell phone rang. She thought it was probably Nancy calling from inside the chateau to say, Helen you *have* to come in here, you've *got* to see this!

But it was her home phone number. A current of fear went down her arms. She thought, news about Margaret.

"How d'you do?" Cal said in his mock formal voice. "You may not remember me. I'm Murray Plymat. I used to be sweet on you in high school, but you took up with that wiseacre Cal Earlywine. Didn't, by any chance, marry the so-and-so, did you?"

Helen smiled. "As a matter of fact, I did."

"Dang. And you're still together, are you?"

"Oh yes. We're still very much together."

"But, now, I heard someone say you were in France. Does that mean things aren't going so well with the guy? I can only hope there's some chance for me."

"Oh Murray, I'm sorry to disappoint you, but things are going just fine. I'm kind of missing the so-and-so."

"No accounting for tastes. By the way, I hear you're traveling with a notoriously pigheaded schemer. How's that working out?"

"It's been fun. But a little tiring."

"Well, who'd have thought?"

"How's your hip?"

"I walked to the mailbox and back today. No pain."

"That's wonderful, Cal! And . . . things with you and Wayne?"

"We're going fishing later on. I expect you'll get home to find an extra freezer in the basement full of all the bass we're likely to catch."

"Be sure you gut them first."

"You don't want the job?"

Their connection started to cut out. Helen said, "I guess we'd better say good-bye. Give Wayne and Margaret my love."

"Will do."

"You visited her?"

"Yesterday."

"She was okay?"

"Yeah. Doing fine."

"Did she know you?"

There was a pause. "She remembered me."

"Is she—" but before she could say more, the connection was lost.

Helen closed her phone, sat quietly looking down on the symmetrical garden beds below, and waited, without impatience, for Nancy to finish her tour.

Acknowledgements ❧

Many thanks to the following for their invaluable suggestions, assistance, and support: Jennifer Leeney Adrian, Eileen Bartos, Bruce Brown, Nancy Ann Carl, Jeanette Carter, Kingsley Clarke, Sandra de Helen, Gary Daugherty, Katie Ford, Michele and George Gerot, Nikki Herbst, Mo Jones, Nancy Lynch, Caryl Lyons, Sally Lee Moore, George Naylor, Jane Olson, Christine Phillips, Tonja Robins, Marcia Smies, Mary Helen Stefaniak, Pam Stewart, Jean and Jon Sutton, Mary Vermillion, Kris Vervaecke, Jean Walker, and Ann Zerkel.